JESSICA SHAY

FROM AWAY

A BELFORT ISLAND NOVEL

Double J Press
Massachusetts

Copyright © 2020

ISBN: 978-1-7353479-0-5 (Paperback)
ISBN: 978-1-7353479-1-2 (eBook)

Author's Note

All of the characters in this novel are figments of the author's imagination. Any resemblance to persons living or deceased is unintentional. Belfort Island is also a fictional location and won't be found on any maps of the State of Maine to the best of my knowledge, but other towns and cities mentioned exist. You should give them a visit!

Systemic injustices in our legal and economic institutions are a challenge we need to address together. Stephan and the other officers portrayed in this novel are the versions of law enforcement I wish for all of our communities. Please listen to those whose experiences are not yours with open hearts and minds, and above all else, be kind to one another. We are all in this together.

Cover Design by 100Covers.com
Interior Design by FormattedBooks.com

ACKNOWLEDGEMENTS

So many friends and family helped over the course of writing this story. I would list you all, but I'm afraid I would forget someone! Please accept my gratitude to all of you for your time, words of wisdom, suggestions, patience, and love especially Perrine and Käthe. A special thanks goes out to my family. Jonathan, Avery, and Ellie I love you more than words can express.

PROLOGUE

Sixteen Years Earlier

Waves rocked Karria as she floated, enjoying the stillness that blanketed the world in the last minutes before dawn. She was making her leisurely way home after a visit that had gone long into the quiet summer's night. The chill of the Penobscot Bay didn't bother her. She turned in a slow roll, luxuriating in the stretch, and slid under the inky black liquid. The powerful tide was shifting. She let it carry her towards the rocky beach by the slumbering town.

Before reaching the shallows, she broke the surface and glanced around. The clanging of the buoy at the other end of the island was a familiar sound that her keen ears picked up despite the distance. Closer by, an owl hooted from a large pine. The slamming of a door disturbed the peace. Karria swiveled her head towards the unexpected noise. After a moment, she noticed two familiar figures creeping down the hill from the historical society's building. A shudder of revulsion rippled through her body. She drew in a deep breath and lowered so only her eyes and the top of her head were above water. Karria stealthily made her way towards the small skiff the men had eased into.

Fragments of their conversation drifted back as she kept a careful distance while following them.

"…right map?"

"Treasure's rightfully mine.…"

"That bitch at the cove.…"

"Can't wait to see their faces when they realize it's gone."

Maps and treasure held little interest for Karria, but the woman they were referring to was another story. Wary and alert, she swam along in the skiff's wake, hoping to hear more snatches of conversation.

The older one drew a flask from his jacket and took a long pull from it. He gave a satisfied sigh moments later. "I'll show them all, bub. I'll show them all."

The younger was busy rowing the small craft and just grunted in agreement.

"I'll buy us the best boat the fleet's ever seen. Hell, I'll get us a goddamn yacht if we want one. We won't need to do a damn thing. We can just sit out there and watch the other poor slobs work their fingers raw while we laugh at them."

He leaned back against the prow and began drinking again. "Maybe we'll just blow this joint. We could go to Aruba or the Keys. I know what they say about me behind my back here." His voice was rough from years of drinking and smoking. "We'll get a cushy bachelor pad somewhere warm. Screw the snow and cold." He trailed off as he gazed out at the colors that were starting to streak the horizon as the sun peeked up over the eastern edge.

A fish leapt out of the water near Karria and splashed back down. The noise drew the older man's attention. Karria ducked her head. Much as she wanted to continue listening, she couldn't risk these particular men seeing her. From under the water, she watched the skiff pull away. When there was more distance between them, she broke the surface and tracked them with her eyes until they rounded a bend and drifted out of sight. Karria drew in a deep breath before diving and hurrying off in the opposite direction.

CHAPTER 1

Maura resisted the urge to rub her forehead. A headache, threatening all afternoon, had bloomed. Tall, dark gray clouds filled the horizon outside the large windows that faced the bay. She forced her lips into a smile as Eliza Thompson nattered on about her grandson Joey and his multitude of accomplishments. As far as Maura was concerned, Joey Thompson gave her the creeps and drank too much. The endless needs of the library, however, always stilled Maura's tongue when it came to Eliza's transparent attempts at matchmaking. The spry, white-haired lady was a generous benefactor. She was also a member of one of the founding families of Belfort. Offending her was something Maura couldn't afford to do. Besides, she genuinely liked the woman. She didn't want to hurt her feelings.

Nodding her head, Maura began to steer Eliza towards the wide pine and glass inner doors. She could lock up the heavy outer oak ones in a few minutes. She sighed in relief when Eliza's blue knit cardigan vanished out the door. The sky was growing unusually dark, thanks to the building storm clouds. Thunderstorms generally skirted the island. This one, however, was bearing down on them. Maura crossed her fingers that she'd get home before it broke. She smiled and waved to Eliza, who'd looked back at her.

Maura knew she'd need to wait a couple of minutes for the chatty lady to leave, lest she get cornered by Eliza's car. She strode to her office and gathered up her bag. She was turning off the lights when she heard a cry of disappointment.

"Daddy, you promised we'd get here in time."

Maura hoped the frustration she felt wasn't reflected on her face as she turned around.

A black-haired pixie of a girl was standing with her hands on her hips, glaring at a tall, equally dark-haired man. He sent Maura a pleading look.

She managed to offer the child a slight smile despite the pounding in her head. "You made it just in time. How can I help you?" She put her bag down on the circulation desk. On Belfort Island, everyone knew everyone else. In the summer and fall, however, enough tourists swelled the population that strangers often wandered into the library.

"I need a library card so I can get my books." The girl gave Maura a worried look and gestured for her to come close. When Maura did, she whispered, "I can't sleep if we don't read them before bed."

"Maisy, remember, I told you the library might not have them." The British accent underlying the father's warm, rich baritone pegged him as definitely from away. "Please forgive us for coming in past closing, but we're desperate." He gave her a lopsided smile.

Maura instinctively smiled back. "If I haven't locked up, we're not closed." She knelt down. "What books are you looking for, Maisy?"

"*Paddington, Chrysanthemum, Green Eggs and Ham,* and"- she leaned close to Maura - "*Goodnight Moon,* but don't tell anyone I still like baby books."

Maura hid her amusement. Instead she nodded gravely. "All excellent bedtime stories. Would you like to come with me and see what we have in?" She offered her hand. There was an old, familiar pang when a small, warm hand slid into hers.

The father trailed behind them as they moved further into the library towards the children's room in the back of the old stone building. The sensors picked up their movements and lights flickered on. George, the resident painted turtle, glanced up and then went back to munching on the lettuce he'd hidden away earlier in the day. Within a couple of minutes, they'd found all but the Dr. Seuss book. Maisy responded to that disappointment by confiding in a stage whisper that "*Green Eggs* is Daddy's favorite. I love the Grinch best." She'd plucked a book emblazoned with the green grump off the shelf and was hugging it to her chest.

Maura grinned at the girl. "He's my favorite, too." She toggled the computer back on when they reached the circulation desk. While it was warming up, she smiled at the duo. "Are you here visiting family?"

"No ma'am, we just—"

"We just moved. That's why my books are lost. And Daddy said we'll get more if we can't find them, but the house is all creaky. I need them tonight."

Maura's hazel eyes moved from one to the other.

The father stuck out his hand. The crow's feet at the corners of his eyes crinkled up as he gave Maura a rueful smile. "Stephan Kirkland."

"Maura Ballard." As she accepted the proffered hand, recognition dawned on her. "Officer Kirkland?"

"One and the same." His hand engulfed Maura's and he gave it a light squeeze before gently releasing it. "Is this a small-town thing?"

She gave him a quizzical look.

"Knowing my job immediately."

Maura chuckled. "You'll get used to it." The computer had come to life. She pulled up the registration screen. "Would you each like your own library card, or a single one for the family? Your spouse will need to get their own if you don't include them today." She watched Maisy's excited expression dim and winced.

Stephan saw Maura's expression falter and hurried to answer. "Maisy would be thrilled to have her own card, wouldn't you, love? And I'd like one as well, if that suits."

"Of course." Maura mentally kicked herself for not paying closer attention to Andy Wickham's monologue earlier in the week. He'd shared some gossip about the new police officer, but it'd been at the end of a ten-minute diatribe on the price of lumber and the damn government taxes and regulations. Her eyes had glazed over. She'd obviously missed an important tidbit.

When Stephan gave her their address, she shot him a surprised look. "3 Briar Road? I hadn't realized the Josephs were selling their house."

"Milly and Sophie—Maisy's mum, my wife—were distant cousins. She and David are letting us stay there while they're in Florida."

"Welcome to the neighborhood." Maura smiled. "I live across the street."

"Yay!" Maisy let out a little cheer, but then a rumble of thunder silenced her. Her blue eyes widened and filled with worry. "Daddy!" She pushed into her father's side.

"I've got you, love. We just need to get food and then we'll go home."

"I can bring some pizza by if you'd like. I was going to stop at Waverly's anyway. You can shop tomorrow after the storms have passed." The offer was out before Maura gave herself time to stop. The fear in the child's eyes went straight to her heart.

Maisy nodded her head vigorously.

Stephan looked down at his daughter and opened his mouth. Then he sighed and looked at Maura. "If you don't mind, it'd be a big help."

"Happy to do it." Maura smiled, despite her worsening headache. "What do you like on your pizza?"

"Cheese will do just fine." Stephan gathered the books up from his daughter and wrapped a protective arm around her shoulders. "Let's hurry home and get ready for Ms. Ballard. Will you and your family join us? My treat."

"Oh," Maura shook her head. "It's just me, unless you count the cats, but I don't want to intrude. Thank you."

A clap of thunder rattled the windows. Maura quickly moved to shut the computer down. Tears started rolling down Maisy's cheeks. "Daddy." She clutched her father's arm.

"I've got you." Stephan scooped the girl up and gave Maura a grateful look. "Thank you. Please be safe. Don't rush on our account."

Rain lashed at Maura's hair and body as she ran from her car to Milly's front door. She leaned over the box to try and keep the pizza from getting soaked by the deluge of cold water. As she hurried up the flagstone steps of the porch, the wide wooden door flew open.

Stephan reached out and plucked the box from her. "Come inside."

Maura hesitated. "I should get home before it gets worse. It's a strong blow." She was cold, wet, and uncomfortable. All she wanted to do was down a handful of Tylenol and climb into her pajamas.

There was a crackle and the hairs on both their arms stood up. A moment later an enormous boom shook the ground and the power went out. The silence that followed lasted only a few seconds before Maisy's scream of fear pierced it. Stephan swore. Maura felt the large box thrust back at her. In the dim light, she saw him reach into his back pocket. A moment later the bright beam from a cell phone lit the area.

Maura stepped inside and moved towards the kitchen. She placed the food on the expansive granite island while she listened to Stephan's footfalls thump up the stairs at a run. Maisy's screaming stopped. She let out a breath she hadn't been aware of holding. As her eyes acclimated to the darkened kitchen, Maura took in the boxes and felt bad that she hadn't thought to grab some paper plates for her new neighbors.

Ready to call it a night, she walked back towards the open front door.

Footsteps echoed in the silent house and Stephan met her at the base of the stairs. Maisy was sobbing in his arms, her head pressed against his shoulder. "I'm sorry, Ms. Ballard. Storms are rough on us."

Maura shook her head. "No worries. If the power stays out long and you need anything, come on over. I'm in the little blue-and-white house at the end of the street, just over there." She waved her hand towards her home, the corner of it barely visible through the dense sheets of rain.

"I can't ask you to go back out in this." Stephan gave her a doubtful look. "You're already soaked. You'll catch a chill. At least let me find an umbrella."

"I'll be inside before you start eating." She eyed Maisy with concern. "Don't worry. Tomorrow is supposed to be gorgeous. It'll look so much better in the morning."

Maisy's face was streaked with tears and her lips wobbled. She managed a bare nod before burying her head in her father's neck.

Maura's heart lurched. She gave Stephan a worried look. He shook his head. "We'll be fine. Thank you for everything, Ms. Ballard. We're grateful."

"Maura." She stepped towards the doorway. "We're neighbors."

"Maura. Thank you." Stephan trailed her to the door.

It only took seconds to back her car out of their driveway and turn into her own. She glanced back across the street and saw Stephan watching. Maisy had her head burrowed into the crook of his neck, but he said something to her and she peeked out. Both waved before Stephan closed their front door.

Maura shut and locked her own door. Three sets of eyes gleamed at her in the low light. A reproachful "merrow" came from the smallest shadowed body.

"I'm sorry, guys. I know I'm late." Maura started pulling off her sodden clothing. "I promise I'll feed you as soon as I get dry."

Once she'd changed into dry pajamas and taken the pain medicine, she turned her attention to the three cats who'd followed her. "Okay. You lot first, then we see about the power."

Greta snaked around her legs. The Persian's silky fur soothed Maura. Tim uttered another impatient "merrow" before leaping into her arms. She nuzzled the anxious orange cat. "I know, I know." Mags, the oldest, was waiting patiently in the doorway. She led the procession into the welcoming kitchen. Tim wriggled out of Maura's arms when she reached the counter. He paced back and forth while she opened the cabinet. Frequent bursts of lightning illuminated the room as Maura rummaged for their food.

The ETA for electricity was only a few hours. No need for the generator. Maura tossed the phone onto the table and ate a bit of her pizza while waiting for the medicine to kick in. Thunder rattled the house from time to time and lightning continued to streak across the sky. Grateful to be inside and dry, Maura set her food aside and stretched out on the couch.

Birds chirping and sunlight streaming through the wide bay window woke Maura. She pried her eyes open and blinked as she oriented herself. A warm orange paw reached up and tapped her lips a few times. She lowered her eyes to see Tim staring at her. He slid his paw over and patted her cheek before extending it towards Greta's fluffy tail, which was lazily waving along the sofa cushion. He stopped when Greta opened her bright green eyes and gave him a piercing glare. A moment later he launched himself off of Maura's chest and began an elaborate stretching routine.

Maura rolled her head a few times and did some stretching of her own to relieve the crick that had developed from her awkward sleeping position. Discomforts she could easily shake off in her twenties had started getting more persistent as she entered her forties. She winced and rubbed the back of her neck as she padded to the kitchen.

She'd given herself the luxury of taking a Friday off and planned on enjoying it. Maura glanced at the time. If she hurried, she could get to Ellsworth to lay in supplies for the next couple of weeks before the tourist traffic picked up and jammed the roads. That would give her the afternoon and evening to catch up with chores and relax.

Her eyes landed on the stack of mail that she'd put down the other day. She'd forgotten about it in her hurry to work on her current painting. Maura thumbed through it while savoring her coffee. A letter made her pause. Milly and David hadn't spent much time at their vacation home this year and she worked long hours, so their paths hadn't crossed more than a handful of times over the summer. She read Milly's chatty note about her relatives who were moving in for a while. Her eyes widened in sympathy when she read that Milly's cousin, Stephan's wife, had passed away. It explained their reaction to her query about library cards.

It didn't take Maura long to finish getting ready to leave. As she was locking up, she felt someone watching her. She turned and noticed Maisy, standing on the wide-planked porch of her new home.

The girl waved and ran over. "Where are you going, Ms. Ballard?"

"To Ellsworth. I need to do my shopping."

The child's black hair was sticking out in all directions. "We need to, too. We ate cold pizza for breakfast because we didn't have anything else besides dry cereal." She leaned in closer. "Daddy's cranky because he hasn't had his coffee yet."

Maura nodded. "I know how that feels. Tell him to go to Jack's. They've got the best coffee on the island, maybe in the whole state."

Maisy scrunched up her nose. "Maine's a big state. It took for-evvvvvvver to get here from Boston. There must be lots of coffee places. We stopped five times." She tipped her head to the side. "I guess that wasn't always for coffee, though." The petite girl shrugged her slender shoulders. "I needed to get out a bunch. It's hard to sit all day."

"There's lots of room to run around here. Our road ends at a small beach, but if you walk through the woods you get to the big town one after about fifteen minutes. I can show you and your dad how to get there later if you want."

Maisy's eyes widened. "That'd be awesomesauce!"

Maura grinned. "When you see my car back here and your dad says it's okay, come knock on the door. I'll show you the path."

"Yay!" Maisy did a little victory dance, then sprinted back across the street with a cheerful wave.

Maura grinned. It'd be nice to have neighbors around this time of year. Hopefully they would stay for a while before moving into their own place.

CHAPTER 2

"Hey, pretty lady. What chuptah?"

Maura felt her shoulders stiffen at Joey Thompson's nasal tones. She put the copy of *Green Eggs and Ham* into her cart and turned to greet him.

The barrel-chested fisherman wore a Red Sox cap over his thinning, sandy hair. Though he gave her a boyish grin, Maura felt the usual niggle of unease in her gut when she met his cool blue gaze. His smile never seemed to reach his eyes. It wasn't the color. His grandmother's were the exact same pale shade. But there was a flatness to Joey's eyes, whereas Eliza's were expressive. He reminded Maura of a shark. She moved so her cart was between them. "Morning, Joey. Errands. How are you?"

He glanced down at the children's book. "More books? Doesn't the town buy them for the library? You shouldn't be havin' to buy them yourself."

"It's for a friend."

He gave her a speculative look and then snapped his fingers. "That's right. The new cop has a kid, doesn't he? Moved in across the street from ya, didn't they?"

She nodded in agreement and figured after another minute of chit-chat, she'd have been polite enough to excuse herself.

Joey pushed closer to her cart until she could smell the coffee on his breath. "Wanna grab a bite when you're done here?"

"Can't, sorry. I've got a tight schedule today," Maura lied.

His expression was skeptical, but he gave her an easy smile. "'Nother time then, Miz Maura."

After a quick goodbye, Maura walked away. She knew he was watching, so she didn't hurry, but she also didn't linger over the books as she'd planned. She frowned. Why was she letting Joey interfere with enjoying her day off? She drew in a deep breath and shook off the discomfort. It was a beautiful day and she had no obligations other than showing her new neighbors how to get to the beach.

She pushed Joey from her mind and focused on her list. Childcare after school was a challenge for many parents on Belfort. For the past decade, she'd been running an informal afterschool program at the library. Maura relied on donations to purchase supplies for the program. It had been a slower than normal tourist season, which meant there wouldn't be a fall influx of cash. She moved further down the row and snagged workbooks, coloring books, a cuddly stuffed dog, and Legos.

Maura studied her cart with a wry expression: cat food and supplies for the library. She'd become a stereotype without noticing it happen. She gave a mental shrug. Things hadn't turned out the way she'd planned, but for the most part, Maura was so busy and engaged in her life that she didn't ruminate on her solitude. There weren't many available men on Belfort and she stayed on-island much of the time. The night scene, such as it was, held little appeal.

When she stepped out into the bright sunshine, Maura shook off the melancholy that had begun to gnaw at her and drove the short distance to the grocery store. As she meandered through the produce aisle, Maura enjoyed the abundance of fresh fruits and vegetables. While she examined the tomatoes, her thoughts turned to a familiar path: the feasibility of building a greenhouse in the backyard of the library. They had the sun and a wide, flat space.

However, getting the materials for her vision was a challenge she hadn't managed to overcome. She could fundraise, but the library had so many more pressing needs. She couldn't justify prioritizing a greenhouse. It would have to remain a dream.

"What did that tomato do to you?"

Maura was snapped out of her thoughts by the amused voice. She realized she was scowling at the crimson fruit cradled in her hand. She shook her head and looked up to see Stephan grinning at her. Maisy was nearby, her attention focused on a pile of dark green cucumbers.

She gave him a rueful look. "Nothing. It was an innocent bystander." She grabbed a produce bag and put several tomatoes in it. "It was reminding me of how much I hate being thwarted."

"By a plant?"

Maura nodded. On impulse, she blurted out, "By a greenhouse. I want the kids to be able to grow fresh produce in the afterschool club, but can't figure out how to finagle a greenhouse."

"Afterschool club?" Stephan's face lit up. "Is that a thing? Can first graders attend?"

Maura nodded. "If you don't mind that it's not super formal. One or two of the high schoolers help out. It's mostly crafts, homework help, and free play."

"That sounds great." Stephan grinned. "What's the fee?"

"There isn't one."

He tipped his head to the side and looked at the bag of tomatoes she was still holding. "How are you going to get a greenhouse if you don't charge anything?"

"It's a conundrum, isn't it?" Maura sighed. "We can't. Most of the families that use the service can't afford to pay much." She put her fruit in the cart and lifted her shoulders in a slight shrug. "Our budget's tight. A greenhouse isn't a priority."

Stephan's expression was thoughtful, but before he could say anything, his daughter returned with two plump cucumbers in her hands. "What'd you pick, Maisy Daisy?"

"These." She plopped them in the cart and looked up at Maura. "Will you still show us the beach later? Daddy said we shouldn't bother you, but I said you didn't mind." Her expression was full of concern, but there was a sparkle in her wide blue eyes.

A grin spread across Maura's lips as she locked gazes with the small imp. "I wouldn't have offered if I minded."

"I'm not sure I believe that, but we're grateful nevertheless." Stephan looked down at his daughter and ruffled her hair. "We've got to finish up here and have some lunch. What time works for you, Ms. Ballard?"

"Maura, please. We're neighbors, remember?" She thought about what she had left to do at home. "Two would be good."

Maisy tipped her head sideways and consulted her father's watch. "That's soooooooo far away."

"It's not that long." Maura laughed.

A big sigh greeted that answer. "I guess."

Stephan shook his head. "It'll go by like *that*," he told his daughter, and snapped his fingers.

Maisy gave her father a skeptical look, but waved goodbye to Maura when Stephan said his farewell. She followed him down to the deli, chattering away.

Maura leaned on her cart and watched the pair for a moment. The sadness she'd felt earlier roared back. Having a family of her own was another secret dream, one she'd nurtured throughout her childhood and slowly abandoned as the years went by. She had to take a moment to stare blindly at the leafy greens while she composed herself. When she was certain she had her emotions well in hand again, the petite woman sighed and focused on her shopping list.

Later, Maura smiled when Maisy handed her a pail and shovel. Stephan looked embarrassed as his daughter grabbed the woman's hand and explained. "I figured you might need something to play with in the sand since you're an adult and prolly don't have your toys from when you were a kid. Daddy didn't think you'd want it but" —she tugged Maura down to stage whisper in her ear—"I wore him down."

"You do realize I can hear you, Maisy, right?" Stephan shook his head.

The girl grinned at her father and grabbed his hand with her free one. "Can we go now?"

Maura chuckled and led them to the small path cut in the back of her property. Decades of use kept the grass from growing in anything more than small scraggly patches. As they walked further, the shade of the trees dappled the sunlight.

"You're sure you don't mind us using your land, Maura?"

"All the neighbors do. I don't mind as long as people don't leave their garbage. You look like upstanding citizens to me." She winked at Maisy, who was still holding her hand.

"We won't litter, promise."

"Didn't think you would." Maura gave her hand a gentle squeeze.

Fifteen minutes later, they left the woods and the path started to become sandy. Soon after, they reached a series of wooden walkways. The steady roar of the ocean became more pronounced. Maura preferred the privacy of the rocky beach at the end of their road, but there was an appeal to the noisy, wide expanse of the town beach.

"Wow." Maisy's eyes were wide as she took in the rolling, crashing waves. Gulls screamed at one another from the sand and air. Cormorants bobbed further out on the rising and falling swells. Several brave souls darted in and out among the frigid breakers to catch rides back to the shore on boogie boards. A line of kayaks was visible rounding the curve of land to the far left of the beach. Colorful blankets, towels, and umbrellas dotted the sand.

"Mind if I hang out with you guys for a little while?" Maura didn't want to intrude, but the lure of relaxing in the sun and sand was strong. She'd worn her swimsuit, knowing it would be.

"Please do."

"Stay! You need to build with me!"

Stephan smiled at Maura. "We'd like you to stay. We brought extra snacks, hoping you would."

"Snacks? I guess that settles it, then," Maura laughed. She pushed off her sandals and dug her toes into the warm sand.

"Where should we build, love?"

Maisy sucked on her lower lip as she surveyed the beach. "There!" She pointed to a spot where the sand was packed down, but still distant from the returning tide. She took off running to claim the coveted location.

Maura reached down to grab her shoes and set off at a more sedate pace alongside Stephan. "She must keep you on your toes."

"You have no idea." He watched his daughter with an affectionate expression. "I think moving here will be a good thing for both of us. I hope it is."

"You're not worried about being bored?" Maura gave him a sidelong look. "It's a very different pace and lifestyle than Boston."

"And I won't have a constant worry about orphaning my child."

Maura winced. "Sorry. I didn't mean anything by it."

"No, I apologize. I know you didn't. I'm still out of sorts from yesterday." He shook his head. "It was a long night after a very long day."

Maura wanted to ask about Maisy's fear of storms, but didn't want to be nosy. She nodded. "Moving's stressful. Oh, that reminds me. I have something for you both back at my house. I'll leave it on your porch later."

"How about you join us for dinner tonight? We were both grateful for yesterday. Besides, I owe you a meal, since you wouldn't let me pay you back earlier. Unless you already have plans." He turned to gaze at her when she didn't answer immediately.

Maura's only plans had been catching up with her DVR. "I'm free. But you don't owe me anything."

Stephan smiled. "Last night would have been miserable if you hadn't helped us. Please, it's our way of saying thank you."

Maura gazed at him for a moment before nodding. "How can I say no, then? What should I bring?"

"Just yourself. Do you like pasta?"

"Come on!" Maisy's impatient voice interrupted. "We have to hurry. There's so much work to do."

"How long till the tide comes in?" Stephan asked.

Maura shot him an amused look. "We have a couple of hours before it gets to us."

"Does six-thirty work?"

"Sure." Maura nodded.

Stephan put the tote he was carrying down in the sunbaked sand. He shook out a plaid blanket and then transferred the bag onto it.

Maura helped secure it and then brushed sand off of her face with her shirt as she pulled it over her head. She dusted her hands off on the cutoffs she'd pulled on over her swimsuit and grinned at Maisy. "How do you want to do this?"

Maisy shrugged her shoulders as she dumped an assortment of buckets and molds out of the tote. "As long as it has the flag, I don't care."

"The flag?"

A shadow fell over the outline as Stephan moved next to Maura. "We brought the special royal flag. It goes over all our sand castles."

"You guys are pros at this," Maura laughed. "You don't actually need me, do you?"

Maisy gave her a quizzical look. "Huh?"

Stephan chuckled. "You wouldn't have stayed to help if we'd told you, would you?"

Maura tamped down the spark of pleasure that Stephan's comment lit in her. He was likely just looking for another adult to help amuse his daughter for a while. "Probably not."

"Thought so."

Several local children soon spotted Maura and joined in the construction. She and Stephan retreated to the blanket.

While they watched the kids, he peppered her with questions about the town and its politics, history, and residents.

"Chief Mason told me there are a handful who tend to be frequent guests in the lockup." Stephan kept his voice nonchalant. "Anyone I should know about in particular?"

Maura frowned. She knew exactly who Ron Mason was referring to, but it felt wrong to prejudice Stephan.

He misinterpreted her expression. "I'm sorry. Friends of yours? I'm not looking for you to rat anyone out."

"What?" Maura turned to him. She stared at him for a moment and then burst into laughter. "I just didn't want to color your impressions of people. I don't like everyone who lives here." She shrugged. "To be fair, not everyone likes me either." She waved away Stephan's automatic placating response before he could do more than open his mouth. "You should make up your own mind about folks without my biases. No one on our road is on Ron's list. Of course, in a month there's only going to be a handful of us until Memorial Day. The Dixons will stay through Christmas, but most of our other neighbors are summer folks like your wife's family."

"I wondered about that. Milly guessed there were ten or so year-round families."

"It's more like five."

"So, we're going to be pretty isolated soon." Stephan looked at Maisy. The concern was evident on his face. Briar Road was a fifteen-minute drive out from town proper in good weather on twisting, bumpy roads. The town center was at the tip of the island closest to the bridge to the mainland. Their neighborhood was at the opposite end, with no direct road in between.

"It's not that bad," Maura tried to reassure him. She gave him a quick summary of their year-round neighbors. She tipped her face back to catch more of the sun's rays as she concluded, "Jackson Prior is the last one. He's a retired banker who moved here about five years ago. His house is down that dirt driveway near where Briar Road starts. He's pretty private, but pitches in on a couple of town committees."

"He's got family visiting, then. Yesterday, I saw a man our age getting the mail at that house."

"That's Jackson."

"You said he's retired."

Maura nodded her head. "He was a successful banker."

"Maybe he could help you with your greenhouse."

Maura frowned at Stephan. "I'm sure he would if I asked. But it should be a community effort. Besides, it'd be rude to ask."

Stephan held up a hand. "I didn't mean to offend." He longed to brush the lock of hair that was gleaming with copper highlights out of Maura's eye, but didn't want to risk raising her ire further.

Maura was protective of Jackson. She knew it was coloring her reaction and worked to lighten her tone. "Small towns are different than cities, Stephan. Have you never lived in one?"

He shook his head. "Born and bred in Bristol and then went to university in London. I met Sophie when she was there as an exchange student. I followed her back to Boston and have lived there since, well, until now." Stephan started to ask Maura a question when Maisy appeared in front of them dancing in excitement.

"A seal! I just saw a seal!"

Maura grinned at the girl's excitement. "What'd it look like?"

"Like a seal? Except it had a white mark between and above its eyes. I've never seen one like that before."

"Seeing her is good luck."

"It is?"

"Yep. She only shows herself to some people. It's unusual to see her here. She doesn't seem to care for crowds. I bet she'll visit with you at our little beach. She likes it there."

"What's her name?"

Maura pondered the question for a moment. "I always call her Belle, because she's so pretty. Milly insists her name is Becky. Chief Mason calls her Blaze." She rolled her eyes. "Not very imaginative, is it?"

"That's Daddy's new boss."

"He's a nice man. His daughter Lana is a couple of years older than you, but I bet you'll hit it off. She's going into third grade this year."

"You seem to know all the kids." Maisy tipped her head at the group of children still clustered around the sand castle.

"We try to keep it interesting at the library." Maura commented.

"Love, are you ready for the flag?" Stephan eyed the encroaching water. "I think we have time for a quick ceremony and photo."

"Right!" Maisy flew to the tote and tossed towels out onto the blanket. She gave a triumphant shout and held up a slim wooden box. "Found it!"

"Fancy." Maura looked at Stephan in surprise.

"We did say it was royal, didn't we?" He winked at her. "It was my grandfather's. He got it in service to the crown during the war. It was given to him by King George himself. It's a family treasure. He was concerned Maisy wouldn't know her roots and sent it over with my parents when she was born."

Suitably impressed, Maura followed them over to the castle. She stood with the other islanders as Stephan solemnly took the box from Maisy. He opened it and drew out a small British flag that was affixed to a slim metal pole. He presented it to Maisy.

The girl curtsied and turned to the castle. "Hear ye, hear ye. All rise for the singing of God Save the Queen."

"Kout! That's not right Maiz. We're Americans." Frank Sewell wore a horrified expression.

Maisy gave him a pitying look. "Duh. I know that. But this is our castle's flag. Are you going to respect it or be rude?"

Frank wore a mutinous expression. His older brother, Charlie, elbowed him. He muttered, "Flatlanders are weird. Let it go, Frankie."

Maisy ignored him and began singing. Stephan joined in. When his baritone hit their ears, the local kids stopped muttering and fidgeting. One thing island life, particularly the long, isolated winters, had taught most of them early on was to appreciate music and art. Stephan's voice appeared to have some training behind it. The children, even the young ones, respected that, at least momentarily.

Maura bit back a smile and stood with her hands clasped loosely in front of her. She hummed along and gave Frank the stink eye when he started to mutter that they were still singing the wrong lyrics.

When the song ended, Maisy bowed to the flag and stepped away from the castle. A moment later, the edges of the waves tipped into the wide, deep moat and filled it.

The cold water splashed over everyone's toes. Some shrieked in delight.

"A quick photo!" Stephan had the kids all grouped up behind the castle before they knew what he was about. He captured the moment on his cell phone before he retrieved the flag and tucked it back into its box.

Maura slid away when she saw Frank reach down to the water to send some arcing towards his older brother. Laughter and complaints broke out in the group as they stumbled around the quickly crumbling structure, kicking and slapping water at one another.

Stephan smiled as he watched the children's antics. He was still smiling when he turned to Maura. She was pulling her shirt on over her head and missed the speculative look that crossed his face.

"I have to do a few chores before dinner. Can you find your way back?"

Stephan nodded. "I think we can manage. If we're not home when you get there later, send out the search parties."

Maura smiled. "I have faith in you. You sure you don't want me to bring anything?"

"Just yourself."

"Okay, then. See you in a bit." Maura picked up her shoes and gave Stephan a small wave.

Walking back down the familiar path, Maura listened to the sounds of the ocean and shrieking children and gulls recede into the background. The pine needles on the dirt muffled her footsteps and she startled more than one chipmunk and squirrel. She grinned at their chittering complaints. All too soon, the woods gave way to her sun-filled backyard and the reality of her responsibilities.

By the time she'd finished her chores, it was almost time to go. Maura hurried up a flight of creaky, wooden steps. For months after her aunt's unexpected passing, Maura had stayed in her old bedroom, feeling odd taking over Jane's room. Eventually, she'd felt foolish leaving the best room in the house vacant and moved herself into it. Maura paused by the pair of wide windows that faced Rose Cove and enjoyed the view. After a shower, she glanced in her closet. There was no point pretending this was a date. Dressing up might make Stephan think she had the wrong idea about his invitation. But she didn't want to show up in jeans and a T-shirt, either. She pulled on a pair of linen capris and a simple green shirt. Earrings and some lip gloss finished off her preparations. She hurried down the stairs and grabbed the bouquet of flowers she'd cut from her garden and the now-wrapped book.

"I was worried you weren't coming!" Maisy flung the door open as Maura walked across the street.

"Why would you think that?"

"Maisy!" Stephan appeared behind his daughter and gave Maura an apologetic look. "We knew you'd be coming."

"*I* was worried," Maisy shrugged. When Maura reached the doorway, she grabbed her by her hand that held the book and pulled her inside. "Is that for us?"

"What do you think?" Maura laughed while Stephan groaned.

"Manners love, manners."

Maisy looked from one adult to the other. "I just wanted to know."

"Yes," Maura grinned. "It's a small welcome gift from me to both of you, as are these." She handed Stephan the flowers and Maisy the present.

"Can I?" Maisy looked at her father.

"*May* I, and yes, you may." Stephan watched his child rip through the floral wrapping paper before the words were fully out of his mouth and sighed. "Thank you, Maura, you didn't have to."

"I wanted to." She felt a surge of pleasure at Maisy's excited squeal. "*Green Eggs*, Daddy! Yay, thank you!"

Maura found her arms filled with a warm, wriggly girl. She automatically scooped Maisy into a hug. "You're welcome. I hope you're happy here, both of you." She smiled at Stephan.

He felt an awareness he hadn't felt since Sophie's passing—before, if he was being honest—when he gazed at Maura with his daughter in her arms. Stephan reached out and clasped her arm gently. "Thank you for making us feel so welcome, Maura."

The moment felt frozen in time as she absorbed the warmth in his expression and touch and the sweet weight of the child in her arms. It would be so easy to be like this. Then Maura remembered herself. She gently disentangled herself from Maisy and Stephan. "Those should probably go in some water." She gestured to the flowers.

"Ah, yes. They're beautiful. Zinnias are my mum's favorites. She always has loads of them growing round the house in pots and in the garden."

"I love sunflowers." Maisy buried her face in the cheerful blooms.

"I'm partial to them, too. They're so friendly-looking."

Stephan and Maisy ushered Maura inside and encouraged her to take a seat at the island. Maisy carefully put out place settings for three. Stephan was busy at the stovetop.

"I feel silly sitting here not helping," Maura confessed.

Maisy tipped her head to the side and then ran out of the room.

"Enjoy it." Stephan winked. "We'll be putting you to work washing dishes."

"One of my least favorite chores." Maura gave a mock shudder.

"We're happy to have you over. This is a treat for us. What would you like to drink?"

"What're you going to have?"

"If you're up for wine I'd enjoy a glass. If not, I'll have a lager."

"I'd love some wine," Maura admitted. "I just didn't want you to open a bottle on my account."

"It can go to waste when it's just you." Stephan appreciated her thoughtfulness. He nodded to the counter near the fridge. "Pick one out for us."

Maura had just settled on a nice Malbec when Maisy skidded back into the room with a stack of books in her hands. She waited for Maura to put the bottle down by the plates and grabbed her hand. "Come on. I'll read to you while Daddy cooks."

"Shouldn't we stay and keep him company?"

Maisy frowned. There wasn't room for her books with all of the dishes and trivets. "We could pick out just one book, I guess."

"Or you could go wash up." Stephan shook his head at the girl. "Dinner's almost ready."

"Yay! I can read to you later, Maura." Maisy put her books down on a counter and took off.

Maura sniffed appreciatively. "This all smells wonderful." In addition to the spaghetti, he'd made a red sauce with meatballs, salad and warmed up some rolls.

"It's one of my better meals," he admitted. "I can handle simple well."

Maura found herself relaxing and enjoying the meal faster and more thoroughly than she'd expected. Stephan and Maisy made her feel welcome. They included her in their conversation and gentle teasing. Both were full of questions about the school and the island's other children. When they finished, Maura helped Stephan clean up while Maisy left with her pile of books.

Stephan refilled their glasses and smiled at Maura. "Are you up to some stories? I have dessert for later."

"I wouldn't want to disappoint Maisy. She seems so excited to read." Maura's voice faltered as they locked gazes. The warmth in his cerulean eyes captured her. The moment seemed to stretch as they studied one another.

"Come on!" Maisy's yell broke the silence.

Maura felt her cheeks warm.

Stephan smiled. The librarian intrigued him.

Stephan placed his hand lightly on her low back and directed her into the sunroom. He grinned when he saw Maura's cheeks turn even rosier. Their new neighbor's blushes were endearing.

Maisy had piled all of Milly's throw pillows into a huge multi-colored jumble on the floor. "Maura, come sit with me!"

"Sure." Maura was glad for the distraction. She could swear the spark of attraction she felt for Stephan was mutual, but wasn't sure what to make of it. She put her wine down and sat next to the girl. When Maisy snuggled into her, the cynical thought that the pair of them might just be looking for a surrogate mother figure surfaced in her brain before she pushed it away. "What're you going to read to me?"

"*Chrysanthemum*, and then Daddy's going to read *Green Eggs*."

"I am?" Stephan laughed.

"Of course."

"Do I get a say in this?"

Maisy frowned at her father. "We have a guest, Daddy. Don't be an imp."

Maura grinned at Stephan. "Being an imp in front of your guests is rude, Officer Kirkland."

"Stephan," he corrected and then putting his own glass down joined them on the floor. "All right, I'll read *Green Eggs* if Maura reads *The Grinch*."

Maisy tilted her head to look up at Maura. "Would you? Please?"

"I'd be happy to."

Later, after bullies had been thwarted, strange food had been tasted, and the Grinch had discovered his heart, Maisy sagged into her father's side. A series of enormous yawns escaped, despite her best efforts to stop them.

"Bed time, love."

"Need a cuddle."

"You're a big girl now. Come on."

"Please, Daddy."

Maura pushed off the floor and piled the books together into a neat stack. "I should be going."

"Please don't," Stephan shook his head. "We still haven't had dessert."

"*I* want dessert."

"You need bed."

"Then I want a cuddle."

Stephan gave his daughter an exasperated look. Her own azure eyes held a mutinous gleam that he knew well as she glared back at him.

"I'm stuffed." Maura studied father and child and decided to take the escape offered by their standoff. "And I have to work tomorrow. Thank you both for a lovely evening." She smiled at them and moved to bring her wineglass back to the kitchen. She rinsed it out and left it in the sink. Father and daughter trailed her to the front door.

Maisy wrapped her arms around Maura's waist and gave her a tight hug. "Thank you for coming."

"Yes, thank you."

Maura smiled at them both. "I'll see you around."

Two dark heads nodded in agreement.

CHAPTER 3

It was the light that woke Maura. She cracked her eyelids open and then shot up. A golden glow filled her bedroom. "Oh, ohohohohoh!" Excited, she pulled her legs out from under Tim, leaving the small cat protesting. She only took a minute to tug on some shorts before racing to get her painting gear and run down the stairs. Maura slid her feet into a pair of ratty sneakers. The cats, who had followed, gave her looks that ranged from indifferent to shocked as she pulled the door shut. "I'll feed you soon," she called when she heard Tim's indignant yowl through the closed door. She ran for the cove with her battered case and easel hitting her leg with every stride.

The color suffused everything. Maura opened her kit with practiced ease. Sliding her phone out of her pocket, she took two quick snapshots and then set to mixing colors.

Engrossed in her work, Maura didn't pay attention to the footfalls until they were near. She gave Stephan a brief nod before returning to her painting.

"Will it bother you if I'm here?" He had a camera slung around his neck and a tripod in his hands.

She glanced at his equipment and shook her head. "Not at all. The color's amazing, isn't it?"

"Spectacular," Stephan agreed, hurrying so he wouldn't miss the unusual light.

Maura began layering colors onto her canvas to try and capture the essence of the golden light. She heard rapid clicking from her neighbor's camera as he worked fast, knowing, as she did, that the light would change within minutes.

They worked in companionable silence until the sun had fully risen. Maura looked at her canvas with a critical eye and chewed the end of a brush. She'd managed to capture some of the iridescent quality, but it wasn't anywhere near perfect. She didn't realize Stephan had put his gear away and walked over, until she heard his exclamation of surprise near her right elbow. She pulled the brush out of her mouth. "I didn't manage to get the color right."

"Maura, this is amazing."

She sighed and shook her head. "No. It's okay, but far short of amazing." She gave him a quick smile. "But thanks for saying that. I took a couple of shots on my phone to try and capture the light, but the quality's not enough."

Stephan looked down at his camera and scrolled through the pictures he'd taken until he found one he liked. "Would this be helpful?" He showed it to her.

Maura's face lit up. "That's gorgeous. Yes." She beamed at him. "Would you mind letting me have a copy? I promise I won't do anything with it other than use it to try and get the light right."

Her smile brought an answering one to Stephan's mouth. "If it helps, I'm happy to share. I just need your email." He unlocked his phone, created a new contact, and handed it to Maura so she could fill it in. "I'll send it and a couple others once I'm home."

"Thank you!" Maura's fingers were itching to get back to work.

Stephan, on the other hand, didn't seem like he was in any hurry to leave. "Have you ever seen "Carnation, Lily, Lily, Rose" before? The light in it is remarkable."

"By John Singer Sargent?"

"Yes."

Maura flashed him a grin. "I spent so much time studying it when I was at the Tate that my roommates gave up and left me there while they took themselves off to a pub." She couldn't stop herself and started filling in some of the blue-gray water she'd only outlined earlier. Mixing and shading the Atlantic where it kissed the shore at Rose Cove was second nature. Maura was able to work and chat.

"You've been to the Tate?" Stephan tried to mask his surprise.

"I spent my senior year at Trinity College in Dublin as an exchange student. My roommates from home went to University of London College. We took turns visiting over long weekends and breaks. I could have stayed at the Tate for weeks." She sighed. "I always meant to go back, but haven't managed to."

"Why didn't you go to London too?"

Maura tapped the end of her brush against her nose as she debated adding wildlife into the image. "My boyfriend was going to the University of Dublin for the year. I wanted to be near him. Besides, getting into Trinity was quite the coup for me. My aunt would have been disappointed if I hadn't taken the opportunity." She flashed him a quick grin. "I tried to avoid disappointing Aunt Jane whenever possible."

Stephan wanted to ask more about the boyfriend, as well as her parents, but couldn't think of a polite question. "Did you enjoy the experience?"

Maura decided against adding more and gathered her used brushes up so she could wash them at home. As she started packing up her kit, she thought about Stephan's question. "It was an amazing school and a wonderful experience, right up until I found Will in bed with an Irish lass halfway through." She shook her head. "I'd thought he was the one. We'd been together for almost three years." She shrugged. "Apparently, he didn't feel the same. It colored the experience for me. I spent a fair bit of time in London after that until it was time to go home. I didn't take advantage of all Trinity had to offer, I'm afraid. I was too busy nursing a broken heart."

"That's a shame."

She shrugged. "It's ancient history." Maura put her canvas on a rock so she could fold up her easel. With the wet paint, she was going to have to make two trips. She laid the palette next to the canvas. "I'll come back for them in a few minutes."

"I can carry something," Stephan offered.

Maura eyed his equipment and shook her head. "I'd feel bad if anything got paint on it. I do this all the time." She smiled. "No one's coming along and bothering my things here."

"I keep forgetting how safe it is." Stephan chuckled.

"Compared to Boston, for sure." Maura's smile was easy as she started walking. "Is Maisy excited for school?"

"She's nervous. She's been enjoying getting to know Lana, but it'll be good for her to meet some of the girls her age too."

"There are a few," Maura glanced over at him as they walked. "My friend Liz has a daughter, Fern, who is Maisy's age. When Liz is at work, Fern comes to the library. But several days a week, Liz is home after school. If you're looking for childcare that's more nurturing, I bet Liz would be happy to watch Maisy for you."

Stephan nodded. "That's good to know. What does she do?"

"Waitressing mostly, but she also has a couple of small side businesses to pick up extra income during the down months."

"And you think she'd be amenable to babysitting?"

"She could use the extra money." Maura was honest. "But, she's also one of the best mothers I know, and Fern's a wonderful kid. I think Maisy would enjoy spending time with them. It might be good for everyone."

"I'll have to meet them both and think about it, but thank you." Stephan looked at Maura as they reached her driveway. "Are you sure you don't need a hand?"

Maura put her gear down next to the front door. She shook her head and tucked a lock of hair back behind her ear when the wind teased it into her eyes. "No, but I'd better get back and grab the rest before the wind picks up."

"Got it." Stephan moved so he wasn't in her way and trailed her back to the road. "Cheers! I'll send those pictures along in a few minutes."

"Thank you!" Maura waved as she headed back to the beach at a jog.

Stephan watched her for a moment, and then turned towards Milly's house. He was whistling a cheerful tune when he opened the front door. Maisy barreled into him.

"Where were you?"

"I just went out to take a few pictures. When did you get up?"

"A few minutes ago. Can I see?" Maisy grinned at him.

"Of course. Go turn on the computer."

"Okay, Daddy." She scampered off to the kitchen where his laptop was sitting on the table. "What are we doing today? Do you have work?"

"I'm off till tomorrow. What would you like to do?" Stephan sat down and reached into the camera bag to fish around for a cable. He connected it to download the new images. Once it was working, he looked at his daughter.

She grinned at him. "We could go to some new beaches. You can take pictures while I look for seals."

"Sounds like a good plan to me, love."

Stephan quickly cycled through the photos until he found a few that he thought best captured the quality of the light.

"Oh, I like that one." Maisy's small fingers reached across the keyboard and tapped on a photo he'd scrolled by.

"Do you, now?" On impulse, Stephan had taken one of Maura. The light was playing in her hair and made it look like the embers of a fire, glowing from within. She was in deep concentration with her profile to the camera.

Maisy nodded. "She's pretty." She gave her father a sideways look. Because he was studying the image, he missed her small grin of satisfaction.

"Yes, she is." Stephan switched back to one of the ones he was sending Maura and sent it to print. He stood up to go to the photo printer he'd hooked up the night before and nodded in satisfaction when the image slid out a minute later. He gave the paper a critical look. It wasn't perfect, but it was a pretty good capture of the light. "Maisy Daisy, can you run this across the street to Maura while I finish up here?"

Maura was just returning home when she heard the girl coming up behind her. She turned and smiled. "Well, hello there."

"Hi, Maura!" Maisy beamed at her and waved the photo. "Daddy asked me to bring this to you."

Maura's hands were full. She smiled at the girl. "Can you open the door for me and bring it inside?"

"Sure!"

"Watch out for the cats." Maura moved so Maisy could go first.

Maisy's eyes lit up. "Can I meet them?"

"Of course." Maura smiled and nodded towards the door.

"Oh, right." Maisy carefully opened it and slipped inside with Maura right behind her. The child dropped to her knees in front of the trio, who were waiting in the small foyer. Maura slipped past all of them and went to the kitchen. She put her palette and damp canvas down, then washed her paint-stained hands.

Maura chuckled when she saw Tim stretching up Maisy's leg with a plaintive cry. "He wants you to hold him."

"Can I?"

"Sure." Maura gently took the print out of the child's hand so she was able to reach down and lift up the small cat. "Wow, this is great." She studied the photograph. "Please thank your dad for me. It will be a huge help." She looked over at the girl and smiled to see the cat hugging her neck. Both had looks of immense pleasure on their faces. "He's really talented."

Maisy nodded. "Uh-huh. He likes taking pictures. What's this cat's name?"

"Tim. And that one around your ankles is Greta. Mags is the old lady here." Maura bent and gave the tabby an affectionate head rub. "They're all waiting for their breakfast."

"Can I stay while you feed them?"

"Will your dad worry about you?"

"I don't think so."

Maisy was rubbing her face against the orange cat's. Tim wore a blissed-out expression and his purr was audible throughout the kitchen.

Maura was loath to interrupt the lovefest, but she didn't want to see the child get hurt when Tim inevitably launched himself into the breakfast scramble. "Sweetheart, you need to put him down now, okay?"

"Did I do something wrong? I've never had a pet."

"Oh, no, not at all. Tim gets excited about eating. I don't want you to get hurt."

"Oh, okay." Maisy crouched down and gently deposited the cat on the ground. She sat next to him so she could keep petting him. Greta shoved her head under Maisy's free hand.

Once the cats were all eating, Maura smiled at the girl. "Thank you for your help." She began moving Maisy towards the door. When they reached it, she opened it and waved to Stephan, who was standing on his porch looking over at her house. His face relaxed and he gave a cheerful wave in response. Maura picked up her easel. "Please thank your dad for me."

"Okay, I will, Maura." Maisy gave her a tight hug and then ran across the street.

CHAPTER 4

On the last Friday of summer vacation, Maura found herself with an unexpectedly quiet afternoon. After driving home, she changed into a pair of ragged cutoffs and an even older Simmons College T-shirt. She grabbed a sweatshirt and made the short trek to Rose Cove.

The small beach was deserted. Maura felt her shoulders drop down and drew in a deep breath. The thick borders of pink and white beach roses sweetened the salty tang in the air. The waters were rougher than usual with a hurricane churning off the coast, but the schussing they made over the rock-strewn beach was still soothing. It only took a couple of minutes to work her way down to the wet sand line. From there she veered left and over to her favorite spot. The little nook was protected by a jumble of large boulders. The long, flat rock she loved best was warm from the early September sun. She sank down and folded her sweatshirt up into an improvised pillow. Once she had stretched out comfortably, Maura closed her eyes. The warmth of the sun and gentle kiss of the breeze soothed her into a trancelike state.

A child's shout of laughter pulled her awareness back.

Maura lay still. She listened for a long moment before slitting her eyes open and sitting up. Once her eyes had acclimated to the bright sunshine, she opened them all the way.

The first thing she noticed was Maisy darting in and out of the shallows. The girl's laugh was full of joy and wonder. Maura smiled when she saw the reason.

A familiar black head with a white blaze bobbed in the agitated surf only feet from Maisy.

As Maura watched, the seal and girl played a rollicking game of their own making. It was all going fine until Maisy, engrossed in the fun, took a few too many steps forward into deeper water. A sneaker wave and the strength of the undertow took her by surprise. The child's legs were knocked out from under her and she disappeared under the turbulent water. Time seemed to pause as dread filled Maura. She saw Maisy's bright pink shoe moving rapidly away. She gasped. Time was suddenly flying along with her feet as she sped across the rocks before she realized that she'd launched herself from her rock. As she charged into the frigid water, Maura heard a horrified shout from the road.

Before Maura could reach the girl, the seal had already gotten to her and was using her own body to push Maisy to the surface and towards the shore. Maura and Belle reached each other as a large wave crashed into Maura's chest, knocking the woman back on her heels. Maisy was coughing and gagging. "Thank you." Maura grabbed the child up in her arms. The seal huffed and watched as Maura fought through the powerful current that was grabbing at her legs. She trembled from the exertion as her feet landed on the sand and rock of the beach. Before she got further, Maisy was plucked out of her arms. Stephan sank to his knees and cradled his sobbing daughter. All of the color had bleached out of his face and his eyes were wide with fear. Maura ran to the rock and grabbed her sweatshirt. She hurried back to the father and child.

"Here, get her out of her clothing."

Stephan gave her a blank look.

"She needs to get warm." Maura reached down and began stripping Maisy's wet dress off of her. Before either of them could protest, she had it off and replaced with her sunbaked sweatshirt.

Stephan nodded but still couldn't speak. He alternated between rubbing circles on Maisy's back and patting it to help expel the water she'd inhaled.

For several long minutes, the only sound either adult noticed were Maisy's wet, retching coughs and shuddering sobs. As they eased, Maura became aware of insistent barking from behind her. She turned and realized Belle was behind her. She gave a startled yelp and jumped out of the way when the seal's cold nose touched her leg.

The seal ignored her and pulled herself forward until she reached Maisy. She rested her head in the girl's lap.

Maisy began stroking the black fur. As she did, her crying slowed and quieted. Once the girl's tears were drying, the seal nuzzled her hand and chest. Maura could've sworn she saw a faint golden light between them, but decided she was imagining things. Maisy bent and gave another retching cough, spat out water, and then after taking in a really deep breath, kissed the seal on the white blaze between her eyes. Belle waited a moment. She rubbed the girl on the cheek with her nose and made her awkward way back to the water.

Maura and Stephan watched the seal retreat into the waves in stunned silence. Maisy was the first to break it. "Her name is Karria."

Both adults looked at the child.

"Her name isn't Blaze or Belle or Becky. She told me it's Karria."

Stephan's face was slowly regaining color. His eyes glistened with unshed tears and sparked as he took in the enormity of what had happened. "Why didn't you wait for me like you were supposed to?"

Maisy flinched at the restrained fury in his voice.

For the first time, Maura noticed he was in uniform. She also realized her own teeth were chattering. She rubbed her goose-fleshed arms with shaky hands.

"You made me a promise, Maisy." Stephan's voice shook as he tried to keep from yelling at his daughter. His emotions threatened to swamp him. The terrible fear that had gripped his heart when he saw her go under and begin to get dragged out by the powerful tide rose again.

Maura hesitated a moment, not wanting to interfere, but she saw Maisy quaking. She reached out to touch Stephan's shoulder. "Maisy should get warmed up."

Stephan looked at Maura and took in her own blue-tinged lips and pale face. Her freckles stood out against her blanched skin. He could feel his daughter shaking in his arms and pushed his anger and fear as far to the back of his mind as he could. He gathered Maisy in his arms and rose to his feet. "Thank you. Thank you, Maura." He held her gaze.

Maisy peeked out at Maura from under the sweatshirt hood that had fallen over her eyes. "I'm sorry. I didn't mean to fall in."

Maura gave her a gentle smile. "I know, sweetheart. Let's get you warm."

"We need to get *both* of you warm." Stephan kept his eyes off of Maura's shapely legs, a task made easier by his immediate need to care for both of them.

They walked as briskly as the adults' unsteady legs could carry them. Maura's soaked tennis shoes squished with every step. She hesitated as they passed her own driveway, but a quiet "Please," from Stephan kept her next to him. She walked up the porch steps and into Milly's larger house with the father and child.

"Could you hold her for a moment?"

"Of course." Maura reached out her arms. Maisy slithered into them. She wrapped her legs around Maura's waist and locked her arms around her neck. Maura instinctively began rubbing gentle circles over Maisy's back and making soothing noises to the child. She shifted the girl in her arms so she could wiggle Maisy's sodden sneakers off. Maura then toed off her own soaked shoes. With a foot, she pushed them onto a mat by the door.

When Stephan reappeared moments later, he had two blankets in his arms. He gently wrapped one around Maura's shoulders. He then held the other out and tipped his head for Maura to put Maisy into his arms, where he wrapped the girl snugly into the colorful quilt. As he settled Maisy onto the couch in the living room, Maura veered left and filled Milly's kettle with water and started heating it.

While the water was warming, she pulled the blanket tighter around her shoulders and body. Maura's hands were still trembling as she gathered mugs. After she found a box of tea and some hot cocoa powder, she perched on a tall stool. The trembling had spread down her legs. The low voices in the living room stopped and a moment later Maura found herself in a tight embrace.

"I saw my world ending and then you were there, saving her." Stephan's voice was rough with suppressed emotion.

Maura could feel his heart beating under her head. She let herself enjoy the warmth and comfort of the hug, but soon the pressure of a button pushing into her temple caused her to shift. Then the kettle began a shrill whistle and she pulled back.

"I thought we could use some tea."

Stephan gave her a wry look. "Mind if I put whiskey in it?"

Maura squeezed his arm in sympathy. "Do you want to call Dr. Beals?"

He ran a hand through his dark hair. It had grown longer than he normally kept it, haircuts not being a priority in the chaos of changing jobs and moving. Stephan nodded. "Do you think I should? Of course, I should. She inhaled God knows how much water." He shook his head. "It's not the same when it's your own child." He pulled his cell phone out and found the number.

"Hello, Carl, this is Stephan Kirkland."

Maura began preparing three mugs while Stephan spoke with the doctor's office. As the tea steeped and Maisy's cocoa cooled, she heard him say thank you and hang up.

"What'd they say?"

"Alex is going to come by and listen to her lungs and do an assessment. We'll go from there."

"Good." Maura nodded. "No whiskey, then."

Stephan's expression lightened a bit. "Yes ma'am."

"Can I check on her and bring her this?" Maura handed Stephan one of the mugs and then picked up the other two. The liquid sloshed around because her hands were still unsteady.

"Let's both go." He gave Maura a slight smile as he took Maisy's mug from her shaky grip.

Maisy was ensconced in her quilt at the corner of the couch. She was propped up by pillows and cuddling a stuffed cow. Her eyes were wide and she was still pale. Giant tears were rolling down her cheeks.

"Oh, love," Stephan put the mugs down on the table and pulled her into his arms.

Maura put her mug down as well and bundled Maisy back up as she snuggled into her father.

"I'm sorry, Daddy. I'm sorry." She buried her face into Stephan's shoulder and wept.

Maura felt like an intruder, but when she moved to leave, Stephan lifted a hand and shook his head. "Please stay, if you can."

"Okay." She sat on the edge of an overstuffed chair and cradled her hot mug in her chilled hands. As Maisy's sobs slowed and were reduced to occasional sniffles, Maura felt the knot of worry in her gut ease up and began sipping her tea.

The sound of a car door shutting had Maura jumping out of her seat. She dropped the blanket from her shoulders. "I'll let her in. You stay," she said to Stephan.

Alex Bright gave Maura a speculative look when she opened the door. "Maura, what a nice surprise."

"Hi, Alex." Maura gave the beautiful blond nurse a polite smile. "They're in the living room."

"Oh, you poor little love." Alex hurried past Maura as soon as Stephan and Maisy came into view.

For all their disagreements over the years, Maura could not fault Alex's professionalism when there was a patient. She took her mug to the kitchen as Alex conducted her exam and spoke with the Kirklands.

When she heard Stephan escorting the nurse to the door, she went back into the living room and sat down next to Maisy. "Want your cocoa now?"

The little girl nodded.

Hearing the change in pitch of Alex's voice from professional to flirtatious, Maura turned so her back was to the doorway and she was fully facing Maisy. She knew it was petty. She had no grounds on which to feel possessive, but Alex's husky laugh was setting her teeth on edge. Maura focused her attention on the child. "How do you know her name is Karria?"

"She told me."

"How?"

Maisy looked around as if to see if anyone was listening. "When the wave knocked me under, I got really scared because I couldn't figure out where up was. There was a voice in my head. It was her. She told me I was safe."

"The seal?" Maura kept her skepticism out of her voice.

"Yes. She's a special kind of seal."

"If she can speak telepathically, I'd say so."

"What's telepathically?"

"Who's telepathic?" Stephan leaned against the doorway. He'd felt a surge of relief when he returned from husting the chatty nurse out to see his daughter looking more and more like herself as she sipped her sweet drink. He sat down beside Maura.

Maura shrugged. She kept her tone neutral as she explained, "Maisy says the seal spoke with her when she rescued her."

Stephan wondered if his daughter had banged her head on a rock and began rethinking the need for further testing.

Maisy saw the look on his face. "I'm fine, Daddy. Really." She gave him a brilliant smile, but then it wobbled. "I'm in trouble, huh?"

"Oh, yes," Stephan nodded in agreement. "You are in big trouble, but not until tomorrow."

Maisy sighed and drank more of her cocoa. She peered owlishly over the rim at her father. "Can we watch a movie tonight, then? And maybe have breakfast for dinner?" She paused to gauge her father's expression and added, "And maybe ice cream?"

Maura's shoulders shook as she held in her laughter. Stephan felt the movement and a smile formed on his lips. He took the opportunity to reach behind her and snake his arm around to tweak one of Maisy's pigtails. He then left it draped across the back of the sofa, touching Maura's shoulders.

"You are pushing your luck, Miss Maisy."

His daughter gave an impish grin. "I just wanted to see you smile. You look pretty upset still."

"I am."

"You worried I was going to die, like Mama, didn't you?" A tear began rolling down Maisy's cheek again.

Stephan nodded. "Yes love, and it terrified me." His voice was rough with emotion.

Maura wanted to give them privacy, but sandwiched between them, couldn't quite figure out how to manage it without making things more awkward.

Maisy solved the woman's dilemma by thrusting her mug into Maura's hand and clambering over her to once more snuggle into her father's lap.

Maura put the mug down on the table and untangled herself from the quilt. She rewrapped it around the quietly crying child and gave Stephan's arm a gentle squeeze. "I'm going to go home. If you need help, just call."

Stephan knew Maisy needed his full attention. He gave a reluctant nod. "I can never thank you enough, Maura."

"Anyone would have done it. And Belle—err, Karria—was the hero."

Stephan noted her discomfort at being thanked. He moved so he could clasp her hand in his larger one. "You both were." He held her hand until her hazel eyes locked with his. "Thank you."

Maura was in her own home feeding the cats before she realized she'd left her sweatshirt and shoes behind. She ran a hand through her tangled locks and sighed. Retrieving them would have to wait. After feeding the cats, she ran a hot bath for herself.

Maura looked at Tim, who sat on the edge of the tub flicking water at her from time to time with his tail.

"I've got a problem, Timmy."

His golden eyes gleamed in the low light as he stared at her.

"They're a grieving family. I have no business being interested in him."

Tim gave her a long, slow blink. "Merrow."

"You think I should focus on you instead?" Maura grinned at the small cat and gave his chin and affectionate rub. His rumbly purrs relaxed her more than the bath.

Maura retreated to her bedroom. Pulling on an intricate shawl Jane had finished shortly before her death, Maura opened the window that faced the cove. When she wore it, she liked to imagine it was her aunt's arms wrapped around her in a hug rather than rows of ocean colored yarn. A heavy, bright moon illuminated the moving water. The clanging of the buoy in nearby Ballard channel and a distant foghorn were familiar sounds. It all seemed so peaceful.

It was deceptive.

Maura shuddered to remember how close to tragedy they'd come. Images from the accident played through her head. If the seal hadn't done what she had, would Maura have been able to get to the child in time? She liked to think so, but the water was cold and the current so strong. The odds hadn't been great.

A complaint from the bed drew her attention. "Are you trying to tell me it's time to sleep?" Maura smiled when Mags replied with a grunt from her nest in the pillow next to Maura's. Deciding the fresh air felt good, Maura left the window open. She eased into the bed and nudged Tim over with her leg. He cracked an eye and gave her a baleful look, but resettled himself on her hip with a groan after she turned off the light. As she settled in, Maura felt a wave of gratitude wash over her. Everyone *was* safe and life would go back to normal.

Across the street, Stephan stood in the larger guest room at the back of the house. He watched Maura's light wink out and turned to study his sleeping daughter. Maisy was snuggling Dot the cow and using her beloved Pooh Bear as a pillow. He could see pieces of Sophie in her as she rested; the shape of her nose, her cheekbones, the slender length of her fingers. Much of her deceased mother was more obvious when she was animated; her wit, the gleam of mischief in her eyes, and her boundless energy.

Stephan let out a heavy sigh.

Maisy coughed a bit and opened her eyes. She smiled to see him. "Daddy." She flexed her fingers at him in greeting.

He smiled back and sank down onto the bed.

"Snuggle me."

"For a little while, Maisy Daisy." Stephan caressed her soft hair when she burrowed her head onto his chest. The child sighed in contentment. He held her for a long time as she slipped back into deep sleep. He knew he could leave and go to his own room, but the fear of losing his daughter was still far too fresh. When Maisy eventually rolled away from him, Stephan stacked his hands behind his head and let his thoughts wander.

The day of Sophie's accident had started like any other. He'd worked the overnight shift and arrived home a half hour before his wife and child were leaving for the day. Sophie had looked beautiful, but remote in her tailored skirt and blouse. Her blonde hair was fixed in a knot at the back of her neck. It showed off a pair of diamond earrings he'd never seen before. Seeing his gaze, Sophie had given him an enigmatic look. She'd been stiff and formal with him, but cheerful with their daughter. Maisy had been eating her Cheerios and watching her parents with eyes that took in everything.

Because of their daughter's intense observance, Stephan didn't comment on the new jewelry. It wouldn't have even led to a fight. He'd given up by then. They'd fallen into a vicious cycle. Not confronting Sophie left him feeling emasculated. And she, in turn, treated him more and more like a lovesick boy than an equal.

They'd talked about little matters: the art project four-year-old Maisy was working on at her preschool, Sophie's plans to go out with friends after work, what Stephan and Maisy would do when he picked her up in the afternoon.

Thunder was rumbling as he'd given Sophie a perfunctory kiss on the cheek. Maisy had thrown herself into his arms with an enthusiastic hug and affectionate kiss. She reminded him to snuggle Pooh Bear if he was worried about the storm when he went to bed. And then they were gone.

He'd only just drifted off when Brian called. His partner's tone had put him on alert even before the words came. He listened, but couldn't process what was being said at first. It didn't make sense. Lightning strike, a drunk driver, accident, dead at the scene, taken to Children's. It had all been phrases. Stephan had mechanically gotten up and dressed. When Brian reached the condo in Jamaica Plain, he found his partner waiting in the rain. Speeding to Children's Hospital, they said little to each other. Brian offered to take care of things in the office, not that there was much he'd need to do. Word of the accident that impacted one of their own had spread like wildfire through the precinct.

A mild concussion for their daughter and a broken neck for his wife. Stephan still couldn't recall all the details of the day. He did remember going to the morgue to confirm that it was indeed Sophie lying there. The primal scream her mother had issued when he told them would be etched in his memory as long as he lived. The way Maisy had cried out in her sleep night after night would never leave him either. He had dreaded the nighttime for months after Sophie's passing.

For his daughter's sake, he set aside his own feelings through the ordeal of the services and funeral. He'd spoken of Sophie's charm, grace, and joy in living. He'd ignored the snide comments and looks from those who Sophie had confided in or partied with. Nicholas, Stephan's brother and best friend, helped run interference from the worst of the offenders. His parents stayed for weeks afterwards and helped care for father and daughter. For the most part, he had been numb. Maisy was his focus. Maisy's heart was broken and she was his world.

He transferred to a desk job and slashed his hours to the bare minimum to keep their health insurance. Life insurance and settlement money ensured he could afford the pay cut. It also meant Maisy's college fund was full. She didn't return to preschool. Stephan hired the retired teacher, Patty, who lived in the unit next to theirs to watch the girl when he was working. By the time kindergarten started, they'd gotten into a routine. Maisy's grief was less sharp and omnipresent. It came in ebbs and flows. She was the center of Stephan's life and he structured their days around getting her all the help she needed to process the accident and her loss. He didn't accept invitations to anything that wasn't a family outing and they only went to some of those. After the one-year anniversary of Sophie's death had passed and they'd settled into the second year of living without her, Stephan had his head above water enough to realize they had become isolated.

With Maisy in kindergarten, he tried to involve them in school and community life. Maisy didn't enjoy her teacher and didn't bond with any of her classmates. Many days she pleaded a stomachache and asked to stay home with Patty. By the time February had rolled around, Stephan decided it was time to make a change. He and Maisy talked about what they most loved and where they'd enjoy living. Both kept coming back to Maine. It was a place they visited every year when Stephan's parents and brother came to stay. When the job on Belfort crossed his desk, he'd flagged it as something to look into. Later that day, Milly, who he only had met a handful of times, contacted him out of the blue to tell him about the position. She offered her vacation home as a place to stay if they wanted to give island living a try. When Stephan had told

Maisy about it over dinner, she'd grown round eyed and told him Sophie had told her in a dream all about the island she was going to move to and how much happier they'd be there. Maisy didn't share all the details of the dream with her father because some were private and others, she thought, would upset him, but she made sure her enthusiasm for going was crystal-clear.

Sophie's parents had been set against the idea of them moving away. Milly again intervened, and Maisy's passionate enthusiasm for the move eased their dismay. Stephan had felt a wave of relief crash over him the day he and Maisy returned to their condo after telling them he'd been offered the position. Keeping up appearances in front of Ruth and Bill had been draining him. It wasn't that he didn't mourn Sophie, but he was tapped out. He had grieved her loss despite everything, but he had been saying good-bye incrementally to Sophie for years before her death. Therapy had helped him sort through it all. By the time they moved, he felt balanced. Most importantly, he felt like himself again.

Maisy's accident today, however, had ripped him right back to when he'd first found her in the emergency room, sobbing in heartbreak and fear. The stab of fear that day had left permanent scars.

Stephan rolled onto his hip and studied his sleeping child until his eyes shut and, despite his intention to stay awake, he slipped into a deep sleep.

CHAPTER 5

"Heard you saved the new guy's kid yesterday."

Maura had been enjoying a quiet lunch when Colleen McQuarrie sauntered into her office. She arched an eyebrow at the tall brunette and continued to chew her food.

Colleen grabbed the free chair and spun it so she could straddle it. She draped her arms over the back as she scrutinized Maura. "He was pretty rattled this morning when he brought Maisy to the station. She's going to hang with Lana and Vicky for the day so Stevie can put in his shift."

"Stevie?" Maura laughed.

"Gotta bust his chops somehow. The nickname annoys him, so we're going with it." Colleen grinned.

Maura shook her head. "How was Maisy?"

"Quiet, but she seemed okay."

Maura gave the younger woman a skeptical look. "Okay?"

"Yeah, I mean, she cried, but she didn't carry on or anything. Vicky and Lana came to get her pretty quickly. She was laughing when they left." Colleen shrugged. "Stevie told us what happened. Did the seal really help?"

Maura nodded. "If she hadn't done what she did, it's hard to tell if I'd have been able to reach Maisy in time. She would've sucked in more water at the very least."

"Damn. That musta been rough." Colleen didn't enjoy children, but she wasn't hard-hearted. "He said he was too far away to help."

"He told you all of this?"

"We might've listened at Ron's door."

"We?"

"Chip 'n me. He's on dispatch today. I was keeping him company."

Maura felt a pang of sympathy for Stephan. He didn't strike her as someone who would want his life gossiped about. Then again, he'd have to get used to it if he was going to make it on the island. Secrets were hard to keep for any length of time when more than one person knew them. Chip Collins was kind, but one of the worst gossips on the island. She groaned when she realized what this meant. "Did you come to warn me about something?"

Colleen grinned again. "If I didn't like you, I'd have let the old biddies ambush you."

"What exactly did you 'overhear'?"

They heard the library door close. Colleen leaned back and craned her neck to look out into the main room. Her eyes were amused when she met Maura's gaze.

"You can thank me later. Want me to run interference while you think of what to say?"

Before Maura could answer, a now familiar face peeked into her office. "Maura—oh hey, I didn't realize you had company." Stephan's accent thickened with his discomfort at seeing his colleague sitting in the librarian's office.

Maura was fascinated with the change.

For her part, Colleen enjoyed watching the subtle interplay between the two. She knew neither was aware how much their expressions and body language were giving away. Chip was so going to owe her five bucks.

"Colleen was just leaving."

"I was?" Colleen gave Maura an amused smirk before she nodded in agreement and stood up. She grinned at Stephan and patted him on the shoulder as she passed him. "Actually, I have things to do and people to see. Till tomorrow, Stevie."

Stephan waited until Colleen was gone before he groaned. "She overheard me talking to Ron, didn't she?"

"Mm, more like she and Chip eavesdropped."

"Chip too?" Stephan let his head thunk against the doorframe. He then straightened up. "May I come in?"

"Of course!" Maura gestured to the chair Colleen had just vacated.

"Are they the busybodies I suspect they are?"

"There's no easy way to break this to you," Maura chuckled at his expression and reached out to pat his hand. "They're probably worse than what you're imagining. Those two put the old men at Jack's to shame, and that's not easy."

Stephan eyed the soft hand that was still on top of his own. Had Colleen told Maura everything she'd overheard? Had she heard everything he and Ron had talked about? He doubted it, or Maura wouldn't be patting him like he was an old dear needing comforting.

"So, anything they heard is likely to be common knowledge by tomorrow."

"By supper actually, but to be fair, as bad as they are about gossiping, they're also good folks. They won't share anything sensitive." Maura gave him a wry expression. "Of course, their version of private and sensitive information is usually more flexible than mine, so…." She shrugged and offered Stephan half an orange. "They heard about the seal rescuing Maisy." Her voice trailed off and she gave Stephan a thoughtful look.

Stephan focused on peeling apart the segments of fruit. He shifted uncomfortably under her gaze.

"Colleen was starting to warn me about some tidbit she thought would cause a stir, but you came in before she could tell me." Maura leaned back in her chair. "Care to enlighten me before the old ladies start parading in here and twittering about?"

Stephan stuffed what remained of the orange into his mouth so he could organize his thoughts. He lifted a finger to ask her to wait a moment. He took his time chewing while mentally reviewing the conversation he and the chief had shared. He could guess at what Colleen had thought the library's patronesses would latch onto. Of course, if Colleen and Chip had minded their own business, he wouldn't even be worrying about this.

Maura arched an eyebrow at the shift in his expression. "That doesn't look promising," she observed.

"Hmm?" Stephan gave her a confused look. "What doesn't?"

"You started scowling at me."

"I did?"

Maura nodded.

"Oh, I'm sorry. It's not intentional. Or at least not aimed at you, Maura."

"Can you tell me what I should expect the gossips to be springing on me?"

Stephan studied Maura in silence for a moment longer. Her russet locks were pulled up in a messy bun. The tendrils that escaped framed her face in lovely waves. She wasn't the kind of knockout who took your breath away, but he thought she was beautiful. Her eyes were full of compassion and good humor, her full lips were frequently smiling, and there was a delicacy about her features that made him want to protect her, something he was willing to admit he found appealing. He wanted to tell her the truth about Sophie. He was tired of living under her shadow.

"I was asking about you," he admitted.

"Me?" Maura wasn't expecting that answer.

He nodded. "I want to talk, but I don't want to rush through it. Are you free tonight?"

"There's a trustees meeting. I have to attend." Maura wasn't sure what to make of his announcement. "They usually end by 9, but I can't promise. It's pretty late, I know."

Stephan couldn't help grinning. "9 is past Maisy's bedtime, but not mine." He winked at her. "I don't have to go to sleep until 10."

Maura laughed at his boyish expression. "If you think you can stay up, then we could talk tonight. If not, it'll have to be another one."

"I can stay up." Stephan's eyes were still warm but his expression had grown serious again. It was better that Maisy would be asleep and not know Maura was over anyway. He didn't want to compete with his daughter for her attention. The conversation he wanted to have wasn't one his child had any need to listen in on.

They both heard the library door open and close. He reached out for Maura's hand. "Please don't listen to whatever they're gossiping about until we've talked."

Maura was surprised when he held and gently squeezed her hand in his larger one. She shivered at the electricity that shot through her. "I usually take the chatter around here with more than a grain of salt anyway."

"Good." Stephan was reluctant to release her hand, but as they heard a "Yoo-hoo, Maura," from the other room he gave her one last gentle squeeze. He then released her hand so that his fingers slowly caressed it as they separated. "I'll see you tonight."

"Tonight," Maura repeated, somewhat bemused by the last twenty minutes, but not displeased. She watched him leave.

As she stood up and straightened her skirt, she heard Eliza introducing him to her cronies Eloise and Clara. All three women had adopted girlish, flirting tones with the Englishman. Maura let him suffer for a minute before leaving her office to rescue him.

"Good afternoon, ladies." she greeted the women. "How are you today?"

"We're just fine." Eloise gave her a sly grin. "But not as good as you two, eh?"

"Officer Kirkland was just letting me know how his daughter is feeling while I finished my lunch." Maura used her best no-nonsense voice.

"Lunch! Is that what young people are calling it these days?" Clara leaned on her cane and cackled.

Maura simply stared at her in silence.

"Oh, be that way," Clara rolled her eyes at the younger woman when she didn't bite. She turned to Stephan. "Our Maura is single. Did you know that? I heard you were wondering." She grinned when he flushed. "She's never been married to anything except the library and that's a damned shame if you ask me."

"No one did, Mrs. Sewell." Maura was mortified.

Stephan winked at her and then nodded to the white-haired lady. "That is indeed a damned shame. What was your name again?"

He peppered the seniors with questions for a few minutes and then gave them a wide smile. "I need to get back to work. Lovely meeting all of you." He winked at Maura. "Miz Ballard, a pleasure as always."

Maura had an urge to stick her tongue out at him. He gave her a roguish grin as he slipped out of the door and left her with three bright eyed, inquisitive women with far too much time on their hands. "What can I help you ladies with today?"

When Maura finally pulled into her driveway at ten-thirty, she closed her eyes and let her head thud against the headrest. Daryl had to be removed from the board. He was going to drive her insane if he stayed. It was bad enough that they'd had to have a Saturday night meeting because of him, but to drag it out unnecessarily was intolerable. She'd sent Stephan a text at nine letting him know she wasn't sure when she'd get home and another as she was leaving the library. She hadn't heard back and assumed he'd fallen asleep. Yesterday had to have taken a toll on him; it had on her, and Maisy wasn't *her* child.

Stepping out of her car, Maura glanced across the street. There were a couple of lights on downstairs, but she didn't want to risk waking them up. As she hesitated, she saw the front door open and Stephan's tall silhouette filled it. When he waved, she grabbed her bag and walked over.

"Long meeting?" He gave her a sympathetic look.

"Our newest board member is in love with the sound of his own voice and the chair is too intimidated to interrupt when he goes off on tangents. But I'm not bitter or anything," Maura gave a half smile. "I'm sorry I couldn't get here earlier. We can talk another day."

"No," Stephan reached for her hand as she started to step back. "Please, come in. I mean, if you're not too tired, that is." He saw she was still wearing the same pretty summer dress she'd had on at lunch topped with a pale green cardigan to ward off the night's chill.

"If you're sure." Maura was too keyed up to sleep and was intensely curious to hear what he had to say. But she was also mindful of the fact that with a young child on her last days of summer vacation, his day tomorrow would likely start well before hers. He was wearing a simple gray T-shirt and blue sweatpants. She bit her lip. He looked like he was getting ready to go to bed.

"Please." Stephan gently ushered her into the dimly lit house. He took her bag and set it by the door. "Would you like something to eat or drink?"

Maura hesitated a moment before sliding her shoes off. "I'd love some herbal tea if you have any. I wasn't really paying attention to what was there yesterday."

Stephan chuckled. "Did you just ask an Englishman if he has an assortment of tea?"

"I didn't want to assume," she smiled.

He continued to hold her hand as they walked. "My mum brought about two dozen boxes when they came to visit in May. I'll still be drinking it by the time she arrives with a fresh batch in December."

"Well then, surprise me, please."

Stephan released Maura's hand when they reached the kitchen. In short order, he had put together a small plate of cheese and crackers and two mugs of steaming tea.

Maura sniffed the fragrant aroma appreciatively. "Is that strawberry?"

"It's more cheerful than chamomile. Besides, I don't want you falling asleep on me." Stephan's expression was warm. "Let's go sit in the back porch."

Maura wrapped her hands around her warm mug and followed.

Stephan sat next to her and angled himself so their knees were lightly touching. "I'm glad you came." He resisted the urge to reach for her hand as he saw her put a slice of cheddar on a cracker.

He gave her a hesitant smile. "Please let me get through this. It's difficult to talk about. I promise I'll answer anything after."

"Okay." Maura angled herself so she could look directly at Stephan as he spoke.

"Sophie and I met when she was an exchange student at Kings College. I was halfway through my course of study in law. We met through mutual friends at a party. I was gobsmacked. I was young and inexperienced. She was beautiful, polished, and confident; so out of my league. For some reason she spent the evening flirting with me anyway."

Maura raised an eyebrow at the notion that the handsome, confident man beside her considered himself inexperienced or out of anyone's league in the heart of his college days.

Stephan saw the look and shook his head. "I was. I'd dated on and off over the years and had a few steady girls and vacation flings, but not an adult relationship. Anyway, Sophie knocked me over. She was brilliant, witty, sophisticated, charming, and in those days, she seemed to find me as fascinating as I found her. When her year in England was over, I couldn't imagine living without her. I proposed. She accepted, but only if we moved back here to the states together, right away." He took a swallow of his tea and then set the mug down. "Obviously I agreed or we wouldn't be having this conversation. My father was upset because it meant I wouldn't become a barrister like he'd hoped and my mum was disappointed I was moving so far away. My brother Nick is my best mate. Leaving him behind was difficult, but I followed my heart. It took a while to get settled. Sophie went on to complete her Masters at BU while I worked and studied American law at nights. It was going to take too long and too much money to earn my JD here with Sophie also in grad school so I changed plans and applied to the police academy. The first ten years or so were good. After Maisy was born things were still good for a couple of years. Then Sophie got a big promotion at work. She began traveling more. I was working full-time as well. Juggling our schedules with a toddler was challenging, but manageable. Sophie started going out with her friends after work a couple of nights a week. They started taking more 'girls' weekends. I figured she was entitled given how hard she worked. It just sort of happened that we saw each other less and less. Then the gifts started. I noticed, but didn't want to know. I thought if I let her have her flirtations it'd pass. She'd get it out of her system. I thought Maisy and I would be enough to bring her back. I was wrong. In the last months, she was talking and texting at all hours with a bloke named Jason. Our marriage was essentially over in all but name for the last year and a half of her life. We'd started working with a mediator a couple of months before the accident. I'd finally accepted I'd never be enough and she wanted the freedom to do what she wanted without pretense. But we didn't agree on how to share Maisy. And then, suddenly, it didn't matter anymore."

Stephan told her about the accident and then paused to take a long swallow of tea. He looked at Maura over the rim of his mug to gauge her reaction.

Maura felt tremendous sympathy for Stephan's situation, but wasn't sure what to say. "It sounds like you've been through so much."

Stephan was familiar with the expression on her face. It was a look he'd become well acquainted with and had, himself, worn in the past.

He let his hand drop so his fingers rested on her shoulders. Her cardigan was soft underneath them. "Coming here is a fresh start for us. I'm ready to start living again, not just for my daughter, but also myself. My plan was to get settled, make sure this is the right place for us, buy a home, and start dating again when the right woman appeared. Instead, we're still settling in and I'm nowhere near ready to buy a house, but I've met a woman I'd very much like to get to know better."

Maura flushed with pleasure but felt compelled to point out, "It could just be the adrenaline speaking."

Stephan lifted an eyebrow. "Pardon?"

She waved her hand as she explained. "When Maisy almost drowned, your—our—adrenaline kicked into high gear. Stressful situations can make people think they're attracted to someone, when it was really just hormones caused by the circumstances."

Stephan was fighting a grin. "So, you think my feelings might be only because of what happened at the beach?"

Maura bit her lip and nodded.

"Why aren't I infatuated with the seal, then?"

She rolled her eyes at him. "Because you're not into bestiality?"

Stephan laughed. "True, I'm not. But, Maura," he slid closer and his voice wrapped around her in a velvet caress. "I wanted to get to know you better the moment I saw you frowning at that tomato."

She looked at him askance. "You're joking."

"Not a bit." He shook his head and reached for her hand. "You looked so serious and beautiful. Then your passion for the library and community lit your eyes up. It got my interest, all right." He winked at her. "I'm also a sucker for the word *conundrum*."

Maura hesitated, unsure of herself and not liking the feeling one bit. "What about Maisy?"

"I don't know," Stephan admitted. "But she's already half in love with you. Maura, I can't keep putting my life on hold. I'm not asking for a commitment, just to see where things between us can go."

"What were you and Ron talking about that got Colleen all excited?"

Stephan took the change in topic in stride. "You." He grinned when she blushed. "I was asking him about you; if you were seeing anyone and trying to learn more about what you like."

"Oh." Maura met his stare and let herself get lost in the vibrancy of it. Her gaze tracked from his eyes down to his lips and back up again. He was handsome, but it was more than bone structure that made him that way. He exuded good humor and kindness. Maura nodded her head.

Stephan reached out and stroked her thick hair. "Was that a yes, you'll go on a date with me?"

Maura smiled. "I'd like to very much. Anywhere we go on the island, people will talk, you know."

"Does that bother you?"

"Yes," she admitted. "But not because of you! I just hate being talked about."

Stephan nodded. "It's good we're neighbors. We can get to know each other with some measure of privacy at least." He was enjoying the silkiness of her hair against his fingers. "Ron told me about a few restaurants in Bar Harbor. Would you like to go next Sunday? Would a lunch date be okay? It's the first weekend after school starts. I'll need to be home for a bit before bed." He groaned. "I sound like an old man."

"You sound responsible. It's kinda sexy."

"Really?" Stephan laughed. "Wait till you see me on a school night. I'll be dead sexy then." He deliberately thickened his accent.

She leaned into his caress, enjoying the feel of his hand against her head. "Why don't we save Bar Harbor for another time, when Maisy's gotten into a routine?" She saw his disappointed expression and hurried to finish her thought. "If Ron and Vicky will take Maisy for a while, you could come over to my house for dinner on Saturday evening. Would that work? That way you're nearby if she needs you. We can make it an earlier meal. I can get a sub for the afternoon at the library."

"I'd love that, but it doesn't seem fair that I ask you out and you end up having to do all the work."

Maura smiled. "It'll be nice to cook for someone else." She couldn't stop a large yawn and hastily covered her mouth, then grimaced. "Sorry. It's been a long day."

Stephan reached for both her hands and helped her up. "And I've kept you out late. Let me walk you home."

"It's just across the street." She laughed, but was inwardly pleased.

Stephan held her hand as they walked towards the front door. He picked up her bag while she put on her shoes.

The cool air held the promise of autumn. The soft murmuring of the ocean and hooting of a nearby owl were the only sounds to break the quiet. The sky was filled with stars and the band of the Milky Way dominated the vista. Maura tipped her head back to take in the view. "It always takes my breath away, no matter how often I see it." Her voice was low and quiet.

Stephan wrapped his arm around her shoulder and enjoyed the beauty of the sky with her. Eventually they made their way across the street and to her front door. They paused there. Maura pulled her key from her pocket and unlocked the door, but didn't open it. She looked up at him. Stephan put her bag down. "May I?" His voice was whisper-soft, but she heard him. She nodded and leaned in close to him, inhaling his scent while he bent down. The kiss was feather soft at first, a tentative greeting. After a moment, they leaned in as the kiss deepened and grew more intimate. When they moved apart, each was breathing raggedly. They held each other as they gathered their own thoughts.

Stephan caressed Maura's cheek and rested his head against hers. "Thank you." He didn't want to break the spell with the wrong words, but needed her to understand just how much it had meant to him. "I—that—you're wonderful."

Maura hugged him tight. It took all her willpower not to pull his head down and kiss him witless. She'd never had a kiss electrify her the way his touch did. She wanted to feel it again, but knew she wouldn't want to stop once they started. "That was amazing," she whispered against his chest.

Stephan was thrilled the kiss had impacted her too. Her words made him want to yell a victory cry. Instead, he held her tight. "I need to let you go," he muttered, "but I don't want to."

Maura started to reply when a plaintive yowl from the other side of the door beat her to it. It was followed by a heavy thumping as a cat launched himself against the structure repeatedly. "That's Tim," she explained. "He's a bit possessive and probably hungry."

Stephan laughed. "I'd better not start off on his bad side, then." He reached down, picked up Maura's bag, and handed it to her. "I'll see you soon." He couldn't resist giving her a gentle kiss before she nodded and opened her door. Stephen saw an irate-looking fluffball glaring at him in the pool of light from the hallway. "Good night, Maura."

CHAPTER 6

Chatter filled the library as children spilled in. Their exuberant voices brought smiles to the faces of most patrons, though a couple frowned at the disruption to the previous quiet. Maura approached the kids and put a finger to her lips. The ones who noticed her first nudged the others and in short order, the unruly bunch became a quiet, respectful group. They followed her to the children's room. A slim, blond teenager stood up from one of the two tables. A couple of other teens lounged on one of the window seats in the back. They didn't even glance up from their phones when the younger kids filed in.

Maura shut the door and turned to them. When the kids had dropped their backpacks and were looking at her, she asked, "How was the first day back, gang?"

"Great!"

"Horrible!"

"Booooooring."

"I got stuck next to Billy and he picks his nose."

"Yeah, well you *eat* your boogers, Charlie."

"They ran out of pizza."

"We already have homework."

"It was okay."

"I'm hungry, Miss Maura."

"Hey, me too."

"Can Isabelle read us a story?"

"No, Izzy should take us outside to play."

Maura raised a hand. After a moment, the group fell silent and all were looking at her expectantly. "First, a snack for everyone who wants one. Then I'll read a story while Isabelle takes those who want to go outside out to play."

A cheer arose. The more experienced kids began helping dole out the snacks. Others led the younger ones to the bathroom to wash up, knowing nothing was going to happen until everyone had pitched in and was cleaned up.

Maura watched Maisy watch the others before attaching herself to Fern Boyd's side. Fern was more reserved than Maisy, but imaginative, kind, and very bright. Maisy wouldn't be able to steamroll her, and Fern would benefit from a new friend.

After everyone was settled and had an opportunity to share about their day, Maura went to check on the adult patrons. Most knew the afterschool routine. A few had come specifically to help out. Sam and Margery Dodd disappeared out back with the kids and Isabelle. Fred Foley had wandered into the children's room and started reading *Charlotte's Web* to the ones who'd opted to stay inside. Maura promised to relieve him as soon as she could. He'd waved her off with assurances that he was happy to read until his voice gave out, which prompted a cheer from the handful of children sprawled out in front of him.

When they saw Maura return to the main room, the Jones sisters hoisted themselves out of the arm chairs they'd been reading and dozing in. There was much complaining as they reached for their canes and cardigans, then made their way to the circulation desk. Rose, the younger at 87, pushed a stack of romances and mysteries towards Maura. Iris was fumbling through a faded change purse for her library card. Years of experience had taught Maura that the elderly woman would not leave until she'd checked out her books the 'proper' way. The fact that the card catalog had given way to a computerized system still rankled Iris. The idea that Maura could look her up without scanning the barcode on her card was nothing short of scandalous.

"We hear the new constable is sweet on you, Miss Ballard."

Maura felt her cheeks warm, which only made the ladies twitter with giggles.

"I think Miss Ballard is sweet on him! Maybe Eliza had it backwards." Rose smiled with delight. Maura suspected it was as much with pleasure at the notion that Eliza might have her gossip wrong as anything else.

Maura hurried through the checkout process and stowed the books in a shopping bag Iris handed her. "They're all due back September 30th." She stood up and went to hold the door open for them.

As the women made their slow way past her, Rose chortled, "Is it possible you're both sweet on each other? That would be delightful." She grinned when Maura's cheeks pinkened again.

"Come now sissy. We've embarrassed the young lady enough for one day." Iris smiled at Maura. "Besides, we need to go to Blanche's and rub it in Eliza's face that we know more than she does."

Rose let her sister get partway down the handicap ramp before loudly whispering to Maura, "Did he ask you on a date?"

Maura was determined not to give them any more to gossip about. She pretended she didn't hear the question and started to step back into the library.

Rose nodded sagely. "That's a yes, then. Good girl! Be bold and daring! Don't let the opportunity pass by, dear." She gave Maura a little finger wave and followed her sister to their tank of a car.

Maura leaned against the doorway and sighed.

"Were they talking about you and Daddy?"

Maura's eyes widened and she drew in a deep breath before turning around to face Maisy.

"I didn't realize you were there, sweetheart."

"It's okay. I wanted to tell you about my day in private, so I waited."

"I'd love to hear about your day." Maura took the hand Maisy was offering and led her to her office. With the door open, she could see if someone was standing at the circulation desk, but not much else. It was the only privacy they were going to get with the library as crowded as it was. She gave Maisy her spinning chair, hoping it would help sidetrack the girl.

"I want to tell you all about it, but was that old lady talking about you and Daddy?" Maisy watched Maura intently. She must have come to some conclusion based on the woman's expression because her lips curved into a wide smile. "It's okay. Mama told me we'd find you here. I hoped it was you the first day, when you told me you love the Grinch too. I'm glad. I like you."

Maura followed the stream of words. They left her baffled, but relieved. Clearly the girl didn't mind her father dating in theory, though her thoughts and feelings when it became a reality were still to be determined. But her mother was dead: what was Maisy talking about? "Sweetheart, why do you say your mom told you I'd be here?"

"Not you exactly, though the woman in my dream really did look an awful lot like you." Maisy cocked her head to the side. "Do you have a lacy shawl, like the kind old ladies make? It's not a regular one, though. It has rows of seals and waves instead of flowers or circles like the ones my granny makes. It's a bunch of really pretty blues and greens and grays, like the ocean."

Maura's jaw dropped a bit. Her special shawl from Jane looked exactly like the one Maisy was describing. Maura loved to wrap herself in it when she was missing her surrogate mother.

Maisy grinned at Maura's expression. "You DO have one! I knew it." She beamed at the librarian. "It *was* you Mama meant. I thought it would be. I know the nurse likes Daddy, but I really didn't think it was her. I hoped it wasn't. She's nice and all, but she's not right. She used that voice when she talked with me. Do you know the one?" Maisy tipped her head to the side as she thought about

Alex for a moment and then spun the chair around. When she stopped spinning the girl smiled again at Maura. "Mama comes to me in my dreams sometimes. She told me we should move here and that we'd be a happy family again."

"Maisy, you already are a family." Maura latched onto the one piece of information she felt she could actually address.

Maisy frowned. "I want to be a happy family with a daddy and mom who are happy together."

Maura wished she wasn't having this conversation. Stephan should be the one deciding what to share with Maisy and what to keep private. "Maisy, your father loves you so very much. I believe he'd do anything for you. Does he know you haven't been happy?"

"Oh, I'm happy. It's just—we're not a family like Lana's family. I want that. I don't remember ever being like that."

The noises of people coming and going from the library receded as Maura focused her attention completely on the girl sitting in front of her.

Maura's heart went out to her. She could relate. Ron's family always tugged at her heart and left her with a bittersweet feeling when she spent time with them. She opened her arms and held Maisy when the girl climbed into her lap. Maura wrapped Maisy in a tight hug. She hesitated a moment, and then decided to be forthright. "I've always been jealous of families like theirs, too," Maura admitted. "Especially when I was younger."

She inhaled the scent of Maisy's shampoo and felt another tug at her heart. "Can I share something private with you? I don't talk about it to most people."

Maisy tipped her head back and nodded. Her blue eyes were wide with interest.

Maura drew in a deep breath. "Okay, then. My parents were always traveling. I don't remember a time when they weren't. It was wonderful when I saw them, but then they'd be gone for weeks, sometimes months, at a time. We lived in Portland. During the school year, my grandfather would stay with me in our house when my parents were traveling. Then, if they were away, I'd spend summers and some vacations here with my Aunt Jane. When I was thirteen, my parents died halfway around the world. I came here to live with my aunt after the funeral. My aunt was only one person, but with her, I always knew I was loved. I knew I was wanted and special to someone. Maisy, family is just being loved, being treasured by someone. You are your father's heart, his joy. Please don't ever think anyone else's family is better than yours."

Stephan had approached the office in time to see Maisy launch herself into Maura's lap. He'd curbed his impulse to rush in. As he heard what was being said, he knew he should step away and give the woman and child privacy, but his curiosity won out. He stood against the wall, out of sight, and listened. He felt a pang of sympathy as Maura shared her story. He guessed there had to be more to it than what she was telling his seven-year-old. He started to move away to give them space when his daughter lifted her head and spotted him.

"Daddy!" She gave a joy-filled squeal and tumbled out of Maura's lap and into his arms. "I'm so happy to see you! I did it! I did my first day of first grade." She beamed at him. Before he could do more than tell Maisy how proud he was, the child wriggled out of his arms and threw herself into Maura. "Thank you."

"Of course." Maura smiled down at the girl and gave her a quick, tight hug. "I'm glad you came to me."

Stephan arched an eyebrow and mouthed, "Is everything okay?" Maura nodded.

Maisy skipped back over to her father. "I have sooooooo much to tell you, Daddy. Come on. Come with me to get my stuff." She grabbed his hand and tugged him towards the children's room.

Maura stood up and followed them out of her office. She grimaced inwardly when she saw Joey Thompson smirking at her as he walked with his grandmother to the circulation desk.

"So that's the way the wind blows, is it, Miz Maura?"

Eliza eyed her grandson. "You'll need to step up your game, young man. There's some competition in town."

"Do I have competition, Maura?" The good-humored expression on Joey's face didn't reach his eyes.

Maura kept her expression even as Stephan and Maisy approached the desk. "Stephan and Maisy, this is Eliza Thompson and her grandson Joey. Mrs. Thompson, Joey, please meet the Kirklands."

Stephan saw the tightness in Maura's expression and the way she was holding herself stiff and as far from Joey as she could without being impolite. He gave the pair an easy smile. "A pleasure to make your acquaintance, Joey; and nice to see you again, Mrs. Thompson." He tweaked Maisy's braid. "Why don't you go pick out a new book before we leave, love?"

Maisy scampered off to where some of her new friends were playing.

Stephan leaned against the tall desk on the side closest to Maura. "What do you do around here, Joey?"

"Lobsta mostly, but a bit of this and that." He shrugged.

Eliza frowned at her grandson. "Joey's being modest. He's an entrepreneur. He has a successful eBay store and invests in stocks. He's quite a catch."

Maura couldn't help grinning at the discomfort that flitted across Joey's face, but she cleared her expression when his eyes turned her way.

"You're embarrassing me in front of Miz Maura, Grandma."

Eliza looked at Maura while she spoke. "If you won't toot your own horn, someone has to do it." Her gaze shifted to Stephan. "Officer Kirkland, you seem like a very nice man. Everyone's singing your praises, but if you've got your eye on our Maura like I've heard, you should know you'll have competition."

Maura resisted the urge to roll her eyes.

"I think Maura's more than capable of deciding her own mind." Stephan smiled at Eliza. "I was wondering how it was that such a beautiful woman managed to stay single on this island, but then I realized how committed she is to the community. I imagine it doesn't leave much time for romance."

Maura bit her inner cheek to keep from laughing. She was used to Eliza's manipulations and had learned to ignore them over the years, but Stephan wasn't and he was laying it on absurdly thick. She decided to put a stop to the conversation. "I've had more than enough people wandering in here discussing my life today. I'm not a prize cow to be auctioned off." She gave Eliza a sharp look. "I haven't given you cause to gossip about me the way you are, and neither has Officer Kirkland."

The older woman had the grace to look abashed.

Stephan winked at her. "A pleasure meeting you, Mr. Thompson. And seeing you again, Mrs. Thompson." He nodded to them both. "Thank you for letting Maisy participate today, Maura." He saw his daughter heading for them with a stack of books in her hands. "I think we're going to be frequent customers."

Joey snorted.

Maura ignored the noise and focused on Maisy. "Do you have your library card, young lady?"

Maisy beamed at her. "I put it in my pencil box so I wouldn't lose it." She plunked it down on top of her books and handed the pile to Maura, who smiled and began checking them out.

Joey wandered off. Eliza found herself a couple of books and left shortly after the Kirklands.

The rest of the afternoon and evening passed without excitement. By the time seven o'clock rolled around, only Fern remained.

"I guess Mom's running late again."

Maura gave the blond girl a hug. "I'm sure she'll be here any minute. Why don't you help me get ready to close? George needs a snack and we need to make sure the back door is locked. Can you do that for me?"

As the girl went to take care of the chores, Maura sent a text to her friend telling her she'd bring Fern home.

Just as the computer shut down, a taller version of Fern blew into the library. "I am so sorry." Elizabeth crouched down and wrapped her daughter in a tight hug. She gave Maura an apologetic look. "A group of flatlanders would not leave."

Maura knew this was still an important time of year for the waitress. She needed the tips to help carry her and Fern through the lean season. "It's fine, Liz. Fern's been helping me." She gave the child an affectionate smile. "She's got a job here as a page when she gets to high school if she wants one."

Fern gave her mom a lopsided grin. "I can help pay the bills then and you won't need to worry as much."

"Ah, girl." Liz draped an arm over her daughter's shoulder. "You save your pennies for yourself." She gave Maura an appreciative smile. "Thanks again, Maura. I'll try to be on time tomorrow."

CHAPTER 7

Since Maisy had made her blessings for Saturday's date known, Maura had felt free to ask about her father's favorite foods. Maura enjoyed cooking, but rarely bothered with complex meals for herself. She wasn't above showing off a bit, however, so she turned a simple chicken dinner into a mini Thanksgiving spread.

Maura had cleaned the house, done all of the cooking that could be done in advance, set the table with Jane's fine china, showered, and changed into a simple-sage colored sheath. She sat down with a magazine to try and distract herself from clock watching. When the bell rang ten minutes later, Maura felt the butterflies in her belly come to life again. She took a couple of deep breaths and then opened the door.

Stephan was holding a bouquet of sunflowers in one hand and a bakery box from Clarks in the other. "Wow." He stared at Maura as she stood in front of him. "You look beautiful."

She started to shake her head and then decided to accept the compliment. "Thank you. You look wonderful yourself." She was inwardly thrilled to see he'd worn slacks and a nice linen shirt. The cuffs were rolled up a bit to give it a more casual look, but he'd definitely taken the time to dress well for the date. "Come in."

"These are for you." Stephan handed Maura the flowers and box. "It smells great!" The aroma of baking bread and roasting meat had filled the small house.

"Thanks. They're lovely. Let's put these in the kitchen and I'll give you the tour." Maura led him down the hallway, past the living room to the kitchen and dining area that took up half of the first floor. As she put the flowers in water, she asked about Maisy.

Stephan assured her that the girl had been happy to go to the Moore's. Concerned she'd worry about gossip, he didn't tell Maura that Ron and Vicky, and Maisy for that matter, had insisted it be a sleepover.

When the sunflowers were settled in a cheerful red pitcher, Maura reached for his hand. Stephan laced his fingers through Maura's as she showed him the welcoming living room. A large bay window faced the beach and offered a lovely frame for the colors starting to streak the sky. They paused in unspoken agreement to stop and admire the view before Maura led him upstairs. "There's three bedrooms, but I use one as a craft room. That leaves a guest bedroom, my bedroom, and another bathroom."

She let Stephan poke his head into all the rooms and then led him back downstairs. The three cats were lined up at the bottom. Tim gave Stephan a suspicious look. Mags studied him with a calm expression. For her part, Greta gave a long stretch and sauntered over to Stephan. She sniffed his shoes and pants leg before twining around him. Maura was amused, but not surprised, to see Greta claim him.

Greta continued to twine around Stephan until he gave in and picked her up. The Persian gave a contented sigh.

"Jealous yet?" Stephan grinned at Maura when she turned back around from getting a bottle of wine out of the refrigerator.

She laughed when she saw the cat smiling at her from the nook Stephan had made in his muscled arms. Maura leaned against the fridge and smiled. "Maybe a little." She showed him the bottle. "Would you like some?"

"I'd love some." Stephan moved to put Greta back down on the ground and found the cat clinging to him rather than hopping down. "Uh, a little help?"

Maura put the bottle on the counter and chuckled. "See, now you're stuck. Once she's comfortable, Greta doesn't give up her spot willingly."

Stephan shook his head. "This is a new one for me." He sat on the chair Maura indicated. "We always had dogs. They'd follow you around, but none of them were ever possessive. They'd go to anyone who offered pets or treats."

Maura took the chicken out of the oven and let it sit on the stove top. "Give her a few minutes and she'll be over here begging for meat."

Stephan gave the cat a dubious look. She was purring away and had begun flicking her tail against his chin with a slow swishing motion. "If you say so." He took the opportunity to admire the table. "This looks as nice as any restaurant. If you put this much thought into the table, I can't wait for dinner." He smiled when Maura looked flustered.

She shook her head at him. "I hope you like it."

"Maisy told me what she said. As long as you didn't believe her about steak and kidney pie, we're good."

Maura grinned. "I nixed that one from the get go, but I'm glad to hear it was a good call on my part." She began to dish up all of the sides and set them on the table. When she started slicing the chicken, Greta jumped out of Stephan's arms.

Freed from the cat, Stephan got up to help.

As they ate, they kept up a light conversation. Each was pleased to discover they had similar taste in music and entertainment. Stephan surprised Maura with the depth of his passion for photography. He peppered her with curious and insightful questions about her painting.

The talk shifted to travel. They both preferred active trips rather than beach vacations. Maura listened, riveted, to Stephan's descriptions of Iceland's rugged, otherworldly beauty. He chuckled at her stories about the mishaps she and her Aunt Jane had in France. Stephan answered all of Maura's many questions about places she hadn't had a chance to visit in the United Kingdom. She answered his queries about the Maritime and Quebec provinces of Canada.

When the remains of the meal were packed away and the dishes dealt with, they took the rest of the wine and their glasses into the living room.

Maura kicked off her shoes and settled onto the sofa. Stephan paused to admire the view from the window. The quarter moon hung low in the sky. He joined her after a moment.

Stephan swirled the pale liquid in his glass and gazed at it for several seconds before meeting Maura's gaze. Her hazel eyes were dark in the low light. "I have a confession to make."

She arched an eyebrow.

"I overheard you talking with Maisy the other day in your office."

Maura nodded slowly. "I figured you might have." She put her glass down. "How much did you hear?"

"Everything from when she climbed into your lap onward, but she told me later that night that she shared that Sophie comes to her in dreams."

He put his own glass next to hers and reached for her hand. When Maura slid it into his own, he gently tugged her closer. Maura nestled against him.

"She's told me about her dreams before. I always assumed they were just the brain's wishful thinking, part of the grieving process, until one this past April. She came tearing into my room at three in the morning, frantic with fear. When she settled down and was able to speak coherently, she told me her mother had warned her that I shouldn't go to work that morning." Stephan gazed off at a point over Maura's head, lost in his memory. "I thought it was malarkey, but Maisy was so distraught. Her therapist had told me to listen to her and take her seriously, even if I thought the dreams were foolishness. She said it didn't matter if they were fantasy. They're real to Maisy." He shifted his gaze back to Maura. "I called in even though it was last minute. Mac—Sergeant Mackenzie—was saving up for a new Harley. He was more than happy to take the extra hours." Stephan swallowed hard. "Mac was sitting at my desk looking through some paperwork I'd left there, when a junkie, out of his mind, came into the station. Someone got sloppy and he got his hands on a gun. The bullet missed Mac's heart and he's been dating a nurse he met post-op since, so all's well that ends well, but it should have been me. Maisy could have been orphaned that day."

Maura had tightened her hold on his hand until she was gripping him hard.

Stephan smiled gently as he loosened her fingers a bit and then dropped a kiss on her forehead. "You have a shawl like the one Maisy described, don't you?"

Maura nodded and drew him up with her. Quietly, she led him upstairs to her craft room and opened the closet. She reached onto a shelf and gave the soft yarn a loving stroke before placing the bundle in Stephan's hands.

He met her gaze for a long moment. His fingers were trembling slightly as he opened the shawl to reveal an intricate design of fanciful seals frolicking in waves. It was the work of a master artist and exactly what Maisy had described.

"This is beautiful," he told her after he'd taken in all the details. He folded it with reverence and handed it back to Maura. "And a bit mind bending."

She put it away with the same care and leaned against the closet door after shutting it. She looked at Stephan. "Does it change anything?"

"No." Stephan reached out and gently caressed the side of her head. He moved towards her with infinite patience, dragging the moment out as long as he could. Before his lips brushed hers, he whispered near her ear, "We'll do what suits us, Maura. Nothing more, nothing less."

She bridged the small distance between them with an impatient sound and stretched up to deepen the kiss when Stephan playfully teased her by holding back.

When they came up for air, breathing heavily, Stephan closed his eyes. He drew in a shaky breath and then opened them. "I need a moment. You're potent."

Maura's lips curved up in a slow grin. "Glad I'm not the only one feeling that way." She reached for his hand. "Let's have dessert."

When Stephan groaned, she added with a laugh, "Get your mind out of the gutter. What'd you get from the bakery?"

He shook his head. His thoughts were a million miles away from baked goods. "I don't remember. It looked good, whatever it was."

Maura led him back downstairs and put the kettle on. He watched as she puttered around, getting down dishes that matched the dinner china. As she started piling things on a tray, he moved to help.

"How did your aunt come to live here?"

Maura looked up from the drawer she was rummaging in. "Honestly? I think she was getting as far away from my grandparents as she could without leaving the coast or state. We're not related to the Ballards who were here before, but it tickled her fancy to purchase the house from a Ballard and live next to Ballard Channel." Finding scissors, she snipped the twine from the bakery box and grinned as she saw the assortment Stephan had brought. "Were you expecting a party?" She couldn't resist teasing him. There was no way the two of them were going to plow through the dozen treats that filled the box.

"I wasn't sure what you like. I didn't want to ask, though I was assured I couldn't go wrong with the lemon or pecan tartlets. The helpful lady behind the counter also informed me that her brownies are a big hit with everyone at the library, right after she shamed me for never having eaten a whoopie pie before."

"That must have been Josephine," Maura laughed. "She brings over bits and pieces at the end of the day to share with the kids sometimes. Years ago, I told her I love her brownies. There's always one or two in the box." Maura smiled fondly, thinking of the plump, white-haired woman. "She and her husband, George, play Mr. and Mrs. Claus every year for the kids at the tree lighting. They're sweethearts. She and Aunt Jane were great friends."

She poured the hot water into a waiting tea pot and tipped her head toward the tray. "Would you carry that into the living room while I bring this and some cream?"

Stephan nodded and followed her. Greta gave an affectionate coo when she saw him. Tim woke up from a nap and launched himself to beat Stephan to the sofa. He stretched his small body out as long as it could go in the middle of the couch.

Maura laughed. "I see we have a self-appointed chaperone." She shook her head and scooped the ginger up. She gave his head an affectionate rub when he gazed at her balefully. "It's okay Tim."

Once they were settled with their tea and treats, Maura snuggled next to Stephan. "What time do you need to be home tonight?"

He shook his head. "I don't. Maisy's staying at Ron's until tomorrow. I'm picking her up around eleven."

"Ohhhhhh."

"There's no pressure, Maura." Stephan gave her a worried look. "Ron and Vicky were just giving us a chance not to be clock-watching. Maisy and Lana seem to have hit it off despite the age difference. The sleepover was Maisy's idea."

"You misunderstood." Maura smiled at Stephan. "That was a pleased 'oh'."

"Oh?"

"Yes." She enjoyed being able to study him. With his strong jawline and piercing eyes, he looked like a Hollywood casting description for a cop. But there was the slightly long dark hair, the warmth that radiated from his eyes, and his expressive mouth that broke the mold. It had been years since Maura had felt more than a fleeting physical attraction for a man. She'd wondered if there was something wrong with her, despite Dr. Beals' assurances that her bloodwork was picture perfect. Now, it was taking an absurd effort not to touch the man beside her at every opportunity. Even when their legs were next to each other and not touching, she felt a crackle of electricity, of connection, between them. It wasn't like her to act impulsively, but in that moment, she felt like throwing caution to the winds.

For his part, Stephan was thrilled Maura didn't try to hide her emotions or play games with him. The laugh lines that crinkled up around her eyes when she was amused or happy were delightful. The seemingly changeable color of those eyes fascinated him. Her rich laughter made him want to join in. And the way she felt in his arms, under his hands, made him feel fully alive again. He was constantly looking for excuses to touch her. It would have been pathetic; except she clearly felt the same way. He didn't want to ruin things by letting his hormones, which were raging like he was a lad again, lead.

They stared at one another in silence for a long moment.

Maura unconsciously licked her lips, which caused Stephan to groan. She furrowed her brow slightly and then realized what she'd just done. She deliberately eased her tongue back out again and let it run along her upper lip. Before she could give herself time to feel embarrassed, Maura shifted so she could slide up and straddle his lap.

Stephan's eyes widened. "Are you sure you want to be doing this?" He held her waist.

"Do you not want to?"

He heard the catch in her voice, the hesitation. "Oh, honey, I can't think straight, I want to be doing this so badly." He tugged her forward until she'd settled into a position that sent a jolt through both of them. "But I don't want to rush you."

"Then we have a problem." She leaned forward and gasped slightly in pleasure, gratified to hear his sharp intake. Maura leaned close to his ear. "I want you to take what I'm offering."

Stephan let his hands roam as she rocked against him in languid movements. It felt so right. He hesitated. "I don't have any protection." He swallowed hard as his hand cupped a full breast. "Are you—do you?" He shook his head at how incoherent he sounded.

Maura had been unbuttoning his shirt and enjoyed sliding her hands across the expanse of his chest before letting her head drop down on his shoulder. "No. Birth control hasn't been an issue in my life for quite a while."

"I had a vasectomy. It should be safe." His voice grew strained as her hands slid lower while he spoke.

She nipped his ear lobe. "I'm willing to take that gamble, Stephan, are you?"

He laced his hands through her hair and pulled her even closer for a carnal kiss.

It was Maura's turn to groan in pleasure. "I can't keep this up. We should go to bed now."

How they ended up, finally, in her bed was a bit of a haze to Maura. As the night wore on, they alternated between making love, dozing, and talking. Neither was ready for reality to intrude when the sun streamed through the windows and a trio of hungry cats woke them.

Maura mumbled a protest when Tim sat on her chest and began poking at her mouth with an impatient paw. Mags started complaining that breakfast was late when she saw Maura stir. For her part, Greta stretched out on Stephan and began giving his chin a bath.

He raised an eyebrow and turned to look at Maura. She looked rumpled, with locks of russet hair going in different directions, but her expression was relaxed. "Is this the normal morning routine?"

She pushed Tim's paw away from her mouth so she could speak. "Not Greta there, but these other two—yeah, this is our normal." Maura ran a hand through her hair, trying to untangle and smooth it down. "Good morning." Her voice grew a bit shy.

"Morning." Stephan tucked a wayward lock of hair behind her ear and drew her over for a kiss. He carefully moved Greta off his chest and settled her down where his feet had been as he sat up.

Maura followed suit, but brought the sheet up along with her to maintain some modesty in the bright morning light. "Would you like coffee?"

"I'd love some. I'll help." Stephan offered. He grinned as she colored while trying to work out how to get out of bed. "Do you have a robe you'd like me to fetch you?"

Maura laughed. "It seems prudish, doesn't it?"

"It's still new. I'm new." Stephan dropped a kiss on her lips. "I get it."

"It's on a hook in the bathroom." Maura was mortified by her embarrassment, but she couldn't manage a nonchalant sophistication that she didn't possess.

Stephan nodded his head and pulled his boxers on and up before she got more than a glimpse of him. He padded down the hall and was back in short order with a soft gold confection. "This can't provide much warmth, Maura." He held the thin garment up and chuckled. "I was expecting a fuzzy housecoat."

She rolled her eyes at him. "I'm not an old lady yet."

"No, you most certainly are not." Stephan handed her the robe and stood there smiling at her as she stared at him. "Oh, you want me to turn around?"

"Please."

He winked at her and did as requested.

When she was done pulling her robe on, Maura found Stephan's shirt where one of them had tossed it. She handed it to him. "I don't want you to catch a chill."

"There's not a chance of that, love." Stephan was giving her an admiring look that made her blush all over again. Taking pity on her, however, he drew his shirt on and buttoned it halfway up. He reached for her hand.

"Would you like some breakfast with the coffee?"

"I'd love some if you're offering, but I don't want to put you to any trouble."

Maura laughed. "I was going to offer you one of the brownies you brought, but I could be persuaded to make eggs and bacon if you have the time to stay and eat."

He grabbed his cell phone from a small table near the door. A quick check revealed no messages and plenty of time before he had to leave, thanks to the early wakeup call from the cats. "Why don't we make it together?"

They worked in companionable silence in the sun-drenched kitchen until each held a mug of coffee. Stephan studied Maura as they drank. He was still learning to read her expressions and moods. The previous night had been amazing for both of them, he thought, but it was just a start. He didn't want to do anything to chase her away. He tried to keep things light. "I have an important question. How do you like your eggs?"

"Fried, you?"

"I'd be a poor Englishman if I didn't enjoy a good fried egg, now wouldn't I?" He grinned at her. "Maisy will only eat them scrambled." He gave a mock grimace. "She's been corrupted growing up in America."

Maura smiled and got the ingredients out of the fridge. "Can I put you in charge of toast?"

Stephan shook his head. "How about you make the toast? I'll take care of the protein."

"Let someone else cook me breakfast while I get to ogle him in his shorts?" Maura smiled. "I think that's great deal for me."

Stephan wiggled his bum in her direction and then set about learning her stove.

Maura sipped her coffee and watched him for a moment, savoring the new experience of having a half-naked man cooking in her kitchen.

Stephan glanced over his shoulder and caught her staring. "I see you take your toast making seriously."

She grinned. "Very." She gave him an arch look. "I only eat my toast hot. I'll start when you're a bit further along." Maura waved her hand imperiously. "Carry on."

Stephan chuckled; glad she was comfortable enough to joke around with him. "As you wish, madam."

When they each had a loaded plate, Maura tipped her head to the back door. "Let's eat out here."

"In our skivvies?"

"Oh, right." She'd actually forgotten that she was only wearing a thin garment that didn't quite brush her knees. "Why not? There shouldn't be anyone back there."

Stephan grinned. "I like the way you think." He followed her onto the deck and over to a small table ringed by a few chairs.

"This is great." Maura closed her eyes briefly as she enjoyed her first bites of breakfast.

"I can manage a few good meals. Hopefully you don't mind repetition." Stephan grinned at her.

"You won't hear me complaining when someone else is cooking."

The backyard was peaceful. Birds called to one another from the trees while squirrels chased each other around the perimeter of the lawn and into the woods. The sound of the tide rolling in provided a rhythmic counterpoint to all the other morning noises.

"I can see why you've stayed here."

Maura wrapped her hands around her mug and leaned back in her chair. She gazed around the tidy yard with its cheerfully painted shed, stacks of firewood, flower beds, and potted vegetables. "It's always felt the most like home to me, no matter where I've been. I couldn't imagine living anywhere else. There's something about this island that speaks to my soul. I don't know if it's because I intrinsically associate it with Aunt Jane or if it's the space itself but," she shrugged, "it's home." She looked at Stephan over the rim of her favorite blue-and-green glazed mug. "Do you miss England?"

He stretched his legs out and considered the question. "Yes and no," was the eventual answer. "I miss seeing my parents and brother regularly, but video chat has made them closer than when I first moved to the States. Bristol will always hold a place in my heart and, well, it's my boyhood home, but I've lived more of my life away from there now. I loved Kings College and London. Boston was fine, but it was home only because it's where we lived. This region feels familiar. I don't know how else to explain it. It's a weird internal recognition. It's comfortable." He frowned. "It doesn't make much sense on the surface. Belfort's not like anywhere else I've lived before, but there's a peacefulness here that I haven't felt since I was a boy. The space seems to resonate with Maisy too. I'm hoping she's able to thrive here. She already has more friends in a month on the island than she did in Boston. I'm a little concerned because the school is so small, but our bigger neighborhood school didn't work out, so who knows, maybe this will be a better fit."

"It's got pluses and minuses," Maura acknowledged. "They're limited in what they can provide, but the kids get lots of hands-on and one-on-one time. Jackson helped them rewire the school with WiFi a bit ago and the principal found a grant for Chromebooks. Distance learning has enabled more enrichment opportunities than they had when I was a kid." She shrugged. "After I moved here, Aunt Jane let me stay in the local school for a year and then insisted I go to Gould Academy. I hated being away from her, but really it wasn't all that different than life before and it was a wonderful experience. I doubt I'd have been able to get into Simmons if I hadn't gone there," she admitted.

Stephan nodded. "I've decided I'm not worrying about high school and college until Maisy gets to middle school. She still hasn't managed a year at public school, so a successful first grade is the goal."

Maura nodded. "Sounds logical."

"My former in-laws didn't think so and my parents, as supportive as they are of us, are in the same camp."

"Give them time to come around. They need to see her happy and thriving. You know your daughter better than anyone else. You know what she needs."

He gave her a speculative look. "Indeed."

Maura had been in the process of bringing a forkful of food to her mouth. She paused at his expression. "Did I say something out of turn?"

Stephan gave her a cheerful smile. "Not at all. You were dead right."

They were finishing washing the dishes when the alarm on Stephan's phone went off. He sighed. "I'd better go. I need to clean up before I get Maisy."

Maura used his shirt to pull him close. "I'd offer to help, but it'd make you late."

"It certainly would," Stephan agreed. "Saying goodbye is going to push it as it is." He leaned down into the kiss she'd offered.

CHAPTER 8

Maura looked out the window and saw the last of the gray clouds scuttling off towards the east. She finished wrapping her hair up into a pony tail and had just moved towards the door when the bell rang. She opened it. Maisy flew in and scooped Tim, who'd come to investigate, into her arms. Stephan gave Maura a swift kiss in greeting and then put a sparkly purple duffel bag down by the stairs.

"Are you excited?"

"I'm grateful I didn't draw the short straw for the dunk tank, even if it means taking the overnight." He reached down to pet Greta as she hurried over to greet him. "Not the uniform, love." He tried to keep the cat from rubbing her body along his legs.

Maura shook her head at the cat. "I'm ready." She plucked her keys from their hook by the door. "Do you want to leave your things here, Maisy?"

The girl reluctantly put Tim down and shrugged off her bright pink backpack. "Can Fern and I snuggle with Tim when we get home?"

"Of course."

"And we'll bake cookies?"

"If you have any room left in your belly, absolutely. Otherwise, we can do it tomorrow. Fern will be here until the afternoon."

"Yay!" Maisy cheered. She squatted down and planted a kiss on the orange cat's head. "We're going to have so much fun, Tim!"

Maura looked at the child. "I hope you don't mind helping me out for a while."

"I can't wait," Maisy started bouncing on her feet. "You said if we help for an hour, Fern and I can have how many tickets?"

"Thirty." Maura grinned when the girl's eyes widened.

"Awesomesauce, we'll be able to do everything! The kids at school told me each thing costs one ticket. That means we can do some things more than once, right?"

Maura nodded her head. "Yes, you will."

Maisy grabbed her father and Maura each by the hand. "Let's go!"

The center of town had transformed overnight for the annual harvest festival. The common in front of the Baptist church was filled with colorful canopies, a large bouncy obstacle course, an area fenced off for pony rides, and a cacophony of voices and music. The waterfront was lined with carnival games and food vendors. Maisy's eyes were huge as she took it all in. Stephan and Maura smiled at each other over her head as they felt her hands quiver with excitement.

Isabelle took charge of the two helpers so Maura could set up her face painting station. As youngsters realized she was open for business, the library lawn got mobbed.

Maura was just adding some sparkly glitter paint to Anna Beals' full faced flower when Fern and Maisy showed up at her side.

"Whoaaaaaa," Maisy gasped as she took in the intricacy of Maura's work. "You're amazeballs at this Maura."

Maura grinned at her. "It's one of my favorite days of the year."

"Will you do us next?"

Maura checked the line. Her youngest, most impatient customers had all been taken care of, but there were several kids who'd been waiting for the better part of the past hour. "Why don't you two go explore a bit. Come back when it's time to eat. I'll be taking a lunch break in a couple of hours and can do your faces then."

Maisy looked disappointed, but Fern nodded in happy agreement. She reached for Maisy's hand. "Let's get our tickets from Isabelle and go jump!"

"Okay," Maisy let her friend lead her over to the teenager.

Maura watched them for a moment and then waved the Myers twins over.

Twenty minutes later, Betty Jo Thompson and her brother, Mike Junior, stood in front of the librarian. Betty Jo's blond ringlets quivered as she bounced up and down with excitement. "I wanna be a beautiful fairy, Miz Maura."

Mike rolled his eyes at his sister but kept his mouth shut. Their Uncle Joey and grandmother Eliza joined them in time to hear Betty Jo's pronouncement. Eliza gave her youngest great granddaughter an indulgent smile while Joey snorted and then coughed at his grandmother's sharp look.

"Do you think you'd be a woodland fairy, or maybe an ocean one, or a flower one?" Maura swished her narrowest brush around in a cup of cloudy water and blotted it dry while considering Betty Jo and ignoring everyone else.

"Which is the prettiest?"

Maura grinned. "They all are. It depends on what colors you want." She tipped her head to the side. "I think you'd be perfect as a flower fairy. I know you love purple and pink. But you swim like a fish, so maybe you'd rather be an ocean one with lots of blue, green, and silver."

Betty Jo gnawed on her lower lip. After a long moment of consideration, she blurted out, "Can I be both?"

Having known the five-year-old since she was born, Maura wasn't surprised by the request. "I think we can do that, Miss Betty Jo."

Mike groaned. "This'll be a while, won't it?"

"You can't rush beauty, Mike," Maura winked at him.

"Can I come back for her?" Mike had drawn babysitting duties, like usual. He hadn't been able to hang out with his own friends or do much of anything all morning, other than follow in his sister's wake.

"You've got twenty minutes." Maura nodded to the eighth grader.

"You're the best, Miz M!" Mike ran off before Betty Jo could protest.

"Yes, she is." Eliza gave an approving smile and nudged Joey.

Joey caught Maura's eye, gave her a slight, boyish grin, tipped his head at his grandmother, and shrugged as if to say "What can you do?"

In rare moments like that, she had a flash of insight into why so many other women found him appealing.

Maura smiled in response and then turned her attention back to Betty Jo. "All right, young lady, you have an important decision to make: rainbow sparkles or gold?"

"We'll be off to look at the book sale." Eliza gave Maura a cheerful finger wave. Joey touched the brim of his Patriots cap before reaching to hold his grandmother's arm as she led them over to the library.

Mike and Stephan both returned as Maura was putting the finishing touches on Betty Jo's face. She handed the child a mirror and felt a surge of satisfaction when the girl beamed as she took in the weaving of flowers and waves that encircled her face and the delicate webbing of color and glitter that dominated the upper part like a mask.

"I'm beautiful," Betty Jo gasped. She saw Mike had come back with a bowl of steaming French fries and reached for them.

"No way. These are for Miz M. I bought them for her with my own money. Mom has lunch for you at the booth." Mike waved towards the direction of the hot dog shack their mother owned with her sister. "She's waiting for you."

"Thanks, Mike," Maura was touched by his thoughtfulness.

"Do you recognize me, Officer K?" Betty Jo stopped in front of Stephan. Before he had a chance to answer, she decided to help him. "It's me, Betty Jo. I'm a fairy queen."

"You certainly are! I didn't recognize you at all, Betty Jo." Stephan's eyes sparkled as he knelt down to talk with the girl. "I don't think I've ever seen such a beautiful fairy princess."

"Queen. I'm the queen of all the fairies in the garden and the ocean."

"Beg pardon, your majesty." Stephan stood up and bowed.

That made Betty Jo laugh. Then she spotted several cousins and started to run off before remembering that she hadn't thanked Maura. She pivoted and threw her arms around the woman. "Thank you!"

Maura hugged her back and watched the girl race off before turning to Mike and Stephan.

She popped a fry in her mouth and sighed with pleasure. "Mike, you have no idea how much I needed this right now."

The boy flushed with pride.

Stephan gave Mike an approving nod. "We were thinking alike, mate." He offered the large cup he was carrying to Maura. "I thought you could use a pick-me-up about now, too." The fragrant aroma of coffee wafted out.

Maura beamed at them. "You guys are the best." She waved her hand at the free chairs. "Mike, it's your turn. Are you thinking full on creepy again this year or do you have something else in mind?"

The youth gave the police officer a sideways look. His embarrassment was easy to see.

"Monster-creepy like Frankenstein or a vampire?" Stephan gave an encouraging grin.

"Ppft." Maura shook her head. "Amateur." She looked at Mike. "Should we show him?"

Mike grinned suddenly. "Yeah, that'd be great. I'm working the haunted house at the church in a little bit. It'd be fun to scare the guys before the kiddies get there."

Maura gave him a fist bump and set to work. Stephan watched for a few minutes, but when it was clear Maura was too focused on her work to chat and Mike was refusing to move a muscle, he decided to leave them in their silence and lend a hand where it was needed.

"Whoa!" Mike admired his face. "Hey, Officer Kirkland," he called over to Stephan, who was organizing a game of cornhole.

Stephan gave a visible jolt of surprise. "I'm impressed."

"You're so gross, Mike." Isabelle shuddered as she took in her cousin's face.

Stephan walked over to them and stared in silence. "You could've been a make-up artist, Maura."

Maura's cheeks pinkened, but she shook her head. "No, I just dabble. But it is fun." She scrutinized her work. "Hang on, Mike." She reached for a spray bottle. "Close your eyes." She gave a quick spritz of setting spray over his face. "There." Maura nodded in satisfaction as she took in Mike's face. Her work was on the left side only. They'd decided to make it look like his skin had been flayed off, exposing muscle and bone beneath. She was happy with the amount of detail she'd managed to achieve. "Go have fun scaring your buddies, but stay out of the tunnel! I don't want a repeat of last year, when you guys got locked in the cellar."

He flashed her a quick grin. "Kevin dared me, Miz M. I had to do it." He scuffed a sneaker on the ground. "Does that mean it's locked at the library end?"

"Yes, it does, young man, and I know Pastor Mills doesn't want to have to trudge down there to fish anyone out again this year, either, so don't sneak in from under the church."

"Yes, ma'am." Mike edged away a bit. "Thanks for my face, Miz M."

"You're welcome, Mike. Have fun!" She winked at him, knowing he and Kevin had already learned their lesson last October. A small reminder, however, didn't hurt.

"Eek!" Maisy and Fern both yelped when Mike turned around and startled them as they approached Maura.

Mike grinned and ran off.

"Is it our turn now?" Maisy practically danced in place in front of Maura. "I've been seeing everyone. Your paintings are so cool."

Before she could answer, Stephan shook his head. "Maura gets a lunch break first."

"But she promised!"

Stephan arched an eyebrow at his daughter's tone. "And she will, but only after she gets a chance to eat." He pulled out his wallet and handed the girls some bills. "Go get yourselves some food and bring us a couple of burgers, if that's okay for you, Maura." At her nod, he continued. "Bring it back here and we'll have lunch together. Then it can be your turn."

Fern was gazing at the money in her hand and then back to Stephan. "You're sure, Officer Kirkland? Mom gave me a sandwich."

"Save it for a snack, sweetheart." He gave Fern's ponytail a gentle tweak. "Make sure you keep some of that for a slushie or candy apple later."

"Thank you!" Fern gave him a shy hug and then tugged Maisy's hand. "Come on. The faster we get the food, the sooner we get back."

Maisy couldn't argue with her friend's logic, but still looked like she wanted to protest.

"You'll be my first customers after we eat." Maura gave her a cheerful wave. "I like mustard on my burger, please."

Maisy sighed and let Fern pull her away.

Maura propped an old "Out for Lunch" sign in the shape of a trout, a gift from Fred Foley one Christmas, up on the table. "I'm officially on break." She offered him the bowl of fries.

"Have you had a chance to enjoy the fair?"

Stephan nodded and unlocked his phone. "It's been a great excuse to take portraits without being creepy." He grinned and began showing her pictures he'd snapped on his phone while making his rounds.

"These are wonderful!" When she came to one of Fred and Sam Dodd with a slight, black-haired woman, her hand rose to her lips. She smiled behind her hand. The older men, caught unawares, had the gentlest expressions she'd ever seen either wear. Fred was clasping the woman's wide, tanned hand in his age-spotted one, while Sam was gripping her shoulder. A careful look revealed what looked to be folded-over money between Fred and the woman's hands. The sun was playing with the highlights in her hair, bringing out deep glossy chestnut and gold tones. Her dark eyes were round, and striking in their fathomlessness. "Josie," Maura murmured.

"Everything okay?" Stephan shot her a concerned look and made a mental note of the picture she was so taken with.

Maura nodded. "I was worried when I didn't see her at all this summer and Liz didn't mention working with her at Molly's at harvest time." She started to explain, but then Maisy and Fern reached them. Each girl was holding two loaded-down plates.

Stephan thanked them, but his eyes sought out Maura's. She smiled at him before turning her attention to the children. "Why don't we have a picnic out back?"

The girls both nodded. Stephan helped Maura gather up her food and drink and as Fern and Maisy went ahead. He quietly probed for more information. "I've never heard of Josie."

"I'm not surprised. She's a recluse." She moved at a leisurely pace. "I think only a handful of us even know she exists. Liz, Molly, Fred, and Sam know her best." Knowing Stephan was still learning about the residents, Maura gave him more details than was necessary. "Fred's a retired park ranger. He spent much of his career out at Yellowstone. He transferred to Acadia after his wife died. He knows the nooks and crannies of the quiet spaces around here as well as many locals. Sam used to be the unofficial captain of the fishing fleet. They tool around on Sam's boat most days, as you must know by now since Ron jokes about deputizing them every time there's a problem out there. They like to keep track of what everyone's up to." She smiled at the girls when she saw them setting up on one of the large flat rocks that dotted the yard behind the library. "I'm not sure if Josie even lives on Belfort. I see her in the summer at our beach. She's quiet, but we've had some lovely chats over the years. Liz knows her better. She helps out at Molly's during planting and harvest season with Liz. That she's here in town today is really rare. She seems to avoid people."

Once the adults were seated, the girls started jabbering away about the things they'd seen and done. After lunch, Maura led the girls back to her workspace, where they requested matching seal faces.

When the girls wandered off again, Stephan leaned against the trunk of a large maple that dominated the library's front lawn and watched Maura. She was animated and engaged with each child as they approached her with their request. Even the most reticent ended up giggling and smiling by the time she was done.

Stephan took a slew of portraits as he watched the crowds ebb and flow past the library.

"That's pretty good."

He started when Ron came up behind him. "Oh, hey, Chief."

"What do you do with all of these?"

Stephan shrugged. "I'll send the good ones along to the people in them if they want them. I delete the junky ones. And a few I keep for my portfolio. I don't do anything with them." He shrugged and showed Ron some of the recent images. "I've entered a few contests here and there, but always get permission from the sub-ject first."

Ron chuckled. "I wasn't worried. We ran an extensive check on you before offering you the job, you know that. I was just curi-ous. Go back two." He nodded. "I really like that one."

Stephan nodded in agreement. The image of a mother and child rubbing noses was sweet and the sun was hitting them just right to form a golden halo around them.

"Can you send it to me? That's Becky and Emma Dale. They're cousins of Vic's."

"Sure." Stephan sent the photo along to Ron, then thumbed over a number of pictures. "Do you know who these fellows are?"

It was a crowd shot that had been focused in on a group of several tough looking men with Joey Thompson. A few women wearing ridiculously high heels and teased out hair were hanging on their arms and laughing.

Ron frowned. "Well, I see Thompson. This one is Roger Collins. He's trouble." He pointed to a lanky man. "I've seen this one," he pointed to a tall, muscular man, "around before at The Point, but don't know who he is. Everyone clams up when I go there. Colleen probably knows him. And this bruiser," he pointed to a deeply tanned, beefy man. "I've never seen before, but I don't like the look about him. She," he indicated a brunette who was hanging on his arm, "is Janice Marsden. She's got a pain pill problem and sticky fingers."

Ron looked at his officer. "What made you take their picture?"

Stephan shrugged. "Most folks were giving them a wide berth. They were being loud. There was just something off, but damned if I could tell you what."

"Trust your instincts," Ron agreed. He glanced over at Maura and looked at Stephan again. "Maura's never liked Joey. I'd trust her instincts, too."

Stephan gave Ron a wry smile. "I would, but she won't talk about most people, other than some old-timers. She doesn't want to prejudice me."

"I don't have any problem doing that." Ron pointed at the phone. "They're trouble and Colleen's not, no matter what she says, clear-eyed when it comes to Mr. Thompson." He waved to Bill Sr. and Doug Jones when the brothers strolled by. "Most of the fishermen are good folks, like them." He tipped his head towards the Jones's. "They have their squabbles, but they take care of one another and the community. The Thompsons are one of the founding families and there's always been several in the fleet. Joey's father and grandfather before him were lobstermen. Joey's father, Cal, taught him and had him crew on whatever craft he was leasing at the time. When Cal died, no one else would let Joey work on their boats, not even his own brothers." Ron gave Stephan a sideways look. "It says something about a man's character when that happens, you know?"

Stephan didn't understand the intricacies of the community yet, but he saw what Ron was getting at. "Why is he so unlikable to the others?"

"Not entirely sure myself. They like to take care of problems in the fleet privately when they can. His father was a violent drunk. Haven't had to deal with the son in that respect. I heard rumors that Cal had a nasty habit of moving traps from time to time. Maybe he taught Joey to do it too. It's hard tellin' what Joey's done to alienate so many, but they've also been careful. He's shunned, but not ostracized. He has some friends among them. A year or so after his father died, he bought himself his own boat. He goes out some days with the rest, but not regularly." Ron frowned. "It annoys me that I still don't know what his deal is. I've always figured drugs, but I've never caught him. Colleen swears he's clean. He's making good money somehow. Eliza natters on about his eBay store and day trading prowess. I don't buy it." He sighed. "Take your sweetheart for a stroll and get some cotton candy in a while. See what you see before things get quiet and everyone heads home or to The Point."

"Do you expect trouble?"

"Nah, just the usual drunken fights and nonsense. Chip'll stay on a bit to lend a hand."

"Cheers." Stephan appreciated the help.

"I'll be off, then."

"Dunk tank time?"

Ron grinned. "Nah, I made Chip take my turn. He's young. He doesn't mind the cold, and he's popular. He'll make more money for the Rescue Squad than me."

Stephan smiled. "Smart move, Chief."

Ron tapped his head. "I'm always thinking."

That brought an appreciative chuckle. Ron grinned and clapped a hand on Stephan's shoulder. "Go help Maura close up shop and enjoy yourselves a bit."

Maura was finishing up the last Spider Man of the day. When she gave Timmy Sewell a fist bump, he loped off with a cheerful, "Hey, Officer K."

Stephan moved next to her. "Can I help you clean up?"

Maura looked around and realized there weren't any more children waiting for her. Isabelle had started packing up the crafts and games. "That'd be great, thank you."

Stephan grinned. "I have an ulterior motive."

"Do you, now?" She swirled her brushes around in a murky cup of water before dumping the liquid out on the ground. "What is it?"

"Now that Ron's planted the idea in my head, I've a hankering for some fairy floss. I'm hoping you'll carry it. It'd wreck my tough-guy image to hold it." He winked at her.

"I see how it is." Maura laughed.

After enjoying the treat and watching a gorgeous sunset with Maura, Maisy, and Fern, Stephan reluctantly said goodnight and headed to the station.

His shift started quietly enough, until the alarm at a vacation home at the southern end of the island was triggered and the station got pinged. He hurried out there and was checking the residence when the call came in for a second alarm on the western side of the island. Chip took it. Both officers finished securing the properties and collecting evidence around the same time. They met up back at the station and made calls to the summer residents who owned the houses when a third call came in. After hanging up with the irate homeowner, Stephan looked at Chip. "Is this normally a busy night for break-ins?"

Chip looked mystified. "No, it's usually only fights at The Point and that's not likely to get going for another hour or so. We normally only see a rash of these once or twice a year in the winter, and never this many on the same night."

"Let's take this one together so we can process it faster."

Stephan let Chip drive and called Ron to give him a heads up. The house they were speeding towards wasn't far from the center of town. Unlike the previous two, this one was occupied. Andy Wickham met them out in his driveway. His face was florid and he was gesturing angrily towards his front door, which gaped open and showed obvious signs of having been at the receiving end of a heavy, blunt object. "This is going to be a pain," Chip muttered as he parked the car.

Stephan had to agree. He didn't find the logger pleasant to deal with on a good day. He sighed.

"If you deal with him, I'll take the photos and check for prints and tracks." Chip gave Stephan a hopeful look. "I need the experience, right?"

Despite himself, Stephan chuckled. "Yeah, you do. Go ahead."

"Got it, Stevie!" Chip slipped out of the car and grabbed a duffel bag from the trunk while Stephan slid a notebook out of his pocket and approached Andy.

"It was Mildred. It had to be!"

"Mildred?" Stephan reached the man.

"My ex-wife. She's bat-shit crazy." Andy's yelling sprayed spittle towards the officer.

Stephan took a closer look at the busted-up door. "Is Mildred a strong woman?"

"Mildred?" Andy snorted. "A gust could blow her over. She was useless in the woods and even worse out on the Calypso. Couldn't haul or lift for beans. She was okay with customers and negotiating, but so am I. Why? What's that got to do with the price of lobster? I'm telling you it was her. Why aren't you writing this down?"

Stephan looked at the splintered door. "Your door looks like someone took a sledgehammer to it."

Andy scowled. "She probably brought that good-for-nothing brother of hers along with her. The inside is totally trashed. All my mother's jewelry's gone and so is my TV. She took my good whiskey, the freaking bitch. That was just spiteful. She doesn't even drink."

Stephan carefully followed Andy into the house and ignored Chip's snicker when he passed by the young officer.

By the time the two finished with Andy, it was close to midnight. On the short drive back, they compared notes. Mildred, Chip insisted, could not have been behind the break in. She had good reasons to be angry at Andy, but the last anyone had heard, she'd fled her belligerent ex in the middle of the night for the warmth of Florida and a man half Andy's age and size. Her brother was not likely involved either, according to the younger man, because he was twiddling his thumbs in the county lockup after getting caught with a pocketful of meth two weeks earlier.

When they reached the station, they found Colleen sitting with her boot-clad feet up on the large desk the three officers all shared. She was dressed in jeans and a form fitting black shirt. Her hair was up and her makeup was heavy. "Hello, boys." She pushed away from the desk and stood. "I brought you a present. He's in the cell."

"Who is?"

"Dwight. Had a bit too much to drink and threw some punches. I dragged his ass here to sober up, since neither of you were available. But since you're back, I'm heading back to The Point. I've got a beer with my name on it waiting for me at the bar."

"Thanks, Colleen." Stephan waved to her as she sauntered out of the station. "Enjoy your night."

She grinned at him. "I'm sure I'll have a better time than you, Stevie." She winked at Chip and left.

"There was either a warning or a taunt in there, wasn't there?" Stephan sighed.

"Little bit of both." Chip gave him a rueful smile. "Dwight's a mean drunk and can't hold his liquor. Hopefully she left a bucket in there with him."

"Great." Stephan grimaced.

"I'll go make sure." Chip liked the older officer and felt a twinge of sympathy for him.

"Thanks, Chip. I'll start dealing with all of this." Stephen waved his notebook. "We'll get the evidence processed when you get back."

"You got it." Chip ducked into the storage closet and emerged with a battered bucket. "Be back in a minute."

CHAPTER 9

The morning after Halloween, Maura joined her neighbors for a companionable brunch. While the adults cleaned up and chatted, Maisy spread her loot out on the table.

Maura laughed at the pile of small black bags. "Was everyone only giving out M&Ms?"

Maisy grinned at her. "They're my favorite, so I picked them every time." She gave her father an innocent look. "Daddy, I ate all my eggs. Remember, you told me I could have some candy if I did that?"

Stephan eyed the child. "I vaguely recall agreeing to something like that last night," he admitted. He watched her hand creep towards the colorful chocolates. "Two bags."

"But there's three of us."

"Are you sharing?" When Maisy nodded, Stephan shook his head. "Fine, three bags."

With a gleeful smile, she ripped them open and chocolate spilled onto the table. With the candies scattered around, Maisy began to sort them into small piles based on colors.

Maura watched in fascination as Stephan helped his daughter. "What're you guys doing?"

"Some colors taste better than others," was Maisy's explanation.

Stephan plucked up a vibrant blue candy and tweaked his daughter's ponytail before he popped it in his mouth. After swallowing he nodded. "I love blue ones the best because they remind me of your eyes." He tipped his head slightly. "I've also grown quite fond of green and brown, especially together."

Maisy laughed. "That's because of your eyes, Maura." She grinned in approval as her father swiped a couple of green and brown M&Ms from her piles. "I like red because it's my favorite color. Plus, they taste the best." She copied her father and popped a red one in her mouth. "I also love yellow because it reminds me of sunny days." Maisy grabbed a yellow and another red for good measure. "What's your favorite, Maura?"

Maura studied the piles of candy. "I'm not sure they taste any different to me. I'd better pick orange, though, because it's being left out. Besides, I do love when the leaves turn that shade of orange in the fall that looks like they're lit from within. This isn't the same, but it'll do."

Stephan winked at her. "Probably best Mars can't make that particular orange. God knows what chemicals it would take to achieve."

Maisy had been studying the candy while her father was talking. She grabbed Maura's hand in excitement and put a red and orange candy next to one another. "We're M&Ms; Maisy and Maura! Daddy, you make us plural with the *s* in Stephan." The girl grinned at the adults, feeling pleased with herself.

"Huh." Stephan looked at the candies she'd placed together. "So we are."

The adults watched Maisy go back to sorting through her loot. Maisy's gaze suddenly grew unfocused and she cocked her head to the side. "Karria! She's waiting for us at the beach." Maisy slid off her chair and grabbed Maura's hand and then her father's. "Come on. She wants to play."

Stephan had reluctantly allowed Maisy to return to the beach if he, Maura, or Liz were with her. Karria often showed up for the women, but Stephen hadn't seen the seal since Maisy's near drowning. He gave his daughter a skeptical look. "If you want to go for a walk, just ask, Maisy."

She shook her head. "I want to go to the beach. Hurry! If we don't come, she'll think I'm ignoring her and will go away. Please." She saw her father's hesitant expression. "I've been good. I've followed all the rules."

Maura stretched. "I could use a walk, and it is a lovely day. There won't be many more like this until late April or May."

"I can see I'm outvoted." Stephan grumbled. "All right, shoes and coats this time, Maisy."

"Finnnnnnne." the girl rolled her eyes at her father. She ran for the hallway closet.

By the time the adults got there, her coat and rubber boots were on and she was dancing with impatience by the door.

"Go ahead, but stay out of the water!" Stephan opened the door so Maisy could bolt out. He helped Maura with her coat and grabbed his camera before locking up. He reached for Maura's hand. "Do you really think the seal is there?"

"I hope so." Maura's expression was troubled. "What are you going to say to Maisy if she's not?"

Stephan sighed. "I'm not sure. Probably just tease her about wanting to go for a walk. I'm concerned about her obsession. I called Maisy's psychologist in Boston and Dr. Brooks assured me she's not going crazy. She speculated that it could be a reaction to the trauma of going under the water like that." He sighed. "She also gave me the name of a colleague up this way, but of course she's an hour away." He was quiet for a moment. "I was hoping we were done with this. I've been enjoying not having to take her to therapy appointments, to just feeling normal again."

Maura squeezed his hand. They topped the rise and were looking at the small cove. Maisy was frolicking on the beach with a large, distinctive seal. "Oh. I've never seen one do that before."

As the adults watched, the seal pushed her head into Maisy's belly and then shoved it under her hands for petting and scratching. Maisy bent her head down to kiss it. Then she turned to beam at her father. "I told you Karria was waiting for me." Maisy knelt down in the sand so she could throw her arms around the seal in a tight hug.

The seal turned her gaze to Stephan and Maura. She gave them a nod before resting her head on Maisy's shoulder and nuzzling the side of her head.

"Is this safe?" Stephan kept his eyes on the seal while he whispered to Maura.

"I," she hesitated. "I think so." She gave a slight shrug. "She's not acting like a sick animal." Maura looked sideways at Stephan. "It's a bit strange Maisy knew she'd be here, don't you think?"

"Yeah, it's a weird coincidence." Stephan tugged Maura forward with him, refusing to let go of her hand while also wanting to get to his child.

As they got closer, Maura led Stephan towards the rocks and urged him to sit with her, rather than hover over Maisy and Karria. He hesitated and then joined her. After a few moments, he slid his lens cover off and began taking a flurry of pictures.

Karria flopped back into the surf and disappeared. Both adults expected Maisy to be disappointed, but she turned to them with a beaming smile. "She has something special to show me." The girl turned away from them to stack rocks and watch for her friend's return.

Stephan and Maura looked at each other. Maura shrugged. "This is new territory for me."

"Me too," he muttered. Stephan's worry about his daughter creating an imaginary conversation with a wild seal eased as the warmth from the sun baked rock penetrated his body. He stopped taking photos and set the camera down with care. Maura's hand was soft and smooth in his. If Maisy having a made-up conversation with a friendly creature was his biggest concern, he decided it wasn't really worth fussing about at the moment. Stephan closed his eyes and enjoyed the peace. When he heard Maura utter a soft gasp, his eyes snapped back open. "What's wrong?" He started to push off from the rock.

She rested a hand against his chest and pressed him back. "Shh, just look."

Karria had come back onto the beach, seeming to understand that Maisy wasn't allowed to go into the water. She was holding something in her mouth that glinted dully when the sun struck it. When Karria reached the girl, she dropped the object gently in Maisy's hand. Maisy's eyes grew round as saucers. "Wowww-www," she breathed, and sat down next to the seal to throw her arms around her in a tight hug. Karria rested her head on Maisy's shoulder and stared at the adults. Her mouth seemed to be smiling. "Come see!" Maisy called them over.

Stephan and Maura bridged the short distance quickly.

"Hi, Karria," Maura greeted the seal politely and didn't make a move to touch her until the animal put her head under her hand. "Oh!" Delighted, she gently stroked the seal's damp fur. "Thank you!"

In the meantime, Stephan had been looking at the gift the seal had brought his child. "I'll be damned."

Maura stopped petting Karria and finally looked. "What is—ohhhh." Her eyes widened as she took in the battered coin. It was mostly circular, but some of the edges were worn away in places. The letters *NE* were stamped in a formal script at the top of one side; *X11* was on the other. The coin had the tarnished look of silver. "Wow, I've never seen anything like this before, Maisy."

All three of them looked at the seal, who gave them a placid look in return.

Maisy offered the coin back to her, but she barked once and gently pushed Maisy's hand back towards the child's body. The girl stared at the seal for a moment and a look of wonder came across her face. "She says it's a gift."

She gave Stephan and Maura a quizzical look. "I can't use a coin like this to buy anything, can I?"

"Love, that coin could be worth a small fortune." He gave the seal a serious look. "Thank you, Karria." There wasn't a trace of self-consciousness in his voice as he addressed the seal. "I'll keep it safe for Maisy."

Karria nodded her head as if she'd understood every word he'd said. She turned and bobbed her head up and down at Maisy until the girl drew close. They gave each other a brief kiss. Then the seal pulled away from the trio and made her awkward way back into the water. She rolled and arced gracefully near the shore before raising a flipper and flapping it as if waving goodbye.

Stephan crouched down in front of his daughter. "Maisy Daisy, this is important. I don't want you to tell anyone about the coin or Karria talking to you."

She tilted her head to the side. "Why?"

"Because it might be valuable, and until we get it into safe-keeping, it should be a secret." Ron's consternation over two more burglaries in the past week was fresh in Stephan's mind.

Maura knelt in the sand and touched Maisy's hand. "Sweet-heart, you and Karria have an amazing, super-special relationship. Other people would be jealous. They might bother her to see if she would speak to them, play with them, or bring them gifts. To keep Karria safe, we need to keep what she does with you secret. I've been on this island since I was a girl and I've never heard of anyone having a seal befriend them like this."

"Huh. You mean, everyone would come hang out here and try to get her to do tricks and stuff?"

"At a minimum." Stephan nodded in agreement; glad Maura had thought about the animal. Maisy would be more likely to keep quiet if it was to protect the seal.

"She'd hate that. She doesn't like lots of people." Maisy sucked on her lower lip. "Okay. It'll be a special secret. But I want to tell Gran. I don't think Grandma would believe me anyway."

"You're probably right." Stephan had to agree with the girl's assessment of her two grandmothers. Sophie's mother would worry the child was having a psychological break and demand they return to civilization where she could get care. His mother, on the other hand, would think it a wonderful lark and reiterate her request for Maisy to introduce her to Karria when she arrived for the holidays in December.

Maisy turned the coin over in her hands. "It looks super old."

"It does." Stephan held his hand out so he could examine it again. After he did, he handed it back to Maisy. "We can do a little research when we get home. Want to help us, Maura?"

"You said research. That's a magical word." She grinned at them. "I'll do you one better, though. We can call Adam Beals and make an appointment to have him appraise it for Maisy. He should be able to tell if it's genuine."

"Adam Beals." The name was familiar to Stephan but he couldn't place it. Finally, he thought he had the right person. "Is he the big muscular fellow at the bank, the one who looks like a biker pretending to be a banker? You know, the one who looks out of place in a suit."

"That's Adam," Maura smiled and nodded in agreement. Her voice grew enthusiastic as she continued. "He collects coins and studies them. He's great. You can rely on him to keep Maisy's gift secret. I've never known Adam to cheat anyone or break confidences. He just loves coins. He usually brings his collection and does a presentation at the library in the spring. It's a popular one. He takes the time to look at every bit and piece folks have unearthed with their metal detectors or found in fish. Even when it's not valuable, he lets them down gently."

"Sounds like a great guy." Stephan's tone was dry.

Maura's eyes reflected her amusement when she looked up at him. "He is, but it's his husband Michael who turns heads. He looks like he was born to wear Armani."

"Brat."

Maura grinned at Stephan.

Maisy was ignoring them and turning the coin round and round in her hand. "Can we go research now?" She tugged Stephan's shirt.

"Sure." Stephan reached for his daughter's free hand and then for Maura with his other hand and began whistling a cheerful tune as they made their way back up the rise towards the road and their houses. As they started to head for Milly's, Maisy shook her head. "Can we go to Maura's? I wanna show Tim."

"You mean you want to snuggle that terror of a ginger."

Maisy grinned at her father. "You're just cranky because he likes me and growls at you."

"He is a jealous boy." Tim was taking longer to accept Stephan's presence in Maura's life than Maura had anticipated. "But Greta has decided you're her favorite human in the world, so there's that. She's far more discerning than Tim."

"Flatterer." Stephan laughed as they walked up the stone path to Maura's door.

When they stepped inside, all three cats were lined up to greet them. Tim brushed along Maura's legs and then put his paws up on Maisy's knee, begging her for cuddles. The girl was happy to comply with his demand and carried the small orange cat into the kitchen, chatting with him about Karria and the coin as they went.

Maura got Stephan and Maisy going on the computer while she called Adam to see about an appointment. When she reached him, he asked her to text a picture. His return call came within a minute. He wondered if he and Michael could swing by for dessert to have a closer look and discussion with them about the gift.

Maura lifted an eyebrow. She muted the phone and asked Stephan if he and Maisy were free and interested. His expression reflected a similar surprise and he nodded in agreement. After making plans with Adam, Maura hung up the phone and looked at the others. "I'm going to venture a guess that Karria gave you a pretty special gift, Maisy."

"It IS a special gift, Maura." Maisy corrected her. "It just might be extra-special, you mean."

"Yes," Maura agreed. "Extra-special." She turned and peered in the refrigerator. "What do you think about pizza? I'm overdue for a shopping trip."

"Yay!" Maisy cheered, which startled Tim into puffing up.

"You could come shopping with us tomorrow if you'd like. And I'll go pick up the food if you'd place the order. Should I get some dessert while I'm there?"

"I'll take that deal." She opened her cupboards and considered their contents. "Michael was baking pies today, so they're bringing one, and I have the fixings for chocolate chip cookies."

"Ooh, can I help make them?" Maisy gave Tim a pat and put him down on her chair after she stood up. "I'm getting better at cracking eggs."

Maura nodded. "You sure are. Wash up and we'll get started." She took the butter out of the refrigerator.

When Maisy had scampered off to the bathroom, Stephan backed Maura into the counter and gave her a quick but passionate kiss. "I adore your cookies."

"I know." She grinned at him.

He pulled back when he heard Maisy coming back down the short hallway. "So, a large cheese and small pepperoni, large salad, and an order of garlic bread so we can scare away any vampires."

"Or at least Adam and Michael?" Maura laughed.

"Okay, maybe just an order of their hot buttered bread. Anything else? No? Right then. I'll head out."

After a pleasant, early dinner, the adults made short work of cleaning up. Stephan leaned against the counter as he finished drying the last plate and quietly asked Maura, "Are you certain it's okay to bring these guys into this?"

Maura nodded. "I would trust Adam and Michael with my life. They're good, honest men."

Stephan started to ask her something, but the doorbell interrupted him. Maura reached for his hand and gave it a squeeze. "Trust me."

Once everyone was settled with a hot drink and a slice of Michael's bumbleberry pie, they brought out Karria's gift. Adam turned it around in his fingers a few times and looked at it with a magnifying glass. After a couple of minutes, he gave a low whistle. "There are a couple of tests I'd run to confirm, but I think you have a New England silver coin shilling. There are high-quality counterfeits out there, but given where it came from, I suspect this'll turn out to be real. They're worth a fair bit to the folks who collect them. This one isn't pristine, but it's in damn—er, darned good shape."

He gave Stephan a serious look. "If you don't already have a safe deposit box at the bank, you might want to think about renting one."

"It's that valuable?" Stephan gave the old coin a skeptical look.

"These colonists in New England produced their own coins for about thirty years before King Charles the second put a stop to it. A sixpence sold for more than four hundred thousand recently. The shillings aren't quite as valued, but you're still looking at many thousands of dollars with a coin in as good shape as this one is."

Everyone at the table stared at Adam with various slack-jawed expressions except Maisy. She gave Adam a serious look. "So, I'm rich, but only if I sell it?" The girl shook her head. "I'm not selling it."

"No, love, you don't need to, but it's good to know what it's worth." Stephan smiled at his daughter, glad that the gift meant more to her than the things it could buy.

After Maisy, bored with the conversation, had wandered off to curl up with the cats and a book, Adam reached for the coin and rolled it around in his fingers. "You know, it's more likely that there'd be more of these around here than any gold from Quelch's rumored treasure. Maura, do you know the story of the *Molly Ann*?"

She shook her head. "The name rings a bell, but I don't know why."

Adam nodded and then looked at Stephan, who had had a blank look on his face.

Michael rolled his eyes. "You just can't help yourself, can you, Adam?" Michael gave them a sympathetic look. "He's the only one on the island who thinks there's more to the *Molly Ann* than an old yarn."

Maura picked up her mug and leaned forward, resting her elbows on the table. "Well, you can't just leave it there. I take it you're talking about a ship?"

"I am." Adam took a long drink and then started his story. "The *Molly Ann* was a sloop out of Boston carrying a couple of spies in service to the British crown; Sir James Wylie and Mathew Moore. They spent much of 1688 visiting the coastal communities of the Massachusetts Bay Colony. Ostensibly, they were merchants purchasing sample goods for a wealthy mercantile back in London. In reality, they'd been tasked with gathering up as many of the illegally minted coins they could get their hands on, as well as gathering intelligence on any rebellious sentiments running through the colony. They were also checking to see what the French and Passamaquoddy were up to. They were headed up towards Mt. Desert to finish their intelligence mission before making the voyage home when they passed our island. This was shortly after King Phillip's War and there weren't any colonists here, only a handful of French fur traders who had spent their summer working along the Penobscot and the natives. The French had come over following moose, though one deluded one claimed to be hunting selkie. They're the ones who later told the British about the *Molly Ann*'s fate.

"It was September. There was a big blow. The trappers had hunkered down in the caves—you know, Maura, the ones under the conservation lands by Doug and Bonnie's weirs. Anyway, they rode out the storm. When it passed, the trappers explored the island. Your cove here was where they found the *Molly Ann*. She was mostly under water. They found two survivors on the beach: Mr. Moore and the ship's cook. Moore had been wounded by flotsam and ended up dying by the time the group reached the mouth of the Penobscot. He was delirious with fever, mistook one of the traders for a Catholic priest, and gave him his last confession. I wish I could find out more about him, but he's lost to history beyond this yarn, far as I know." Adam sighed.

Maura sipped her coffee in silence for a moment as Adam waited for her and Stephan to react. A grin formed on her face. "Is this why you're always scuba diving around here?"

Michael laughed. "Busted."

Adam gave her a boyish grin. "Maybe. Maybe you just have some cool fish out there."

Stephan gave Adam a thoughtful look. "Did they find anything valuable?"

"Who?"

"The trappers."

Adam shrugged. "Doubtful. The *Molly Ann* hit rocks on that spit of land on the other side of the channel, and then drifted towards your cove with the tide while taking on water. Mathew described a couple of lock boxes with several pouches in each. There were other items of value on the ship, but nothing extraordinary and nothing that'd survive out there," he jerked his thumb towards the water, "for this many centuries and retain value to anyone but a historian or collector. Even the coins aren't particularly valuable for their metal. It's the history and rarity that make them special." He smiled at the table. "I've gotta admit, your find here has given me hope. I'll be back in the water searching."

His husband rolled his eyes. "Which means you're going to be needing me to come along too."

"You know it's not safe to dive alone."

"I hate how cold this water gets."

"A few dives before Thanksgiving and then we wait until summer. I want to explore that cave complex with the petroglyphs more, anyway."

Michael's voice was dry when he replied, "Or we could spend the winter by the woodstove working on puzzles, organizing the back room, going to Aruba, even skiing. You know, the things people normally do in the winter."

Adam stared at his husband, aghast. Then he saw the twinkle in Michael's eyes and laughed. "We're not normal people, Mike."

"What caves are you talking about?" Stephan broke in before the men could continue their banter.

"Oh, Lord," Michael sighed and looked at Maura. "Would you like more pie, sweetheart? You know we're going to be here for hours."

Maura grinned and pushed her empty plate over to him as Adam turned his attention to Stephan after giving them both a chastising look.

"There's a bunch of caves and tunnels in the granite of Belfort. One runs underneath the library and Baptist Church. Another cluster is on the west side of the island near the Jones' weirs. I think they're connected, but they're hard to explore. There's lots of dead ends and narrow passages. Some flood at high tide. There are several deep ones on the southern end of the island. A couple have some wicked cool petroglyphs."

"Most folks leave them be unless they need shelter in a storm, but Adam's been obsessed with all of them since he was a boy." Michael handed Maura back her plate. He gave Stephan an inquiring look and smiled when an empty plate was handed over in return. "There's nothing special in most of them, but every now and then you'll come across interesting odds and ends."

"Some folks around here are also still convinced that there's pirate treasure to be found in the caves." Maura's eyes were twinkling as she grinned at Adam.

"Hey, it kept me out of trouble when I was a kid, didn't it?" Adam's cheeks had warmed. "You never know what might have washed into them. Plenty of treasures have been lost at sea here, and with the tides we've got, things get moved around. It doesn't need to be pirate booty to be valuable." He waved a fork at Michael and Maura. "You two lack imagination sometimes."

Michael eyed him. "You might want to take that back."

Adam grinned at his husband. "Or what? Will you prove me wrong?" He gave him a cheeky grin.

"You're so juvenile sometimes."

"I'm going to go check on Maisy." Maura stood up. "I'll be right back."

As she moved out of the room, she heard Adam start telling Stephan more about the tunnel under the library. Maura poked her head in the living room and didn't see the girl. She walked upstairs and saw soft yellow light spilling out from the craft room. She peeked into the doorway and smiled. Maisy was sprawled out on the futon. *Charlotte's Web* was on the floor. Tim was tucked up against her and her right arm was thrown around the small cat's body. He gave Maura a long, slow blink and pushed his head back into Maisy. Mags was snoozing near the foot of the mattress. Maura quietly picked up a throw blanket. She covered the sleeping child and turned the lamp down to the lowest setting. Tim's quiet purr, Maisy's soft breathing, and Mags's gentle snoring brought a smile to her face. Maura took a moment to enjoy the peacefulness of the scene before tiptoeing out of the room and back down the stairs.

"Everything okay?" Stephan asked as soon as she re-entered the kitchen.

"She's sacked out with Tim and Mags upstairs."

"We should get going," Michael nudged Adam.

"But—oh, yeah," Adam glanced at the time on Maura's microwave. It read 8:01. "It's really late."

Maura's lips quirked in amusement.

"Uh, anyway, I'd be happy to show you the spot any-time Stephan."

"I'd appreciate it," Stephan nodded in thanks and rose as the other men did.

After the couple left, Maura shut the door and smiled at Stephan. "That was an unexpected evening."

"Indeed." he reached out and wrapped his arms around her waist, pulling her close. "I'll help you clean up before I wake Maisy."

"We could," Maura hesitated and then plowed ahead at his inquiring look. "We could just let her sleep."

Stephan gave her a thoughtful look. "She's comfortable here. I don't think she'd be scared if she woke in the night." He twirled a lock of Maura's hair around an index finger. "If I get Dot and Pooh and tuck them in with her, she'll go back to sleep even if she wakes. I could get my toothbrush and pajamas then too."

"Did I say *you* could spend the night?" Maura grinned up at him.

Stephan smiled in response. "You never said I couldn't."

"Hmmmm," Maura leaned back in his arms so she could fully see his face. The warmth in his expression made her heart skip a beat. "It would be nice."

"Only nice?"

"It'd be lovely."

"Lovely?"

"It'd be delightful."

Stephan pulled her close. "You're getting warmer."

Maura linked her arms around his neck and tugged him down. "It'd be amazing," she whispered against his lips and smiled when she felt his curve upwards before they met hers in a heated kiss.

CHAPTER 10

Wrapped in her quilt, Maisy's pale face was the only part of her visible when Maura opened the door. "Oh, sweetheart, come on in." Maura held her arms out to the girl. "Let's get you settled."

"Okay," Maisy's voice was listless.

Maura helped her into the living room while Stephan set a duffel bag down and shut the door.

Her eyes were glassy as she looked at Maura. "I don't feel good."

"I heard. I'm sorry, sweetie." Maura's voice was soft and sympathetic. "Would you like some toast and ginger ale?"

Maisy nodded briefly before shutting her eyes.

Stephan watched the cats settle themselves around his daughter and followed Maura to the kitchen. "I'm sorry."

"For what?"

"Your Thanksgiving plans didn't include getting exposed to the flu."

Maura shrugged. "It's not Maisy's fault she's sick and couldn't go on her trip."

Stephan gave her an appreciative smile. "I know, but you had plans."

"The same ones I've had for the past six years. I don't mind skipping it, and the cats will be thrilled to get some turkey this year." She smiled at him. "And I'm looking forward to celebrating with both of you tomorrow."

"If you need me, just call. I expect I'll mostly be at the station."

"It was thoughtful of you to take the whole holiday for everyone."

It was Stephan's turn to shrug. "It's not one has a lot of meaning for me. I don't have any childhood memories tied up with it." He smiled. "I've never minded working it. This year has the added bonus of getting me more time at Christmas with my family. You're sure you're okay with this?"

"We'll be fine. I'll make us some chicken soup later. We'll watch TV and read some stories. She can nap. Hopefully she'll be feeling a bit better tomorrow and can enjoy a quiet Thanksgiving do-over. Don't worry about things here."

He bent and gave her a gentle kiss. "You're a gem, Maura. I promise I'll make this up to you."

"There's nothing to make up." She shook her head at him. "I'm happy to have a quiet day at home. Stop fretting. Is she taking any medicine?"

"Here." He pulled out his phone. "I wrote up a schedule. I'll text it to you now. Call me if you have any concerns. She may get a bit whiney. She sometimes does when she's ill."

Maura chuckled. "It's okay, Stephan. We'll manage."

"I know you will." He gave her a rueful smile. "It's hard not to worry anyway."

Maura gave him a push towards the hall. "Go give Maisy a kiss and get going. I'm not going to get blamed because you're late to work and Chip has to miss the kickoff."

Stephan grabbed her hand and hauled her against him. "What about your kiss?" He wrapped his arms around Maura and held her close. "I do like the custom of saying what we're grateful for on this holiday. Maura Ballard, I am grateful for you. I am grateful our lives have intertwined." He tucked a lock of hair behind her ear and lowered his head to give her a long kiss.

With Maisy asleep, Maura went back into the kitchen to prep food for the next day and for the two of them to celebrate when Maisy was awake and up to eating.

That evening, Maura felt the girl's forehead. "How are you doing, sweetheart?" Maisy was heating up again. A glance at the clock showed that it was time for more Tylenol. "Think you can take your medicine?"

"The one that makes me feel yucky or the grape kind?"

Maura smiled at her. "Grape. The yucky one isn't till later, and hopefully it sits better tonight. I've been told the first dose or two are the worst."

"Okay." Maisy pulled herself into a semi-reclining position and held out her hand. After she was done washing the tablets down with the flat soda, she sniffed the air. "The soup smells kinda good. And I smell something cinnamony."

Maura squeezed her hand. "I'm glad. Want to try a cup of soup?"

Maisy thought about it and then gave a slight nod.

"How about we watch the Grinch while we eat our dinner?"

The girl's lips curved up ever so slightly. "Okay."

"Give me ten minutes and we'll be all set."

As she set her own food up on a small table that matched the one Maisy was using, Maura checked the girl. Her face was still pale except some flushing from the fever, but her eyes were less glazed looking.

"Hey, Maura?"

"Yes, Maisy?"

"I'm really grateful for you."

Maura smiled at the child and reached over to gently caress her cheek. "I'm grateful for you too, Miss Maisy. You've made life much more exciting and interesting around here and it's been so much fun getting to know you."

"And Daddy."

"Yes," Maura felt herself blush. "Your daddy too."

"I'm glad you like each other."

"That makes me happy to hear."

"Good." Maisy spooned some soup into her mouth. "This tastes really good. Thank you for taking care of me. I love you." Tears wobbled out of her eyes.

"Oh, sweetheart," Maura put her own food aside and gathered the child in her arms. "I love you too."

"I don't know why I'm being a baby," Maisy wailed as her tears picked up.

"You're sick, honey. It's normal to cry when you're not feeling well." Maura held the girl close and rubbed her back.

"I'm gonna get you sick."

"Hopefully not, but it's not the end of the world if it happens."

"I'm sorry. I'm really, really sorry." Maisy kept crying.

"Shhh, it's all okay." Maura held her tight. "You're going to feel better soon."

"I'm not dying and leaving Daddy alone, am I?"

"Oh, honey, no." Maura felt tears prick her own eyes. "Have you been fretting about that?" She felt Maisy's head nod against her chest. "Sweetheart, you're going to be fine. You feel rotten right now, but your dad's been doing all the right things to take care of you. You're already feeling better than yesterday, aren't you?"

"Yes," Maisy's voice was muffled against Maura's sweater. "I hurt everywhere yesterday, even my eyelashes. I only hurt some places today."

"See," Maura murmured, stroking her head, "already mending."

"Okay." Maisy's tears had stopped and her voice was sleepy. "Can we watch the Grinch later?"

"Of course. Take a little rest. I'll be right here reading my book."

"Kay." Maisy slid back down and snuggled in with Dot.

Tim merrowed from the floor before jumping onto the child's legs.

Maura gave his head an affectionate rub before she settled back to her end of the couch to eat. "Happy Thanksgiving, buddy."

When Stephan knocked on the door the next morning, Maura greeted him in an old pair of flannel pajamas and a serious case of bedhead. He leaned down to kiss her and she waved him away. "I haven't brushed my teeth." She sniffed the crisp, salty air that he brought in with him. "You smell good."

He laughed as he pulled her close. "You look and smell worlds better than Dwight."

"Ugh. He went on a bender?"

"Oh, yeah," Stephan agreed and stepped inside. "All the way around the bend and into the harbor. His car is never going to dry out."

Maura's eyes widened. "He drove off the pier?"

"Sure did." Stephan shook his head. "Lucky for him, Fred and Sam were out for a post-feast constitutional. They saw it happen and fished him out before the car sank. I'm more worried about them than him. He was so pickled; I doubt he'll remember any of it. None of us wanted to dump him home alone, so I brought him back to the station. Thankfully he fell asleep quickly. He was still snoring away when I left. Ron'll get the pleasure of dealing with him when he wakes up. I stopped at the Dodds on my way here and found Fred and Sam already up. Margery had them swaddled up like babies in front of the woodstove, lathered in Vicks and enjoying what smelled like hot toddies for breakfast."

Maura smiled at the image. "It's probably driving Fred nuts. He hates being fussed over. Are you okay? Did you have to go in the water too?"

"No, they'd already gotten him back onto the pier before I got there. We attached a buoy to his car, but how it gets fished out is a question for people whose pay grades and experience in these matters are above mine."

"I'm glad you're all safe."

Stephan nodded in agreement. "Mind if I make some coffee?" He'd had several plates of Thanksgiving dinner appear at the station throughout his 24-hour shift, but hadn't had a coffee since waking from a nap at five to go deal with yet another break-in at a summer cottage.

Maura waved at the kitchen. "Feel free. We had a bit of a rough night."

"How's Maisy doing? Is she awake?"

Maura shook her head. "She's still sleeping and she's doing better. I think the fever finally broke around three. Unfortunately, the Tamiflu didn't agree with her again, but she was a trooper. She fell into a really deep sleep after the fever broke. I'd just as soon let her sleep herself out, if that's okay, rather than waking her up to move her."

"It's fine with me." Stephan pulled her close. "Thank you for taking such good care of her, Maura."

"I was happy to. She's a great kid."

"I know we'd talked about celebrating Thanksgiving today, but why don't you rest? I can cook up something simple later."

Maura shook her head. "The turkey's easy and has to get cooked anyway. I already made some of the sides, and Liz brought pies by when she picked Fern up on Wednesday. They shouldn't sit another day without being enjoyed."

"You didn't have some yesterday?" Stephan looked surprised.

"I figured I'd wait until we were together." She shrugged.

Stephan patted his flat stomach. "Maybe I'll have some for breakfast." He pulled her close for a hug and kiss. "Let me help cook. A turkey's pretty much like a big chicken, isn't it?"

Maura laughed. "Similar for sure. Feel free to have all the pie you want." She reached for his hand. "But my vote is for a nap."

"I like how you think," Stephan smiled. "Let me check on Maisy and run home to get some fresh clothes. I'll meet you in bed."

She gave him a tired smile. "I make no promises about being awake when you get back."

Stephan gave her an affectionate kiss. "Get some rest. We have the rest of the day to visit."

Maura nodded in agreement and trudged back to her room. As she was sliding under the covers, she heard the front door click shut. She had the best of intentions to keep her eyes open, but when Tim sprawled out across her chest, his rumbly purr lulled her back to sleep.

The sound of giggling and smell of coffee and roasting turkey woke Maura. Disoriented, she stared at the clock in her sun-soaked room before it registered in her brain that it read one in the afternoon. Appalled, she hurried out of bed and threw on a clean pair of jeans and a sweater. In the bathroom, she dragged a brush through her hair and put it up in a loose bun. She hurried to brush her teeth and then rushed down the stairs.

Maisy grinned at her from the couch. "Hi, Maura! Happy day-after-Thanksgiving-Thanksgiving!" Her face was still pale, but her eyes were clear. "Guess what?" She kept talking before Maura could reply. "The yucky medicine didn't make me sick this morning and I'm all done with it. I already ate some eggy toast Daddy made me and feel way better. Will you share your pecan pie with me later? I really want to try some. I've never had it before. Did you have a good nap? Daddy said you were exhausted. Thank you for taking such good care of me. I was scared, but you held my hand and helped me. I'm glad you're so nice. Maura, I'm really thankful for you."

Maura leaned against the archway to the living room as she tried to figure out where to start with the torrent of words. "I'm really thankful for you too, Maisy," she managed.

Stephan came up from behind her with a chuckle. He put a warm mug in her hands. "Maisy, remember we talked about giving Maura a chance to wake up slowly?"

Maura gave him a grateful smile as the aroma of freshly brewed coffee reached her nose. She looked at Maisy over the rim. "I'm glad you're feeling better."

Maisy grinned at her. "Me too. Did I tell you I realized why you named Tim, Tim? I watched the Muppets' *Christmas Carol* this morning. He's named after Tiny Tim because he's so small, isn't he?" Maisy tipped her head to the side. "Why is he so small, anyway? Aren't boy cats usually big?'

Maura's shoulders started shaking as she tried to hold in her laughter.

Stephan shook his head at his daughter. "You've got a lot of chatter pent up in that body of yours, don't you, love?"

Maisy shrugged. "I didn't feel much like talking when I felt sick, but now I do." She looked back to Maura. "Is that why he's Tim?"

Maura nodded. "He showed up on my doorstep three Christmas Eves ago. I have no idea how he got here. I'd just finished watching *A Christmas Carol* when I heard noises by the front door. This little orange furball stuck his head out from behind the bush and started crying at me. It was bitterly cold. I couldn't leave him out there. He looked like he'd been on his own for a while, so I adopted him. And yes, he's named after Tiny Tim."

Hearing his name, the cat in question came crawling out from under Maisy's blanket where he'd been having a nap. He chirruped at Maura and trotted over to her for loving after giving Stephan a halfhearted, obligatory growl. Once he was nestled in Maura's arms, he made a contented noise and nuzzled her head with his before resting his chin on her shoulder and purring in her ear.

"Did you already have Mags and Greta?" Stephan eyed Tim warily before giving the ginger's head a quick rub.

"I did. I inherited Mags from Aunt Jane along with the house. Greta kept showing up at the library as a kitten. When no one claimed her after she stayed there for a few weeks, I brought her home. Did you already put the turkey in or is my nose deceiving me?"

"I followed instructions I found online and added a few herbs and spices to the butter rub. I hope you don't mind. I wanted to let you sleep."

"Mind?" Maura started laughing. "You're welcome to cook anytime! I think I've mentioned that before."

From her spot on the couch Maisy's eyes darted between the adults. She smiled. "When do we eat?"

Stephan checked his watch. "The turkey should be done in an hour."

Maura sighed. "I'd planned on cooking for *you* after you worked such a long shift."

Stephan smiled. "I got a few good naps in and was well-fed by the folks who live near the station. I don't think we're going to be out of things to eat there for days."

Maisy giggled. "It's a funny kind of Thanksgiving after Thanksgiving, isn't it?"

"We can make our own traditions, right love?"

"Right," Maisy nodded. She looked at Maura. "Dr. Kate taught us that after Mama died."

"It's good advice."

Maisy nodded. "I keep asking Daddy to start the ice cream sundaes on Sunday tradition, but he always tells me no." Maisy's eyes gleamed. "Maybe you can ask, Maura. He might say yes to you."

Stephan shook his head. "The answer is still no."

"Awww," Maisy gave a mock frown and then looked at Maura. "Can we turn on the tree lights again? I really liked that last night, even if I was sleeping a whole lot."

Maura put her mug down on the sideboard and crossed the room to plug them in. The warm lights weren't all that visible in the still sunny room, but with the early sunset, they'd be providing a cheerful glow soon enough.

The timer from the microwave dinged. "I've got to baste the turkey."

"Do you need a hand?"

"Sure," Stephan smiled. "You can make sure I'm doing it right."

Maura chuckled. "I don't cook turkey often. I'm not sure I'd know if you're doing it wrong."

"Excellent." He winked at her. "I'll look competent as long as I don't drop it on the floor, then."

She grinned at him. "The cats would like that, but, yeah, it would blow your image as a master chef." Maura gave Maisy a kiss on her head and grabbed her coffee before following Stephan back into the kitchen. "How can I help?"

They worked companionably, laughing and teasing as they put the meal together.

In fairly short order, the living room was converted to a dining room. Maisy was still in her spot on the sofa, with Stephan further down. Maura had pulled her favorite armchair over so that it faced them.

Despite the fact that it was only 2:30 in the afternoon, the sun was already starting to fade and the tree's lights were casting a warm glow. Maura turned on a few of the small lamps that were scattered around the room. It was warm and cozy as the three of them sat with their holiday meals.

Stephan started to cut into his turkey when Maisy shook her head. "Daddy, no! Before we eat, we have to say things we're grateful for."

"Oh, right." Stephan put his utensils down and gave his hot food a longing look. "Okay, why don't you start?"

"It's Maura's house." Maisy objected. "She should go first."

Maura had snuck a generous spoonful of stuffing into her mouth while Maisy's attention was diverted. She shook her head and put her hand in front of her mouth. "Guests first, please." Her voice was muffled.

Stephan started laughing, which prompted Maisy to glare at both of them.

"You two aren't doing this right!"

Maura managed to choke down her food and Stephan caught his breath after a moment. Each smiled at the other. "I haven't eaten since dinner last night," Maura explained. "I'm starving."

Stephan gave his child a "don't you dare make a fuss" look that she knew well.

Maisy gave a sigh. "I'll go first then, so you can eat more, Maura. I have a lot I'm grateful for anyway."

As they ate, the conversation bounced around topics that ranged from food and holiday traditions to school, work, and family, and back to food.

"Who's ready for pie?" Maura asked a bit after everyone had finished eating.

"Could I take a nap first?" Maisy was snuggling Dot again and had slid a bit deeper into her pillows.

"Of course," Maura stood up to clear away the plates.

The adults cleaned up in the kitchen. When all the leftovers were stowed away and the last of the dishes were washed, they sat together at the table with mugs of tea.

"Did you ever think about trying to make it as an artist?" Stephan was admiring a couple of her landscapes that hung in the kitchen.

"For about a semester," Maura grinned. "I earned a minor in fine arts because I took so many classes, but it was never a practical choice. I knew I'd need to do something that would enable me to take care of myself." She idly traced a pattern on the wooden table's surface. "Aunt Jane had saved all my inheritance for school, so I was able to go debt free, but there wasn't any left after. I'd always liked libraries and bookstores. They were places where I could lose myself in other worlds. I worked at the library here every summer from ninth grade until I graduated from college. I suppose I should have taken internships or stayed in Boston and worked other places to try and make connections and gain other experiences, but I never wanted to. Jane encouraged me to explore. I don't know if it was homesickness or something else, but I've always needed to return. I took a job in Boston for a few years after I finished my Master's. A couple of my girlfriends convinced me to room with them and give it a chance." She gave him a rueful smile. "I tried, but when Mrs. Brown decided to retire, I put my application in here without telling anyone." She took a sip of tea. "Aunt Jane was disappointed that I didn't spread my wings more, but I think she understood. She certainly made me feel welcome to come back and live at home. I'd intended to share an apartment with Liz, but she and Fern's dad got serious so quickly that by the time I started work, rooming with her was no longer an option."

Stephan covered her hand with his when it had stilled. He gave a gentle squeeze. "I'm glad you decided to settle here." He smiled at her. "Your parents traveled frequently. You didn't share the urge?"

Maura shook her head. "I've always been more of a home-body. I always just wanted to belong somewhere, and here," —she waved with her free hand— "turned out to be my place."

"Do you think you'd have found your way here if it hadn't been for your aunt?"

Maura gave him a thoughtful look. "You know, I've consid-ered that. Jane's the whole reason I started coming here, and I'm sure she's the main reason it feels like home, but there's something about the space that's always spoken to my soul, too."

"There is something about the island, isn't there?" Stephan looked out the window towards the cove. Small clouds scuttled across the darkening sky. The bare trees were dancing in the brisk breeze while the pines were hunched over like old women from years of relentless winds pushing on them. "It's not an easy place to live, but it's soothing and healing all the same."

Maura nodded. "You get it."

"I think I do," Stephan agreed. "Aside from the connection with the physical space and spirit of the place, in practical terms, I know moving here was right for me. Ron's philosophy around policing and our role in the community is much more aligned with mine than my old precinct. I am really enjoying working with the teenagers. I feel like I'm actually making a difference in tangible, meaningful ways. I haven't felt like that in years. I was pretty jaded about my job in Boston. I just hope I made the right choice for Maisy."

She flipped her hand under his so their palms were touching and gave a light squeeze. "Maisy is thriving right now, and civiliza-tion's not so terribly far away."

Stephan smiled. "All true words." He gazed down at their joined hands for a moment before breaking the silence. "My par-ents worry Maisy will miss out on too many of life's opportunities living out here. The school can't compete with the ones in Boston. But she's actually going to school here and enjoying it. That wasn't the case in JP." He gave her a wry smile. "Ruth and Bill have been appalled whenever Maisy describes how small her class is and how the grades mingle and share teachers. It's funny, but the one who's been the most enthusiastic is my brother. Nick lives in London and is always traveling. I expected the most pushback from him, honestly. But he keeps saying how well he thinks Maisy is doing and goes on about how much happier we both are."

Maura smiled. "I'm glad he sees it."

Stephan nodded in agreement. "Me too. And he's right, you know." He squeezed her hand and then released it so he could cradle his mug of tea. "Why doesn't Fern's dad help out more?"

"Oh." Maura shot him a look of surprise and then chagrin. "No one told you, huh? I guess we all figured someone else did, and everyone knows how private Liz is. We're pretty protective of her and Fern." She gazed out the window for a moment, then sighed and looked back at him. "He was an addict. He OD'ed on Fern's first birthday."

"Christ." Stephan sank back in his chair. "And his family doesn't help?"

Maura shook her head. "They've had nothing to do with her since Billy died. She could pass her grandparents on the street and not even realize they're related."

"Ouch," Stephan winced.

"Daddy?" Maisy's voice sounded fretful.

Stephan shot up from his chair and hurried into the living room. Maura followed close behind him. Maisy's cheeks were flushed and her eyes were fever-bright again. "Daddy." She stretched her arms up.

"Hey, love," Stephan gathered her into his arms.

"Daddy, I don't feel good again." Maisy frowned up at him. "I want my bed."

"Okay, sweetheart. I need to pack up your things first."

"Can you hurry?"

"I'll do my best, Maisy." Stephan carefully put her back on the sofa. He gave Maura a regretful look. "I'm sorry to have to cut the evening short."

She shook her head. "I understand. Let me help get her things packed from upstairs. It'll go faster with two of us."

Maura helped Stephan bring everything across the street so he could carry Maisy. After she shut their door behind her, she whispered, "I'm thankful for you, Kirkland family," before slipping back into the warmth of her own cozy home.

CHAPTER 11

Stephan stamped his feet. Despite his wearing the warmest socks that could fit in his boots, they were still cold. He stood on the periphery of the crowd and watched his daughter run around with all the other kids. They moved in a pack, screaming like banshees with their coats flapping open, hats askew, and mittens and gloves flopping in pockets. He was tempted to tell her to zip up when she raced by, but seeing her joy, kept his mouth shut.

"You look half-frozen." Maura's amused voice reached him through the earmuffs he'd donned the moment Colleen had wandered off to check on Santa's ETA.

He gave her a grateful smile when she put a hot cup of coffee in his gloved hands. "Thanks, Maura."

She gave him a sympathetic look. "Can you take a minute to warm up inside?"

A wry smile flitted across his face. "And have Colleen call me Wimpy Stevie or Stevie Weevey or whatever other god-awful nickname her devious mind comes up with? Not a chance."

"Am I allowed to snuggle you when you're on duty?" She grinned at him and slid her hand out of a thick mitten long enough to run it along his cold cheek.

Stephan groaned as she cupped his cheek. He leaned into the precious heat coming from her palm. "You tempt me, woman."

Maura laughed. "I was coming to tell you they're about to get started. George is buckling up." She tugged her mitten back on.

The piercing wail of the fire sirens silenced everyone and the night was suddenly lit with red and white flashing lights. A moment later, the trees on the common blazed with twinkling lights. A booming "Ho ho ho," came from on top of the ladder truck. That was the signal for the combined choirs of the Baptist and Catholic churches to begin belting out "Santa Claus Is Coming to Town".

Stephan felt a wash of pleasure rush through him as he took in the sight of Maisy watching with unbridled glee, her hands clasped with Fern's and Lana's. He heard Maura singing along in a soft voice next to him and pulled her close in a one-armed hug, protocol be damned.

The choirs led the celebrants through a rollicking sing-a-long before they turned the mood down a drop with a reverent Silent Night. That was Santa's cue to lead the children into St. Michaels for visits, cocoa, and cookies.

Maisy came running over with Fern and Lana. "Can I go in too, Daddy?"

"Of course," he laughed. "If you can't find me later, look for Maura."

"'K!" Maisy gave each of them a fierce but distracted hug before running off with her friends.

"Are you allowed to come inside now and thaw out, or is Ron requiring you to become a popsicle?"

"Nope, in ten minutes I'm off duty unless there's an emergency." He offered her his arm. "Shall we?"

Maura nodded. "I love this time of year."

Stephan had to agree. Aside from the stress the unsolved burglaries were causing the small police force, life was feeling damned close to perfect. Maura and Maisy continued to get on well. They'd spent the Sunday after Thanksgiving trimming Maura's tree as a quiet activity with Maisy. Later that week, he and Maisy came home to find that Maura had hung a large wreath with a cheerful, sparkly red-and-gold bow on their door. It matched the one on her own. This morning, he and Maisy had cut down a huge Christmas tree. The three of them were going to decorate it the next day. Stephan wasn't sure who was looking forward to that the most, him or Maisy. Not being able to go to sleep and wake up with Maura beside him each day was a frustration, but he was a patient man. They'd agreed Maisy's comfort and sense of security needed to be kept in mind as their relationship progressed. Stephan sighed. His parents and Nick were due to arrive in another week for an extended stay through the New Year's holiday. It would make carving out private time with Maura even more challenging. She didn't seem to share those worries. It was that or she was keeping them to herself. He looked down at her. Her cheeks and nose were red from the cold and her gorgeous hair was stuffed under a cream-colored beanie cap with a silly pompom bouncing on top. He smiled. He loved her. It wasn't a new revelation to him, but he still hadn't said the words out loud.

"Maura." He stopped as the heat and noise from the church hall hit him.

"Yes?"

A crowd of teenagers jostled them as they hurried by to get inside. "It can wait." he gave her hand a squeeze.

"Okay." She gave him a quizzical look, but accepted him at his word. Her lips curved into a broad smile as she took in the festive decorations, barely-contained chaos with children running everywhere, and holiday music blaring from an old sound system in the corner. She adored the quiet elegance of the library's holiday decorations and music, but this raucous cacophony also appealed. She hoarded the memories of the busy, social holiday season to carry her through the quiet that came in winter and early spring, when the last of the snowbirds had fled for their southern trailers and the number of children in the afterschool program thinned out because of winter colds and flus and parents out of work for the season.

Maura tugged her hat off and stuffed it in her pocket. Stephan chuckled when she reached up to smooth down her flyaway hair. "Don't." He gave her an affectionate smile. "You look wonderful."

Maura wrinkled her nose. "I doubt it, but I don't care right now. I'm happy to get warm."

Stephan saw the urns of soup. "Let's get in line." He reached for her hand.

As they moved through the soup line, the couple endured some light-hearted ribbing and laughter when Maurice LaCroix showed up next to them with a sprig of mistletoe on a pole and waved it over their heads until they obliged the crowd with a kiss. He then moved on to Josephine and George Clark, a.k.a. Santa and Mrs. Claus.

Maura's cheeks were now rosy from the attention as well as windburn. Stephan drew her over towards a table in a quieter corner. Fred and Sam made room for them and continued their quiet conversation about new regulations and the idiots in Augusta. Stephan wrapped his hands around the cup of chowder Margery Dodd had offered him. "I was wondering if you'd like to come over for brunch tomorrow and make a full day of it."

Maura started to answer when three wound-up girls raced over to their table. Fern gave her a hug, while Lana and Maisy surrounded Stephan on either side.

"Daddy, Lana invited us over for a sleepover. Can I go? Can I? Huh?"

"Do Lana's parents know about this?"

All three girls nodded their heads vigorously.

Vicky and Liz appeared at the table. "They got to you before we could."

Stephan smiled. "I hear you've invited this imp to spend the night."

Vicky nodded. "I thought it'd be nice for the girls. We're going to make gingerbread houses tomorrow and trim the tree. It's always more fun with friends. Liz has already said Fern can join us."

Stephan laughed. "Who am I to stand in the way of holiday merriment? I'll need to run Maisy home to get her things."

"Can't you just get them and bring them back to me? I can tell you what I need."

"You're sure you want to take this on?" Stephen gave Vicky a skeptical look.

The chief's wife smiled. "They'll run around here and play, and then settle down at home with holiday movies. It'll be fine."

"Let me finish my soup and conversation with Maura, and then I'll go get your things, Maisy."

"But you'll have all night to talk."

Maura felt a blush spread across her face.

Stephan, however, took his daughter's careless words in stride. He observed that Vicky and Liz didn't look concerned. "I hadn't considered that." He grinned at Maura's blush. "We can have a sleepover too."

Maura looked like she wanted to crawl under that table.

Fred and Sam both chortled. "We won't tell the old biddies, Maura," Fred assured her with a twinkle in his eye. "I know your reputation is important to you."

"Reputation's not worth letting life pass you by, though, gell," was Sam's observation.

Maura was looking at all of them, wide-eyed, when Fern wrapped her arms around her in a fierce hug. "Don't let their teasing bother you, Maura. We're all happy you're happy," she whispered in Maura's ear.

Maura hugged the sweet child back and drew in a deep breath. "I haven't had a sleepover in ages," she commented, with as much dignity as she could muster.

Stephan grinned at her while the old men smirked at him.

Maura rolled her eyes at the three of them, but gave each of the old men an affectionate hug after she stood up.

Fred gave her a gruff "Scram," but Stephan noticed he was patting her hand much longer than politeness dictated.

The retired park ranger caught him looking. He narrowed his eyes at the younger man. "You'd better have good intentions or you'll be answering to us." He jerked a thumb towards himself and then Sam.

"Yes, sir," Stephan nodded.

"Daddy, I need Dot, my pillow, PJs, and red sweatshirt for tomorrow." Maisy started edging away. "I'm gonna go see Santa now. Love you!"

"Whoa, wait, little girl. I want to get pictures."

Maisy made a face at him. "Fine, but don't embarrass me."

"How does me taking a couple of photos—never mind." Stephan shook his head. "I won't do anything embarrassing."

Liz reached for Fern's hand. "I'd like a picture too," she announced.

Fern smiled at her mother.

Lana shrugged, trying to act nonchalant, but her eyes were sparkling and lips curled up into a smile. "It could be fun."

Vicky did a poor job of hiding her delight at her daughter's reaction. "Let's go see Santa then, ladies—and gentleman." She nodded at Stephan.

He started to follow, but paused to whisper in Maura's ear. "We're having a sleepover." He laughed at the way her cheeks pinkened and dropped a quick kiss on her lips before hurrying to catch up with the rest of the group.

After the girls left with Vicky, Stephan and Maura slipped out of the party. Because they'd come in separate cars, they each drove their own home. Maura pulled into her driveway first. She was just about to turn off her headlights when her brain caught up with what her eyes were seeing. Her front door was gaping open.

She froze behind the steering wheel and a shiver of apprehension ran through her. She knew she'd shut and locked it. She *always* locked the door. The cats! Her eyes frantically skimmed the yard for any telltale gleams.

Headlights illuminated her yard briefly as Stephan swung his car into Milly and David's driveway. Maura hurried across the street.

"My house." Her teeth were chattering as adrenaline spiked in her. "My front door is open."

Stephan's smile fell away. He glanced at his own door. It was shut. He squeezed Maura's hand and reached for his flashlight. He flicked on the powerful beam and played it over his own yard. There were no prints in the snow other than ones he recognized. He hadn't had a chance to shovel after the last round of squalls and was suddenly grateful for that. "Stay in my car with the doors locked while I do a quick circuit around my house first."

Maura shook her head. "I'm staying with you."

Stephan didn't want to waste time arguing. "Put your hand on my shoulder, then, and keep it there. Stay behind me as we go." He unlatched his revolver from its holster and drew it. He kept it in his right hand, using his left to play the light around the yard. The dry snow crunched and squeaked under their feet as Stephan led them on a thorough, but quick trip around his house. He hurried more than he normally would have. Maura needed to get warm.

"Okay. If anyone's still here, they know we're back. I want you to do exactly what I say. No arguing on this, Maura." He pulled her close with the hand holding a flashlight. "I want you to stay in your car while I make sure there's no one still here. Keep it running with the doors locked. After that, we'll go back in together and see if anything is missing and make sure all the cats are safe. I'm calling Ron. If you see anything while I'm inside, text me. If you hear gunshots, I want you to call 911. If anyone other than me comes out, you get to town as fast as you can." He put his weapon away so he could get his phone.

Maura nodded and wrapped her arms around herself. As he was talking to Ron, Stephan nudged her forward so that they were walking back across the street to her car. As they neared the vehicle, she heard a plaintive meow from the tree line. Maura crouched down. "Tim?" she called.

A small orange ball of fur rocketed out across the snow and into her arms. Maura burst into tears as she snuggled his cold body. She quickly unzipped her coat and pulled him close to her chest, then carefully zipped up so he was half-covered.

Stephan ended the call. "Into the car, you two." He gave Tim a gentle caress. The cat bumped Stephan's hand with his head instead of giving the usual growl. "Too bad you can't speak, buddy. It'd be helpful." He turned his attention to Maura as she slid back into the driver's seat. "Ron is on his way in the cruiser. Lock the doors. You stay here until one of us comes and gets you, okay?"

Maura nodded. "Okay."

After Stephan gently shut the car door, Maura turned the heat up to full blast and examined Tim for any injury. Satisfied he was unhurt; she went back to cuddling him close. Stephan had finished a circuit around her house. He stopped by the front door and took pictures of some footprints. He had already entered the house and begun methodically turning on lights and examining every nook and cranny of each room by the time Ron arrived with the cruiser lights flashing.

"Shut the front door, will you, Ron?" Stephan had closed the back door before examining the partial basement that lay under the utility room and bathroom area.

"Is it like the others?"

"No." Stephan shook his head. "We'll need Maura to check, but nothing seems to be missing, near as I can tell, and it hasn't been trashed like the others. It's more like they wanted her to know they were here." He startled as something bumped his legs and then smiled in relief. "Oh, good, Greta. Where's Mags, girl?"

As if her name had been the magic word, Mags slunk out from behind the washing machine and gave him an uncharacteristic earful. Stephan knelt down to give both of them affectionate head rubs before looking back at his boss. "I still need to check upstairs. It'll go faster if we do it together. Then we can get Maura and Tim in here with you while I check my place."

Ron nodded. "Helluva a way to end the night." He shook his head. "I told Vicky, but made sure the girls didn't hear. I'll bring Maisy's things back home with me. You should stay with Maura."

"Thanks," Stephan sighed in relief. As they reached the top of the stairs, he went right to check the bathroom and her bedroom, while Ron took the craft and guest room. After that, they pulled down the attic steps and did a quick survey of the tidy space.

"Did you get pictures of the footprints? They sure look the same as the others, which means diddlysquat since everyone and his brother wears Carhartts. Snow's too dry to get a good impression, but we should grab one anyway."

"Yeah, I got images of the ones from the back and front. I'll send them to you now." Stephan's fingers flew across his phone and moments later Ron's dinged in response.

Ron glanced at them and nodded. "Let's get Maura in here. Take your time at your place. I won't leave until I know you're set."

By the time Stephan returned, he found Maura wrapped in her aunt's special shawl. A fire was blazing in the woodstove and she had a cup of tea wobbling in her hands. The three cats were snuggled up against her and Ron was patting her knee reassuringly.

"I don't understand who would do this, Ron," she was saying as Stephan entered.

"I think I have an idea." Stephen's voice was grim. He handed Ron a piece of white printer paper that he'd stuck in a storage bag. "Piss Off Pig" was typed out in large boldface print. "I found it slid under the back-porch door at my place. I had missed the footprints earlier. I'll have to get pictures of them in the daylight. My flashlight battery is going. It wasn't bright enough."

"I'll get some on my way out." Ron frowned at the paper. "Probably someone's taunting us about the break-ins. I'm sorry, Maura. I assume you got dragged into this because Stephan's leading the investigation." He patted her leg again and then stood up. "I'm going to take those pictures and then be on my way. I'm sure Vicky is worrying."

"Oh, here." Stephan dropped a small black duffel bag down by the coffee table and handed him a bright purple backpack. "I think I got everything Maisy asked for, but if I forgot something, please cover for me. I don't want her to know what happened right now. She feels safe here."

"Of course." Ron smacked his forehead with the heel of his hand. "I forgot. Vic figured we'd be distracted. She sent a list while I was driving over." He unzipped the backpack and compared the contents to the items his wife had requested. "Looks right. I'll be on my way. "

After walking Ron to the door, Stephan looked back toward Maura. She was silent, but tears were rolling down her cheeks. Tim was wiping at them with his paw, but couldn't keep up. He gave Stephan a plaintive cry.

"Oh, love," Stephan took in the scene and hurried over to the sofa. He scooped Maura up and pulled her and Tim onto his lap. He felt a surge of anger at the hooligans who'd invaded her privacy as he felt her shaking against him.

"I thought I was better, but I can't stop crying and shivering again," Maura whispered.

Stephan held her close, hoping his body heat would help. He slid further down towards the warmth of the roaring fire. Waves of heat were rolling off the woodstove. If that didn't penetrate her body, he didn't think anything would.

After a while, Maura shifted uncomfortably in his lap. "Something's poking me in the side," Maura muttered.

Stephan felt a surge of relief and smiled. "I'm still in uniform," he reminded her. "It'd be more comfortable for both of us if I change. Are you okay if I go do that?"

Maura nodded. "I should feed the cats. Tim was a popsicle. He must be ravenous by now."

"Okay. I'll change down here. I can be right out if you need me."

Maura gave him a wobbly smile. "Thank you."

Stephan reemerged into the kitchen in a pair of comfortable sweats and a T-shirt. He leaned against the door as he watched Maura take a pound of butter out of the refrigerator.

"What're you doing?"

"Making cookies."

Stephan gave her a puzzled look. "At ten at night?"

Maura nodded. "I need to do something normal. I need the house to smell normal again." She waved her hands around. "I can't explain it, but I need to do it."

"Okay." Stephan shrugged. "Let me put my bag upstairs and then I can help."

She chewed her lower lip for a moment. "I'll come with you." Maura shook her head. "Not because I'm scared to be alone down here, but I need to see upstairs. Ron told me nothing looked disturbed and it didn't seem to be when we got my shawl, but I know someone went through my things. Stuff was a bit out of place." Anger entered her voice for the first time. "I want to put it all back the way it's supposed to be and then we bake cookies." She gave him a challenging look, as if he were going to argue.

Stephan held up his hands. "You're the boss. We do whatever you need tonight. Want to go first, or should I?"

"I will." Maura walked in front of him. She led him to her bedroom first. While Stephan was putting his bag down, she pulled the comforter and sheets up and peered under the pillows.

He watched in silence.

"I don't want any surprises later. In fact, I want clean sheets." Maura explained as she yanked the bedding off and dropped it all on the floor. She went to the closet. "Please take the pillowcases off."

Stephan did as she asked and piled the naked pillows up on the armchair. When Maura returned with a set of flannel sheets, he smiled. "These are cheerful." Colorful snowflakes dotted the soft material.

Maura nodded. "Here," she handed him a corner. "You do your side. It'll go faster."

"Of course." Stephan got to work. As he was tucking the second corner down and under the mattress, he looked over at her. "Maura, I'm so sorry."

She tossed him part of the flat sheet. "Don't be." The anger was back. "You didn't do it. You are doing your job protecting all of us. You. Did. Not. Do. This." She frowned when she realized she'd started shouting. "Seriously, don't apologize."

"This wouldn't have happened if you and I weren't involved."

Maura snapped her part of the sheet with more force than was necessary. "You don't know that." She shook her head when she saw his face. "No, really, you don't know that. It's true that most of the break-ins have been at summer places, but not all of them have, have they?"

"No, several have been occupied houses." Stephan was convinced that some were a diversion meant to distract the police, but which? It galled him that they were missing something. The items taken from all the homes had all been run-of-the-mill, though without owners present, it was hard to get a complete inventory of what had been stolen from the vacation homes. He'd gotten calls from two of the year-round occupants a few days after each of the break-ins, telling him that they couldn't account for books or maps, along with the other missing items. He leaned toward the idea that the unoccupied houses were the diversion, but couldn't figure out what the thieves were actually after if that was the case. He gave Maura a speculative look. "Hey, Maura, do you have any old maps of the area or books about the island?"

She tilted her head to the side. "I do, why?"

"Can you show them to me after we finish up in here?"

Maura shrugged. "Sure. They're in the craft room."

"Thanks," Stephan smiled at her and helped her shake out her spare comforter and spread it across the bed. They made short work of putting the pillows in fresh cases and piling them back up at the head of the bed.

Maura reached for Stephan's hand. "Don't laugh. I know this is going to seem weird for an old map but Aunt Jane made me promise to keep it hidden. I figured it was best to put them all in here so I'd know where everything was."

His curiosity piqued, Stephan followed her into the craft room and watched as she pulled a watercolor of the cove off of the wall. Maura carefully slid it out of the frame and his eyes widened. What appeared to be the frame actually masked a second frame that the picture sat in. Maura grinned at his expression. She eased out a piece of parchment that was sandwiched between the painting and dust cover. She laid everything but the old paper down on the desk and nodded to the futon. "Come on over. I'll show you a bit of Belfort history."

With careful movements, she laid the hand-drawn map out on her lap. Notations in the waters indicated deep water, inlets, and shoals. In one intriguing spot near the weirs, there was a sketch of a seal that had markings like Karria's, but along the side of its head rather than the top. What drew Stephan's eyes, however, was the intricate network of caves and tunnels. He traced them with his finger. One went all the way from under the library out to near the weirs on the western part of the island. Several tunnels branched off from it, including one to the large cave Adam had told them about as well as smaller ones. "Maura, this is amazing."

"It is, isn't it?" Maura leaned in next to Stephan so she could study the map. "It's been so long since I've looked at it. I'd forgotten how much detail is in here. It's the only one I've ever seen that seems to document tunnels and caves so well. Look, a bunch even have dimensions noted on them. I don't know if these all even exist. Adam would've told me if there was one from the library out to the big cave."

"May I take a picture of this?"

Maura hesitated, remembering Jane's admonishment that the map was secret. "What for?"

Engrossed in what he was looking at, Stephan didn't see her wary expression. "For one, this is amazing. I'd love to study it. The other reason is, I am seeing a pattern here that relates to the break-ins, but I can't quite grasp it. I'd love to spend time with it to see if I can figure out what I'm missing."

Maura bit her lip. "I promised Aunt Jane I'd keep it secret and safe. If it were just you, then yes, but as part of a criminal investigation, well—that's not keeping it so secret, is it?"

Stephan had already pulled his phone out, assuming she'd say yes. He put it down when her answer registered. He drew in a slow, deep breath. "I suppose so." He frowned down at the map.

Maura shifted uncomfortably next to him. "I don't know. Can we talk about it tomorrow? I'm not thinking clearly tonight. I'd like to sleep on it."

Stephan forced a smile. "Of course." He moved so she could put it away. "May I look at it again sometime?"

Maura gave him a relieved nod. "Anytime. I wouldn't have shown it to you if I didn't trust you. I just don't know about letting it be used where it could become public. I don't know *why* Jane was so adamant that it be kept secret, but it was one of the only promises she ever asked of me. It was a really big deal to her. I need to respect that." She made short work of sliding the map back into its hidey hole. Once the frame was sealed up and the picture was put back to rights and hung, she gave Stephan a rueful look. "I really am sorry. I just need to think about it more. You can come see it whenever you want."

He reached out for her hand and gave it a gentle squeeze. "It's okay Maura."

"I have other old maps and books you're welcome to take with you for as long as you want." She made her way to the closet. "Huh." She began moving boxes around. "That's weird. They're not where I left them." Maura sat down on the floor and began pulling out all the boxes that remained and piling them in a neat stack on the floor. She gave Stephan a puzzled look. "The entire box is gone. I had it here, between my father's papers and Aunt Jane's sketches. It's labeled *Belfort Maps and Historical Society*." She began looking at the labels on the remaining boxes again. "Jane was a member of the historical society. A decade or so before she died, they lost their building and had to winnow down the collection to fit in the room they have now at the town offices. A few big maps and some books are at the library. There are other maps and pictures scattered around the town hall, but many got stowed away in the attics and closets of former and current historical society members."

A strange expression crossed Stephan's face. "Is Maurice LaCroix a member?"

"Yes. He's the current chair."

"What about Terry Beals?"

"He was the chair in Aunt Jane's day." Maura studied him. "Why?"

"I think you've just given me the break I've needed on this case, or at least an avenue of investigation I hadn't checked out." He leaned down and gave her an enthusiastic kiss. "Thank you, love."

"You're welcome." Maura was bemused but glad. "You can kiss me again if you're that grateful."

Stephan laughed and proceeded to show her just how appreciative he was.

After a while, when both were breathless, they broke apart. Stephan caught his breath first and grinned at her. "What kind of cookies are we making?"

"That's a silly question." Maura responded to his shift with an easy smile of her own.

"Chocolate chip it is." He squeezed her hand. "My favorite."

"We *could* go crazy and make chocolate-chocolate chip or cherry-chocolate chip."

Stephan smiled and wrapped his arms around her. "What's your preference?"

"Comfortable, familiar chocolate chip," Maura confessed. "Right now, I'd like comfort."

"You know…" He pretended to be thinking. "We could skip the cookies tonight and head straight to bed. We could make them for breakfast. Put in some oatmeal and cherries and we can call them breakfast bars. What do you think?"

Maura ran a hand down the front of his body and slowed when she reached his waistband. "I think you got sidetracked."

"Is that so bad?"

She shook her head and let her hand slide further down. "It's pretty good, actually."

"Only pretty good?" He gave her a look of mock indignation.

Maura shrugged. "That's better than okay."

Stephan pulled her close, "I'm going for wonderful. Spectacular, even."

She nuzzled his neck. "I'd enjoy that."

"Enjoy? Good god, I hope you'll do more than *enjoy* it." Laughter laced his voice and prompted a grin in return from Maura.

She nipped lightly at his neck. "Why don't you show me?"

"I think I will." Stephan's voice grew husky as their lips met again.

CHAPTER 12

After dropping Maisy at school on Monday, Stephan settled in at his desk and began calling the theft victims. Maura had, of course, catalogued the contents of the missing box. Unfortunately, the list was inside it. She was only able to give him vague details about what was missing. While cooking dinner back at his house on Saturday, Stephan had sketched everything he remembered from the hidden map. Maisy had been tired from her sleepover and didn't protest putting the tree-trimming off until Sunday. By then, he and Maura both managed to keep the atmosphere light, and they'd ended the weekend on a happier note.

He hung up the phone. Maurice LaCroix was heading to the town offices in an hour to talk. When he looked up from his notes, Stephan saw Colleen giving him a funny look.

"What is it?" He gave her a wary glance.

"You think the break-ins have something to do with old maps and books?"

"I'm not sure, but some of the year-round residences that were hit were storing documents for the historical society."

Colleen got a thoughtful expression and started tapping her pencil on her side of the large desk they shared. "What was taken?"

"Aside from the usual easily sold items and liquor, maps and books. Maurice says he also had a box of old postcards and an old tackle box stolen."

"Hmmm." She pushed away and strode over to the filing cabinet where they stored old case files. After a few minutes of rummaging around, Colleen gave a victory shout and slapped a manila folder on Stephan's desk. "Sixteen years ago, the historical society was burglarized. It was pretty soon after that they moved into the town offices."

"You were what, ten?" Stephan looked at her.

Colleen rolled her eyes at him. "My dad was chief before Ron. This case always bothered him."

"How so?"

She perched on the edge of the expansive desk. "Why steal from the society? They've always made all their stuff available to the public. Anyone could just go in and study their maps and books. And whoever it was didn't just steal. They totally trashed the building and everything left in it."

Stephan thought of Jane's hidden map and wondered if there were others like it. He kept silent and nodded to Colleen.

"Yeah, and even though it happened in the summer, he always thought it was a local, something personal. He never had any solid reason that I know of, just his gut, but with work at least, it was reliable. It stuck in his craw that a local would steal from the town and destroy community property." Colleen shrugged. "Never happened again far as I know, but maybe there'll be something useful in there."

"Thanks, Colleen."

"I might bust your chops, but I want this figured out too. If you ask me, they're not really looking for anything from the summer places but stuff to sell."

Stephan nodded. "I agree."

Colleen looked surprised with his agreement. "Hey, I ran those prints through the scanner. We can still send them out for analysis, but they match up with ones from most of the other break ins. Ron said no fingerprints like usual either, huh?" She blew out an annoyed sigh. "How's Maura handling it? I know she's never minded living so isolated, but it's pretty remote out there in the winter."

Stephan had lain awake for hours on Friday. Maura had slept fitfully until he'd gathered her in his arms and held her close. Saturday, her bedroom light was on late into the night. He'd almost invited her over, but Maura had expressed her need to feel safe and comfortable again in her own home before he could extend the offer. Stephan's expression was troubled when he finally answered Colleen. "I don't know. She's not talking about it. She's angry and upset her space was violated. She didn't seem concerned about the stolen box itself. She told me I was being ridiculous when I changed her locks and installed the video doorbells, especially in the back. I wanted to put up motion lights, but she worried they'd be going off all night with the animals."

"I'm impressed you got her to agree to that. Did you put some in at your place?"

Stephan nodded. "I did. How about you?"

"Chip insisted." Colleen rolled her eyes. "Honestly, I don't think they're going to target me, but I did it to humor him."

"Why do you think you'll be left alone?" Stephan sat back in his chair. His eyes were sharp as they gazed at her.

"Intuition." Colleen brushed off the question with a grin, but there was a tightness around her eyes and her hand clenched the pencil she'd been fiddling with.

"What aren't you telling me?" Stephan's voice was mild.

She shot him an annoyed look. "I don't have anything concrete. If I do, I'll let you know, okay?"

It wasn't okay as far as he was concerned, but Stephan decided pushing her wouldn't help, so he nodded. "Sure. You know where to find me."

Colleen slid off the desk and stood up. "Tell Maura I asked about her."

"Tell her yourself," Stephan suggested. "She said she hasn't seen you in a while."

She shrugged. "I've been busy. She's been busy. But yeah, all right. I'll swing by the library today."

"I'm sure that'll make her happy." Stephan picked up the folder. "Thanks for this, Colleen."

"No problem. Like I said, I want this resolved too, and if I can give my old man an answer, even better."

"Where is he?"

"Florida. Left five years ago and hasn't looked back."

"Think he'd mind talking to me?"

Colleen shrugged. "Not sure. He's prickly. Here." She pulled the pad he kept on the desk over and scrawled out a name and number. He waited until Colleen started gathering up her things before opening the folder. The edges were coffee-stained and well worn. Colleen's father, John, had neat handwriting. Stephan pulled his pad close and began to make his own notes as he read.

When he finished, Stephan reached to take a sip of coffee and grimaced at how cold and bitter it was. He stood up and stretched before taking his mug to the kitchenette. As he rinsed it out and put a fresh filter and grounds into the coffeemaker, he thought about John's notes. The former chief had been convinced that members of the historical society were hiding something from him that hindered his investigation. His frustration was evident as the notes in the file went on. He interviewed some more than once, including Jane Ballard. Another tidbit that stuck out in Stephan's mind was the last name Thompson. John had it underlined several places, with no frame of reference. Given the clan's numbers on Belfort, he assumed it was a relation of the fisherman Ron and Maura disliked. It could've been the society member, Cal Thompson. Thompson's interview notes were sparse. He'd have to see if Ron knew.

With his fresh coffee, Stephan walked over to the bank of windows that looked out on Water Street. He could see the small fleet tied up in the inner harbor. It looked like most of the boats were in their slips. As he watched, he noticed Colleen walking briskly towards the floating dock. He took a swallow of the hot drink and watched her move down the slippery ramp with sure-footed grace. She strode to a twenty-footer in one of the middle slips. Joey Thompson stepped off to greet her.

Stephan arched an eyebrow as he watched them embrace. It was more than a friendly kiss. He tapped his forefinger against his mug. Interesting. He recalled Ron's off-hand comment about Colleen and Joey at the harvest festival as the couple disappeared into the cabin of the boat. When they didn't quickly reemerge, he turned back to his desk. He grimaced when he saw the time. He was late to meet Maurice. Stephan took a gulp of his coffee, grabbed his pen and pad, and left for the other wing of the building.

A whip-thin, stooped man greeted him with a congenial smile when Stephan entered the historical society's room. Stephan smiled back. "Mr. LaCroix, I owe you a thanks."

Maurice gave a bark of laughter. "We've been taking bets on how long it'd be until you two kissed in public. I decided to make sure I won." He winked. "George tells me that since I cheated, I've lost and the wager's off."

Stephan's amiable smile fell away, replaced by a fierce frown. Maurice started laughing so hard he had to hold his sides. When his laughter slowed to wheezing gasps, the old man sank down into a chair and gestured to one across from him. "Oh, your expression. Young man, we wouldn't bet on such a thing, at least not with Maura. We're all mighty fond of Jane's girl. Sit, sit." He waved again at the free chair that Stephan was standing beside.

Once Stephan was seated, Maurice gave him a considering look. "It's about the maps, isn't it?"

Stephan's eyes narrowed. "Which ones?"

"The missing ones, of course. And perhaps some that haven't gone missing." He cocked a bushy white eyebrow.

Stephan gazed at him in silence.

"You're no fun." Maurice sighed. "George and I stopped by the library this morning to check on Maura. We also wanted to know if Jane's piece was safe."

"It's only a piece?" Stephan leaned forward, eager to hear more.

Maurice nodded. "Go shut the door and I'll tell you more. Oh, and turn on that sound thingamabob over there while you're up."

Stephan glanced at where he was pointing. He was surprised by the sight of a white noise machine. What were these history buffs up to that required privacy? He strode over to the door, gently shut it, and turned the device on.

When Stephan turned around, he discovered Maurice had also gotten up. He led Stephan to a broom closet at the back of the room.

Stephan stepped inside to look around. Maurice followed. A wrinkled hand reached past Stephan to turn on the lights, shut the door, and then flipped a lock. An intricate set of wires and sensors webbed the inside of the door and frame. A pair of cameras were mounted above the frame. Green lights blinked from their bases. One was angled down at the door and the other into the room.

"What are you up to?" Stephan started to glare at him, but then noticed the unusual items on the shelves and walls. His eyes widened. "What is all of this?" He slid past Maurice to examine some of the artifacts. His hand encountered something soft when he gently shifted a box that looked precariously balanced. Startled, he peered behind it and sighed in relief when he realized it was a seal pelt that had been tucked away. Markings on it were similar to Karria's and the fur was silky. Maps of all sizes were preserved in frames stacked on the shelves. Some looked ancient. Stephan picked up one that was no bigger than a large cell phone. He furrowed his brow as he tried to make out the language it was written in. After a moment, he gave up and then tried to identify what it was depicting.

Maurice was watching him in silence. His chocolate brown eyes danced with amusement at Stephan's amazement as he took in the treasure trove that was tucked away in the closet. "Sometimes," Maurice commented, "keeping things in plain sight is the best way to keep them hidden and safe."

Stephan put the odd map back down and examined a pair of old boots. They looked like something from a pirate movie, except they were water-stained up the calves and pieces of dried mud drifted off when he handled them. He quickly put them back and gave Maurice a quizzical look. "Why is all of this hidden in a closet? It belongs in a museum, doesn't it?"

Maurice nodded. "If Belfort could afford the security, ayuh, it would. But we can't. This is our heritage. The youngsters all go on about pirate booty, but these are genuine, honest-to-God treasures that belong to the town."

"Who knows about them?" Stephan gave Maurice his full attention.

"Members of the historical society. It's a need-to-know thing. You needed to know, so now ya do."

"How many members are there?"

"Seven of us. But two are new. They've only been on the board for a term or two so they— Jackson and Vicky—don't need to know just yet."

"Will you give me the names of everyone who knows about this room?"

"Sure." Maurice shrugged. "If our homes hadn't been burgled and had certain items stolen, we wouldn't have let you in. Maura's cinched the deal, though. George finally agreed. If all five of us don't agree, then the room doesn't get opened." He looked around the small room. "This," he waved his hand, "is what we think they're looking for."

"But how would they, whoever 'they' are, know about it, if only five of you are aware of the contents in here?"

Maurice nodded. "We've been puzzling over that one. Other houses of former members haven't been struck, though two of the flatlander houses that were hit were previously owned by members before their families sold 'em off—the Richardson house and the one at Barrel Cove. There are plenty of others who've been members over the years who haven't been bothered. But Jane—Jane knew our secret. She helped set this room up."

"Who else was on the board at the time?"

Maurice rubbed his chin as he thought. "Cal Thompson, Eliza's middle kid. He's been dead for a dozen years or so. Jane and the Clarks had real issues with him. He wasn't allowed in on all this." Maurice waved his hand and then continued his recitation. "Asher Whitcomb's in South Carolina now, living with his son and daughter-in-law. Ethel Richardson, she's been gone about four years, and Maeve O'Connell. She lives in a tiny cottage on Seal Point. She doesn't come out much these days." Maurice waved to the camera. "George and Josephine Clark are watching us. Me. Terry Beals and Molly Harrison."

"And they all know?"

Maurice nodded. "Except Cal. He wasn't all that likable, and like I said, Jane hated him. George and Josephine too, for that matter." He shrugged. "None of us, other than Terry, wanted to include him, to be honest, so we cut him out of the discussions. He was suspicious, but he was suspicious of everything and everyone except maybe his mother." He shrugged.

"Wait, back up." Stephan looked puzzled. "What do you mean when you realized how much you had here?"

Maurice nodded. "That's a bit more complicated a story." His phone dinged and he fished it out of his cardigan pocket and smiled after a moment. "Josephine says we should come over to the bakery in an hour. They're closing early today. Terry and Molly'll meet us there, too."

Stephan rubbed his forehead. "Won't that seem odd to folks?"

Maurice gave him a blank look. "Why in God's name would it be odd for us to be enjoying a cup of coffee and muffins?"

"The five of you and me sitting in a closed shop won't seem at all odd?" Stephan's expression was skeptical.

"Ohhhhhh, hmm, yes I see what you're getting at." Maurice glanced at the camera. "Boy's got a point, Jo."

While Maurice stared at the camera, Stephan took the opportunity to look around more at the hodgepodge that was crammed into the small room. His eyes lingered on a book that he didn't dare touch. It looked like it would crumble if his fingers pressed too hard. Nathaniel Hawthorne's name was embossed on the cover and what looked like a handwritten letter poked out from between the pages.

"That came from a wreck. The letter's from Hawthorne to Franklin Pierce—ya know, President Pierce. They were friends." Maurice had noticed what Stephan was looking at. His phone dinged again.

"You sure? Better call Molly and Terry first," Maurice again addressed the camera and then nodded. "Right then. Time's up in here, Officer Kirkland."

Stephan was reluctant to leave the room without fully examining the contents, but he didn't want to antagonize anyone so he nodded. "I'd love to come back here another time," he offered.

"Hmm, well, maybe we'll have an opening on the board sometime." Maurice gave him a sly smile. "You're going to have to work for it if you want back in here."

Stephan glanced back at the room as Maurice hustled him out. "It'd be worth it."

"That's the spirit." Maurice clapped him on the back, a surprisingly strong thump given how fragile he appeared. He turned and locked the door once they were both clear of it.

Stephan glanced up. For the first time, he noticed a small camera angled out into the conference room.

Maurice followed his gaze and grinned. "Not bad for a bunch of old hicks, eh?"

"You certainly surprised me," Stephan had to admit. "I wasn't expecting any of this."

The elderly man nodded. "Ayuh." He brushed his hands off on his pants legs after pocketing a silver key. "I'll call when we're ready to meet."

He nodded to the old man. "Thank you for trusting me with your secret."

"Yeah, well, we'll have to kill ya if ya go blabbing about it." Maurice gave him a cheeky grin.

Stephan bit his inner cheek to keep from saying anything. He offered a bland smile and nod before leaving the room. He was deep in thought as he made his way back to the police offices. When he got there, he checked the time on his watch. He could get a call in to Colleen's father. It wasn't until he'd sat down and was going over his list of questions for Chief McQuarrie that Stephan realized Maurice never explained what he'd meant about Jane's map only being a piece of something larger. He'd have to remember to ask when he spoke with him next.

Stephan started to dial Colleen's father and then hesitated. It'd be better to wait until after he'd spoken with the old-timers. The former chief wasn't likely to welcome repeated calls. Sighing, Stephan decided to get some fresh air to clear his head. When he stepped out, he glanced down at the harbor and hesitated. Would Colleen think he was spying on her if they bumped into each other? He decided to stroll the other way, up Water Street, and visit the shopkeepers who were still open.

The street was quiet. By his calculations, at least a third of the buildings were vacant or underutilized, and another third of the businesses were closed for the winter. Stephan paused in front of a stately old stone building that he often admired. Large windows were boarded up, but he imagined they let in a tremendous amount of light when uncovered.

"I think it'd make a wonderful artists' collective."

He was startled Maura had been able to come right up to his side without him realizing it. "Hey there, beautiful."

"You looked lost in thought."

He nodded in agreement. "I was." Stephan's blue eyes slid back to the building. "What did it used to be?"

"It was the shop associated with the cannery in that part," — she pointed— "and the rest used to be the municipal offices."

"Hey, Maura," Jackson. He nodded to Stephan. "I don't want to interrupt your lunch, but do you have a few minutes afterwards, Officer Kirkland?"

"Why don't you join us?" Maura gave Jackson a quizzical look when she saw a funny expression cross his face. "I'm sorry—it's private, isn't it?" She glanced over at Stephan and inferred from his expression that he wanted to speak with the other man. "Why don't I go get our food and you can talk now?"

Stephan gave her a grateful smile and fished out his wallet. "I promised to treat you to lunch." He handed her a couple of bills.

Maura took Stephan's order before winding her way through the maze of tables to reach the front counter. She glanced back and arched an eyebrow to see both men already engaged in conversation. It usually took Jackson a while to open up. She hoped everything was all right. Maura was still frowning when Jack Thompson grinned at her from the other side of the counter. "Miz M., whatcha getting?"

She found a smile for Eliza's youngest son—her favorite Thompson on the island if she was being honest. "Hiya, Jack. I'd like a roast beef special, a ham and swiss, and three large coffees." A platter of festive-looking cookies caught her attention. "Can I add in a few of those too?"

"Of course." Jack cocked his head to the side. "I think the stocking for Jackson, the tree for Stephan, and the angel for you." He winked at her and set the plate of cookies to the side. "I can bring it all over when it's ready."

"It's okay. I'll wait up here.".

Jack looked back at the table where Stephan and Jackson's heads were bent close together. "I bet it's about the break-in at your house."

"How do you figure that?" Maura gave him a quizzical look.

"All your neighbors have been in. Most are worried they're next. Not that many of you out that-a-way this time of year." Jack shrugged. "It's got folks on edge. Normally its only vacation homes hit, eh?"

Maura nodded.

"You okay, sweetheart?" He reached out and caught her hand in one of his large calloused ones. "That musta been upsetting."

Maura gave the older man an affectionate look. Like all his brethren, Jack was a barrel-chested, muscular man. His salt-and-pepper hair was turning saltier as the months went by. She nodded. "I am. It was a shock and I was upset, but I'm all right now."

Jack patted her hand with his free one. "Good. Don't let them win. But," —he let go and reached down below the counter, then brought out a large can of wasp spray— "I'd feel better if you kept this with you at your house. Go for the bastards' eyes if they come back and then run like hell outta there."

Maura started to demur, but found the cold can thrust into her hand anyway.

"I've got about ten of 'em under here. You take one and let this old man rest easier."

"Thank you, Jack." Maura felt tears form in her eyes. If it weren't for the red, battered Formica counter between them, she'd have hugged him.

Maura went over to the beverage station and had just finished capping Jackson's coffee when she heard June shout, "Order up! Hey, Maura girl, it's yours. Tell that hunk of yours I made his just the way he likes it; a little extra pepper and some mustard instead of mayo."

"Thanks, June." Maura smiled at the matronly woman who beamed at her from the kitchen.

"Be right there." Jack brought two overflowing plates to one of the trays he'd set aside. He handed Maura the other for the drinks.

As he led her back to her table, Maura bit back a smile. She knew Jack was hoping to hear a snippet of gossip before the men realized he was there. After they set the trays down, she gave him a hug. His cheeks reddened and he patted her on the back awkwardly. "Always thought of you like one of m'nieces, though I like you better than some of 'em." Jack winked at her and wagged a finger at the two men. "You'd better take care of my girl."

"We will." Stephan gave him a nod.

Jack looked from one to the other, clearly disappointed he didn't overhear anything juicy. He started to say something, but June bellowed, "Order up, I said. Get yer butt back here, Jack!"

He shook his head. "Not sure I should've ever taken her on. She forgets who the boss is in this joint." He glanced back at June and hollered, "Coming, sweet cheeks!" She gave him a single fingered salute in response. He winked at the younger people. "She keeps me on my toes."

Back at their table, Maura handed Stephan his change and put the small plate of cookies in the center of the table. Stephan moved to clear the trays and picked up the can of Raid. "Jack must have put this down by accident"

"Oh, that's for me." Maura held her hand out for the can. "He wants me to spray the bastards in the eyes if they come back to the house."

"Huh." Stephan handed her the black can. "That's not a bad idea, I guess." He shook his head. "I'll just get rid of these and be right back."

"Are you okay?" Jackson asked Maura in a low voice when it was just the two of them. "I would have come by, but I didn't want to intrude."

She smiled at the soft-spoken man, but her grin faltered as she got a better look at him. His black hair had grown shaggy and long. The normally trim beard he sported was unkempt. His gray eyes were ringed by dark circles, and his lips had a tight, pinched look to them. "I think I should be asking you the same."

Jackson gave a slight shrug. "Not my best time of year."

"I know," Maura's voice was sympathetic. "But I've never seen you look quite this—" she hesitated.

"Bad. You can say it, Mo."

Stephan rejoined them.

"What's bad?"

Jackson pointed a thumb to his chest. "Mo's too polite to say that I look like shit."

"Mo?" Stephan couldn't help it. He grinned at her and then gave Jackson a critical look. "Is there anything we can do for you?" He'd noticed the man's haggard look, but hadn't wanted to comment when they had more pressing issues to discuss.

"Nah." Jackson shook his head. "I'll be back to my usual self in a few weeks." He shrugged off their looks of concern. "I didn't intend to crash your lunch date." He nodded to Stephan. "Thanks for the coffee. I'll see you later." He stood up, then bent to give Maura a brief hug. "I'll stop by the library to catch up."

"Please do." Maura tried to hide her concern, but her eyes were troubled as she watched him walk away.

Stephan reached for her hand and gave it a gentle squeeze. "Can I ask you something personal?"

"Of course."

"Why did you and Jackson never—or did you?" He stumbled over his question.

Maura rested her chin on her hand and grinned. She gave him a feigned look of innocence. "Did we never have lunch together? Did we never what?"

He rolled his eyes at her. "Were you ever a couple? He's a nice guy, rich, funny, and seems like a good person."

"Nope." Maura shook her head. "We dated for a bit, but mutually decided we're great as friends and neighbors, nothing more." She looked like she might say more, but instead took a bite of her sandwich. When she was done chewing, Stephan was still looking at her, patiently waiting for whatever thought she hadn't completed. "Jackson is a wonderful man and has become a really good friend, but he's not my type and I'm not who he needs as a lover."

Stephan mulled over the last few words as he ate. "That's a bit cryptic, Maura."

"It's all I have to say on the subject, Stephan." She gave him a sweet smile. "Are you going to tell me what the two of you were discussing so intently?"

He gave her a rueful look. "It's been suggested that I consider joining the historical society. I wanted to pick Jackson's brain about that a bit, and he wanted to talk to me about security on our road."

Maura arched an eyebrow. "The historical society? Who suggested that to you?"

"Maurice LaCroix."

Maura sat back in her chair and gave him a long, considering look. "There's more to it than community involvement, isn't there?"

Stephan nodded. "Yeah, but I can't talk about that part. I'm sorry, love. I'm also intrigued. Maisy and I are finally settling into the community. It seems like it might be a good fit. Besides, he's the first to ask me to join a group."

"That's only because everyone else was being polite and letting you get settled in first."

"Isn't there something about early birds and worms?"

When they'd finished their meal, the couple began bundling up again. Maura stepped away first to wend her way towards the door. Once they were outside, Stephan smiled at her. "You forgot something."

"I was going to kiss you when we got closer to the library."

He smiled. "I'm glad to hear that, though how do you know that's the direction I was going?"

Maura paused. "It's not?"

Stephan grinned. "Of course it is. We need to get the most out of our lunch date. But that's not what you forgot."

She furrowed her brow and touched her head to make sure her hat was back on and looked at her gloved hands. Next, Maura patted her pocket to see if she could feel her wallet and keys. She couldn't think of anything else she'd be missing. "What is it?"

Stephan handed her the can of bug spray.

"Oh," Maura chuckled. "My new self-defense kit." She took it from Stephan and shoved it into one of the deep pockets of her jacket.

"It's sweet that he worries about you; they all do, you know."

"All of who?"

"The old-timers on this island. Every single one of them always wants to know about you."

Maura shrugged. "Aunt Jane was pretty popular and very active around town."

"No, Maura," Stephan shook his head. "They're concerned about you." He reached for her hand and held it as they walked back up towards the library. "They care about *you*."

Her lips curved into a soft smile. "They're my family, at least of sorts. It's not the same thing, but they're who I've got." She shrugged. "I care about them, too."

"I know you do." His voice was gentle.

They finished walking to the library and snuck around the side of the building for a bit of privacy. Their long good-bye kiss was interrupted by Stephan's cell phone. He pulled away reluctantly to check who was calling and groaned. "I'm sorry, Maura, but I've got to take this."

"Kirkland speaking." He nodded his head a few times and then said, "I'll be over in ten." He strode back over to Maura to give her a quick embrace. "Talk tonight?"

"Of course." Maura smiled and waved.

Stephan waited a moment to make sure she was safely inside before heading to the bakery.

He reached the fogged-up glass door the same time as Vicky Moore. "Hey, Vic." He smiled and held the door open for her.

She hesitated.

"Maurice invited me," he explained and followed her in.

"Huh." Vicky glanced at him. "You're being roped into the historical society? I would've thought you'd have been grabbed by the Library Friends first." She winked at him.

Stephan cleared his throat.

"Colleen's right. You're easy to tease." Vicky gave a merry laugh.

He felt his cheeks flush.

Josephine bustled out of the kitchen, wiping her hands on a flour-dusted apron. The cheerful green ruffles that bordered the red fabric along with her bouncing, white curls made Stephan feel like he'd stepped into Mrs. Claus's kitchen. The scents of sugar, butter, and gingerbread wafting through the building cemented the image into his head. When she pulled him into an enthusiastic embrace, the aroma of vanilla filled his nose. Stephan decided he was in heaven.

George saw his expression and burst into laughter. "She's already spoken for, young man!"

Josephine gave Stephan a smacking kiss on his cheek and then fondly patted it. "I have a box for you to bring Maura when you leave here."

"Yes, ma'am," Stephan smiled. "I'm sure she'll appreciate that."

"Did you make a box up for me, Jojo?" Terry Beals had slipped in without anyone noticing.

"You're getting a free muffin, that's plenty on the house for you." Josephine gave the small man a hug. "Of course, I did. I have boxes for everyone."

"How do you have anything left this time of year?" Vicky waited for her hug.

"She insists we make extra," George gave his wife an affectionate look before greeting them. His apron featured an image of a merry St. Nick enjoying a cookie. "We'll get started when Jackson and Molly arrive."

"We're here!" The gentle bell above the door tinkled as it was pushed open again. A frail-looking, elderly woman stepped in, followed by the quiet young man.

"Jackson, will you flip the lock and sign for me?"

"Sure, George." Jackson wondered why they were meeting in private and gave Vicky a sideways look as he did what the bakery owner asked.

"Folks, I don't mean to be a wet rag here, but isn't it illegal to have a meeting without posting a notice at least two days in advance?" Vicky decided to ask what Jackson wasn't prepared to.

"But Vic, dear, this is just a Christmas party. It's not a formal meeting." Josephine smiled and began handing out mugs to everyone. "Cream and sugar are on the table in the corner. Take your cup and find a seat."

Vicky, Jackson, and Stephan ended up seated next to one another, with the older members of the group forming the rest of the circle.

Once everyone had settled down with their snack, Vicky gave George and Josephine a narrow-eyed look. "What exactly is going on? You've all been edgy. Don't think Jackson and I haven't noticed you all linger after the meetings and don't leave with us. I know some of you've had your homes burglarized. And now Stephan, the one leading the investigation, is suddenly here to join us for a holiday party we've never had before. So, what gives?"

Molly gazed at Vicky over the rim of the bright red mug George had given her. "Can you let us get to it in our own good time, please?"

Stephan brought his mug to his lips and took a long, slow swallow as he watched the play of emotions over Vicky's face. Annoyance settled into resignation before she sighed. "You lot are some of the most stubborn people I've ever met."

"Do you have other plans that we're making you late for, hon?" Josephine's expression and tone were sympathetic.

"No." Vicky couldn't bring herself to lie, though she was tempted. "Just my sewing for the play, and that's not going anywhere."

"We'll try to keep things moving," George chimed in. "Maurice, why don't you take the lead since you've already talked a bit with Steve here."

Maurice nodded. "First off, I think we should bring Stephan formally into the historical society, but that'll be a vote for an official meeting. Based on our discussion earlier today, I assume you're interested."

"You're correct." Stephan nodded in agreement. "I'm quite keen to join now, in fact."

"As you should be." Molly's voice was tart.

"Let it go, Moll," Terry gave her a conciliatory look. "We knew this day was coming sooner or later. We need to let some of the younger folks in. We can trust them to help carry on our mission."

Vicky sucked in some air, but before she could start asking questions, Maurice held up his hand. "We have a special collection that isn't available for public viewing because of security concerns. We agreed to make Stephan aware of it as part of his investigation into the burglaries that have recently targeted members sitting around this table."

"Maura's not a mem—oh." Vicky sat back and gave the old man a narrow-eyed stare. "Jane."

Maurice maintained a placid expression as he smiled back at Vicky. "Yes, Jane is connected to all of this, if our guesses are right. Now, Jackson and Vicky, we will bring you over to see the collection, but we can't draw attention to what we're doing, so we'll have to do it another day."

He took a swallow of his tea. After giving Vicky a sharp look, he then proceeded, in general terms, to describe some of the collection the society was hiding. He also explained that each of the members had some pieces stored in their homes because they'd all agreed that it'd be best not to keep the entire collection in one place.

When he was done speaking, Maurice looked at Vicky and Jackson. "Now, we'll answer your questions."

"Have you had some of these valuables stolen from your homes?" Vicky's sharp gaze roamed over the faces of the senior citizens.

"Yes." Terry nodded. "We have."

"If they belong to the town, why are you keeping them secret?" Jackson looked from one senior to another.

Molly shifted uncomfortably in her chair and picked her words carefully. "We didn't realize everything we had until our old building was broken into, oh my, sixteen years or so ago. There was a secret space, a false wall, none of us knew about. We only discovered it when we were cleaning up. None of us had ever been told about it. It was a generation before us, at least, who hid it all away. We think some came from wreckers. We only know the origins of a handful of the items, but we do know they're valuable both historically and financially. Belfort can't afford the kind of security we'd need to keep them safe and we all agreed they shouldn't be sent off-island. They belong to our community, not in Augusta or Portland."

"What were you planning on doing with all of it when you all retired from the board?"

"Well, Vic, we've been pleased with you and Jackson. We were planning, in our own time, to bring you two in on the secret and let you help us decide how to proceed. Recent events have changed our timeline. It made sense to bring Stephan in after they hit Maura's house and stole Jane's box." Josephine gave the officer a fond smile and then returned her gaze to the chief's wife. "We didn't want to burden you young people with the responsibility too soon."

"Can you tell me about Cal Thompson?" Stephan knew his question was out of left field, but he was curious about their responses.

All of the older board members fixed their gazes on him. George and Josephine's expressions hardened. Maurice looked amused, while Terry and Molly both gave him considering looks.

"Cal's name rang some bells for you, did it?" Maurice broke the silence that had fallen.

"I read the file on the break-in you're talking about."

"But Cal didn't do it." Terry looked at the others.

"I still think he did." George's voice was harsh.

"He had access to the building, the same as all of us. We've been over this so many times." Molly sighed and leaned back in her seat. "George, I know you had good reasons for not liking the man. I share the sentiment, but why would he have broken into and vandalized a building when he had a perfectly good key? He was free to borrow anything anytime, the same as the rest of us."

George grumbled something under his breath and then frowned at the group. "I still think it was him. Joey was the only alibi Cal had, and he'd have buried a body for his old man, no questions asked."

Stephan looked at George.

"Well, he would've. Cal and Eliza are the only people I've ever seen that man respect, even when he was a boy. He would do anything for his father and grandmother, anything."

The others around the table nodded in agreement with that assertion.

"It doesn't do us any good to rehash old arguments right now," Josephine finally interjected while reaching for her husband's hand. "We are concerned someone is looking for the collection. We need your help figuring out what steps to take next and the best way to preserve this legacy for the town. Now, Vicky and Jackson, we would like to show it to you. We can't do it at a meeting, since those are public. Perhaps we can set up some time with each of you for next week? And Stephan, there's some paperwork you'll need to fill out with Bernice to get appointed to our board. It'll only take a minute or two. They just have to approve you at the next Select Board meeting. We meet the first and third Thursday of every month."

Before anyone could ask more questions, Josephine stood up. "Let me get the little holiday boxes George and I made for all of you. This is a party, after all, though we need to cut it short. With the blow expected tomorrow, we need to run to Ellsworth."

Vicky was gazing at the older folks and shook her head. She leaned over to Stephan and whispered, "Here's your hat, what's your hurry?"

CHAPTER 13

Maura put *Treasure Island* down on the table and gazed at the dozen faces that were staring back at her. A windstorm was howling outside, rattling the library's windows from time to time. "How many of you know about the pirate treasure that's rumored to be hidden here on Belfort?" All of the hands shot up.

Maura grinned at a fifth grader who was bouncing up and down on his knees. "Charlie, why don't you go first."

"John Quelch was a nasty, rotten old pirate from Marblehead, Taxachusetts. He and his crew robbed a bunch of ships in South America and got rich. People thought they hid their loot on Star Island in New Hampshire before they got arrested, but my grampy says a few of them smuggled a bunch of it here. They married local girls and kept from getting arrested because their new families liked 'em and didn't rat them out. Plus, they didn't like the snots from Taxachusetts nosing around their business so they prolly wouldn't have told, even if they didn't like the pirates."

"The Joneses are supposed to be ancestors," chimed in Billy.

"My Uncle Sally says we are, but Aunt Polly says he's full of shite cause Quelch was before Americans lived here and we ain't French." added Tommy Templeton.

"Language," Maura chided the excited eleven-year-old. "And it's *Massachusetts*, Charlie, you know that."

Tommy nodded but kept talking. "Uncle Sally says great-great-great-great-grandpappy John was on the ship, but got excused by the judge because he was just a kid and only a cabin boy. He thinks that John and a couple others brought the loot here and hid it."

"Tommy, your Aunt Polly is right about the timing. Americans weren't settled in this area during Quelch's time; it *was* the French. But yes, that's the legend, more or less," Maura agreed. "Judge Sewell caught some of the crew in the Isles of Shoals in New Hampshire with a bit of gold dust. Because there was an awful lot of treasure that's never been found, people speculate that Quelch, or some of his crew, hid it before they got caught. Since they were New Englanders, this region is certainly possible. No one has ever come across any piece of evidence that there's any hidden here, despite generations of treasure hunters poking around. Still," — she grinned at the children—"it's a fun thing to imagine on a cold, blustery day, isn't it?"

She stood up. "I bet you can come up with some fun pirate activities to do while you wait for your parents. You know the drill. If you don't want to participate, find a quiet activity to do by yourself or with friends. You can always add on to our holiday chains or snowflakes. We also need more cards for the shut-ins and old-timers." She doubted anyone would be interested in working on those particular projects at the moment, but made the suggestions anyway.

Maura nodded to Isabelle, who pulled out the cardboard box they'd turned into a treasure chest. "Let's open it up and see what's inside."

Isabelle's announcement was met with cheers and general jubilation by the children, who quickly mobbed her.

Maura grinned, snapped a few photos on her phone, and then shut the door to the children's area on her way out so the merriment wouldn't disturb the other patrons.

Back in the main part of the library, she leaned against a stack and paused to enjoy the cheerful lights on the Christmas tree and soft glow the electric candles in the windows were throwing against the glass. They made the inside feel inviting on a decidedly unfriendly-looking day. It was only 3:30, but the gray sky was darkening fast.

Humming along with Bing Crosby, she began to check in the stack of books that had formed on the desk. After the fourth geological tome, she began to get curious. Someone was doing extensive research on the physical topography of the region. Maura scanned the book to see who had last checked it out. Her eyebrow lifted in surprise. She checked the rest and sat back as she mulled over what Joey Thompson could want with these books. He'd taken them out on her day off the previous week. It was unusual for him to check out anything other than an occasional dvd. Maura gave a mental shrug; it really wasn't her business. She should, she supposed, be glad he was reading and using the library.

Before she could continue to ruminate, Charlie and Billy approached her.

"Miss Ballard, are there any books on John Quelch?"

"And we'd like to know if there are any books about the tunnels and caves on the island."

Maura glanced down at the title she was holding and handed it over to the seventh grader. "You might as well start with this one, Billy. And Charlie, we don't have any books about Mr. Quelch specifically, but there's a small assortment on piracy in New England. I'm happy to show you where it is."

"Cool beans! Thanks, Miss B." Jack looked at Charlie. "Let's check it out and then we can go through them."

Maura spent a quiet hour catching up on library correspondence before parents began trickling in to collect their children. She moved back out to the circulation desk to continue her work so she could keep a better eye on the comings and goings. As she worked, Maura's mind wandered to the upcoming visit.

Stephan and Maisy were going to pick up his family in Bangor on Thursday. After that, they were going to take a day to get acclimated. The plan was for her to meet everyone over a casual brunch on Saturday. Every time she thought about it, she got butterflies in her belly. It'd been so long since she met a lover's family and even longer since it was someone she was actually in love with. Maura held the happy thought in her heart. She was in love. Who'd have thought it? A few months ago, she didn't even know Stephan Kirkland existed. Now she loved him and his child. The thought warmed her.

Both had assured her on their own, and together, that Andrew, Evelyn, and Nicholas Kirkland were going to adore her. Stephan insisted they were thrilled that he and Maisy were so happy. Maisy had confided that she'd been grilled by her grandmother and told her how awesome Maura was. But it didn't matter how many reassurances they gave her. She knew that with the history of Stephan's first marriage, his family was likely to be protective. She sighed. She could only be herself. Hopefully that would be enough.

"That was a heavy sigh." Liz observed as she passed by the circulation desk.

Maura smiled at her friend. "Just fretting."

"About the impending visit."

Maura nodded.

"If they don't love you, that's their problem, Maura." Liz gave her an encouraging smile. "They'd be crazy not to at least *like* you." She laughed.

"Thanks. You should be a motivational speaker."

"Hey, there's no need for sarcasm." Liz leaned on the desk and gave Maura a surprised look. "You're really worried, aren't you?"

"I keep telling myself not to be, but I am."

Liz drummed her fingers on the wood. "I don't think there's anything to fret about with the parents. The brother is another story. But that's just my guess from what I've gleaned by Maisy's descriptions and the bits Stephan's said, which really hasn't been much."

Maura nodded in agreement. "Nicholas is who concerns me most, too."

The women looked at one another in silence for a moment before Liz shrugged. "Can't do anything about it right now, can you? Might as well set it aside and not borrow trouble."

"True words." Maura wished it was as easy as just turning off a switch.

"Mama!" Fern hurried over and threw herself into her mother's arms. "I'm so happy you're here. You're early tonight!"

The worry lines in Liz's forehead deepened, but she smiled at her daughter. "I was able to convince Sandy that I needed to get out early to spend some time with my baby girl."

Maura was embarrassed to realize she'd never even asked Liz if something was up. She was indeed early. She gave Liz a questioning look.

Liz's grim shake of her head and frown was an answer in and of itself.

Maura's own worries suddenly seemed petty. She watched with concern as Fern led Liz back to the children's room to gather up her things.

CHAPTER 14

"This is where I come after school on the days Fern's mom has to work."

Maura looked up from the stack of mysteries she was shelving when she heard Maisy's excited chatter.

"It's just lovely, isn't it, Andrew? It's so welcoming." A cheerful voice answered the girl. The woman's accent was more pronounced than her son's and had a distinctive Scottish burr to it.

Maura put the books down on the ground and straightened up. She pressed a hand to her belly to try and steady it.

"It is, Evie." Stephan's father's voice was a warm, rumbly thing. His accent matched Stephan's, though thicker in sound.

Maura peeked her head around the corner and swallowed hard when a plump, blond woman noticed her and waved before striding over with open arms. Her eyes were a familiar shade of blue and they seemed to be taking in every detail as she moved forward.

Maura only had time to wipe her now-damp palms on her skirt before she was enveloped in an enthusiastic hug.

"I am so, so happy to meet you, Maura." Evelyn released her after a fierce squeeze.

Before Maura could catch her breath, Maisy had flung herself into her arms. "Did we surprise you, Maura?"

The girl had an impish grin on her face as she leaned back in the Maura's arms. "We did, didn't we? It was all my idea."

Maura saw Stephan give a vigorous nod in agreement.

"And I overrode Stephan when he said no; grandmother's prerogative." Evelyn gave her son a benevolent look.

"Maisy Daze, let go of Maura so she can come meet everyone properly." Stephan came over and dropped a light kiss on Maura's lips as he extricated her from his daughter.

Maura felt her cheeks warm as she gave the remaining Kirklands a shy look. "You must be Andrew." She extended her hand towards a tall man with silvering hair and green eyes. She felt immediately at ease with him as he clasped her hand between both of his larger ones in a gentle, warm grip.

"It's a pleasure to finally meet you, Maura. Evelyn and I have been looking forward to finally making your acquaintance."

Nicholas was about an inch taller than his younger brother. His hair was a light brown rather than black and longer than Stephan's. By and large, however, the brothers bore a striking resemblance to one another. His expression was reserved. He extended his hand for a polite handshake when Andrew had released her. "Nick." His voice was as cool as well.

Maura tried not to take his less-than-enthusiastic greeting personally. Evelyn frowned at her eldest but didn't comment. She turned to Maura and gave her a bright smile. "Stephan tells me you're dining with us later in the week. I'm looking forward to getting to know you better while we're here. Maisy and I were wondering if you'd like to join us for tea and cakes tonight."

"Oh." Maura's eyes widened in surprise. "I don't want to intrude on your first night together."

Maisy grabbed one of Maura's hands. "Please say you will. Please, please, please."

"Don't you want family time tonight?"

Stephan saw the worry in Maura's posture. He wrapped an arm around her waist and looked down at his daughter. "We talked about this," he reminded the child. "We aren't going to overwhelm Maura."

"But it's just Gran, Gramps, and Uncle Nick," Maisy protested. "You wouldn't be overwhelmed by three extra people, would you, Maura? There's loads more here at the library all the time." Maisy's expression shifted as though a thought had just occurred to her. "Ohhhhhhhhhh, but you know all of them, don't you? They aren't strangers." She adopted a contrite expression that Maura almost fell for until she saw the sparkle in the girl's eyes. "Maura." she started grinning widely. "Uncle Nick *is* strange, but he's the only one." She started giggling at her own audacity while the uncle in question dropped his guard long enough to laugh.

Maura smiled at Maisy as she leaned into Stephan's half-embrace. "If I'm not intruding, I'd love to come over for a bit this evening. What time is best?" She directed her question to Evelyn.

"I will probably be asleep by nine, so maybe half seven? Is that enough time for you? Stephan tells me you work long hours here."

Maura nodded. "Plenty." Her mind was racing, trying to figure out if she'd have enough time to get to the bakery or if she had anything in the freezer she could thaw out and bring.

Evelyn nodded in satisfaction. "Brilliant. Now don't fash yourself about bringing anything. We stopped at a lovely bakery before walking over here. We picked out all sorts of treats."

"I don't feel right coming over empty-handed." She leaned into Stephan's hand as it rubbed slow, lazy circles around her low back.

"I bet Mum would enjoy a nip of the elderberry elixir you introduced me to at Thanksgiving." Stephan spoke softly.

She gave him a grateful smile for solving her quandary. It was the perfect solution. She still had a couple of the small bottles that Liz had made her.

"That sounds intriguing." Evelyn had a wide smile that put Maura's nerves at ease. "Now, where is this George I've heard so much about?"

"Come on. I'll give you a tour." Maisy grabbed each of her grandparents by a hand and started chatting away at them about the different features of the library. Soon they were in the children's wing, leaving Maura alone with Stephan and his brother.

Nicholas's eyes were the identical shade as his mother, brother, and niece's, but didn't hold the same warmth as he studied Maura.

She drew herself up, refusing to be intimidated by his appraising stare. "How was your flight, Nicholas?"

"A bit bumpy, but otherwise unremarkable. We flew into Boston yesterday and only had a quick jump to Bangor today. The car ride was almost as long as the flight."

Maura nodded. "It's great that you were able to take this much time off. Maisy has been so excited about your visit," she offered.

"I plan on working while I'm here, so it's no trouble."

"Has she told you about the play?"

"In great detail." Nicholas's voice was dry. "Great detail."

Stephan gave his brother a sharp look. "And you will find something positive to say to her about it, no matter how bored you are, Nick."

"Hey, mate, you know me better than that. I'd never hurt our girl's feelings."

A veteran of the school's annual holiday musical extravaganza, which was really a community effort, Maura felt confident that none of them would be bored. She didn't, however, want to ruin any surprises, so she kept her mouth shut.

Iris and Rose Jones waved to Maura from the circulation desk. "Excuse me. I need to check them out." She hurried over to the elderly sisters. She sat down across from them to begin scanning their books.

Along with Stephan, Nick followed her. Stephan introduced his brother to the sisters. He winked at Maura when they started asking Nick about his wife or girlfriend.

Maura couldn't contain her amused grin.

Nick was a good sport and began flirting with the sisters. When Maura had put their books in the bags they'd brought, he reached for them. "Let me help you out. I need to stretch my legs." He continued the good-natured banter he'd started up with them as they made their slow way out of the library.

Stephan chuckled. "He's a decent bloke at heart."

"So I see. Should I really come over tonight?"

"Yes. Mum and Maisy are looking forward to it, but if it's too much for you, it's okay to plead off."

Maura shook her head. "No, I don't want to do that."

Soon, Maisy returned with her grandparents in tow. After a flurry of farewells, the Kirkland family left and Maura returned to her work.

Between having to hurry home, take care of the cats, and grab the gift, Maura had little time to catch her breath before walking across the street to Stephan's house. The lights from their large tree were warm and inviting. Maura put her nose near the lush wreath and drew in a deep breath of the faintly pine-scented air before pressing her gloved finger down on the bell.

Stephan opened the door so quickly that Maura could hear Maisy's voice yelling "I'll get it!" from the back of the house. He smiled at her and bent to give her a brief kiss. "Your arrival has been much anticipated." He helped take her coat once she'd stuffed her gloves in the pockets. As he hung it up, Maisy skidded to a stop in front of Maura and gave her a fierce hug before grabbing the woman's free hand.

"Come on! We're in the porch."

Stephan drew in a breath, but stopped himself from saying anything when Maura gave her head a brief shake. She grinned at him and then Maisy. "I've been looking forward to this all evening."

As they walked into the back room, Maura felt her jaw slacken. The space sparkled and glittered with holiday decorations. Strands of delicate lights were strung along the windows and walls. A small tree had been added to the round table in the back corner. It was laden with candy canes and foil-covered chocolates. Christmas crackers and envelopes were tucked between branches and tiny colored lights glowed, lighting the dark corner. "When did you do all of this?"

Evelyn came up behind them. "Maisy and I have been busy all afternoon. Your friend Liz helped gather everything for us."

Stephan put an arm around Maura's shoulder. "These two are always plotting and scheming. But," he had an affectionate look for his daughter and mother, "I'm not complaining."

"It's wonderful." Maura grinned in delight as she took in the small collection of Santa figures that ranged from traditional to whimsical and lined the mantle above the propane fireplace. A simple nativity scene sat on the top of a low bookcase near the door. "Oh." Maura turned and smiled at Evelyn. She held out a pretty, glass bottle filled with a pale lavender liquid. "This is for you. Liz is a woman of many talents."

"I think I'll enjoy a nip before bed tonight. I always struggle to sleep the first night or two in a new place." Evelyn slid her arm through Maura's and led her over to the chairs and loveseat that were grouped around the low table. "Andrew will be bringing the tea in shortly, and then we're kicking the lads out so we can enjoy ourselves and have a natter without them."

Maisy grabbed Maura's other arm. "I told Gran you like the strawberry tea best."

Stephan chuckled. "YOU like the strawberry tea best, Maisy Daisy."

"It makes me feel happy inside."

Maura smiled at the girl. "Me too. It's a perfect choice." Her eyes landed on the three-tiered tray that dominated the center of the table as they approached the seats. "Oh my. You went to an awful lot of effort." Tiny sandwiches, cookies, and pastries filled the plates. Delicate teacups with small matching plates were set out, along with festive red-and-green linen napkins. "This looks amazing."

Evelyn smiled at Maura's obvious appreciation. She dropped a kiss on her granddaughter's head and gave Maisy a half-hug. "We had a grand time preparing it. Ah." Her eyes lit up as she saw her husband come into the doorway. "Excellent timing. Thank you, love."

Once the teapot was set on the table, the Kirkland matriarch gave her husband and youngest son each a fond look. "Off with you both."

Stephan caught Maura's eyes. "We're just going to be watching football in the living room if you need anything."

She smiled. "I'm sure your mom and Maisy have everything well in hand."

Evelyn's eyes twinkled with amusement. "Indeed. Don't fash yourself, Stephan Ian Kirkland. I'm not going to do anything to embarrass you or upset Maura."

"I didn't say." Stephan shook his head and held up his hands in mock surrender. "I'm leaving now."

Maisy grinned at the two women and plopped herself down cross-legged on the loveseat. Her grandmother joined her. Evelyn reached for the teapot as Maura sat in the chair by the remaining place setting.

Once everyone had their tea and all their plates were filled, Evelyn leaned back in her seat and cupped Maisy's face with an affectionate look. "You're looking wonderful, young lady, and so grown-up." She turned her smile to Maura. "I hear you've helped Miss Maisy Daisy settle in. Thank you."

"It's been a pleasure."

"Gran, did I tell you about the ornaments we made for the tree for our school play?"

Evelyn listened attentively as the child chatted away.

Maura sipped her tea and enjoyed observing the duo. She forced herself not to gobble down the treats on her plate, even though she'd skipped dinner. When there was a lull in the conversation, she turned the pretty white teacup around in her hands, admiring the green and purple cluster of thistles that snaked around the side. "These are so pretty. I've never seen this pattern before."

"They were great-great-great-granny Glynis's. They're from Scotland, like Gran." Maisy sighed. "I love them, but Daddy won't let me use them. He only brings them out for special occasions."

"Which this is." Evelyn gave her granddaughter an indulgent smile. "And I'm sure we'll find plenty more occasions to bring out the china while we're here, lovey."

Maisy gave a contented sigh and leaned into her grandmother. "I can't wait to show you everything, but I especially can't wait for you to meet Karria."

"I'm looking forward to that, too." Evelyn had put her cup down and was holding the child in her arms. She gave Maura a quizzical look. "Stephan tells us the seal behaves unusually with our Maisy."

Maura nodded. "They have a pretty special relationship. I've never seen anything quite like it."

Evelyn's lips curved into a contented smile. "I cannot wait to meet this lovely creature."

"Karria can't wait to meet you either." Maisy beamed at her grandmother. "We talked all about you last week."

Evelyn gave the girl a thoughtful look. "Should we make some fish cakes for her, do you think? I don't know if seals eat cooked fish, though. Maybe we should just bring a whole fish?"

Maisy shrugged. "Dunno. I've never asked."

Both looked at Maura.

She shook her head. "I haven't a clue if they eat cooked food or not. I imagine a fresh fish would be appreciated."

"I bet Betty Jo's dad would sell us one from his boat, dontcha think so, Maura?"

"I'm sure he would, though I wouldn't tell him it's for Karria, okay? He has—" Maura paused. "Strong feelings regarding seals."

"He hates 'em," Maisy explained to Evelyn. "Betty Jo tells some funny stories about him." Her eyes twinkled. "So does Karria. She likes to play games on him since he can be mean to the regular seals."

Evelyn sighed. "I sorely hope your Karria will speak with me. I have so many questions."

Maisy laid a hand on her grandmother's age-spotted one. "Gran, don't be disappointed if she doesn't. She told me there's only been a few people she's spoken with in sixty years and I'm the first in six. But maybe she'll at least sing for you. Her songs are beautiful. Sometimes she sings me to sleep."

Unbidden, a memory of her aunt Jane laughing and dancing on their little beach on an unseasonably mild December day popped into Maura's head. A distinctive-looking seal had been frolicking in the surf, barking and splashing along with music that only she and Maura's aunt seemed to hear. Jane and the seal mimicked each other's movements while a young Maura sat on her favorite rocky perch, watching them. Maura had assumed that Karria was descended from that seal. Now she gave Maisy a speculative look. Jane had always talked about her friend at the cove. Had they actually *been* friends? Maura had assumed it was an expression of affection for the wild creature that often popped up there and was friendly to her aunt. Could it really have been Karria this whole time? Jane had passed away suddenly six years ago. How could Karria be at least sixty? Seals didn't live that long.

"Maura, dear, you look like you're deep in thought."

Maura blinked and shook her head. "It's been a long day. I'm sorry." She gathered up her teacup and saucer. "This has been such a lovely evening, but I should go home. You must be exhausted."

"I am a bit knackered," Evelyn admitted. "But I am so glad you came over. I look forward to getting to know you better."

Maura gave Stephan's mother a shy look. "I'm looking forward to it, too."

"Wonderful." Evelyn patted Maisy's hand. "Young lady, you take the teacakes back to the kitchen. Maura and I will bring the china."

Between the three of them, cleanup was quick and easy. Maisy and Evelyn each gave Maura a long hug before going upstairs and leaving her alone to say goodnight to the men.

Maura stopped in the living room. Andrew was asleep in the recliner, snoring gently, while Nicholas was stretched out on the sofa with his eyes closed. The volume on the soccer game was low.

Stephan eased out of the armchair. He reached for her hand when he got to her side. "Tea's over?"

"Yes, your mother's taken Maisy up to bed."

Stephan nodded. "I'll walk you home, then."

After they'd bundled up, the couple slipped out of the house, shutting the door quietly behind them. The moon was hanging full and low, bathing everything in a gentle light. The usual breezes had stilled, and the air was cold but not freezing.

"Want to go to the cove for a minute?" Stephan asked on impulse.

Maura shot him a surprised look, but nodded. As they walked at a leisurely pace, she told him about Liz's hours getting cut back for the winter. "She's proud. She won't want charity, but I want to help her. She's going to need every penny to pay for heat and bills over the winter. That doesn't leave much for Christmas."

Stephan gave her a thoughtful look. "I don't think it'd be charity if we bought some gifts for Fern. She wouldn't take money for helping Mum and Maisy even though she had to have spent hours on it."

They reached the beach and settled on Maura's favorite rock. The waves were making a quiet murmur with slack tide.

Maura drew in a deep breath and let go of her residual anxiety over meeting Stephan's family. "Karria was a big conversation topic tonight."

"I'm not surprised. Mum's been beside herself with excitement to meet her." Stephan wrapped his arm around Maura and she nestled into him. "I'd try to keep her from filling Maisy's head with fairy tales, but that ship has long sailed." He was quiet for a moment before adding, "What do I know anyway? Karria is unique, in my experience. Maisy's conversations with Sophie have proven to have some validity, whatever they may actually be. Still, I need her to stay here in reality. I worry that fantasy land will be too alluring for her. I'm struggling with it."

Maura smiled in the dark. "I love that you are willing to see things others aren't." She clasped his free hand and told him about the memory that had surfaced earlier and Maisy's offhanded remark about the seal's age.

Stephan dropped a kiss on her head and inhaled the citrusy smell of her shampoo. "I love that you don't think my family is barmy, even when I question it." He felt her shiver next to him and gave a regretful sigh. "I'd better get you inside and myself home." He cocked his head to the side. "Do you hear that?"

Maura listened intently for a moment and then furrowed her brow. There was a delicate sound that felt like it was teasing right at the edge of her hearing. Then all she heard was the gentle breezes of slack tide and the soft rustling of the water. She shook her head. "No. What do you hear?"

Stephan frowned. "I couldn't quite catch it and then it was gone. It was silvery sounding music, crazy as that sounds." He rubbed his head. "I think I need the time off next week. The investigation is getting to me."

Maura slid off the rock and stood up. She offered her hands to Stephan and helped him stand. "I'm glad you're getting a chance to spend time with your family while they're here."

"Me too." He held her hand as the made the short walk to her house. "I'm also glad you agreed to spend Christmas with us."

"You're really sure about that?"

"Positive. Everyone was adamant that they want you there too." He saw her expression. "Even Nick. I know he wasn't as friendly as my parents today. Give him time. He's protective of us, even when he's been told there's no need."

Maura nodded. "Okay then." She turned her face up to kiss him goodnight. "I'll see you for breakfast on Saturday?"

"Absolutely."

Stephan gave her a lingering kiss and waited until she was inside before hurrying back home to make sure everyone was settled in for the night.

CHAPTER 15

"You've met a Selkie!" Evelyn's voice was filled with wonder. "What a gift, my love."

"A what?" Maisy puzzled over the unfamiliar word.

"A Selkie, one of the seal folk. They live in the sea, but can come ashore, shed their seal skins, and appear as human as any of us sitting round this table."

"Whoa." Maisy sat back in her chair. Her eyes gleamed as she mulled over the possibility that Karria was more than just a seal.

"Karria speaks to you. She saved your life. She's given you a fabulous gift. And now that I've seen her, I can say she's certainly bigger than the average seal, isn't that true, Maura?"

Maura paused as she lifted her tea to her lips. Her eyes widened and went from the blond-haired woman to her son. Andrew caught her gaze as it was darting between the two. He put his index finger to his lips and gave the slightest shake of his head before reaching for a biscuit to dunk into his tea.

Evelyn, Maisy, Maura, and Stephan had enjoyed an early morning stroll to the beach and a couple of visits: first, to Karria, who'd enjoyed her fish, and then to see Maura's cats, before returning to Stephan's for breakfast. It'd been lovely, but there was some underlying friction between mother and son after the seal left. It had carried over through breakfast.

"Mum, what are you talking about? Please don't feed Maisy any more folktales as reality." Stephan interrupted before Maura could feel compelled to reply.

"Stephan Ian Kirkland, don't you dare patronize me. I know a Selkie from a simple harbor seal, young man. What our lass has befriended is certainly a special being."

Stephan saw the mulish set to his mother's mouth. He didn't want to get into a fight the first family meal they were sharing with Maura. "I can agree with that. Karria is special."

Maura let out the breath she was holding and smiled at all of them. "She is, and though she's friendly to many of us around here, I've never seen her bond with anyone the way she has with Maisy. That's a lovely gift." It was neither the time nor place to mention that she'd read a chapter on Selkies the night before and had been struck by some of the correlations with Karria. The notion that Selkies really existed, however, was too much of a stretch for her mind.

"Oh, well done, Maura," Nick chortled. His laughter stopped when both his mother and brother turned their gazes in his direction, but he kept grinning. "What?" He shrugged at them. "I was impressed. That was a nice bit of verbal dodgeball."

Maisy looked at her uncle like he was speaking a foreign language. She turned her back on him and grinned at her grandparents. "You promised to take me Christmas shopping in Bar Harbor today. Can we go soon?"

Andrew stood up and grimaced when his knees cracked. "Are you sure you want a decrepit old man like me tagging along? Ouch, hey." He rubbed his arm where Evelyn had lightly smacked it. "Yes, dear. Let's clean up. Then Nick will drive us."

"Have you forgotten me?" Stephan inquired. "I'm fully capable of driving you around."

"How am I going to buy your present if you're with me?" Maisy frowned at her father.

"What she really means to say is, how is she going to finagle some treats from your father with you hovering nearby saying no every time?" Evelyn gave her granddaughter a conspiratorial wink. "And how indeed is she going to buy a present for you if you're like a burr on her side?"

Stephan looked at Maura as she gathered up plates with his father. He wanted to stay behind and spend more time with her, but didn't feel right sending his family off when they'd only just arrived.

By the time he reached the kitchen with his mother and brother, Maisy was beaming at him. "You can come with us Daddy. Gramps asked Maura if she'd keep you company."

In the end, they added Fern to the mix and crammed into Stephan's SUV. As the group congregated on the sidewalk, Evelyn suggested Stephan make a late lunch reservation at Madras. Fern promised she'd keep everyone from getting lost. The larger group walked off, leaving Maura and Stephan standing in the cold air looking at one another. He smiled at her and reached for her hand. "This is unexpected. Do you mind?"

Maura shook her head. "Not a bit, but I feel bad keeping you from your family."

Stephan shook his head. "They're all thrilled, even Nick, though you won't catch him admitting it. This gives them a chance to spoil Maisy and, by extension, Fern, without any interference."

"It's a treat for me too." Maura smiled up at him. "Maybe you can help me find presents for your family?"

Stephan knew better than to tell her not to get them anything. "I'd be happy to."

When they wrapped up a couple of hours later, Maura and Stephan added half a dozen bags to the ones that already filled the trunk of the car. Stephan whistled. "Wow. I hope Maisy appreciates Santa, too."

Maura looked at the mounds of bags. "What did she ask him for?"

"An iPad." He chuckled. "She was covering her bases in case I didn't come through. And an American Girl doll like Lana has." His expression was troubled. "I want to get it for her, but Fern will be left out. I don't think Liz would be pleased if I got Fern one too. I've been holding off. I have to decide by tomorrow. It's the last day of guaranteed shipping."

"Let's go in on it together. It can be from both of us."

"You bought Fern a bunch of things today. Liz is already going to feel it's too much."

"What if she doesn't know who it came from? What if Santa leaves it on their balcony?" Maura's expression was thoughtful. "We'd have to enlist some help getting it up there, but that shouldn't be hard. Plenty of people would help Liz if she'd allow it. She accepts help to make sure Fern has what she needs, but when it comes to *wants,* she's hard to convince."

"If it's there anonymously, would she let Fern keep it?"

Maura shrugged. "I don't see why not. It's not like she would know who to return it to."

"Can you stay tonight and help me pick them out? The only trick is going to be getting Maisy to bed. Hopefully today will help wear her down or—" He sent off a quick text. "If Fern spends the night they'll hole up in her room and we'll have all the privacy we need." He closed the trunk.

It was a boisterous group that reconvened at the harborside restaurant. The elegant venue was decorated and a roaring fire greeted them as they gathered in the lobby. Seeing Fern in the group, the hostess, Cheri, made sure to seat them at Liz's largest table. The girls' eyes were bright with excitement. They pounced on Maura and Stephan as soon as the group was seated. The normally reserved Fern was jabbering away at the two like it'd been years since they'd last seen her. Maura arched an eyebrow at Stephan and tipped her head slightly towards the youngster when Fern turned to show Nick something on the menu. Stephan smiled in agreement with the silent comment. It remained on his lips as Liz approached the table.

"Good afternoon, everyone! Welcome to Madras." The willowy woman stood behind the two girls and affectionately ruffled both their heads. "It's a pleasure to see all of you." As much as she wanted to visit with them, Liz was acutely aware of the manager entering the dining room. "What can I get all of you to drink, and do you have any questions about the menu yet?"

After the initial order was placed, Fern and Maura excused themselves from the table. When they got back, Maisy was bouncing in her seat. "Fern, your mom said you can spend the night!"

A mug of coffee and glass of water sat at Maura's spot. She splashed in some milk and paused when she saw Maisy staring at her.

"You could stay too, you know, Maura. You never have sleepovers with us. I wish you would."

Maura carefully put the creamer down before milk went everywhere.

Stephan's cheeks warmed and his brother started laughing. His parents both hid their smiles behind their mugs of tea.

"What'd I say?" Maisy looked around in confusion. "Adults have sleepovers too, don't they? You had one when we stayed at Lana's, didn't you?" She narrowed her eyes at her father and then her uncle. "You have sleepovers, don't you, Uncle Nick? I've heard you and Daddy talking. It sounds like you have a lot of them."

Nick regained his composure. "You've got me there, you cheeky thing. I do enjoy the occasional sleepover with a friend. But," —he gave his brother a distinct 'you owe me' look— "I think your dad was hoping Maura would sleep over on Christmas Eve, and you know how cranky you can get after a sleepover because you don't sleep a whole lot, right?"

When his niece gave a reluctant nod, Nick continued, "I'm sure your dad and Maura don't want to be crabby this week at work."

"I guess that makes sense. Will you sleep over on Christmas Eve, Maura?"

Liz picked that moment to return to take their orders.

Maura gave her friend a grateful look.

Liz shot her a silent question, but addressed Stephan's parents first. "Do you have any questions about the menu?"

Andrew peered at her over his half-moon reading glasses. "I do indeed, young lady. Could you tell me more about the seafood specials today? I'd love to hear your recommendations."

With everyone's attention diverted, Maura sipped on her ice water, hoping it'd help cool her still-warm cheeks. She felt Stephan give her knee a gentle squeeze and looked at him.

He leaned over and his breath brushed her cheek as he murmured, "I'd love it if you would spend the night Christmas Eve. Think about it, okay?"

Maura nodded and gave him a soft smile. "I'd like that."

He smiled back and then realized the table was silent around them. Stephan looked at the others. "Pardon, did we miss something?"

"We're all waiting on you two to order so the lovely Liz here can get on with her day." Nick's voice was laced with amusement.

Even Liz was grinning at the couple as they both flushed.

"I'll have the salmon with a baked potato and broccoli." Maura hadn't intended to order fish, but it was the first thing her eyes landed on as she stared at the menu.

"That sounds good. I'll have the same, Liz, thanks." Stephan ignored his brother's smirk.

Liz winked at them both and then told the table, "I'll put this in and have your appetizers out in a moment."

Evelyn beamed at all of them. "I'm having a lovely day."

"Me too." Maisy grinned at her father. "Gran helped me get the best presents."

"For you or other people?" Stephan gently teased his daughter, causing Fern to giggle.

"Everyone," Maisy retorted.

By the time the meal was over, the sun had set. The servers had gone around lighting the thick pillar candles wreathed with evergreens at all the tables in preparation for the dinner diners. When Liz came back with the check, Nick plucked it out of her hand with a wink. "Thank you." He handed it back to her with a credit card he'd palmed moments earlier.

After she walked off, Andrew and Stephan both started to protest. Nick grinned at them. "You're going to have to be faster next time."

Evelyn whispered something to her husband. He nodded in agreement and smiled at his eldest. "Well, thank you for dinner, then, lad."

"You're welcome." Nicholas gave them a magnanimous smile.

Stephan had wanted to make sure Liz got an extra-generous tip, but there was no way to say anything with the girls seated at the table.

Maura sensed his discomfort and looked at the youngsters. "Why don't we go visit the restroom before the drive home?"

"That's an excellent idea." Evelyn stood up to join them.

After the two women herded the girls away from the table, Stephan leaned forward to Nick. "I'll give you the cash, but I want you to—" He trailed off as Liz approached the table with the folio.

She smiled at Nick and handed it to him. "I hope you all enjoyed your meals."

All three assured her they had. Before Liz walked away, Maisy came rocketing back, with Fern close behind. The girl wrapped her arms around Liz. "It's great here, Liz! Thank you for taking such good care of us."

Liz hugged her back. "I'm glad you enjoyed it, Maisy."

Fern gave her mother a hug when Maisy released her. "I love you, mama."

"I love you to the moon and back, pipsqueak." Liz gave her daughter a kiss and tight hug. "Be good for the Kirklands."

All but Nick had left the restaurant when Liz hurried into the foyer. She grabbed his arm. "It's beyond too much."

Nick shook his head. "It's not nearly enough. Stephan's told me how much time Maisy spends with you and Fern when he's working and I know how much time you had to have spent helping

Maisy and mum pull together their surprise. Take it and enjoy the holidays."

Liz gave him a searching look, trying to see if there was pity in his expression. Finding none, she smiled. "Thank you. It's the nicest Christmas gift anyone's ever given me."

Nick frowned at that. His voice took on a gruff tone. "I should hope not, but you're welcome."

Liz nodded and reached into her apron for the large bill she'd found on the table. "Your father dropped—" She trailed off when Nick shook his head.

"He insisted."

Tears sprang to Liz's eyes. "I don't know what to say."

Nick impulsively leaned over and gave her a chaste kiss on the cheek. "Say you'll enjoy the holidays."

Liz hesitated a moment and then nodded. "We will. Thank you."

Stephan stuck his head in the door. "Nick, it's freezing out here. Are you coming? Oh, hey, Liz."

Liz blinked her tears away and smiled at Stephan. "Call me if Fern gives you any trouble."

"She never does," he assured her and waved goodbye as Nick joined him at the door. A bitter wind hit them both in the face. The rest of their group was nowhere in sight.

"Where is everyone?"

"Maura's taking them to the car. It was too cold to stand around waiting for you. What was going on in there?"

"Nothing."

"It didn't look like nothing."

"Well, it wasn't something you need to fash yourself about."

"You can be a pain in the arse sometimes. You know that, right?"

Nick grinned at his brother. "Takes one to know one."

"Whatever." Stephan laughed and punched him in the arm. "I'm glad you're here, mate."

"Me too." Nick stuffed his hands in his coat pocket. "So, it seems pretty serious with Maura. Maisy's in love with her."

Stephan nodded in agreement. "We both are."

"You sure you're not jumping into things too soon?"

"Too soon?" Stephan glanced over at his brother. "You know what my marriage was like. And Sophie's been gone two years."

"I just don't want to see you get hurt. And I really don't want to see Maisy's heart get broken again."

"We have to live our lives, Nick." Stephan's words came with a puff of white vapor. "Maura's worlds different than Sophie."

"But you haven't known her that long."

Stephan gave his brother a sideways look. "I know her well. Nick, do you want me to be alone until Maisy is grown and flown?"

"Yes, maybe—okay, fine, no." His brother's grudging tone resembled his niece's when she didn't want to admit something.

"Then be happy for us. If it doesn't work out, be sad for us." Stephan shrugged. As they neared the running car, he slowed and put a hand on his brother's arm. "Give Maura a chance."

Nick nodded. "I'll try, mate. I am trying."

The two hurried the short distance to the car and slid inside the warming vehicle with everyone else. With the radio playing holiday tunes, the trip back to Belfort was spent in an enthusiastic singalong.

When they reached the building where Liz and Fern rented a small second floor apartment, Stephan left the car idling. "I'll take you up, kiddo."

Nick had to get out of the car for Fern to exit. Rather than get back in, he shut the door. Stephan gave him a quizzical look, but didn't want to linger in the cold. Fern paid no attention to the men and unlocked the door that led to the stairwell. Once in, she flicked on the light and led them up the narrow flight of stairs to the apartment door. She hurried into the small, drafty apartment. "I'll be quick," she promised Stephan as she ran to her bedroom after turning on a couple of lights.

Nick looked around the cramped space. The kitchen island doubled as a table, with a few barstools lining one side. A dilapidated sofa delineated the living space from the kitchen space. A couple of colorful throw blankets were draped over the top of the faded plaid fabric. A rickety bookshelf leaned against the wall opposite it, and a battered but well-polished coffee table and a couple of mismatched chairs were in between. A sliding glass door led to a small balcony. A small Christmas tree stood in the corner where the door met the far wall. Tinsel sparkled in the low light.

While Stephan studied the balcony, trying to figure out the logistics of getting presents up there unseen and unheard, Nick stuck his head in Liz's bedroom. It was small. A few pictures hung on the walls and a colorful quilt covered the bed. Her closet door was open and showed a pair of sensible black shoes, much like the ones she'd been wearing at the restaurant, a pair of boots, a pair of battered sneakers, and a single pair of red heels. A few sweaters, a couple of dresses, and some tops hung from the bar.

"What're you doing?" Fern peeked into her mother's room to see what had captured the Englishman's attention.

"Just coming to see if you needed help."

"My room is across the hall," Fern pointed to the now-dark doorway. "Do you want to see it?"

Nick followed her the two steps into a room that mirrored her mother's in size. Her bed was draped in a cheerful yellow quilt covered in white daisies. A couple of stuffed animals sat on the pillow. There was a small desk and chair along the wall opposite the bed. A pair of rubber boots, a pair of snow boots, and a pair of well-worn black flats were lined up against the wall at the foot of the bed. It didn't resemble the colorful clutter of toys and clothing that filled Maisy's room at all. "What are your friends' names?" Nick pointed to the two stuffed animals.

"The bunny is Clover and the cat is Gus."

"Won't they be lonely without you tonight?"

Fern nodded. "That's why they're staying together. I don't have much room in my bag, so I'm only bringing Ted, my bear."

"That's thoughtful of you." Nick smiled at the girl.

Nick was silent as they drove out of town and out to the far end of the island. When they reached Milly's large house with the bright, colorful lights and lamps glowing in the windows, he was struck again by the contrast between the girls' homes. Wrapped up in his own thoughts, he helped bring packages inside for his mother while Stephan and Maura brought a few bags over to her house.

"Nicholas." Evelyn gave him a concerned look. "Are you feeling well?"

"I'm fine, Mum." He straddled the chest in Milly and David's room, where his mother had wanted the bulk of the bags. "They're poor."

"Excuse me?" Evelyn blinked at him.

"Fern and Liz."

Evelyn nodded. "They don't have much money, true."

Nick frowned. "How does she not resent coming here and seeing everything Maisy has, when she has so little?"

Evelyn sat down at the foot of the bed and patted her son on the knee. "They're rich in love. That counts for a lot. And upbringing matters. She's being raised well."

Nick nodded. After a moment, he gave her a wry smile. "We spoil Maisy rotten, don't we?"

"Yes, but Stephan is keeping her from becoming a brat. Maura's a good influence on her as well."

"Fully in the pro-Maura camp, are you?"

"Of course." Evelyn swatted his leg and stood up. "You should be too. She's good for them. They're all happy and well-suited for each other. Now let's get back downstairs to your father and the girls. I promised we'd bake biscuits before they start their movie. There's no reason we shouldn't spoil Fern when she's here either, you know. It'll do her no harm."

"I'm not baking." Nick shook his head at his mother.

"No, but you're not sitting up here brooding either."

"I have work to do."

"Do it downstairs."

"You're relentless woman."

"That's mother relentless to you, young man."

"Yes, mother relentless," Nick replied in a sassy tone.

"Cheeky lad." His mother laughed and led him down the stairs. As they reached the bottom of the stairs, the front door opened and Stephan and Maura came in.

"Are your furry friends fed?" Evelyn smiled at Maura as Stephan helped her out of her coat.

"They are, thank you. What are the girls up to?"

"We're baking and then they're watching movies."

Stephan and Maura exchanged a look. Evelyn and Nick both gave them questioning glances.

"We're going to play Father Christmas's Elves," Stephan grinned. "We'll show you when the girls are doing their own thing."

Evelyn tucked her arm through Maura's and led her into the warm, well-lit kitchen, where Andrew was brewing a pot of tea and entertaining Maisy and Fern with a rollicking tale of Henny Penny.

Later, when the girls were ensconced in a blanket fort piled high with stuffed animals and pillows and a platter of finger food, Stephan cleared out a space on the kitchen table for his laptop. He pulled up the American Girl Doll website. He knew which doll Maisy was coveting and added it to the shopping cart. He then went back to the list of dolls.

"Should we go for the same or different?" He tried to keep his words vague in case either girl came in.

Maura reached over and scrolled down the page. When she reached the one Fern longed for, she pointed.

"You're sure?"

"Positive. They wrote letters to the big guy a couple weeks ago. I peeked at a few. She asked for the miniature version. She's also read every book we have on this one at least five times."

Stephan added the doll, Kit, to the cart. His mother reached over and turned the laptop so it was facing her. After a few minutes of deliberations with Andrew, she added several more items to the cart.

Nicholas had been studying his own laptop. He looked up. "Maura, can I have your opinion for a moment?"

"Sure." She pushed away from her spot, which Stephan slid into to finish processing the order with his parents, and walked around to Nick. "What's up?"

"Which of these would be best?" He showed her a couple of women's parkas on the LL Bean web site. "I want to get her something that'll be warm enough for the weather up here, but that she'd enjoy wearing."

"Liz?"

"Of course."

"Ah." Maura focused on the screen and tried to blank out her expression. Both of the coats he was looking at were the company's higher-end ones. After a few minutes' deliberation, Maura pointed to the full-length one.

"That's what I thought too. But good to have confirmation." Nicholas clicked on the parka. "Medium, right?"

"Yes."

"I like this burgundy for her myself, but what do you think?"

"I think she'll love it," was Maura's response after she studied the colors.

He nodded. "Cheers."

Maura took that as a dismissal and went back to her spot.

Stephan was giving his brother a thoughtful look, but didn't say anything.

"May I use the computer for a few minutes?"

Evelyn slid it over to Maura. The younger woman's fingers flew across the keyboard as she quickly composed a note.

Stephan turned so he could read over her shoulder. He grinned. "Good thinking."

Evelyn and Andrew both came around to read from behind Maura's chair as well.

Dear Fern,

Every year Santa lets his Naughty and Nice list helper elves pick a few children from around the world to give a special surprise to. We look for girls and boys who are kind, who help their families, who don't ask for much for themselves, and who we think deserve a little extra holiday cheer. There are so many wonderful children in the world, but even Santa's sleigh and magic have their limits. Unfortunately, we can't do this for everyone who deserves it. That's why you've probably never heard of us before.

This year we picked you!

Merriest of Christmases, to you Fern! We love you and are so proud of the young woman you are becoming. Keep up the good work!

Love,

Jingle, Jangle, and Edna
Team Naughty and Nice

Andrew chuckled and Evelyn smiled and dropped a kiss on Maura's head. "Well done, dear."

Nick came over to read the note, nodded, and reached around to pluck the computer away from Maura.

"Hey!" Stephan started to stand up.

Nick shook his head. "I'm just forwarding it to myself. I have to go Ellsworth on Monday to take care of some work. I can get this printed on special paper while I'm there." He finished sending the file to himself and gently placed the computer back in front of Maura.

Maura murmured a thanks and forwarded a copy of the document to herself as well after Nicholas had wandered back to his side of the table.

Evelyn shook her head at her sons and turned to Maura after the younger woman had shut the laptop. "Dear, we haven't talked about the holiday meals with you. Do you have special traditions you'd like us to include?"

Maura's eyes widened in surprise at the question. "Oh, that's nice of you to ask." She smiled at Evelyn. "I don't. The only thing I do that would be a tradition is watch *A Christmas Carol*. If I'm longing for company, I'll stay up and go to midnight mass in town. Most times I'm in my pajamas by then and can't bear to go back outside. Since my aunt passed, I've taken to lighting a candle in her memory that I let burn until I go to bed. She used to do it in honor of her mother. It seemed natural to do it for her."

"Well, that's a lovely tradition," Andrew touched her shoulder as he passed by to refill his mug. "Would you mind if we incorporate it? I rather fancy the notion, what about you, Evie?"

His wife nodded in agreement. "I think it's a wonderful way to honor your aunt, Maura." She reached for the younger woman's hand and held it in her own. "Would you mind if we included a few for our parents as well?"

"Of course not!" Maura shook her head. "It'd be nice."

"Brilliant." Evelyn squeezed her hand and then stood up to help her husband. "Lads, I am planning our usual meal. Do either of you have any problems with that?"

"Nope." Stephan smiled at his mother.

Nick was tapping away at his keyboard, oblivious to the conversation flowing around him. When the room grew silent, he glanced up after a moment. He blinked when he saw everyone staring at him. "What'd I miss?"

When he looked at his brother, Evelyn winked at Maura. When her son's eyes returned to her, she beamed at him. "Nicholas, we were just discussing the Christmas menu. I decided I'd like to share my family's traditional meal with Maura; you know, the one Grandma Glynis made when I was a wee lass?"

Nick blanched. "Haggis?" The word sounded strangled.

"Just so." Evelyn nodded in agreement.

"And you agreed to this?" He gave Maura an accusing look.

She just shrugged in response. "I'm a guest here."

"You." He turned to Stephan. "I thought you like her." He pointed at Maura.

Stephan grinned at his brother. "It was that or Granny Cate's steak and kidney pie. You know my feelings about that."

"I'll just skip dinner," Nick muttered under his breath.

Evelyn chuckled. "*I* like Maura too much to do that to her." She then turned back to Maura with a merry look. "Now we find out if you're allowed to stay for supper. Which version of *A Christmas Carol* is your favorite?"

"George C. Scott is my favorite. I also like the Alistair Sims version."

Evelyn beamed at her.

"I still say Mr. Magoo was the best." Andrew noted as he plucked a piece of shortbread off the platter on the countertop.

Stephan grinned at his father. "Maisy's watched the Muppet version on repeat since she found out Maura loves the story. It's grown on me." He looked over at his brother. "What about you, Nick?"

"Bah, humbug." Nick didn't look up from his laptop screen. "It's not my cup of tea."

Stephan grinned at Maura and his parents. "That's right. Nick's more of a *Love Actually* lad."

"You're an arse, Steve." Nick made a face at his brother before returning to his computer.

"What about you, Evelyn?" Maura was curious to learn as much as she could about Stephan's parents.

"I adore the Sims version because it holds a special place in my heart. Mr. Scott was an outstanding Scrooge as well. My absolute favorite holiday movie is *A Child's Christmas in Wales*." Her eyes lit up. "Would you like to join me on the porch to watch?"

Stephan slipped out of the kitchen. He returned a couple of minutes later with the platter and two mugs. "Their movie's almost over. They're going upstairs after. In about ten minutes you can have a better tv." He gave his mother a quizzical look. "What exactly are you going to watch?"

"*A Child's Christmas in Wales*, of course. I brought my DVD with us. I'll go get it now. Why don't you make us up a plate of snacks to enjoy, dear?" She patted Maura's hand as she passed her.

Andrew helped Maura while Stephan went to the living room to put it back to rights as the girls gathered up their pillows, stuffed animals, and blankets to bring back upstairs.

Stephan smiled at Maura when she and his father joined him. "Come sit with me." He patted the spot next to him. Once she'd put the plate down, he wrapped his arms around her waist and tugged her down and onto his lap, shifting his position a bit so that he was angled into the corner.

Maura's exclamation of surprise caught Andrew's attention. He glanced over at the couple and chuckled when Maura's cheeks flushed with color.

The elder Kirklands snuggled up together at the opposite end of the expansive couch. Andrew plucked a blanket from the back and tucked it around himself and his wife. Evelyn shook her head and smiled at Maura. "He's going to fall asleep within ten minutes." She turned her attention to the screen with a contented expression.

Stephan grabbed the other throw that was still resting on the back of the couch. "Are you comfortable or do you want to move?" He whispered his question into Maura's ear.

She shivered against his chest when his warm breath tickled the sensitive hairs by her ear. "Should I?" She whispered her reply back.

Stephan's response was to settle back deeper into the cushions and pull the colorful afghan over them. Once they were tucked in, he made a quiet, contented sound and held her close.

True to Evelyn's prediction, Andrew was snoring softly fifteen minutes into the movie.

The low lighting and feeling of security in Stephan's arms lulled Maura into a deeply relaxed state as well. The anxiety of the week and excitement of the day caught up with her. She promised herself she'd only shut her eyes for a moment as she rested against Stephan's shoulder.

"Maura, honey, it's time to wake up." Stephan's voice sounded regretful as it pierced her consciousness.

Maura struggled to come awake. She heard Andrew's low, rumbly voice as well as Nicholas's coming from the entry to the kitchen. She grimaced as she saw the credits rolling by on the screen. She glanced over at Evelyn, who gave her an affectionate look.

"We'll watch it again sometime when it hasn't been as full a day."

"I'm so sorry." Maura's voice was still thick with sleep.

"No worries, dear."

Stephan gently stroked a lock of hair off her face and tucked it behind her ear. "I'm sorry I had to wake you. I need to check on the girls and Nick wants to go to bed."

Maura nodded. "I didn't mean to fall asleep."

"I know, love. You needed it, though." He dropped a gentle kiss onto her temple. "Let me check on the girls. Then I'll walk you home."

"You don't need to." The response was automatic.

"I want to." He gave her a brief hug before sliding her off his lap and onto the cushion so he could stand. Stephan stretched and winced when his arm cracked. "I'll be back down in a couple of minutes."

Maura nodded and started to gather up plates. She felt Evelyn's cool hand rest on her own. "Nick can take care of that. Don't fuss." The other woman gave Maura's hand a gentle squeeze. "This has been a lovely day. I'm so glad you shared it with us."

"Me too," Maura gave her a sleepy smile. "Are you sure, though? I can help clean up."

"Don't fuss. Here, Nick. Take these into the kitchen. Now, Maura, tomorrow I'd love it if you'd join me and Maisy at the cove again for a bit if you have the time."

"Uh." With her brain as sleep fogged as it was, Maura couldn't pull up a mental image of her schedule.

"Get a good night's rest. I'll talk to you tomorrow." Evelyn stood up and helped Nick begin to take the plates to the kitchen.

"Thank you, good night." Maura was stumbling over her words and felt a surge of embarrassment over her awkwardness, but was too befuddled to do anything about it. She rubbed at her eyes and then covered her mouth so her yawn was hidden.

She was sliding into her boots when Stephan reached the bottom of the steps. He held her hand as they stepped out into the bitter air.

Maura shivered as the icy blast of wind off the ocean hit the exposed skin of her face.

"Come on." Stephan wrapped an arm around her waist and guided her across the street at a brisk pace. When they reached her house and she was fumbling with her new keys, he gently took them from her and slid them into the locks to open the door.

Maura was still tugging off her boots and jacket when she noticed Stephan was heading into the kitchen. She blinked slowly as she realized he was feeding the cats. Her lips curved into a sleepy smile. Once she was out of her boots, she padded into the kitchen after him. "You're pretty wonderful, you know."

He grinned at her. "I'll get on Tim's good side yet." He put their dishes on the floor before reaching for Maura's hand. "Come on, I'll tuck you in and then head home."

"You don't have to do that," she protested.

"I want to." He laced his fingers through hers and walked up the stairs with her.

"I'd like that," she admitted in a sleepy voice. She stopped at the bathroom door. "I'd better brush my teeth first."

"I'll meet you in your room," Stephan's voice was soft and low and sent a frisson of pleasure skittering down Maura's spine.

She hurried through her ablutions. "Oh." Maura took in the turned-down covers of her bed in the low light that Stephan had turned on.

He was holding a soft flannel nightgown. The blues and greens were faded from being washed over the years and the cuff of the left sleeve was fraying, but Maura couldn't bear to part with the comfortable sleepwear.

"Let's get you ready."

Her eyes widened in surprise. "Uh—"

Stephan's arms wrapped around her, gently tugging her sweater up and over her head. He then slid them back down her torso, lingering at her breasts and hips before gently tugging the simple silken shirt that remained out from under the waistband of her jeans. He took his time sliding it up, letting his hands roam on her soft skin.

Maura's breath hitched as the sensations flooded her. She started to reach to help but stilled when he shook his head and whispered, "Let me, please."

"Okay." She lowered her hands and rested them on his hips.

Once her undershirt had followed her sweater onto the nearby armchair, Maura shivered as the cool air hit her skin.

Stephan bent to kiss her as he undid the clasp of her bra and let it fall to the floor.

She sighed against his lips. Maura wasn't quite sure how they finally ended up in her bed. She gazed at Stephan in a pleasured stupor when he was sliding her nightgown down over her body and tucking the blankets around her before pulling his own cloth-ing back on. "I could get used to this," she murmured.

"Me too, love, me too." Stephan gave her a lingering kiss and then, with a regretful expression, reached over to turn off the small lamp. Stephan ran a hand down her cheek and dropped a gentle kiss on her lips before whispering, "I love you."

She smiled as she slid back into a deep sleep.

CHAPTER 16

The next few days passed in a flurry of activity. Maura spent long hours at work and helping with various civic projects. Her remaining free time was spent lending a hand over at the school for the final rehearsals of the annual holiday play.

Stephan was busy with his family and with the ongoing investigation into the break-ins that continued to periodically happen across the island. Most continued to be summer homes, but there were a couple more occupied homes hit. People were on edge and the officers on the small police force were all feeling the pressure and frustration that came from not being able to stop the burglaries.

The day before the play, Stephan decided to take advantage of the mild air to take a long circuit around the town and harbor on foot. His path eventually led to Liz's apartment.

Stephan leaned against a tree and studied the balcony. He thought they could bring a ladder and carry it from the parking lot. Maura had expressed concerns that it'd be too noisy and Nick had been skeptical that they'd be able to drag one out that would be tall enough. Studying the lay of the land, Stephan was forced to acknowledge they were both right. He frowned as he mulled over the problem.

"Are you casing my house?" A familiar voice called out from above Stephan's head.

He looked up and a wide smile formed on his lips when he saw Chip leaning against the railing of the balcony next to Liz's. There were only a couple of feet between the two structures. "Your house?"

Chip rested his elbows on the railing and let his hands dangle. "Well, I don't own the joint, but I've been renting here for a while now. Seriously, dude, what're you doing?"

"Can we talk?"

"Sure." Chip shrugged. "Come on up."

Stephan jogged back around to the front of the building and reached the door just as Chip was unlocking it.

"Welcome to *mi casa*, or something like that. I failed Spanish. Heck, I barely passed English." Chip chuckled, made a grand flourishing gesture with his arm, and indicated Stephan should go up the stairs first.

The apartment was a mirror image of Liz's in layout, but that was where the similarities ended. A huge TV and sofa dominated the main room. A dining room table was pushed against the kitchen wall. Video game cases and controllers were strewn across a long coffee table, along with a bunch of empty mugs and beer bottles.

Chip dropped down onto one end of the sofa. "So, what're you doing?"

"We're trying to play Santa to Fern without Liz knowing." Stephan tipped his head towards Chip's slider. "I was looking to see if a ladder could reach."

"You'd need a construction one, and that'd be hard to get back here without anyone noticing. We all keep an eye out for one another. Everyone's extra jumpy lately." Chip gave him a considering look. "Liz cooks for me and my roomie sometimes, and Fern's a good kid. She's wicked at Mario Cart. Liz doesn't like charity, you know."

"That's why I can't tell her what we're doing. She'd say no."

Chip nodded. "Use my side. You can at least toss things over, unless they're fragile." Chip's face lit up. "Or, even better, Matt can hop over and we can pass things to him. He can set it up, all pretty-like."

"Are you sure that's safe?" Stephan glanced towards the balcony.

"Matt's like a cat. It's an easy hop for him."

"You know this from experience?" Stephan couldn't help the amusement that entered his voice.

"Ya want our help or not, flatlander?" Chip waggled his eyebrows at the older officer.

"I'd be grateful for your help."

"Awesome. It'll be fun. Matt and I'll get something, too. They're pretty chill neighbors to have."

Stephan grinned. "Fantastic. This is a huge help."

"You got it, dude. It's for a good cause." Chip stood up. "Just glad you weren't out there because you were worried about us getting hit."

"I have no reason to think you would be. No one on Water or High Street has been bothered. Too many people around, I think."

Chip nodded. "Lots of busybodies around here." He said it without a trace of self-awareness. "Enjoy the play tomorrow."

When Stephan reached the street, he started whistling a cheerful rendition of "Santa Claus is Coming to Town" as he went about the rest of his circuit.

Concerns about more break-ins during the performance, when many in the community would be filling the large gymnasium, were high in the police department. In the end, they decided Colleen and Chip would manage dispatch and patrol, while Ron and Stephan would attend the performance. Both men agreed they'd each take note of who was and wasn't there. It was the best the small team could do.

Large, puffy flakes of snow floated through the air, drifting on breezes from the sea, before lazily spiraling down to the ground as Stephan helped his mother out of the car. He held her arm as they walked towards the two-story building that stood on one of the higher hills on the island. Every light in the school was on.

Nick shot his brother an inscrutable look. "They teach all the levels in this building?"

"They do." Stephan pointed to the side of the building. "There's a wing over there that you can't quite see for the lower school. They have a nice playground back there. The younger kids only share the cafeteria, gym, and arts spaces with the older kids." He shrugged. "It's more cost-effective and keeps them from having to get bussed to Ellsworth. Apparently, the issue of consolidation comes up every few years, but the townsfolk have resisted it and pushed back on the state successfully so far. Ron tells me it's likely to happen for the older grades the next time there's a budget crunch."

Nick nodded and followed their parents into the building. The large, wood-framed outer doors were propped open and the interior glass ones were being opened by a pair of smiling teenagers in gaudily decorated sweaters.

"Hey, Officer K!" A lanky boy with a mop of blond curls greeted Stephan as he opened the door for the Kirklands. "I finished that essay for my application."

"I look forward to reading it, Pete. Are you working the evening shift tomorrow?"

"You know it." The kid gave him a thumbs-up. "I need to earn extra money to pay for Deirdre's Christmas gift."

Stephan patted him on the shoulder and quickly introduced the young man he was mentoring through a state-sponsored vocation program to his family before noting, "We'd better get in and find some seats so we're not stuck way in back."

The dark-haired girl who was helping at the other door grinned at Stephan and chimed in. "Miz Ballard already reserved seats for all of you up front."

Stephan chuckled. "Thanks, Maggie. How will we know which seats are ours?"

"You'll see." The girl's eyes were gleaming. "She wanted to surprise you."

"I'm surprised already." He nodded in greeting to a boisterous group of teenagers who were jostling one another through the doors. "We'd better get out of the way."

"See you inside, Officer K!" The kids waved and turned to greet their friends.

The family made their way down the wide hallway, pausing periodically for the Kirklands to admire artwork that filled the walls above the lockers. When they reached the wide entryway to the gym, Maura smiled at them. A cheerful Santa hat with her name written in gold glitter on the ruff was pinned at a jaunty angle on top of her russet curls. "Hi!" She gave Evelyn and Andrew friendly hugs hello, nodded to Nick, and gave Stephan a brief kiss. She handed them each a colorful program. "I still have to help out up here, but I'll show you to our seats."

"Pete and Maggie said something about that." Stephan was meticulous about reading all of the information that came home from the school. It concerned him that he'd missed something.

Maura grinned at him. "The PTO does a fundraiser every year. I made sure your notice was diverted. I wanted to surprise you and make sure you can take pictures unobstructed. The Moore's and their extended family are next to us, except Ron. He asked me to tell you that he'd stay in the back corner to keep an eye on everyone." She gave him a questioning look. "I didn't think you'd mind. Do you?"

"Not at all," he assured her and reached for Maura's hand as she proceeded to lead them into the cheerfully decorated gym. The stage was lit with strands of twinkling lights. Ropes of fresh greenery hung below the footlights. Row upon row of chairs filled the space. Many had hats with names set on the seats.

"How does this work as a fundraiser?" Evelyn was charmed by the setting.

"The PTO sells the hats every year. With an extra donation, you can pick your seats early. You put your hats on the seats to reserve them in the order that you turned in your money."

"What's to keep someone from moving them?" Nick was busy watching people shout greetings across the large space and glanced at Maura only briefly.

"The honor system." She shrugged. "If someone wants to cheat, they can, but it doesn't go over well. The current PTO president, Janice Beals, is a stickler for following the rules. She has a master seating chart. She fills it out as each seat is reserved. She knows if any shenanigans go on and steps in."

Stephan commented, "She scares me. I wouldn't mess with her."

Maura grinned. "Most people feel that way." She chuckled. "The PTO has become a model of efficiency the past few years under her leadership, from what I've heard."

As they reached the front center row Stephan squeezed Maura's hand. "You must have been on top of this from the start to get these spots."

He dropped an impulsive kiss on her lips and then moved so his parents and brother could choose their seats while Maura hurried back to her post. Vicky Moore waved to them from a few seats down and before he knew it, Stephan was being embraced and introduced to her and Ron's parents, siblings, and assorted spouses. By the time all the family members from both clans were introduced and had made small talk, a group of adults and teens dressed in black and carrying a range of instruments made their way down the left-side aisle and arranged themselves in seats angled to face the audience. A mismatched assortment of stands stood in front of the musicians. Belatedly remembering he was supposed to be observing the crowd, Stephan studied the room behind them. He heard a slight hiss nearby and noticed Nick scowling. Stephan elbowed him in the ribs. "It's only an hour of your life. You can cope with it, mate."

"Huh?" Nick registered what his brother had said and shook his head. "Who's that?" He gestured towards the aisle nearest them without taking his gaze off of the person in question.

Stephan's eyes narrowed when he saw Joey Thompson had snaked an arm around Maura's waist. She sidestepped away from him but couldn't move far because she was boxed in on the other side by Eliza Thompson and her sister. Her back was ramrod-straight, and he could read the discomfort in her body language as Joey moved closer to her.

"A tosser." His voice was tight. He was about to go to Maura when he saw her reach behind to grasp Joey's index finger and start bending it backwards. There was a brief war of wills before the brawny man dropped his arm and gave Maura a sardonic smile. He turned his head and winked at Stephan and Nick before moving down a long row filled with members of the extended Thompson family.

Joey picked up a cheerful Santa hat and stuffed it in his back pocket before sprawling out in his chair.

Joey's brother, Mike, had witnessed the entire interaction. He was frowning when Joey looked his way.

"What?"

"Are you still stuck on Maura?" Mike searched his younger brother's face. "I thought you got over that crush years ago, bro."

"I did." Joey grinned. "But I like yanking her chain, and did ya see the looks the flatlander and his brother gave me? Totally makes having to sit through this bullshit worth it."

A number of thoughts flitted through Mike's brain as he glanced back at the woman their grandmother was now holding onto and then at his sibling. His eyes reflected the worry he often felt when thinking about his brother. Joey's secretiveness and the rough crew he hung with bothered the rule- and order-loving man. "I wish you'd find a nice woman and settle down, Joe. Don't you want a family of your own?"

Joey's eyes tracked up and down the five rows of folding chairs filled with members of their immediate and extended family. Several bounced fretful babies and toddlers in their arms, while others tried to distract preschoolers who wanted to run wild in the crowd. He chuckled and smiled at Mike. "Nah, I'm good."

When the microphones issued an ear-piercing screech of feedback, Maura winced and glanced at the stage. Her eyes landed on Stephan and the tightness around her eyes and lips eased. As he watched, she gave each women a squeeze and hurried down the aisle to him.

"Sorry. Eliza and Mary wanted to finalize plans for the new book club they're trying to start after the holidays."

Stephan stood up and gave her a hug. He whispered in her ear, "Was Joey bothering you?"

Maura grimaced. "I thought he'd finally gotten the message when you and I started dating." She shook her head. She wasn't going to let the other man intrude on the evening.

Stephan clearly wanted to ask more, but the lights flickered and went out. He and Maura took their seats. She didn't see the sharp look Nick gave her, but Stephan did. He shook his head at his brother and reached for Maura's right hand. He laced his fingers through hers and felt her relax next to him.

It wasn't the time or place, but there hadn't been an opportunity all week so Maura gave in to the impulse. She leaned over so she was as close to Stephan as possible and whispered "I love you," into his ear.

The makeshift band burst into a rousing rendition of 'Jingle Bells' before he could respond. Stephan had to settle for squeezing her hand and nudging his chair closer to hers. Maura turned her attention to the stage and snuggled close.

A series of colored lights illuminated the backdrop of a painted forest. It was effective at mimicking the late afternoon sun dappling a shadowed wood and helped set the mood.

Five minutes into the show, Stephan glanced over at his family and saw they were all transfixed by the play, a series of vignettes interspersed with songs and poetry readings. There was a breadth of musical and artistic talent in the community that constantly surprised him. It spilled over into even a school play. The youngsters were hardly polished actors, but the storyline was good and the production simple enough that they were able to do a credible job carrying it off. The music was excellent for an amateur performance, and the set design and costumes were surprisingly professional. He knew Vicky and Maura had lent their considerable talents to that part of the production.

When the lights came back on and all 235 students from the school crammed onto the stage and floor in front of it, they were met with thunderous applause and a standing ovation. A pair of seniors brought out a bouquet of flowers and called for the school's music (and middle school science) teacher Sally Jeffries to join them up front. They made a short, funny speech that lauded her patience and talent before inviting the audience to the cafeteria for refreshments.

"Well, that was just delightful!" Evelyn's face was glowing as she turned to Stephan and Maura. "I had no idea they'd do such a fine job."

Because there was a crush of people behind them, the families in the front few rows congregated together to chat.

Vicky approached Stephan and Maura. "Maura, can I borrow you for a few minutes? I need help wrangling costumes and you know what to do."

"Of course," Maura smiled at the Kirklands. "Please excuse me. I'll find you in the cafeteria."

The two women slipped out a side door that led outside and offered a shortcut to the elementary wing. Stephan and his family made their slow way towards the main entrance with Ron's parents, who were peppering the Kirklands with questions.

The group followed the masses to the noise-filled cafeteria. There were far too many people to fit inside and groups spilled out into the hallway.

Stephan waved to Liz when he spied the tall waitress. She smiled and waved back. Fern was already by her side, glowing and chatting with an older, smaller version of Liz.

"Daddy!" Maisy plowed into Stephan's side, knocking him into his brother.

Nick steadied him and reached over to swing Maisy up into his arms. "You were, to quote a girl I know, *amazeballs*, Maisy Daze."

Maisy laughed and hugged her uncle. "You have to say that. You love me. Put me down. I don't want to look like a baby."

Nick laughed and hugged her before setting her back on her feet.

"Did you like the play, Gran? Gramps?"

"Oh, we did indeed, love."

"It was brilliant, dear."

"Daddy?"

Stephan knelt and gave his daughter a fierce hug and kiss on the cheek. "I loved it, sweetheart. You all did such a fantastic job."

She beamed at him and then grabbed her grandparents by their hands. "Come meet my teachers! I've told them all about you. They're super stoked to meet you!"

Stephan straightened up and smiled at Nick. "Did you enjoy yourself?"

"I did, far more than I was expecting at that." Nick kept glancing over at Fern and Liz. "Let's go say hello to Fern. I'd like to compliment her on her acting."

Stephan's eyes sparked in amusement. The quiet girl's only line had been "What's that?" and singing in the chorus.

"What?" Nick's tone was defensive. "It took guts to get up in front of all these people."

"I'm not disputing that." Stephan held his hands up and then gestured for Nick to go first as they worked to wend their way through the press of bodies.

Stephan was stopped frequently by youth and adults alike. Nick quickly grew bored standing and smiling politely as one person after another wanted to either compliment Maisy or ask Stephan a question. He slipped away and made a beeline for Liz.

When he reached the mother and daughter, they were standing and chatting with a couple of mothers and children. As he approached, the others smiled at Liz and moved towards the table that was loaded down with refreshments. Fern gave him a wide smile when he approached. "Hi Nick! Did you like the play?"

"Mr. Kirkland," Liz corrected her automatically.

"I told her she should call me Nick the other night. Mr. Kirkland is my father."

Fern's eyes were dancing with amusement when she told her mother. "And he told me to call him Gramps because Mr. Kirkland was HIS father."

Liz shook her head and rested her hand on her daughter's shoulder. "As long as you're being respectful, I suppose it's okay."

Nick gave both of them an easy smile. "I thought you did a brilliant job, Fern."

The child's cheeks pinkened with pleasure. "I didn't have to say much."

"Yes, but you conveyed so much emotion with your expression. You could be a fine actress, if you chose."

Fern shifted uneasily and gave her mother a wary look.

Liz looked like she'd just tasted a sour lemon, but managed to give Nick a tight smile. "That's kind of you to say, Mr. Kirkland."

"Nick." Nicholas wasn't sure why, but it was clear his words had put the unhappy look on Liz's face. He frowned in response.

Hyperaware of her mother's feelings toward all things related to drama and acting because of her aunt, Fern tried to change the subject. "What'd you think of the backdrop?"

Nick gave her a fleeting smile in appreciation for her effort. "It was lovely. It looked just like a winter wood. You must have some talented artists in the school, or did the teacher do it?"

Fern was grinning at him and even Liz's smile had reappeared. "We do, but it was Miss Ballard who did most of it. She always helps with the holiday play." Fern's eyes darted between the adults. "Would you like a cookie? Mama, would you like one?"

"Oh, uh—" Liz hesitated.

Nick glanced over at the spread. "I'd love to try whatever you think looks good Fern. Thank you."

"She's a great kid," Nick commented after Fern scampered off.

Liz nodded in agreement. "The best."

"She's a good influence on Maisy."

Unsure of how to respond to that, Liz gave a noncommittal shrug. "The girls play nicely together. I'm glad Fern has a friend her age. It's hard sometimes in such a small school."

Nick looked around and nodded. "A lot of these kids are related to each other, aren't they?"

"Yes," Liz glanced over at the table to check on her daughter's progress.

"Does Fern have cousins here, too?"

Liz studied Nick's face for a moment, trying to discern if he was just making small talk or if he had an unnatural interest in her child. She blew out a sigh of relief when Stephan came up next to her and gave her a brief, one-armed hug. "Fern did great tonight, Liz. They all did."

She gave him an easy smile. "Maisy did, too. I was impressed she remembered that entire poem."

Stephan laughed. "She's been reciting it endlessly for weeks. I think I have it memorized too."

"I bet." Liz chuckled.

"Do they put on the same show each year or does it change?"

"Some bits stay the same and parts change," Liz explained. "The singalong at the end is always there, and Sally tries to reuse as many costumes as possible in the production, so there's usually snowflakes, snow sprites or snow fairies, and always wild creatures."

Fern returned with a plate loaded with cookies and a couple of frosted brownies. She smiled at the adults. "I brought enough for everyone to share." She was quick to explain, wanting to make sure no one thought she was being greedy and taking more than her share of the treats.

"That was thoughtful, Fern." Stephan grinned at her and eyed the baked goods.

"Mama, which would you like?" Fern offered the plate to her mother first.

"Why don't we see what Mr. Kirkland and Officer Kirkland would like first? Thank you, sweetheart."

Stephan raised an eyebrow at the fact that he'd become Officer Kirkland again for the first time in months. He noticed a flash of annoyance cross Nick's face. Figuring he'd missed something between the two of them, Stephan looked down at the plate Fern was holding and asked the girl, "What do you recommend?"

"All of it. I picked my favorite things."

"Clever girl." Stephan plucked a butter cookie with a bright red cherry in the center. "I'll try this. I don't think I've ever had one before."

Fern's jaw dropped. "Never?"

Stephan shook his head. "Never ever."

The child gave him a pitying look and then offered the plate to Nicholas, who selected a brownie in silence. Liz encouraged Fern to take something before choosing a simple piece of shortbread for herself.

Fern grinned at her. "Maisy's gran made those. They're so yummy."

Liz laughed. "Since you gorged yourself on them last time you were over at the Kirklands, they must be." She took a bite and smiled in pleasure at the rich flavor and flaky texture. She gave her daughter a nod of approval.

Nick forced himself to stop staring at Liz's mouth and looked down at the brownie in his hand. "I'm going to go get a drink to go with this. Can I get anyone anything?" When the others shook their heads, he stalked off.

Liz watched him go with a furrowed brow.

Stephan shook his head. "Don't pay any attention to him. He gets cranky when we pull him away from his work." He snaked an arm around Maura's waist as she joined them. He noticed the tension leave Liz's expression and wondered what his brother had said.

CHAPTER 17

The fragrant smell of roasting chicken hit Maura's nose as Maisy let her in.

Maisy's eyes gleamed as she studied Maura's two large shopping bags that held cheerfully wrapped presents as well as her contributions towards dinner. "That's a lot of gifts, Maura."

"Some are even for you," Maura teased the girl.

Maisy gave her an irrepressible smile in response. "I know."

"Sure of yourself, are you?"

The child pointed to a package wrapped with a festive candy cane ribbon and a tag that read "Maisy," in Maura's neat script.

The woman laughed. "Want to help me put these under the tree?"

"Yes!" Maisy was eager to feel the packages and try and guess what they contained before her father came along and squashed the game. "Want me to carry a bag?"

"Sure." Maura gave her the lighter one. "Be careful with it, though. Your uncle's gift is fragile."

"Okay." Maisy took the bag and carried it with care as she led Maura into the living room. A bunch of festively wrapped presents already spilled out from under the tree. "Can I help you?"

"Of course." Maura set her bag down. "Just let me take care of these two." She reached in and eased out Andrew's gift and the clamshell with a painting of the cove inside it that she'd made Nicholas. After a moment's deliberation, she stowed Nicholas's shell on a bottom bough of the tree, where the branches formed a net of sorts.

"Ooh, that's a good idea!" Maisy took some of the smaller, lighter boxes and put them in the tree as well. "I'm so excited. I might jump out of my skin or burst."

Maura laughed. "You'd miss Christmas if you did that."

Maisy grabbed her hand. "Come on. Let's bring your bag upstairs and then go hang out in the kitchen with Gran. You can help me set the table."

"I'd love that." Maura let the girl tug her towards the stairs.

"Maisy, did I hear—ah, it was you." Stephan met them in the hall and kissed Maura hello. "I see the welcome committee found you."

"We're bringing Maura's stuff upstairs and then going to the kitchen."

"I'll come with you." Stephan rested his hand on the small of Maura's back as they made their way up the stairs.

Maisy started to lead Maura into her room and stopped to give her father a quizzical look when he cleared his throat. "Ohh, right." She backed out and continued down the hall to the small guest room Stephan had claimed as his own.

Aside from the full-sized bed, a simple dresser, night stand and lamp there wasn't much more in there. A few framed pictures dotted the dresser and a couple of books were on the night stand. The attached bathroom held personal items, but on the whole, it looked like he was staying in a hotel.

Stephan reached for Maura's hand when Maisy liberated it to go bounce on the bed.

"When we move into our own house, Daddy promised he'd hang his pictures up and that we'll have our old furniture back from storage. He has the coolest chest. It's like a treasure chest.

There're all sorts of old things from his grandparents in there. My favorite is the zoo animals."

"It's a Noah's Ark," Stephan corrected her. "My great-grandfather carved it."

Maisy shrugged. "The animals are really cool, Maura. You'll love playing with it with me."

Stephan opened his mouth to say something and then shut it when Maura squeezed his hand. "I look forward to that, Maisy."

"Let's go back to Gran!"

"Scoot on down. We'll be there soon." Stephan nudged his daughter out the door and on her way.

When they were alone, he wrapped his arms around Maura. "I love you and am glad you agreed to spend the night."

She tipped her head back to smile at him. "Tim might feel otherwise, but I'm happy I'm here."

"I'll buy Tim a chicken and cook him a feast."

"Bribery might work."

Stephan brushed a lock of hair back behind her ear and lowered his head. "I'd like to enjoy the few minutes of privacy we have until God knows when."

The afternoon and evening passed with plenty of banter, laughter, and comradery as the Kirklands and Maura got to know each other better over baking, cooking, and, later, feasting. When a Monopoly game turned cutthroat, Maura gratefully lost and joined Andrew and Evelyn on the couch with a small glass of sherry as Maisy, Nick, and Stephan battled it out.

Evelyn swirled the amber liquid around. "Maura, how does Liz get her cordial to have such a pretty purple tone? I've never had elderberry that color before."

"Lavender and I think a bit of wild blueberry, but she's pretty tight-lipped about her exact recipe."

"I don't blame her. It's wonderful stuff. She should be selling it."

"I know she looked into it at one time, but the costs were prohibitive. She could try the farmers' market in the summer, but it didn't make financial sense. It's her busy season at Madras. She'd never see Fern if she did that."

"It must be hard being a single parent." Sympathy washed over Evelyn's face.

Stephan glanced over at his mother and cocked an eyebrow.

"Yes, dear, we know you're a single parent too, but I mean without resources to help ease some of the burdens."

He nodded in agreement and returned his attention to the game, taking advantage of Nick's distraction by the conversation to neglect paying him for a stay at the hotels lining Boardwalk.

Maisy started giggling when she saw what her father had done, but didn't tattle on him. "Your turn, Uncle Nick."

"Huh? Okay." Nick rolled the dice and took his turn.

Maisy quickly took hers, too, and then handed her father the dice while chortling.

Nick gave her a bemused look as she toppled over and started rolling around on the floor with laughter. "How many cookies did you let her eat?" He glanced over at his brother, who was moving the shoe around Go.

"Only a few."

"Are you sure about that?"

"Positive."

Nick gave his niece a dubious look, handed his brother $200 for passing Go, then picked up the dice.

Maisy's face was red and she was gasping, but she managed to sit up. She wiped tears away from her eyes. "Uncle….Nick…. Daddy….got you!" She went off in gales of laughter again.

Nick's eyes narrowed as he took in Stephan's place on the board. "Did you just cheat?" He shot his brother an accusatory look.

"It's not cheating in Monopoly if you don't get caught." Stephan gave him an unrepentant smile.

"Did you all see it and not say anything?" Nick looked at his parents and Maura in disbelief.

"Maura and I were chatting, dear. We weren't paying attention to the game."

Andrew smiled at his older son. "I learned to stay out of things that don't concern me with you lads a long time ago. It's saved me a world of grief over the years."

"You." Nick pointed an index finger at Stephan. "You are going down."

Stephan shrugged. "Going to have to keep your head in the game for that to happen, Nick."

A half hour later, Maisy flopped onto the couch across Maura and her grandparents' laps. "Can we read some stories before we put out milk and cookies? Oh, and we need to put out the reindeer food Ms. Meg helped us make at school. And carrots; we need to put out carrots too. Maura, do you think Rudolph will be coming? Gramps, was Rudolph alive when you were a boy? Gran, how old do reindeer get?"

Evelyn gave the child an indulgent smile. "Go get your books, lass. We'll read and see if we can answer some of your questions."

"Okay." Maisy rolled off their laps and scampered upstairs. She'd just returned with a stack of books when Nick let out a shout that caused everyone to look over at the two men.

"Victory is mine! Even cheating, you couldn't break my streak!"

Stephan slowly untangled his legs and stood up stiffly, shaking his limbs out to regain feeling in them after hours of sitting cross-legged on the floor. "Good game, Nick. Enjoy cleaning it up."

"Arse."

Stephan just smiled at his brother and wandered into the kitchen. When he came back, he handed Nick a beer and put a simple cheese and cracker board out onto the table before sitting on the other end of the sturdy coffee table. "Which book are we reading first Maisy?"

"Maura's going to read *The Grinch*, of course. Gramps will read *The Night Before Christmas* last. Gran wants to read *The Polar Express*. I'm giving Uncle Nick *Llama Llama*. That leaves you *Red and Lulu*."

"That's a lot of books," Nick commented.

"You can go first if you want." Maisy gave him a sweet smile. "I gave you the shortest book."

"And then it'll be time for you to head to bed, young lady."

"After we put everything out. And I still have to hang my stocking."

"Yes, after that," Stephan agreed. He stood up and picked up one of the armchairs to move it closer to the corner of the couch Maura was seated in. He waved her back when she moved to stand up and give him her spot.

Maisy reached for her grandmother's hand and then Maura's and gave a happy sigh. "I love Christmas." Her eyes lingered at the pile of presents that had been steadily appearing under the tree all day. "Are you sure I can't open just one tonight, Daddy?"

"We'll see after the stories."

By the time Andrew's deep voice uttered, "Happy Christmas to all and to all a good night!" the child's head was resting against Maura's shoulder and her eyes were drifting closed.

Stephan considered his daughter for a moment. He knew she'd be likely to pop up in the middle of the night if he put her to bed without putting out all the goodies. He slid out of his chair and picked Maisy up. "Love, time to get the cookies and milk."

Maisy forced her eyes open. "And carrots. And we need to sprinkle the reindeer food outside."

Stephan shook his head. "You're not going outside."

Maisy frowned at him.

Maura interceded. "I could use some fresh air. What about if you tell me where you want it and watch from the window while I sprinkle it around?"

The girl nodded. "Thanks, Maura. I'm worried Santa might not realize I'm here and the sparkles will help the reindeer find me."

Maura smiled. "I understand."

After a small plate and glass of milk were filled and placed near the fireplace, Maisy gave Maura the baggie she'd filled at school. Stephan picked a gold-wrapped present out from under the tree and handed it to his daughter. "Still want to open one tonight?"

Maisy nodded her head vigorously. She ripped through the paper and squealed when it opened to reveal a soft plush seal. "I love her so much! Thank you, Daddy!" She hugged the stuffed animal to her chest.

"I'm glad, love. Okay, reindeer food and then bed."

"Okay. Oh, wait." She wiggled away from her father. "I need to kiss everyone goodnight!" Maisy scampered around hugging and kissing everyone. She whispered something in Maura's ear and then reached for her father. Together, they watched Maura slip outside into the cold, calm air. She walked down the road a bit towards the cove.

She started sprinkling bits of the oat and glitter mixture along the roadway and then up the path to their house. She shook the bag out at the front steps and then hurried inside, bringing the crisp tang of the ocean and night air with her.

"That was perfect, thank you, Maura." Maisy reached over from her father's arms and wrapped her own around Maura in a fierce hug. "Merry Christmas!"

"Merry Christmas, sweetheart." Maura returned the hug with a tight squeeze of her own and gave Maisy a kiss on the cheek. "I'll see you in the morning."

"Yay!" Maisy leaned back into her father's arms. "I'm ready to go to bed, Daddy." She hugged him hard and then wiggled out of his arms. "Can I have just a little snuggle?"

"Of course." He walked up the stairs with her as she chatted with him about names for her seal.

When Stephan came back downstairs twenty minutes later, he flopped down onto the couch between his mother and Maura. "She's asleep." He put his cell phone down on the table. "Hopefully she's out for the night."

"We'll manage if she wakes when you're not here." Evelyn handed him a cracker with cheese.

"Thanks, Mum." Stephan popped the snack into his mouth and rested his head back on the pillow. "Maura, would you mind if I shut my eyes for a few minutes?"

"Of course not." She reached for a soft throw blanket and carefully draped it over him. "I'm going to go check on the cats and make sure they're set for the night. I'll be back in a bit." She leaned over and gave him a kiss.

Stephan gave her a sleepy smile and nodded before shutting his eyes.

"Maura, dear, would you mind if I came with you?"

"Not at all." Maura tried to hide her surprise at Evelyn's request.

"Just give me a moment and then I'll be ready."

"Okay." Maura took the opportunity to bring her dishes to the kitchen and put them into the dishwasher. She then picked up the platter and brought it over to the table where Andrew was working on a crossword puzzle and Nick was tapping away on his laptop.

"Thanks, love," Andrew gave her a smile and returned to his crossword puzzle. Nick glanced up and gave her a fleeting smile before turning his attention back to his work.

Maura wandered back into the living room. Stephan was breathing deeply. She sat in the armchair and watched him sleep, wondering if he had learned to fall asleep that fast because of his work or if it just came naturally.

"He could always do that. Me, I lie awake for hours some nights. He gets it from his father." Evelyn showed up next to Maura and gave her son a fond gaze. "I hope I didn't keep you long."

"Not at all." Maura stood up.

The women bundled up to head out into the bracing air. Maura looped her arm through Evelyn's, wanting to make sure the older lady didn't slip on any icy patches in the road. Evelyn slowed her pace as she took in the brilliance of the starry sky.

"The sky was like this in Aberdeenshire, where my grandparents lived in a small town. My sister, brother, and I would spend most of our summer holidays there. The sun stays out long hours that time of year but the times we went in the winter, well, it was like being in church and seeing God all around. You feel like there must be something more when you see how vast the universe is, even in our tiny corner of it."

Maura had tipped her head back and was gazing up at the Milky Way as well. The earlier calmness was shifting with the tides. She couldn't help shivering in the icy wind that skated in off the cove.

"Ah, you're getting chilled, lass. We can't have that." Evelyn patted her arm and started walking again.

Maura's house was only dimly lit with the outside porch light. After she shut the door, a plaintive meow came from the top of the stairs. Maura smiled as Tim raced down and practically jumped into her arms. He wrapped his paws around her neck and began rubbing his head against the side of hers, his purr loud and rumbly in her ear. Maura giggled. "I missed you too, Timmy."

Mags and Greta showed up a moment later, twining around the women's legs. "Mind if I feed them first?"

"Of course not." Evelyn was patting the female cats on their heads.

After getting the cats settled, she offered Evelyn a drink to be polite.

"Actually, I was hoping to see your art room."

"Oh." Maura was surprised but nodded. "Sure. It's just upstairs." She turned lights on to ensure Evelyn could see the stairs clearly. When they reached the top, Maura led Evelyn into the peaceful space.

"This is so cozy." The Scotswoman smiled. "It must get beautiful sunlight during the day with those windows."

"It does." Maura hesitated, curious why Evelyn had wanted to come upstairs.

Evelyn roamed the room, admiring Maura's paintings and Jane's weavings. After several minutes, she sat down on the futon and patted the seat next to her. "I wanted talk where we'd have privacy."

Maura felt a flutter of anxiety in her belly as she sank down onto the plush cushion.

Evelyn reached for Maura's hand and clasped it between her age spotted ones. Her skin was soft and warm to the touch. Tears pricked the back of Maura's eyes. They reminded her of Jane's, except her aunt's had had small callouses on her fingers from years of knitting and weaving.

"I've watched you trying to juggle giving us privacy and letting us get to know you. It hasn't been an easy dance and you've been doing a wonderful job. We are so happy you and Stephan have found one another." Her gaze slid away from Maura's face and to a point over her shoulder for a long moment as she gathered her thoughts and then shifted her eyes back. "Sophie was a beautiful woman. She was vivacious, ambitious, clever, and for years she truly loved Stephan. But over time it became clear, at least to me, that she loved herself more. I think if Maisy hadn't come along, they'd have gone their separate ways. We are all grateful she's with us, but having Maisy meant they stayed in an unhappy marriage longer than was healthy for anyone." She squeezed Maura's hand and released it before settling into the corner of the futon where she could rest and still meet the younger woman's eyes. "Stephan's grown up since those early days. What I've seen between the two of you is so good. Sometimes love that comes later in life is better because we already know who we are." She gave Maura a fond smile. "I promised I wouldn't stick my nose into your private business, but I want you to know how pleased I am and tell you how very welcome you are in our family."

Maura was touched by Evelyn's words. "Thank you. This means so much."

Evelyn patted her on the knee. "It's just the truth. Now, there is a shawl I've heard much about. May I see it?"

Maura shifted uncomfortably. "Maisy told you?"

"About her dreams, yes, and I'm a believer, but I also believe in free will. Stephan was the one who was gobsmacked by your aunt's talent and told me how amazing it is."

"Of course." Maura stood up and went to the closet. With loving hands, she brought it down and handed it to Evelyn. Together they laid it out on the futon and opened it up.

"Oh, my, that's a work of art." Evelyn gently explored the knit seals and waves with her fingertips. "Was she self-taught?"

"No." Maura shook her head. "Her mother was a weaver and her grandmother knit. She learned from both of them before they passed away."

"Did you know your grandmother?"

"No, she died when I was an infant. I have a few pieces of her work here in the house, but not much. She sold most of it. What she did keep, my grandfather gave away to friends before he passed. He didn't think Jane or I would want them, so he didn't bother asking." She shrugged. "He had some strange ideas about family."

"Stephan told me your parents traveled extensively."

Maura nodded. "They were anthropologists. Their research kept them away from home a lot."

Evelyn's expression was filled with sympathy, but Maura didn't see it because her gaze was fixed on the shawl.

"How did your aunt end up here?"

Maura smiled. "She always told me she was drawn to the island. She was already living up here and eking out a life working as an editor and doing her art before I was born. Her grandmother had left her and my mother both inheritances. Aunt Jane used hers to put a down payment on this house." Maura fingered the edge of the shawl. "I was very lucky to have Aunt Jane."

Evelyn gave her an impulsive, tight hug. "I would have loved to have met her."

"She'd have loved you and Andrew."

"That makes me happy to hear."

Maura felt her phone buzz in her pocket and pulled it out to read the brief text. "Santa time." She grinned at Evelyn. "May I walk you home?"

"Don't be silly. Just come outside with me and start warming your car up. I'm sure the lads will be right over."

After Maura turned her car on and stepped back outside with Evelyn, Stephan and Nicholas showed up. Evelyn kissed everyone on the cheek and waved Stephan off when he tried to walk her back to the house. "Get on with you."

They hurried into the car to get out of the cold. Stephan grinned at Maura from the passenger seat. "I'm looking forward to this." He glanced back at his brother and laughed to see Nick's long legs folded up practically to his chest in the small back seat. "You okay back there?"

"I'll survive." Nick sounded cranky.

Stephan grinned at Maura. "Chip said their apartment's been quiet for a half hour now. Matt slipped across to their balcony once already to peek inside."

As they continued to drive down the dark, winding road with Maura's headlights cutting the black, Nicholas broke the silence that had fallen. "Don't you get lonely living out here?"

"Not as much as I thought we would." Stephan gave Maura a smile and then winced when a hand hit the back of his head. "What the?"

"I was asking Maura, you twit."

"Oh." Maura glanced at Nick in the rearview mirror before focusing her eyes back on the road. "Not often. In the deep of winter when there's a gale blowing for days it can be isolating, but the handful of us who live on the road year-round tend to check in on each other and Liz will usually call for a long chat. I also catch up with my childhood and college friends in the winter."

"But aren't you lonely, I mean, at least before Stephan and Maisy moved across the street?"

She felt Stephan's hand tighten on her leg, but a smile played around Maura's lips. "No, Nick. I wasn't. I mean, I've had my moments, but doesn't everyone? Mostly, I've been happy and content. I keep busy. I have good friends. I enjoy my own company. Stephan and Maisy are wonderful and I'm so happy they're here, but my life was hardly empty before they came."

"That's not what I was—," Nick stopped himself, shook his head, and had the grace to look abashed. "I guess it was."

"Do you ever get lonely, Nick?" Maura glanced at him in the mirror before returning her eyes to the road.

"I live in one of the busiest cities in the world. How could I possibly get lonely?"

"You can be lonely even whilst surrounded by people." Stephan shifted in his seat so he could turn and get a better look at his brother.

Nick gave him an annoyed look, but finally shrugged. "Yeah, sometimes. But most of the time my work and my mates keep me too busy to worry about it."

"You understand, then." Maura nodded.

"I guess I do." He returned to gazing out the window.

As they got closer to the center of town, the houses were closer together and many were lit up against the dark with cheerful displays of lights and lawn ornaments despite the late hour.

When they reached the parking lot, Maura parked as close as she could to the path leading to the front of the building. A figure wearing a cheerful Santa hat appeared in one of the windows above them.

"Load me up," Stephan stretched out his arms. Nick and Maura began piling boxes and packages up. When his arms were full, Maura repeated the process with Nick. By this time Chip had jogged over to them. "Matt's holding the door open, Stevie. You can head on in."

"Stevie?" Nick snickered at his brother as they began walking down the path.

"Stuff it, Knickynack."

"Ouch, I haven't heard that one since we were in nappies."

A trim, dark-haired man with a thick beard waved to them from the top of the stairs. "Come on up." He gestured with a flannel-covered arm toward the interior of the apartment. "I'm Matt, by the way. Let me help you guys with that stuff." As soon as they started into the apartment, he began plucking boxes out of their arms and setting them down. Once Maura and Chip came in and added their packages to the pile, Matt strode over and swung Maura in the air as he gave her an exuberant hug. "Thanks for all your help."

She returned the hug and gave him a fond smile. "I love your aunt and uncle. I'm glad things worked out."

"They're loving Florida. I'm going to spend January with them."

"Give them my love."

"I will." Matt rubbed his hands together. "This was a wicked awesome idea. I hope you don't mind that we decided to get in on it."

"Of course not." Stephan smiled at the younger men.

Maura started laughing when she saw the mischievous looks on their faces. "I wouldn't be so quick to say that, Stephan."

He raised an eyebrow. "Should I be concerned?"

Chip and Matt exchanged a look and gave identical shrugs. "Nah, we'll help Liz rehome it if Fern can't keep it."

Stephan blanched. "You didn't get her an animal, did you?"

Nick looked at the men with fresh interest.

"Sorta, maybe you should just come see." Chip led Steve out to the balcony. They all heard Stephan's burst of laughter.

"Shhhhhh," multiple voices reprimanded him.

Curious, Maura stuck her heads out of the door to look.

"Oh." Maura's eyes were dancing with amusement as she looked over at Matt. "Liz might just kill you."

He was grinning. "I know. It's great, isn't it?" He held out a necklace with flashing lights in the shape of Christmas tree lights. "I'm going to put this around his neck. I had to cobble six of them together to make it fit."

"It's the size of Fern's bed, Matt."

Nick gave them both skeptical looks. "It can't possibly be that large. It wouldn't fit on the balcony. And I still don't see the problem with a stuffed animal."

Both shrugged at him. "Hopefully there won't be one." Matt gave him an easy smile. "But like I said, if it's too much, we'll rehome it for her. We already have a waiting list. I got this little dude, just in case." He pulled a smaller version of the stuffed bear out of a bag that was sitting on by the door. "I have a necklace for him, too. Wouldn't want him to feel left out." He winked at Maura, who grinned.

"Of course not."

Nick's eyes narrowed as he observed their friendly expressions and easy banter.

Stephan and Chip came back in. Seeing his brother's expression, Stephan gave him a quizzical look. When Nick tipped his head at Maura and Matt, who, with Chip, were sorting out the packages by size, Stephan rolled his eyes and shook his head. "Come on. Let's have some fun."

Once everything had been ferried across, Matt turned on the flashing necklaces before making the jump back to his own balcony.

After a chorus of Christmas wishes, Maura, Stephan, and Nicholas were back outside and heading for her car.

They took care entering the house without speaking and walked in stockinged feet to the living room. The tree was still lit and a few small lights had been left on.

"Wait for me while I lock up and put Father Christmas's gift out? Mum took care of filling her stocking."

"Sure." Maura sank down into a corner of the sofa and tucked her legs under her. "I'll be right here," she mumbled through a jaw-cracking yawn. She let her eyes close as she listened to the low rumble of Nick and Stephan's voices as they spoke in the kitchen. She was slipping into sleep when the cushion next to her sank down and an arm snuck around her shoulders. Maura let out a contented sigh and snuggled into Stephan's embrace. She felt a blanket gently fall around her body and let herself slip into sleep while Stephan and Nick continued their conversation.

"What're you all doing down here? You had a sleepover downstairs without me? Did you see Santa? Did you? Oh, Father Christmas definitely was here!! He filled my stocking so much it overflowed! I'll go tell Gran and Gramps!"

Maura's eyes were gritty and dry as she pried them open.

Nick was snoring loudly from the loveseat. The matching ottoman was pushed up against it and his feet dangled off. A thick quilt was draped over him. He had a pillow mashed up between his head and the corner of the oversized chair. Maura discovered a throw pillow had been put under her head. She'd stretched out and been sleeping with her head on Stephan's lap. His legs were propped up on another ottoman. He gave his daughter a weary smile. "Happy Christmas, love. Maybe take some time to explore what Father Christmas left you in your stocking before you get Gran and Gramps."

"Okay, Daddy. Why aren't you in your PJs?" Maisy looked at Maura. "You're not either. Is Uncle Nick?"

Maura's voice was raspy when she said, "We tried to stay up to see Santa."

Stephan gave her head a gentle caress as she started to sit up. He shifted so she could snuggle back in against his chest.

"Did you see him, Maura?"

"Nope. We fell asleep. But it looks like he covered us all up."

"Santa's nice like that," Maisy agreed. "I'm going to bring my stocking over to you. Move your feet, Daddy."

Stephan gave Maura a gentle kiss and whispered, "Happy Christmas, Maura."

"Merry Christmas, Stephan."

After her initial restraint at bringing a gift to each person and waiting for them to open their present and thank the giver, Maisy became too excited by the bounty of presents. She eagerly burrowed through the mound and began dropping gifts in the adult's laps.

Maura arched an eyebrow as she came to the third book-shaped gift from Nick. She glanced at the ones already beside her; *The Pilot's Wife*, *Nantucket Nights*, and *Anna Karenina*. She carefully slipped a finger under the tape that bound the thick silver and blue paper. When *Lady Chatterley's Lover* and *Madame Bovary* slipped into her lap, unease bloomed in the pit of her stomach. She murmured a thank you to Nick and noticed he was having trouble meeting her gaze. Stephan, Maisy, and Evelyn were all oblivious, but Andrew had taken note of the titles and shot his eldest son a sharp look.

When all of the presents were unwrapped, Maisy did a last check under the tree and backed out with a triumphant grin. "Maura, there's one last gift to you. It was pushed way back in the corner. It's from Uncle Nick." She glanced at the crimson-wrapped package and rolled her eyes at her uncle, whose cheeks were flushed. "It's another book."

"Thank you, Maisy, Nick." Maura didn't want to reach out for the gift. She kept her head down as she broke the tape sealing it shut. She closed her eyes briefly against a flash of pain when she saw a familiar cover for *The Scarlet Letter* appear.

Stephan and Evelyn were already trying to gather up the mounds of paper. Maura kept her head down as she gathered up her pile of presents. She didn't notice when the last book slid to the floor. She whispered something to Stephan. He gave her a kiss before nodding and turning his attention back to Maisy, who was jabbering away. His mother had gone into the kitchen.

Maura mustered up a smile for the other two Kirklands. "Thank you for such a generous Christmas. I need to take care of a few things at my house, but I'll be back in a bit."

She gave Maisy a kiss on the head and headed for the door.

Andrew waited until he and Nick were alone in the living room. He spotted the book Maura had dropped on the floor and picked it up. He glanced at the cover, then strode over to his son and smacked him in the arm with it.

"What was that for?"

"We raised you better than this, Nicholas Ewan Kirkland. What were you thinking?" He kept his voice low, but his anger came through anyway.

Nick didn't try to pretend he didn't know what his father was upset about. "I bought them before we knew her. But they're all classics or popular novels. She might enjoy them."

"She might have enjoyed books if you'd asked your brother who her favorite authors are and gotten something by them, or better yet, something other than books. This was a poorly veiled insult." Andrew smacked him in the arm again with the book before tossing it onto the coffee table and stalking out of the room.

The cold wind coming off the cove brought tears to Maura's eyes. If those tears started flowing faster and harder than the bracing air justified, Maura didn't care and there was no one to see. She hurried to the sanctuary of her own home. The house was cool and dimly lit in the early morning light. She put the gifts down on the first chair she came to and shuffled into the kitchen.

Once her coffee was brewing, she got the cats a special breakfast treat. Tim gave her a lecture about not being home, but purred loudly in her ear when she held him close for a snuggle.

Maura forgot about her coffee and went upstairs. She gathered what she wanted from her room and headed for the shower. She carefully took off the earrings and necklace set Stephan had given her and placed them on the counter. She felt her shoulders drop a bit as she examined the whimsical cat shapes the beautiful stones had been cut into. He'd whispered that he'd tried to find tomatoes, but had been forced to admit defeat and picked out something else that reminded him of her.

Nick's message had been hard to miss. Every single book he'd given her had to do with infidelity. Did he think so little of her? All this time he'd been polite, even friendly. He was more reserved than his parents, but she'd thought they were getting on fine. Now she had to pretend nothing was amiss. Maura was exhausted from the lack of sleep and feeling raw. She wasn't sure how good of an actress she was, but she'd do her best to make sure Maisy and Stephan's Christmas wasn't marred on her account.

She finished up her shower and dressed. Maura was just passing the front door when she heard a gentle knocking. She glanced out the side window and saw Andrew. She hurried to let him in.

He stepped inside and gave a shudder. "It's brass monkeys out there."

She gave him a bemused look.

"It's cold, love, it's damned cold."

Maura nodded. "I made some coffee. Would you like a cup? Or I could make you tea instead."

"I'd love to have a coffee with you, if you don't mind me interrupting your peace."

Once they were seated at the table with steaming mugs and a plate of cookies between them, Andrew reached for Maura's hand and gave it a firm squeeze. "Evelyn and I are delighted that you and Stephan have found each other."

She gave him a tired smile. "Thank you."

He let go of her hand and sat back in his chair. The moment he did, Greta jumped into his lap. She gave a happy purr, sank down, and wiggled around until she was comfortable. "Well, hallo, puss." Andrew gave the longhaired cat's head a gentle stroke.

Maura chuckled. "Stephan's become her favorite person in the world. It looks like you may be auditioning for runner-up. He's the only other person I've seen her do that with." She sipped her coffee. "Do you want me to move her?"

"No." Andrew shook his head and continued to pet the purring cat. "She's quite a sweet thing, isn't she?"

Maura nodded. She stared into her coffee for a long moment, trying to formulate her question in a way that wouldn't be offensive.

Andrew was the first to break the silence that had fallen. "Nicholas was wrong. His worries for Stephan and Maisy blind him sometimes. I want to you to know it's not you. It's just what you represent. He's not normally like this, I promise. Stephan and Maisy have both sang your praises since they moved here. They're close in age, but sometimes he can be an overprotective older brother." He sighed and took a swallow of his coffee. "We've all worried about Maisy these past years. Evie and I have delighted in seeing the changes. We were concerned about how school would go and if she'd ever manage to make friends her own age again after Sophie died." Andrew reached for Maura's hand again and patted it. "She's thriving here. You've played a part in that, a big part, I'd wager. It's the best gift we could have ever been given, Maura. Thank you."

Tears sprang to Maura's eyes and she tried to blink them away. "I'm sure she'd be doing wonderfully without me, but that's nice of you to say."

Andrew squeezed her hand again and then let it go. "It's just the truth, love. Seeing Stephan happy and relaxed in ways we haven't seen in many years is a gift, too." He reached for a cookie. "Please try to bear with Nicholas. He'll come around."

Maura nodded. "It's depressing he thinks I'd do what Sophie did." She shook her head. "That's not who I am."

"We all know that, even Nick." Andrew assured her. "You're strikingly different women. I won't speak ill of my former daughter-in-law, but I think that you are absolutely wonderful for Stephan. I can only hope you feel the same about him." His eyes twinkled at her.

Maura grinned at him. "I do."

"Good. Then you won't let my one son's ninny move ruin your Christmas?"

"I won't," she assured him.

"Cheers." He gave her coffee mug a gentle tap with his own. "Tell me how it went last night. If I were twenty years younger, I'd have been out gallivanting with you."

Maura's face lit up. "It was so much fun. Chip and Matt found an enormous stuffed bear, the local university mascot. Stephan took pictures. Oh," she glanced down at her phone when it started ringing. She gave Andrew an apologetic look. "It's Liz. I'd better take it."

"Of course, dear. I'll just enjoy some more cookies."

Maura answered the phone. "Merry Christmas, Liz."

"I should be furious at you, but I can't be, not with the wonder and joy all of you put on my girl's face." Liz's voice was thick with emotion.

"She liked her surprise?"

"She is over the moon." Liz chuckled. "Of course, being the sweet child she is, she wanted to make sure I knew how much she loved the little doll I got her."

Maura could visualize the conversation.

Liz's voice grew hesitant. "I know the Kirklands and the boys next door were involved, but was anyone else?"

"No," Maura assured her. "It was just us."

"I know I shouldn't be worrying about it, but that relieves me."

"I get it." Maura hesitated. "None of us was intending to embarrass you."

"I know." Liz nodded, even though she knew Maura couldn't see her. "The gift cards were too much, though."

"What gift cards?" Maura looked at Andrew, who shook his head and shrugged.

"The ones tucked into the mittens."

"I don't know anything about them, Liz." Maura felt conflicted all of a sudden. She was still hurt by Nick's implication that she was going to be unfaithful, but she did appreciate his concern for her friend.

"They were for the gas station, Hannaford, Wal-Mart, even a couple of places in Bar Harbor." Liz cleared her throat. "Was he this generous to everyone else? He already gave me a tip the likes of which I've never gotten."

Maura swallowed hard and blinked back tears that pricked her eyes. Nick was clearly capable of great kindness and generosity. She had to clear her own throat before continuing. "I think Fern made a big impression on him."

"In a weird, creepy way? I was a bit concerned at the play, but I thought maybe he's just awkward."

"No, in a 'wow, she's a great kid' kind of way."

"You're sure not in a creepy way? Never mind, it's still weird, Maura, but I'm not going to look a gift horse in the mouth. We can use these. They'll help get us through the winter. What'd he give you?"

Maura gave Andrew an uncomfortable glance before simply saying, "Books."

Liz was silent for a beat. "Books? Books for a woman who is surrounded by more books than she could possibly read in a lifetime?"

"Yes, it was a, um, theme."

"Which was?"

"Some other time."

"I have to get us ready to head over to my mom's. Catch up tomorrow after story time?"

"I'd love to. Tell your parents and Fern I said Merry Christmas!"

After she hung up the phone, Andrew gave her a thoughtful look.

"So, my boy was unexpectedly and overly generous to the point of worrying your friend and a prat to you. Does that sum things up?"

Maura struggled to answer, not wanting to be petty.

Andrew nodded and patted her hand. "He'll come around. I'm sorry he's being an arse, though I'm glad he's choosing to help Fern and Liz out. He can well afford to. It's good he does something useful with his money. He has pots of it."

She smiled in response, which eased the remaining worry from Andrew's face.

He drained the remainder of his coffee and began gathering up the dirty dishes to bring them to the sink. "Will you come back over with me now, or do you need some alone time?"

Maura hesitated a moment. Going back with Andrew would be easier and with work the next day she could plead off after helping clean up after the main meal. "It's an early dinner, right?"

Andrew nodded. "Yes. Evie loves to have the big meal around two and then everyone picks at leftovers the rest of the day."

"I'll come with you and help. She must be getting ready to start cooking." Maura glanced down at her outfit. She'd donned a pair of basic black slacks and a favorite simple green sweater that complemented her eyes. "Am I dressed appropriately?"

"You look beautiful." Andrew walked with her towards the hallway and front door. "If I were a betting man, I'd wager that

Maisy'll try to wear those pajamas you gave her rather than the dress her father bought her."

True to Andrew's prediction, Maisy greeted them by the door decked out in the soft, fluffy seal pajamas Maura had been unable to resist. "What took you guys so long? Gran is ready to start cooking. You're staying for dinner, right Maura? Will you start reading Harry Potter with me? I love the drawings so much. I can't wait to read the book. Is it different than the movie? I wasn't supposed to watch it, but it was on the holiday channel when Fern and I stayed at Lana's after the Christmas party at the church and—" she paused when her grandfather started snorting while trying to contain his laughter. She looked at him askance for a moment and then grinned. "I'm being a jabber walkie talkie again, aren't I, Gramps?"

"Just a bit, love, and it's Jabberwocky."

"Maura doesn't mind, do you?" She gave Maura an anxious look.

"Of course not. I love your exuberance, Maisy."

Maisy frowned at the word and mulled it over for a moment. After tugging off her boots, Maura offered her hand to the girl. "Exuberance is like excitement."

"Ohh, I thought it might be like that." Maisy slipped her hand into Maura's. "Gran and Dad both say I have to change for dinner, but I can wear my PJs while we cook. They're soooooo comfy, Maura. I love them! I'm so excited you were here this morning right when I woke up. Why were you, Dad, and Uncle Nick all sleeping in the living room? I wanted to jump on the bed and wake you up yelling 'Santa's been here! Santa's been here!' like the girl in *The Polar Express*, but you were already down here." Maisy stopped walking so abruptly her grandfather almost tripped over her. Her eyes grew large. "Did you see Santa?"

Maura shook her head. "No. I was asleep."

"Even with Uncle Nick's snoring?" Maisy gave her a look of disbelief.

"I was tired," Maura replied.

"You must've been. He's so loud." Maisy giggled when her grandfather let out a loud snorting snore that was an accurate imitation. "I'm glad Fern and Lana aren't noisy like that when we have our sleepovers." She gave Maura a pitying look. "You must be really tired, huh? After we help Gran, maybe you can snuggle in my bed with me and I'll read to you."

Maura rested a hand briefly on the girl's head. "I would absolutely love that."

Andrew gave his granddaughter an approving nod. "Let's let Gran put us to work."

Maisy gave them a cheerful grin and continued chattering away as they walked into the kitchen.

"Happy Christmas." Stephan walked over to Maura and gathered her into his arms for a hug and kiss.

She leaned into the embrace and rested her head against his chest, enjoying the familiar crisp, woodsy smell of his soap.

Stephan kept an arm around Maura's waist as he looked between her and his father. "Was everything all right?"

Andrew nodded. "I wanted to get a few minutes of peace and quiet and get to know Maura and her cats better."

"Greta loves your dad almost as much as she loves you," Maura's eyes reflected her amusement.

"Oh, I'm wounded. My Greta is that fickle?" Stephan started laughing.

Maura gave Andrew a grateful look for diverting the conversation. He winked at her and then called Stephan over. "Where's the roasting pan stored around here?"

CHAPTER 18

Maura was shelving books when Joey Thompson came in. She gave him a polite smile and went back to her work for a few minutes, but he kept drawing her attention. He was pacing around rather than looking for anything. She sighed. Maura put down the book she was holding and walked over to him.

"Is there something you need help finding today, Joey?"

He smiled laconically at her, but his eyes were fixed on the door. "Well, as a matter of fact, Miz Maura, there is something you can help me with."

She waited. When the silence stretched out, she asked, "What?" The door opened. Out of politeness, she didn't turn away from Joey to greet the newcomer. She saw Joey coming, but couldn't process what was happening quickly enough to evade him. Maura started to turn her head away as his face neared, but he grabbed her upper arms in a harsh grip. Her face swiveled back towards his to protest. When it did, he yanked her forward and had his lips fused to her mouth at the same moment. Maura's eyes widened. As she yanked her head back, she registered the door slamming.

"Let me go!"

Joey smirked at her and held her tight. Furious, Maura drove the heel of her shoe down hard onto his foot. It couldn't penetrate his work boot, but got his attention. He chuckled and loosened his hold. She yanked her arms away and moved to the desk to grab the phone. "Get out," she demanded.

Joey tipped the brim of his Patriot's cap to her and waltzed out of the library, whistling a cheerful tune.

Shaken, Maura rounded the circulation desk and sat in stunned silence for a long moment as she pondered what to do. She slid off her shoes. One heel was snapped right off from slamming it onto Joey's foot. In a daze, she slid on a pair of flats she kept under her desk and went to look for the missing heel. After several minutes of searching, she was successful. She turned the broken bit around in her fingers and stopped to think about who had come in and then left the library so abruptly without helping her. Everyone on the island knew she and Stephan were a couple. At a loss, she dropped that train of thought. Instead, she dialed Colleen's cell phone. "Colleen, it's Maura. Can you come to the library? I need to talk to you."

Her hands had started shaking when she set the phone down. By the time the off-duty officer arrived five minutes later, Maura had put her cardigan on and buttoned every button. She'd also turned the heat up in the drafty building in an effort to ward off the chill that had settled into her body.

After Maura told her what had happened, Colleen's expression was inscrutable. Her eyebrows lifted at the sight of the broken shoe. Maura knew Colleen had had a crush on Joey years earlier, but she'd dated a number of men since. In their conversations, Joey's name rarely came up. It hadn't occurred to Maura until she finished talking that the other woman might still have feelings for him.

Maura felt a sudden wash of guilt. She should have called Ron. She'd discarded the idea of calling Stephan first almost as soon as it'd entered her mind. She didn't know what his reaction to Joey would be, and he'd looked so worn out when she saw him at supper the previous night. Another break-in the day before had left him frustrated and troubled. She was safe and unharmed. There would be time to talk after his family left in a few days.

Colleen saw Maura's expression and waved it off. "I've wasted too much time and energy on that man." She leaned back in her chair and gave the other woman a long look. "Do you want to press charges? You can, you know."

"No." She hesitated and then added, "No, I don't want to press charges. Besides, it's my word against his and I'm not injured. But I wanted to make sure I reported it in case he does it again. That isn't overreacting, is it?"

"No, not at all." Colleen shook her head. "Did you see who came in?"

"No. My back was to the door. I heard it open and then slam shut. When Joey left, there was no one else in the library. Someone must have come in and gone right back out."

Colleen's expression was troubled, but she kept her thoughts to herself.

Maura hesitated. "I'll tell Stephan, but I think I'm going to wait until his parents and Nick leave. I don't want to upset him when they're here. He's already so stressed with the burglaries and has been trying to enjoy the time with his family. I don't want to wreck the last few days of his family visit over this."

"Are you sure that's a good idea?" Colleen looked doubtful. "It's the kind of thing he should hear directly from you."

"It is, but Joey's not likely to go telling him."

"But someone came in."

"True." Maura frowned and wrapped a lock of hair around and around her index finger as she thought about it. An unsettled feeling flared in the pit of her stomach. Colleen's logic was irrefutable. Maura realized she wasn't thinking it through well. "If I can get him alone tonight, I'll tell him."

"Good." Colleen gave a decisive nod. "You should be perfectly safe. Do you need me to stay or can I head out?"

"You can go." Maura gave her a slight smile. "Thanks for coming so quickly."

"You're welcome. Call me if Joey comes back." Colleen patted Maura's hand and headed out of the library with a long, decisive stride.

The rest of the day went slowly. When the clock hit seven, she was grateful to be able to lock up. She only had to work for another day and a half before getting a break. Maura was looking forward to the downtime and chance to celebrate the new year with the Kirkland family.

While she was waiting for the heat in her car to kick in, she sent a text to Stephan telling him she was heading home and asking if she could see him. His reply was uncharacteristically short, but affirmative.

After getting home Maura kicked off her shoes and fed the cats. She was contemplating what to do next when there was a knock at the door. She glanced out the small side window and saw Stephan standing there. She had a sense of foreboding at his grim expression. Maura opened the door and gave him a slight smile. "Hi, thanks for coming over."

He nodded and shut the door. All the words Stephan had mentally rehearsed fled when he gazed at her. He spoke without thinking. "Nick told me what he saw. I want to hear your side of the story."

"Nick?" She gave him a puzzled look and then her eyes narrowed. "At the library?" Taken aback at the abrupt greeting, Maura wanted to make sure they were on the same page.

"Yeah."

Maura shifted. She tipped her head towards the living room. "I'd rather sit while we talk."

"Okay." Stephan's expression was inscrutable.

After Stephan sat across from her, Maura studied his face and body language with growing apprehension. He was eyeing her like she was a suspect. Maura didn't like it one bit. She clasped her hands together. The surge of nervousness that flooded her, kindled her temper. She'd done nothing wrong. It rankled her that Stephan seemed oblivious to his own tone and expression. "Out of the blue, Joey Thompson grabbed me. He wouldn't let me go and kissed me. After he left, I called Colleen to make a report." As Stephan continued to sit and watch her, Maura felt the unease continue to grow in her gut. "Someone came in, but left very quickly. Was that Nick?"

Stephan nodded in confirmation.

Maura frowned. Why hadn't Nick stayed to see if she needed help?

Silence stretched on for several moments.

"Why'd you kiss him, Maura?" Hurt laced his voice. It was the first emotion that Stephan showed since he'd come into the house.

Maura felt a pang at the pain she heard in his voice, but also anger that he hadn't seemed to hear her. "I didn't kiss him, Stephan. He forced himself on me."

He winced and ran a hand through his hair. "Did you ask for help? Yell, try to get away?"

Maura's temper flared. "Why are you being a jerk?"

He flinched.

The anger pushed away everything else she was feeling. Maura shot to her feet and wrapped her arms around her waist as she stepped away from Stephan. "You're treating me like a suspect. I didn't do anything wrong here."

The expression on his face was remote. "Nick doesn't lie."

"Neither do I."

"I know." Stephan tried to backtrack. The conversation wasn't going the way he'd planned. When Nick had cornered him about what he'd seen, Stephan had immediately assumed Joey'd been harassing Maura. His brother had been more suspicious. Maura, he'd said, hadn't cried out for help and didn't look like she was struggling. Stephan had planned on listening with an open mind, but Sophie's betrayal was a wound that had left scars. Despite his best intentions, he'd had hours to brood and retreat into a protective shell.

"Nick's been waiting for me to make a misstep since he arrived."

"This isn't about Nick."

"Are you sure about that?" Anger felt better than the anxiety and confusion that had been with Maura through the afternoon and evening. There was a relief in letting it all out. "It's my word against Nick's. He's involved, whether anyone wants him to be or not."

Stephan was taken aback by the fury in her voice. He'd never seen her like this. He swallowed. "I, I don't know what to think Maura."

Her eyebrows lifted. "You don't know who to believe, you mean?" When he was silent, she glared at him. "I love you. I've spent years avoiding any entanglements with Joey Thompson. Yet, you're willing to believe Nick when he says I wanted that man to kiss me? Hell, Stephan, it's my word against Joey's, too." Her eyes drilled into him. "When did my word become so meaningless to you?"

"He didn't say you wanted—," Stephan trailed off. He sighed. "I do believe you. What do I say to Nick, though?"

"You're kidding me, right?" Maura looked at him askance. "You tell him he only saw what he wanted to see. He wanted to see me cheating on you."

"That's not fair." Stephan felt his own temper rise. "Nick worries about me and Maisy."

"It's more than worry. Every book he gave me at Christmas was about infidelity, Stephan. Did you know that?" Maura drew in a deep breath. She forced herself to slowly count to ten. She loved Stephan and knew he loved her, but love without trust wasn't enough. As rapidly as it had bloomed, her fury evaporated. She took in the conflicted expression on Stephan's face. It left her feeling hollow. "Maybe you should leave. Maybe we shouldn't see each other for a few days until you've had a chance to decide who and what you believe."

"Maura." Stephan started to protest and then sighed. It'd be easier to sort it all out after his family was gone. Maura wasn't going anywhere and neither was he. It didn't feel right, but he was tired, out of sorts, and didn't want to fight with her or his brother. "Okay." He nodded. "Let's take a few days and hash it out after the holidays." He stood up and moved towards the front door.

Tears sprang to Maura's eyes at his easy acquiescence. She wasn't sure what she'd wanted when the words had tumbled out, but this all-too-easy agreement wasn't it. "You never even asked how I was, Stephan." She shook her head. "I love you, but if you don't trust me, well, a few days won't change that, will they?"

Stephan felt his equilibrium vanish. "What are you saying, Maura?" His hand trembled on the handle of the door.

She shook her head. Her voice had grown bleak. "I don't know. But you cared more about what Nick thought he saw than whether or not I was all right." She managed to keep her tears from falling. "I deserve better than that."

Stephan wasn't sure how it had all spiraled out of control so quickly. He wanted to reach out to her, hold her, have her hold him. He wanted everything to go back to the way it'd been just hours earlier. The chasm that had opened up between them stunned him with the speed with which it had appeared. "Maura, that's not—" He took a step towards her and began to reach out when his phone went off with the ring tone for the station. He frowned. "I have to take this." The conversation was brief. Stephan looked over at her after he hung up. "I can't do this right now. I have to go."

She nodded. "Ron's voice carries."

He hesitated as he moved towards the door. "Can we still talk? I guess after my family leaves, if that's what you want?"

She tried for a casual expression and shrugged. "Sure. You'd better go."

"Maura," Stephan started and then shook his head. He didn't even know where to start to get out of the mess the conversation had devolved into. "Okay." He nodded, stepped out, and gently closed the door behind him.

After he left, the tears flowed out of Maura's eyes and down her cheeks. She swiped at them, but more followed.

The next morning, she almost called in sick. If it had been a regular week, she would've reached out to the substitute staff, but it wasn't. She couldn't ask any of them to sacrifice their family time. The day passed in a blur. Thankfully, it was busy, with patrons coming in to load up on movies, books, and magazines for the long holiday break. Maura was able to keep from having too much time to sit and stew.

For the first time in ages, she shut early when the library had emptied out by 6:00. As she turned the lights off, Maura drew in a shaky breath and let it out. She'd gotten through the day. She only needed to work a few hours the next day. Then she could crawl into her bed and not leave it for four days.

For his part, Stephan had been so short-tempered that everyone at the station had given him a wide berth. Colleen decided to wait it out and approach him on New Year's Eve if he was still a bear. Whatever conversation Maura had with him clearly hadn't gone well. While she was disinclined to discuss her own complicated relationship with Joey with anyone, it bothered her that Stephan and Maura were at odds because of him.

When Colleen showed up to near the shift change on New Year's Eve, Stephan was still ill-tempered. She demanded he come speak with her in the staff lounge before he left for the night.

"I want to talk to you about a report I took, Stevie."

"Is it about the break-ins?" Stephan tried to muster up some interest in the open investigation that was consuming most of the department's attention.

"No." Colleen waited until he made eye contact with her. "It was a reported assault two days ago."

Stephan drew in a breath, but that was his only visible reaction. He continued to lean against the wall and gazed at her. After a long beat, he managed a neutral tone and asked, "Assault?"

"Yeah." Colleen flipped open a small notebook she liked to jot notes down in while talking with witnesses. It helped to have detailed recordings when her fellow islanders were slinging complaints against one another. "'Adult female called to complain that she'd been assaulted at Belfort Public Library on December 29 at approximately 1:15 pm.'" Her brown eyes were sharp when she looked up to see if Stephan was paying attention. Satisfied he was, she continued her recitation. "'Upon arrival, found victim wholly believable, despite no visible injuries and no witnesses left at the scene. There was evidence supporting victim's claim of stomping on perpetrator's foot in the form of a broken heel. Victim declined to press charges, but wanted an official record of the complaint filed,' which it will be in about five minutes. And I have had just about enough of dealing with you in such a pissy-ass mood." Colleen shut her notebook with a snap and stared at Stephan. "I told Maura I'd let her tell you what had happened before I filed the official report. Hell, I wanted her to talk to you immediately. You've been a major pain in the ass the past couple of days, so I figure that didn't go well. That or you're just being a dumb fuck about it and need to readjust your priorities."

She sat down and crossed her long legs. "So, which is it Stevie?"

"Tell me exactly what she said happened."

Colleen gestured to one of the other chairs and refused to speak until he'd sat. She then gave him a more thorough, dispassionate recounting of what Maura had told her. She added in Maura's worries about protecting him as well as her own observation that Maura shouldn't try to spare his feelings or family visit. When she was done, she added one last thought. "I was eating lunch at Jack's with Joey Thompson, the alleged assailant, prior to the incident. He didn't mention Maura once. He's been sleeping with a cashier from Ellsworth and an office manager in Bangor when he gets down there. He didn't say anything about the library at all. Your brother walked in and sat down near us. The three of us made some small talk before I left. If you're half the detective those yahoos in Boston claimed you are, you might want to have another chat with Nick." She shrugged. "Anyway, that's just my thought. But I'm a hick from Down East, so what do I know?"

Stephan didn't rise to the bait. He gave Colleen a distracted look. "I need to get home."

She nodded in agreement. "Probably a good idea."

"You can file your report."

"I planned to."

"Be safe out there tonight."

"You too."

Colleen smirked at him. "Would it kill you to say it, Stevie?"

He scowled at her. "Maybe."

Colleen grinned in response.

"Thank you, Colleen. Thank you for telling me about Miss Ballard's report and your lunch."

Colleen rolled her eyes at him. "A word of advice?" She didn't bother waiting for an affirmative response. "Get over yourself, and certainly get over what other people think they might have seen and try talking again with the woman herself. Happy New Year, Stevie. See ya on the flip side."

With that last remark, she sauntered out of the staff lounge and towards the desk to clock in.

Stephan sat in silence for several minutes and then noticed the time. He swore under his breath. Dinner was supposed to have started 15 minutes ago. He sent his brother a quick text to let everyone know he was on his way.

Maisy scowled at Stephan from across the dinner table. "May I be excused?"

"You haven't eaten much."

"I'm not hungry."

"You need to eat."

"I don't wanna eat with you."

Stephan ran a hand through his hair in frustration. He didn't want to eat either, but here he was, sitting at the table with everyone trying to pretend nothing was wrong. Maisy had clearly decided where her loyalties lay. He eyed his child, who was staring back at him in defiance. "Fine, don't eat, but you may not be excused yet."

He heard Maisy grumble under her breath, but had averted his eyes to stare down at the spread his parents had prepared.

He'd been looking forward to it, they all had. Now he was just enduring it.

"More peas?"

"No thanks, Mum."

A spoon laden with the small green orbs dumped its contents on his roast beef.

He looked up and over at his mother with a raised eyebrow.

She was staring back at him with a mutinous expression similar to her granddaughters.

Stephan briefly wondered if she'd spoken with Maura. They needed to talk, but he wasn't sure where to even start.

Andrew took pity on his son and began to engage Evelyn and Maisy in conversation as best he could to divert their attention.

When the meal was finally over, Stephan grabbed his brother by the arm and dragged him to the back room. He shut the door so they wouldn't be overheard.

"What exactly did you see, mate?"

Nick sighed. "Again? I'm not the suspect here. Why are you grilling me?"

"Humor me."

"Fine." His brother sighed and sank down into an armchair. "I walked into the library. Maura's back was to me. Joey had his arms around her—"

"Like in a hug?"

"No." Nick closed his eyes as he replayed the moment. "More like his hands were on her shoulders, or actually her upper arms, you know, by the deltoids or biceps, holding her." He tipped his head to the side as he went through it again. "He pulled her forward and she stumbled a bit. Might've been the heels she was wearing. Then they kissed. I got disgusted and walked out."

Stephan sank down on the sofa. "Did anyone know you were heading for the library? What had you been doing before?"

Nick had seen how much his brother and niece had been hurting over the past two days, so he was willing to go along with the interrogation. "I had lunch at Jack's and chatted with Colleen.

Told her I needed to pick up lager and some DVDs for Mum and Maisy. Joey was there too, sitting with her. I thought they were a couple, but I didn't ask. Obviously, they're not. I don't think she's the type who'd stand for her lover cheating on her." He ticked his fingers as he went through his actions. "Anyway, after I left the café, I went to the store and then walked over to the library for the DVDs."

Jesus. Stephan felt a chill go through him, deflating the last bit of indignation he'd clung to. Colleen was right. Nick might not have seen everything. Hell, Colleen pretty much spelled out her thoughts that it had been a set-up right from the get-go. But why hadn't Maura called him? Why did she go to Colleen? Despite what Colleen had said in that regard, he still felt it was something Maura should have come to him with first. It didn't matter that he'd been off duty. Stephan then thought about how stressed he'd been with the newest rash of break-ins. He also thought about how much Maura wanted to make a good impression on his family and how she was trying to make sure she gave them time to visit without her presence. He groaned and let his head flop back against the cushion. "Colleen had something to say to me tonight right before I left."

"Oh?"

"Maura called her over to the library maybe fifteen minutes after you'd left." He shared the conversation with Nick. Afterwards, Stephan let out a heavy sigh. "Colleen had asked her why she hadn't called me. She said Maura told her she didn't want to add to my stress. She wanted me to enjoy the time with my family." Stephan snorted. "Bollocks. That worked out so well for all concerned, didn't it?"

"You think the tosser set me up?"

"You and Maura and me, yes. It's possible, Nick."

"What a wanker." Nick liked Maura, despite his determination to keep her at arm's length. He replayed what he saw through the filter of her side of the story. It certainly was plausible. He hadn't stuck around more than a minute. Seeing all his worries proven out, he'd stormed out of there in high dudgeon. He should have stayed and interrupted. He would have gotten a better sense of the situation if he hadn't overreacted. Nick groaned. "I cocked that up, didn't I?"

"We all did." Stephan's voice was bleak.

"Go talk to her."

"And say what?"

"That your brother's an arse. That you're an arse." Nick shrugged. "You could start there and see how it goes. I don't think it could go to hell more than it already is."

"There's a cheerful thought." Stephan opened his eyes. He stood up and opened the door. His mother and Maisy practically tumbled into the room. "Seriously?"

"We were just walking by and heard you talking. We came to see if you wanted some tea and biscuits."

"Are you going to go bring Maura back?" Maisy wasn't going to pretend she'd been doing anything other than eavesdropping.

Stephan knew he was going to have to address that with her later. "Should I?"

"Duh!" Maisy looked at him like he was an idiot. "I have something important to ask her. You need to bring her back home with you."

"She might not want to come."

"If you don't ask, she won't."

"True. All right, love. I'll go ask."

"Be nice."

"Apologize."

"Tell her I'm an arse."

Stephan glanced over at his father who had just appeared in the hallway. "Do you have anything to add?"

"To what?" Andrew looked puzzled to find them all clustered by the porch door.

"Daddy's going to bring Maura back."

"Oh good." Andrew smiled in relief. "I've grown fond of her. Tell her I'll make us hot toddies. Oh, and Stephan, it's okay to lose the battle to win the war."

"Right."

"Give her a kiss and say you're sorry," was Maisy's contribution.

"Make it a good kiss," added his mother.

Stephan shook his head. "Right. Carry on with your celebrations. Hopefully, I'll be back with Maura."

Nick gave him a thumbs-up. "Brilliant. Make sure you tell her what an arse you are."

Stephan paused long enough to smack his brother before stepping out into the cold.

The wind was bitter as it swept up off the cove. Stephan shivered as he stood in front of Maura's darkened house. He tried knocking on the door. With no answer, he rang the bell. When he put his ear to the door all he could hear was faint music. He tried the bell again. Finally, he resorted to holding it down with his index finger.

He heard Maura swear from the living room, but hadn't pulled away in time to keep from half falling over the threshold when she jerked the door open.

"May I come in?" His teeth were chattering. Stepping outside without a coat had been a monumentally dumb idea.

"Looks like you already have." Maura frowned at him. "Come in all the way so I can shut the door. It's cold."

"No kidding." Stephan rubbed his arms as he stepped in and shut the door for her.

She frowned at him again, but nodded toward the living room. The woodstove was throwing off waves of heat. Stephan held his hands out in front of it and soaked in the warmth while he tried to figure out how to start. The light from the fire and her Christmas tree bathed Maura and the room in a soft glow. She was wrapped in her aunt's shawl and wearing a pair of thick, fuzzy socks over old gray sweatpants and a green hoodie. Her face was tear-streaked and pale. He wanted to pull her into his arms and pretend their fight had never happened, but knew that wouldn't work. When she arched an eyebrow at him, he realized he'd been standing there staring at her in silence for too long.

"I'm sorry." It wasn't how he'd planned to start. Stephan decided to go with it anyway. "Maura, I am so sorry that I didn't just trust you straight away instead of listening to my fears and old pains. I was an idiot and a fool."

She didn't stop him, so Stephan figured she either agreed and wanted to hear him debase himself some more or she was waiting to hear why he was there. "What happened with Sophie left scars. I know." He raised a hand. "I know you're not Sophie. I also know you aren't having an affair with Joey Thompson or anyone other than me." He sat on the other end of the sofa so he could look directly at Maura. "I knew all that, but reacted anyway. I was already kicking myself when I stepped out the door. Colleen told me you called her because you were trying to protect me. Maura." He shook his head. "There was nothing to protect me from. I would have done my job and bashed his nose in."

Stephan smiled when his absurd remark caught her notice.

"Okay, I wouldn't have done that, though I'd have been tempted. I'm furious that he laid a finger on you, but I wouldn't risk upending our lives for the pleasure of punching him." His hands were resting loosely between his knees. Stephan stared down at them. "I overreacted and didn't take you at your word. I never asked if you were all right when you told me what had happened. I was an idiot. I'd like to add that my brother's a bigger one, because if he'd stayed for a couple of seconds longer, he'd have seen it wasn't consensual. He could have punched Joey for all of us." He looked up at her. "Can you forgive me? Will you forgive me?" Stephan gave her a boyish grin. "And before you answer, know that I've been forbidden from returning home without you, so if you say no, I'll either have to camp out here or turn into a human popsicle out there."

Maura shook her head at him, but she'd started to smile. "I'd give you a quilt before I threw you out, and Milly's shed doesn't lock. You have to have noticed that by now." She rubbed the fringe of her shawl with anxious fingers. "You should have trusted me Stephan. And I guess I should have called you first instead of worrying about upsetting you and calling Colleen instead." She gave him a sad look. "I would never hurt you or Maisy on purpose, Stephan. Haven't you realized that?"

He nodded.

A couple of tears rolled down Maura's cheeks. "These have been some of the worst days of my life."

"It's been awful." Stephan's voice was rough with emotion. "I don't want to feel like this ever again, but I guess that's the risk with loving, isn't it?"

Maura gave him a sharp look.

"Of course, I still love you, Maura. I knew I would come crawling over here to try and work things out even if you'd kissed that slimeball on purpose, just not when Nick was here and willing to remind me how badly Sophie hurt me and warn me away from risking that pain again."

"I've been avoiding kissing that man for years now. I have no reason to start now. And Nick is an ass, but," she amended, "one who was trying to protect his younger brother."

Stephan smiled. "I cannot argue with a word of that." He stroked Greta when she jumped onto his lap with a happy greeting. "Are you willing to give me, give us, another chance?"

"You really are an idiot." Maura smiled. "I love you. How can I not? But you need to promise me that the next time I say or do something you don't like or you *think* I've said or done something that upsets you, we talk first. You don't go believing the worst of me on someone else's say-so. And I'll come to you first with things, no matter what."

"Agreed. And Maura, if we ever part ways, it's because you decide you want to leave." Stephan hadn't planned on laying his soul bare, but he wanted to start the new year off right between them and full honesty seemed the way to go.

"Oh." Maura brought her hand to her mouth and slid down the sofa until she could move Greta aside and climb into his lap herself. "Don't say things like that if you don't mean them."

"I mean it with all my heart. I can't formally propose without talking to Maisy first, but I know what my heart feels. I know what love feels like. I've found my home, and it's with you."

Maura swiped at the tears running down her cheeks and leaned in to kiss him. "Me too. I will wait as long as Maisy needs. We can do whatever we need to for this to work for all three of us."

Stephan cupped the back of her head and deepened the kiss.

Neither was aware of how much time had passed, but eventually Stephan's FaceTime alert went off. They broke apart. He was still catching his breath when he answered Maisy. "Hi, love."

"Daddy, are you and Maura coming back to see the ball drop with us?"

"Yes, I think we are." He gave Maura an inquiring look. When she nodded in the affirmative, he looked back at Maisy. "I think Maura's going to want to change first. She's in her pajamas."

Maisy shrugged. "So are we." She craned her head, trying to see Maura.

Stephan angled the phone a bit so Maura would appear on Maisy's screen.

"Happy New Year, Maura!" Maisy grinned at her. "I have something important to ask you. Can you please come over soon?"

They all heard Evelyn calling for Maisy.

Stephan saw the guilty expression on his daughter's face. "What did you do?"

"I wasn't supposed to bother you," Maisy confessed. "But you were taking foreverrrrrrrrr." She looked up at someone off screen. "I'm coming, Gran. Maura's coming over, too." The girl waved at them and then disconnected the call.

Maura looked down at her clothes. "I'd better change."

"Stay comfortable. But," Stephan hesitated, not wanting to upset her.

"But what?"

"You might want to brush your hair or put it in a pony."

Maura touched her hair and winced. She hadn't taken care with it that morning and had been tugging at it and twirling it around her fingers all day and night. "Good call." She gave him a brief kiss. "Give me five minutes."

"I'll bank the fire and unplug the tree." Stephan stood up after Maura had slid off his lap. "Just in case you decide to stay with us."

"What about Maisy?"

"We'll just tell her New Years is a big sleepover night. She's certainly fond of them." He grinned at her. "I am too."

Maura rolled her eyes at him.

"If you promise you'll stay, I'll feed the cats now too, so you're not worrying and Tim doesn't break out to come and drag you home."

Maura folded her aunt's shawl and brought it upstairs. She put it in her dresser and gathered up a few odds and ends so she'd be comfortable as well as presentable. She eyed the goofy seal slippers Maisy had given her and shrugged. Why not? She slid them onto her feet, stopped in the bathroom to wash her face, run a brush through her hair, and then went downstairs. Stephan was waiting by the door with her coat and keys. "Everyone's fed. Tim gave me the obligatory growl, but his heart wasn't really in it."

Maura slid into her coat when he held it open for her.

He saw her footwear and laughed. "Lucky it's a quick dash across the street."

When they stepped into the warm, brightly lit house, Maura found herself knocked backwards into Stephan when Maisy raced down the stairs and launched into her arms. "I missed you!" Maisy held her in a fierce embrace.

Still holding the girl, Maura returned Evelyn and Andrew's warm greetings. She offered a cooler hello to Nick. Maisy finally was willing to disengage from Maura long enough for Stephan to help her get her coat off before she clambered back up into her arms. As they lagged behind the others heading into the living room Maisy whispered in Maura's ear. "I need to talk to you in private, you and Daddy."

"Okay, sweetheart. Is something wrong? Honey, I have to put you down so I can see you properly." Maura set Maisy down and knelt so they were eye to eye. Stephan had come back to the hallway to see what was keeping them.

Maisy was fighting back tears. "I hated these two days. I know you and Daddy were fighting, but I love you and don't want you to leave me. Can you marry me, even if you and Daddy don't love each other? Is there a way you can be mine even if you don't want him?"

"Oh." Maura rocked back on her heels.

Having heard Maisy's little announcement, Stephan hurried to them. He scooped his daughter up in one arm and took Maura's hand with his free one. When they'd reached Maisy's room, he set her on the bed before they joined her. Maisy climbed into Maura's lap and snuggled into her.

"The past two days were hard on all three of us, weren't they, love?"

Maisy nodded. "Super awful."

Maura tightened her embrace around the girl.

Stephan rubbed his daughter's cheek. "Maura and I agree with you on that." He studied the child for a long moment. "No matter what happens between us, you can always have a relationship with Maura, we both promise you that, Maisy Daisy."

"I love you so much, Maisy," Maura added. "Even if your Dad and I fight, that will never change."

"But if you love him and then stop because you fight, then why wouldn't you stop loving me too, maybe? I know it happens."

Maura wiggled her way back until the wall was supporting her. "First of all, I never stopped loving anyone. People can fight and still love each other. Second, my love is unconditional, Maisy. No matter what, I will always love both of you more than I ever thought possible. You've changed my life and I'm grateful." She kissed the girl's forehead.

"Can I be yours, too, then?"

Maura looked at Stephan, who had started laughing.

"This isn't how I'd planned on doing this, and I don't have a ring for you; but, Maura, would you marry us? We will always love you, even when we argue." He winked at Maisy. "Will you make a new family together with us?"

Maisy squeezed Maura's arm in excitement.

Maura gazed at each of them in turn with tears in her eyes. "Yes, I would love to be a family with you both."

"YAY!" Maisy threw her arms around Maura and gave her cheek an enthusiastic kiss before hugging and kissing her father and taking off down the hall. They could hear her thudding down the stairs screaming, "We're getting married!" at the top of her lungs.

Maura started laughing. Stephan had been leaning in to kiss her and instead rested his forehead against hers and began laughing as well.

"For the record, I planned on coming up with a romantic way to ask you."

"You've thought about this?"

"Ever since Thanksgiving."

Their lips met.

A clanging of pots and pans and shouts of "Happy New Year!" interrupted them. The room filled a moment later with everyone else in the house.

They got up off the bed and Maura found herself being embraced with warm words of welcome and congratulations from his parents and brother. Nick whispered an apology in her ear as he bent to embrace her.

When Evelyn asked to see the ring and was told there wasn't one, she got a funny expression on her face and hustled off, after telling them to stay put. Andrew smiled in understanding, but didn't offer to illuminate anyone.

When she returned, Evelyn pressed a blue, velvet-lined ring box into Stephan's hand. "This was your grandmother Cate's. It's the funniest thing. I had set it aside for you after she passed, but it never felt like the right time to bring it over." She glanced at Nick. "Maude's is gathering dust waiting for you, dear." Evelyn's gaze shifted back to the couple. "Cate's ring is a bit old-fashioned. It's not a traditional engagement ring. But I think it might just suit Maura a treat. I kept hearing Cate tell me to bring it with us on this visit. I swear she wouldn't leave me alone. I'd be doing the laundry or the dishes and I'd hear her voice as if she was standing next to me lecturing me to remember to bring her ring with us. You don't need to use it as an engagement ring, but it is yours, and I'd like you to have it now." She glanced at the ceiling. "You hear that, Cate? I did it. You can leave me alone about it now." Evelyn shook her head. "Go on; open it up and let Maura look."

Stephan took care opening the old box. He knew the ring his mother was referring to and agreed that it would suit Maura, but didn't want to presume. He angled it so Maura and Maisy had a clear view when the delicate teardrop emerald came into view. It sparkled under the light. The gold band was shaped into fanciful curls, evoking the feel of the movement of waves around it. Tiny sapphires, diamonds, and emeralds set in the band helped convey the notion that the ring was an homage to the sea. None of the stones were especially valuable, and the ring wasn't a classic engagement ring, but it was beautiful and unique.

Maura's hand had gone to her mouth and her eyes were wide. Maisy was gazing at it with admiration. "It's amazeballs, Gran."

Stephan was studying Maura. "Want to try it on, love?"

She nodded and held out her hand.

He slid the ring onto her finger. It hugged her as if it were meant to be there. "Do you like it?"

"It's gorgeous, but are you sure?" She looked at Evelyn when she asked.

Evelyn and Andrew were watching the scene unfold with their arms around one another. It was Andrew who answered. "My mother would have loved you, Maura. I can think of no one else who should wear her ring."

"Is that a yes?" Stephan's voice held a gentle teasing tone.

Maura nodded. "Of course, it's a yes."

Everyone in the room cheered when Stephan took advantage of the moment to give Maura another kiss. They then paraded down to the living room for a quiet celebration. Maisy fell asleep on her grandmother's lap. Stephan carried her up to her bed with his parents trailing behind. He promised Maura and Nick he'd be right back.

When they were alone, the future in-laws eyed one another with some discomfort.

"So." Nick ran a hand through his hair. "I, I jumped to the wrong conclusion about you and the situation. After what happened with Sophie, I just don't want to see Stephan or Maisy hurt again. I was wrong."

Maura was feeling magnanimous. She reached out and touched his hand. "I understand how it must have looked from your perspective. Joey's enough of a jerk to have done it on purpose. I don't know what his game is, but it was no accident that he did that when you came in. Shall we start over?"

Nick's grin was so like his brother's that she had to smile back at him. "Nah, I'm bound to behave like an arse again. Might as well be up front about that here and now. Sophie hated me for it."

"She struggled with you because you saw who she was," Stephan corrected Nick as he rejoined them. "Even when we were in love and well before the affairs, you saw who she was, both the good and bad. She resented it. You never sugar-coated your words for her or politeness's sake, even when it would have been the done thing."

"I did like her." Nick felt guilty.

"I know you did."

"It's hard not to worry about you and Maisy Daze."

Stephan laughed. "I worry about *you* all the time, Nick."

"Me?" Nick looked taken aback.

"Yes, you. Your business is thriving, but all you do is work."

"That's not fair. I play rugby with my mates. I visit Mum and Dad and the cousins. I date occasionally."

"Dating? Is that what you call it?" Stephan grinned at his brother and turned to Maura. "He's afraid of commitment that goes beyond a single night, maybe two."

Nick threw a pillow at his brother. "Am not."

"Are too."

Maura listened to their petty bickering and smiled. She'd been a lonely child and often longed for a sibling. There was a mix of pleasure and jealousy in listening to the brothers' squabble.

"Are we amusing you?"

"I'm living vicariously through you, Nick."

"Huh?"

"I'd have given away all my treasures when I was younger to have had a brother or sister to fight with."

Nick and Stephan looked at each other in silence for a moment before each burst into laughter.

"Nick tried to sell me to tinkers one time," Stephan informed her. "Luckily they weren't the sort who trafficked in children. They dragged him home."

"By the ear." Nick's grin was rueful.

"By the ear, to Granny Cate, and told her what he'd done."

"I couldn't sit for a week and didn't get any pudding for longer than that." Nick gave her a mournful look. "Mum and Gran didn't understand what an annoying prat Stephan was when he was three."

"You tried to sell him?" Maura was looking at Nick in astonishment.

"For a pound and a silver whistle." Stephan threw the pillow back at Nick, aiming for, and hitting him in the chest. "I don't know which was worse, that he did it at all, or that he thought I was worth so little."

"I was five!" Nick laughed. "A pound was a fortune and that whistle was way fancier than those beat-up tin ones Gran had given us. Besides, I figured they'd get annoyed with you too. I assumed you'd be home before tea."

Maura laughed. "Your mother must have been appalled."

"Ask her about it in the morning." Stephan's eyes were dancing with amusement.

Nick started to protest and then shrugged. "If you do, I'm saying we're even."

"Hmm, I think I should wait for something more important then. I rather like having some leverage over you, Nicholas."

"And here, I was worried you were too nice to handle our Maisy."

Stephan laughed. "Maura holds her own with our girl just fine." He squeezed her hand. "I don't know about you, love, but it's been a hell of a day. I'm past ready to go to bed."

Maura gave him a shy smile, acutely aware of Nick's gaze on them. "It has been," she agreed and put her feet back on the floor.

Nick stood up. "Thank god you're leaving. I've been wanting to turn in for ages." He gave a melodramatic sigh and grinned at them. "I'll keep Maisy entertained as long as I can in the morning."

"Cheers." Stephan gave his brother a hug before helping Maura to her feet.

They made their way upstairs and slipped into Stephan's small room. Once the door was closed, he pulled Maura close.

She sighed as she wrapped her arms around him, content to breathe in his familiar scent and soak up the warmth from his body. She felt the residual tension fall away from her own.

They began touching one another tentatively, each remembering how close they'd come to giving up the other. When Maura's shirt eventually drifted to the floor, Stephan saw the marks on her upper arms. His hands stilled as he took them in. The bruising was an ugly greenish yellow. The shapes of fingers were distinct and easily identifiable as such. "I was a complete idiot, Maura. And I still might bash his bloody nose in."

Maura caressed his cheek. "Not worth it." She drew him down for a kiss.

When New Year's morning dawned, they slept through it. It wasn't until the smells of coffee, bacon, and maple syrup wafted up the stairs, riding on laughter and cheerful voices, that either woke. Stephan oriented out of dream-world first and smiled to see Maura nestled up next to him. He rolled onto his hip and studied her face. She looked peaceful. Her russet hair was mussed and silken to the touch. There were fewer freckles dotting her cheeks and nose than in the summer. The faint lines in the corners of her eyes were dear and familiar. He let a hand run down her hair and arm. She wrinkled her nose and sighed. Maura's lips curved up before she opened her eyes. "Happy New Year," she whispered.

"Happiest New Year," he replied, and sealed the sentiment with a kiss.

CHAPTER 19

After the holidays, Stephan's family flew home and the quiet rhythm of winter took over. David and Milly had been told about the engagement on New Year's Day, since they were tapped into the island grapevine. That had necessitated an immediate conversation with Sophie's parents, Bill and Ruth, as well. Both went better than anyone anticipated.

Maura and Stephan began to slowly integrate their households. They agreed they'd live in Maura's house, since she already owned it. As a bonus, it allowed Maisy to remain near the cove and Karria. Stephan had also suggested they add on a guest suite. He had enough money set aside to pay for it. It'd give them space to have visitors stay at the house, and for their artwork when there weren't house guests. They made arrangements with a local contractor whose stepdaughter was a frequent participant in library activities to draw up a proposal.

It was with those happy plans and activities in progress that Maura went to work one blustery day near the end of January. The weather had been unpredictable: warming and then freezing, raining and then sleeting and snowing. She decided to close the library after a couple of hours when the current storm unexpectedly shifted to ice. Before she could lock the doors, however, a group of her Wednesday regulars from the school showed up. Isabelle explained to Maura that they weren't sure where they should go during a chaotic dismissal. At a loss, they had gathered up and trudged over to the library as a group.

Maura monitored the weather reports with increasing concern. She had spent the hour since the children's unexpected arrival texting and calling parents to see if they could come pick them up. She sighed when the power suddenly went out. The library was filled with shadows. Ice pinged off the windows, louder now that the heating system had gone silent.

In the children's room, five-year-old Betty Jo Thompson began to cry while her brother Mike lectured her to stop being a baby.

Isabelle bent down and hugged Betty Jo. "See, Betty, it's all okay. We're here and you're safe." She rubbed the girl's back and reached over to smack her cousin on the back of his head when he started to mock his sister's tears.

"It just startled me." Betty Jo glared at her brother as she used her fists to wipe away her remaining tears. Amber and Maisy patted her back and scowled at Mike as well.

Knowing the drafty building would cool quickly with the heat off, Maura had the kids put their coats on or keep them close by. She gave the younger children the spare blanket from the closet. Snacks were then passed around. Once they were all settled, Isabelle began reading more of *Treasure Island* to them.

Maura shut the door to the children's room and went into her office. She reached for her cell phone. Though it took a moment, she was able to access the weather forecast and grimaced at the ominous warnings. She peered out the window, but in the dim, gray light there was little to see. The clicking of ice encased branches against one of the side windows in the main room didn't bode well. Sighing, she took stock of the supplies she had in the office. There was no telling when someone would think to come get them, and the parents she'd been able to reach were all either off-island or working essential jobs that wouldn't let them break away anytime soon. She had to be prepared to have the kids there into the night.

Her phone vibrated in her pocket. She smiled to see Stephan's name.

Are you okay there?

Yes.

How many are with you?

Isabelle, Betty Jo and Mike, Kevin, Tommy, Amber, and Maisy. She came to me instead of going home with Fern.

Okay. Stay put. Chip or Colleen will try to break away to help you get everyone over to the station ASAP. Generators are up and running. Don't leave until they get there. It's a sheet of ice everywhere. I'm stuck at the weirs. Be safe.

Maura nodded to herself and started to type a reply when a loud banging from the rear supply room took her by surprise. As she reached the door, it was flung open. The blow made her stumble and fall backwards onto the floor. Pain blossomed from her tailbone. Her eyes focused on a booted pair of feet. She gazed up and blinked in surprise to see an unwelcome face.

"Joey?" Before she could say anything else, three more men emerged from the room and eyed her. Maura pulled her legs closer to her body and started to move so she could stand.

"Gimme your phone, Maura." Joey held out his left hand. His right was holding a gun. "Can't have you calling lover boy for help, not that the flatlander would do ya much good in this."

Maura thumbed the screen to close the text messages and lock it as she moved to hand it over.

"What're you even doing here?"

"I work here, Joey."

He rolled his eyes at her. "Why're you still here in this weather? It's wicked out there, if you hadn't noticed. Nobody's coming for a book. There's no book-reading emergencies, for Christ's sake."

His partners snorted as if Joey had cracked a hilarious joke.

Maura hesitated too long. Joey swore.

"Rugrats are here, too? What the hell, Maura? Don't their parents give a damn about them?"

"Dude, you said there wouldn't be *anyone* here."

"What're we gonna do with them? What're we gonna do with her?"

"How many kids, Maura?"

Maura's eyes were focused on Joey's gun. She swallowed hard and met his harsh gaze. "Seven."

"Damnit." Joey looked at the men with him. "Cover your faces, boys. If they can't identify us, we won't need to worry about the kids." He gave Maura a malevolent smile. "Sweetheart, you can't save yourself, but you can help them."

Maura thought she was going to get sick, but nodded her head. She watched them pull ski masks down over their heads and surround her.

"Get up."

She wasn't certain her now-shaking legs would manage the task Joey demanded, but Maura forced herself to think about the youngsters and did what she was told. Once she was standing, she felt him come up behind her.

"It's a damned shame you're so responsible about this place. If you'd gone home early like everyone else, you'd all be safe and sound." Joey's voice was dulled by the layer of yarn, but Maura understood each word and felt tears prick her eyes. The gun pushed against her back and she moved forward. "They're in the kiddie room, right?"

"Yes."

"Let's go, then. T, you come with me. Rog, you and Colin get started in here just like we planned."

Hearing Joey use his cohort's names drove home the reality that he wasn't planning on letting her live. Maura felt her mind detach from her body as a cold sweat broke out across her skin.

"Tell them to be quiet and cooperate. If they do that, they'll go home to their mommies and daddies."

She nodded.

They reached the door to the children's room. Maura forced herself to open it. She moved toward the children and tried to speak, but couldn't make the words leave her mouth. She felt Joey jab the gun further into her ribs and grunted at the stab of pain. She found her voice. "We need to do what these men ask. If you do that, they promise you'll be safe."

Betty Jo immediately shrieked.

"Fuck." Joey's voice was soft when he realized his niece and nephew were there. He saw Isabelle and swore again. She was one of the handful of cousins he genuinely liked. The other two, Betty Jo especially, annoyed him, but they were family. He tipped his head toward the kids and stopped pushing the gun into Maura's body.

Maura quickly moved away and towards the children. She sat down with them. Maisy and Betty Jo climbed into her lap. Tommy and Amber slid their hands into Isabelle's. Kevin and Mike Jr. moved away from the game of chess they'd been playing and stood behind the group.

Using his biggest voice, Mike demanded, "What's going on here?'

Joey sighed inwardly at the eighth grader's reaction. He'd be like a dog worrying a bone; the same as his father, Joey's older brother. The kid was a freakin' carbon copy of his old man. He did the best he could to convey to Maura that she should answer the boy, but she sat there mutely, staring at him. Joey glared at all of them and showed them his gun. "Stay here," he growled.

Betty Jo had been staring at his feet. "Uncle Joey?" Fortunately, she whispered it and Maura gave her arm a warning squeeze. She followed the child's eyes. There were sparkly stickers affixed to the toes of his boots. Maura hoped he didn't realize, or the children's lives were in far more jeopardy.

Joey nodded at the large man who had accompanied him and handed him the gun.

The man sat down on the edge of the table and stared at the silent group. Amber was crying, but didn't make a fuss otherwise. The other children were being quiet. Betty Jo was trying to get her brother's attention, but every time she did, Maura squeezed her arm, so she finally stilled.

There was a sudden ruckus from the main room, followed by a muffled explosion that rattled the windows and shook the floor.

Several of the kids yelped in surprise. Maura pulled the girls on her lap into a tight hug. The man with the gun yelled at them to shut up. He glanced at the door before focusing back on the hostages. "Keep quiet. There's gonna be a few more booms."

Pieces clicked into place in her mind. Joey had been studying the topography of the island. Was this all because of the old yarn about Quelch's long lost treasure?

Maura always figured it lay under the Atlantic somewhere. Something must have convinced Joey the old tales had truth to them. He wouldn't have broken into the library on a whim. He had three other men convinced there was something of value hidden in or under the library. She thought about the books he'd been borrowing. They would only have been helpful in understanding the island's physical structure better. Her eyes narrowed as another thought occurred to her. The break-ins. What exactly had been stolen from Jane's friends on the historical society board? Did they have "special" maps or documents in their homes, too? Had those been taken? She tried to remember everything Stephan had shared with her about the investigation, but her thoughts kept skittering away as her fears over the situation grew.

The muffled booms continued for several more minutes. Maisy and Betty Jo cuddled in Maura's lap. She felt Kevin shifting behind her and hoped he wasn't doing anything foolish. The man watching over them was bored and kept looking towards the door, but he glanced back at the hostages every time there was the slightest rustle or cough.

It felt like a cell phone was bobbing up and down against her back. Maura closed her eyes and paid close attention to what she was hearing and feeling. Yes, it felt like Kevin was texting. She offered up a prayer that he could get a signal and had his phone silenced. Mike was nudging his friend when their guard's attention was once again focused on the door.

Maura couldn't do anything to help the boys other than remain still and silent. To distract herself from the pins and needles hurting her legs, she mentally reviewed what she knew of the tunnels from experience and the maps she'd recently pored over.

On Jane's map, one tunnel went all the way out to the caves that Adam and other treasure hunters loved to explore near the weirs. There were a couple of others that seemed to start from the library and head in that general direction as well. It was the only map she'd ever seen that showed unbroken tunnels going that far. If you wanted something from the caves, it'd make more sense to access them by sea. But what if you were trying to get to a spot that was blocked?

Maura couldn't stop the shiver of apprehension. Joey hadn't expected anyone at the library, so whatever his plans were, he and his friends didn't need her or the children.

The door to the Children's Room smashed open. "Everyone up," demanded the voice of the burliest man—Colin, if her memory was accurate—as he strode into the room. Maura's legs wobbled as she tried to balance on them. She held Maisy and Betty Jo's hands as the group stared in silence back at the two intruders.

"We're going on a walk," Colin announced. "Keep yer coats, on kiddies. Bitch and moan and you'll regret it."

They followed Colin into the main room, with the gun-toting "T" bringing up the rear. When they reached the door in Maura's office that led to the small basement and the tunnel, Joey and the fourth man, Roger, were standing there waiting for them. When Colin again started issuing directions, Maura viewed it as confirmation that Joey was rattled by the presence of his young relatives. He was worried they'd recognize him. That he was trying to keep his identity from them was the tiniest bit reassuring. Her jacket was shoved into her chest.

"Follow us, brats."

Mike, Kevin, and Isabelle glanced at each other and Maura. Mike squared his shoulders and was the first to follow two of the men down into the dark stairwell. The rest of the hostages made their way down the creaky stairs, with Kevin and Isabelle in the rear. There was a bunch of swearing, banging, and crashing from Maura's office. Colin and Joey appeared a few minutes later at the top of the stairs and quickly joined the group.

Their kidnappers had swiped the library's solar lanterns and were using them to see as they finished trooping down the rickety steps and gathered in a tight clump at the narrow base. Maura looked at the gaping hole in the wall with dismay. The sturdy door to the tunnel between the Baptist Church and library was ajar. That explained how the men had gotten in, but not the blown-out wall.

Roger turned on a bright lantern and stepped into the dark maw. Everything inside her protested bringing the children into what she assumed was a newly uncovered tunnel, but the guns in their hands convinced Maura to usher the younger children through with her. She tried to go slowly to keep from stumbling over the rubble that littered the floor. It was a challenge with Betty Jo on her arm and Maisy clinging to her free hand.

Once everyone was in what was indeed an uncovered tunnel, the men sorted the hostages out so that the older kids were separated from one another and the younger four were with Maura in the middle of the group. They put on headlamps and handed the lanterns to the older kids.

The air in the tunnel was stale and thin as they started off. As the group walked further in, the rock walls went from smooth-cut to rough and the pathway narrowed, forcing them to walk single file. After twenty minutes, the air changed. It grew cold and damp. The sound of waves became audible. It started off as a soft murmur above their shuffling footfalls. As the waves grew into a more distinct crashing sound, the walls of the tunnel become damp to the touch, and they had to step through occasional puddles of water.

Maura tried to picture the tide charts for the week in her head. She felt a small measure of relief that they were just entering low tide. She knew her situation was bleak, but held on tight to the hope that the children could get away to safety. It was all that let her keep putting one foot in front of the other instead of screaming. When she saw Amber and Tommy both wiping tears away from their cheeks on the mostly silent trek, Maura reached out to give their shoulders reassuring squeezes as often as she could. Most of the time, Maisy and Betty Jo clung tight to her hands, and all she could give the two fourth graders were words of encouragement and, what she hoped were, reassuring smiles.

After maneuvering around yet another puddle, Maura let the image of Jane's map build in her head. The focus helped. There had been two branches off of the main tunnel under the library. This had to be one of them. But where exactly did it go? She chewed on the inside of her cheek as she thought about it. Based on the noise and water, this was likely the one heading towards the western caves.

As the group continued to make its way, the temperature began plummeting and the ambient light began to increase. The younger children held hands and moved closer together. Amber's teeth began audibly chattering and she started steadily crying again. Maura felt her heart ache, as she couldn't do anything else to ease the child's fear other than hand her the scarf that she still had stuffed in her coat pocket. When she passed the soft knit fabric to the girl, Maura gave her a gentle smile and squeeze. After that, Maura gave up trying to visualize the map. In the increased light, she forced herself to look for anything that could be used as a weapon.

Fred and Sam had been nursing mugs of hot tea and listening to the weather updates and police scanner from the comfort of Sam's cozy cottage on Water Street when the power went out. Sam had everything rigged to switch over to battery backup during outages, so their entertainment wasn't disrupted when the lights went.

Fred frowned when he heard Stephan's voice reporting that the library had children trapped in it. The two men had a pretty good idea of where the town's officers were based on the chatter they were listening in on. Colleen was the only one at the station, and she needed to stay there to handle dispatch unless one of the EMS volunteers made it in to free her up. The weather was forecast to continue deteriorating. None of the town's first responders were going to be able to get the kids to a warmer building anytime soon.

Sam nodded in agreement to Fred's unspoken question and went to get crampons out of the closet. "Marg, we're going out," he called to his wife. "Maura has a bunch of kiddies stuck with her at the library."

His wife appeared from the kitchen. "Why on earth did the school send them there?"

Sam shook his head. "Who knows?" He shrugged. "Fred and I will bring the lot back here. That okay with you?"

"Of course!" Margery nodded her head. "I'll add to the chowder I've got cooking on the fire. They'll all need something warm in their bellies when they get here."

"You're a good woman, Marg." Sam gave her a cheerful kiss and then handed Fred a pair of crampons to fasten on over his boots. "Better bring all the extra blankets we've got down here so they can warm up."

"I know what to do for a bunch of cold children, Samuel." Margery shook her head at him and then wagged a finger at the men. "The two of you had best take care, though. I know you're excited to have an adventure, but no one is going to have time to come and rescue you if you do something foolish like break a leg or hip on the ice."

Fred grinned at his friend's wife. "I'll keep him out of trouble, Marg."

"Just get the kiddies and Maura back here safely, along with yourselves." She tried to hide her concern, but saw it reflected in the expressions on their faces anyway. She gestured to the bindings Sam had in his hand. "Bring my set for Maura to wear. You'd best take some ropes for the kids to hang on to, and maybe the sleds. You three can pull some of them back here that way. They're on the porch where Benny left them."

"Good thinking, dear." Sam nodded. He grabbed his emergency backpack and tucked in the extra pair of crampons, along with all the hats and mittens their grandchildren had left behind with their sleds. He looped a sturdy length of rope through a strap. "Call Colleen and let her know what we're doing?" He began strapping the traction devices onto his boots.

Margery nodded her head. "Take your cells with you in case you run into trouble," she reminded them.

Fred patted his pocket.

"Don't stand there wrecking my floors with those things on your feet, then," she admonished them as she shooed them out the door.

The men chuckled and gingerly left the house. The wind was harsh and biting as they stepped out into the icy mess. Fred briefly wished he had his own gear, but let the thought go almost as quickly as it happened. There was no point in wasting time on wishes. He tucked his scarf around his face to protect as much of his skin as possible and slid his hands into his warm gloves. When he saw that Sam had finished doing the same, the two set off the quarter mile to the library. An easy stroll in good weather, it had become a perilous slog in the worsening storm. Neither complained as they trudged along.

The wind was howling and whipping ice pellets at their heads as Fred and Sam reached the darkened library doors forty minutes later. They stood in the vestibule shaking out their hands so they could remove the crampons from their boots before stepping through the doors into the library proper. As he was releasing the straps from around his boots, Fred sniffed the air.

"Hey, Sam, do you smell smoke?"

Sam furrowed his brow. "I thought my nose was playing tricks on me."

Both men gave each other worried looks and hurried into the library. The smell of smoke was strongest from Maura's office, but by unspoken agreement they first went to the children's room. Fred and Sam took in the blanket and snacks strewn on the floor and the abandoned backpacks. They explored the rest of the library in short order and couldn't find anyone. They went to Maura's office last.

"Christ." All of her knickknacks had been strewn around the room. Many were shattered. Books were ripped apart and tossed around and framed paintings had been smashed on the ground. Sam looked at Fred.

A cool breeze wafted up from the entry to the basement. The door had been shut, but was hanging loose and only upright because the upper hinge was still screwed to the frame.

"Why in God's name would she take them down there?" Sam wondered aloud.

Fred was at a loss as well. He flicked on his flashlight. He slowly looked around the room more carefully for clues as to what had happened and why Maura would have taken the children down there, if indeed that was where they'd gone. "Let's make sure all the other doors are still locked and that they didn't leave out the back."

Sam nodded in agreement and the two did another careful circuit of the building. There were small signs of disruption throughout; the turtle's aquarium was broken and books had been knocked off of shelves. The main door was the only unlocked one. They returned to the office and stood and stared at the broken door in silence.

"Better tell Colleen where we're going, then," Fred finally acknowledged and pulled out his cell. He moved around the building until he was able to get a decent signal and called over to the station. He explained what they'd found.

Colleen sounded as mystified as they were as to what could have happened. As they were talking it out, she put him on hold; someone was calling the 911 line.

After several minutes, she came back. "They could be in trouble. Kevin Jones sent his father a text almost 50 minutes ago that there were armed men in the library. Bill didn't see it until just now."

Fred swore. "We'd best be going after them, then."

"That's a negative, Fred. You don't have weapons and we don't have any info. You stay there. Ron and Chip are heading your way. Stephan's stuck out at the weirs with Doug and Bonnie and can't get out. I've already notified the Staties and Coast Guard, for whatever good that'll do."

"Where're Ron and Chip coming from?"

There was silence for a moment.

"Colleen, tell me the truth."

Fred heard her blow out a sigh before she answered. "They're at the Huberts'."

Sam shook his head as he listened in. "We ain't waiting the time it'll take them to get here in this weather." Fred nodded in agreement.

"We're going after them, Colleen. Let Ron know." Fred ignored the young woman's swearing and hung up on her. The two men gave each other grim looks and looked around for possible weapons. Fred grabbed a can of wasp spray that was sitting on a shelf and tucked it into a deep pocket. Both grabbed stout pieces of wood that had been blown out from the doorway. Sam ripped a shirt he found hanging behind the door and carefully wrapped some of the soft fabric around the bottom of a piece of jagged glass from a shattered picture frame to turn it into a makeshift knife. Fred nodded and followed suit.

While they were preparing, a text message came through on both their phones from Margery. *"Be careful. I expect ALL of you for dinner. Bring those kiddies home."* Clearly, a message had gone out on the scanner.

In silence, they began following the larger group that was ahead of them. Fred slipped ahead of Sam. Years of tracking in Yosemite and of observing the wildlife at Acadia had taught the retired park ranger to move with stealth. He kept one ear open to make sure Sam wasn't struggling and the other for any indication that they were approaching the larger group. They made good time now that they weren't slipping and sliding on ice. Knowing the children were in danger added urgency to their steps.

A rumble and vibration down the tunnel made both men pause and share a grim look before picking up their pace. The tunnel grew damp and the noise of the ocean increased as they drew closer to where the explosion had come from.

Voices and the lingering smell of smoke made them slow their steps. As they came to a bend in the tunnel, both froze and turned off their flashlights when a shadow formed on the wall. Fred waved Sam back and tried to blend in with a piece of the rock that jutted out a bit.

"Thought I saw something. Go on. I'll catch up."

The reply was faint.

Fred gripped his makeshift knife in a tight fist as footfalls drew closer. A headlamp played along the walls of the tunnel. He crouched lower, hoping to make himself less visible. Out of the corner of his eye, he saw Sam step away from the wall and into the middle of the tunnel. He gave his friend a fierce frown, but couldn't do anything because a burly man came into view. A ski mask covered his face.

Colin eyed the man standing in the tunnel. His weathered face was a testament to years on the sea. Colin had seen the old-timer around. The younger man glanced back behind him, towards the cavern that opened up near the weirs. He hadn't noticed a boat, but also hadn't been looking. "Bad day to get caught out, old man." He eased a crowbar he held into a better grip for swinging.

Sam kept his eyes on the hooligan and away from Fred. "Eh? You got caught in the storm too? Shit luck to have the engine give out in such crap weather. Didja get swamped? Didn't see another boat."

Colin passed Fred without noticing him. His eyes widened in surprise when his knee buckled from behind and a sharp burn spread down his leg. As he twisted to see what had happened, the fisherman bore down on him and clocked him hard with a steel barreled flashlight.

He managed a strangled cry before there was an intense burning sensation in his other leg. Colin tried to swing his iron rod at the old man, but found it wrenched out of his hands and used against his already-throbbing head. The tunnel tilted and everything went dark.

"Christ, you scared me, Sam." Fred took the rope Sam handed him and began to truss the unconscious man up. He yanked the man's ski hat off and grunted in recognition.

Sam took it and forced a good part of it into Colin's slack-jawed mouth before wrestling with the puzzle of how to keep it in place. When Fred handed him a small roll of duct tape, he beamed. "That'll do." He gave his friend an admiring look. "You always keep the best junk in those jackets of yours."

Within a couple of minutes, they had Colin well gagged and immobilized. Sam felt around his pockets and took his wallet and a cell phone. He turned the phone off and stuffed it and the wallet into his pack.

"Wonder how many there are. I always see this one with a group." Fred gave the kidnapper a disgusted look as Sam double checked all his knots.

"Dunno, but Quinn ain't going anywhere." Sam gave a satisfied grunt of approval. "We'd better get a move on. They're going to miss this clown soon."

Fred nodded in agreement and began moving forward again. They passed the wide cave most islanders knew and soon came upon the spot where a hole had been blasted.

"I'll be damned." Fred studied the surrounding stone. The seam of where the tunnel had been sealed up was nearly invisible. "Some impressive craftsmanship went into this. How'd they find it?"

Sam's expression was shuttered and he kept his thoughts to himself as they gazed down at the rubble scattered on the ground from the artificial wall's destruction.

They could hear voices wafting back periodically. Sam gripped the crowbar and nodded at Fred, who stooped down and shielded the beam from his light to keep it from spilling out beyond the radius of his feet as he gingerly eased himself into the tunnel. A couple of rocks shifted and fell with his passage. He pressed back against the wall and held his light so Sam could see where to place his feet as he slipped through the opening and joined his friend. They crept forward through a dark, narrow tunnel. As they moved, heading due east by Fred's reckoning, the sound of the waves receded and light once again faded. There was one turn that was a tight fit, but they managed to squeeze past the unforgiving granite.

After ten minutes of painstakingly cautious movement, voices began drifting back to them with greater clarity. The older men slowed their pace and turned their flashlights off. As they eased forward, a dim light began making it easier to see where they were going and the sound of gentle water could be heard. The tunnel began widening. Fred almost stumbled into the room before they realized it was there. Sam caught his arm and hauled him back. They pressed against the wall and behind an outcropping that framed the entrance. The air that wafted out was warmer than the ambient temperature in the tunnels they'd been traversing. There was a faint, acrid smell of smoke to it. Fred started to ease forward to get a better look, but again Sam pulled him back and pointed to his ear.

Fred frowned, but nodded in resigned agreement as they settled in to try and get a better sense of what they'd be walking into.

"Where the hell did Colin go?"

Sam arched an eyebrow. The voice was muffled, but he still recognized Joey Thompson's nasal tone.

Fred's frown deepened.

"Probably can't get past that narrow bend," came a deep voice neither man recognized.

"Want me to go find him?" A third voice chimed in.

"Nah. He'll find his way back. If he's stuck, we'll deal with it later. We've got bigger fish to fry here." There was some shuffling and the sound of crying filtered down to the men.

"Now kiddies here's the deal. You're going to do some work for us. If you do anything other than what we say, Miz Ballard here pays the cost." A woman's cry of pain could be heard. "Or maybe you'll be more motivated if you see that we mean business."

A piercing scream rang out. It was followed immediately by an aggrieved voice yelling. "Uncle Joey, stop being so mean! You're hurting Miz M."

Sam's eyes widened at Betty Jo's voice.

"Godddamn it, ya brat! I'm gonna hurt her a lot more, and you'll be next after I'm done." Joey's roar reverberated down the tunnel.

"What are you doing here?"

Soft as it was, the newcomer's words cut through the shouting. There was sudden silence.

"Oh, Lord," Sam whispered. Fred's face went white as he recognized Josie's voice.

Keeping track of the four children next to her took most of Maura's focus. Amber's crying was still quiet, but hadn't eased up. The group stopped in a decent-sized cavern while Joey and T set their charges against the far wall.

Colin and Roger pushed the hostages closer to the tunnel they'd just walked through. In the dimming light, Maura caught a glimpse of the sea down a side branch. She felt a pang in her chest as she realized how near the weirs—and most importantly, Stephan—they were. When Maisy started squeezing her hand in quick bursts, Maura looked down at the child.

Maisy tipped her nose towards the same direction Maura had been looking. A small smile played at the corner of her lips and the look she generally got when "speaking" to Karria was on her face.

Maura squinted and felt her eyes widen as she noticed a seal bobbing in the waves by the cave entrance. Based on Maisy's reaction, she assumed it was Karria. Even if it wasn't, Maisy was finding some comfort and that helped. She shifted her gaze to check on the rest of her charges.

Amber was plastered to her cousin Kevin's side. She was wiping her eyes with the colorful scarf Maura had given her. Kevin was saying something in her ear and awkwardly patting her back. Isabelle stood next to Kevin on his other side and Tommy kept reaching for her hand and then dropping it. After a moment of this, Isabelle grabbed the fourth grader's hand and held it tight. Maura watched some of the tension in his body ease as he let the teenager comfort him.

When they'd stopped, Betty Jo had launched herself into her brother's arms. Mike was holding her close and listening intently as she whispered something in his ear. Maura saw his eyes look towards the direction Joey had gone.

Please, she prayed, don't let either of them say or do anything foolish that would put themselves or the other children in any more jeopardy.

Maura squeezed Maisy's hand to get her attention. When the girl looked up at her with a question in her vibrant blue eyes, Maura whispered, "I love you."

Maisy whispered back, "I love you too. Karria will help us. She says we'll be okay."

Maura didn't share Maisy's faith that the creature could do anything to aid them, but she was grateful the girl had something to ease her fear.

A couple of booms followed by the sound of falling rock rolled down into the chamber.

Maura blinked back tears as the two men rejoined the group.

The one called T addressed them. "We're going on a treasure hunt. You kiddies are going to help us. If you do anything we don't like, we'll leave you down here alone in the dark to die. Got it?"

The children all stared at him in sullen silence.

T shrugged his shoulders. "Same groupings as before." When the chilled and frightened hostages didn't move quickly enough for them, the men started pulling them roughly by their arms to where they wanted them.

As the first group, led by Joey, started across the pile of unstable rocks by the new opening, Colin glanced behind them. "Thought I saw something. Go on. I'll catch up."

As they reached a narrow passage, Maura found herself pushed into T's back when Betty Jo stumbled and fell into her.

The man turned his head and smacked it on the rock. He swore loudly and looked down at her and the girls. "You're gonna regret that."

"It was my fault. I tripped." Maura had to clear her throat to find her voice.

He gave the girls and then her a sardonic look. "Whatever." He leaned close to her ear. "Do you really think he's going to let them go?"

Maura had been holding on to that very thought. Keeping the children safe was all that had been keeping her steady. Her throat tightened convulsively against the bile that was rising in it.

He nodded, pleased to see the fear that was starkly evident on her face. T turned and finished wiggling his way through the tight squeeze.

When Maura stumbled into a wide cavern behind him, she reached for the girls.

Joey started crowing. "It's just how my old man described it, dude! The treasure has to be here." He dropped his pack on the floor and pulled out a camping lantern. Within moments, the bright light from the lantern added to the dimming lights from the solar lanterns and headlamps.

T lowered his pack and pulled out an identical one. A minute later, all of their shadows flickered on the walls of the cave.

Roger followed suit and, though roomy, the cavern became reasonably well-illuminated.

Maura saw a couple of openings branching out of the room. One was dimly lit and along the ocean side, if the murmur of water was any indication. The gray stone was cool but dry to the touch. The rock above their heads was high enough for all of the men to stand comfortably. Her examination of the room was cut short when Joey yanked her hard by the arm, causing her to stumble into his body.

The predatory look in his eyes chilled her. He spun her to face the children.

"Now, kiddies, here's the deal. You're going to do some work for us. If you do anything other than what we say, Miz Ballard here pays the cost." He twisted one of her arms behind her back until she cried out in pain and then held a filet knife to her throat with his other hand. He let it sink in enough to spill blood down her neck before wiping it on her jacket and tucking it back into the sheath clipped to his waistband.

Tears leaked from Maura's eyes despite her best efforts not to respond to his assault. After making sure the kids saw the blood trickling down her neck, Joey brought his forearm to her throat and pressed it in. "Or maybe you'll be more motivated if you see that we mean business."

Maisy let out a piercing scream of protest and would have thrown herself at Joey if Kevin hadn't grabbed her and pulled her into a tight embrace.

From her spot by Mike's side, Betty Jo yelled. "Uncle Joey, stop being so mean! You're hurting Miz M." Her brother stiffened and reached for his sister as Joey dropped Maura's arm and yanked off his ski mask, sending his headlamp flying across the space, to glare at his youngest niece.

"Godddamn it, ya brat! I'm gonna hurt her a lot more, and you'll be next after I'm done." Joey's roar reverberated through the room. He proceeded to apply more pressure to Maura's neck, causing her to make involuntary sounds of protest as she struggled to get air into her lungs.

"What are you doing here?"

Soft as it was, the newcomer's words cut through the shouting and silenced them all momentarily.

"This doesn't concern you, freak." Joey's tone was harsh as Josie came into the lamplight. "Grab her, T." He grunted. "Gonna finish this."

Amber shrieked, "Stop it, you mean man!"

CHAPTER 20

Stephan kept glancing down at his phone after the last exchange with Maura. It had looked like she was still typing something, but then nothing arrived. He sent a quick message asking her to give Maisy a kiss for him and tell her he'd see them back at the station. He then pocketed his phone and clipped his radio to his belt before exiting the cruiser. Slipping and sliding, he made his way back to the small building attached to the dock that led out to the weirs. A generator chugged loudly from under an awning off the left side of the shack. It took a couple of hard yanks to get the door open, but once he did, the wind caught it and shoved it towards him with a force that almost knocked him off his feet.

"Sorry you got stuck out here with us," Bonita Jones handed Stephan a mug of hot soup after he finally wrestled the door shut against the whipping wind and ice. "Your daughter safe and sound?"

"Not your fault." He gratefully accepted the hot cup of tomato soup. "Thanks. Yes, Maisy's with Maura at the library. They've lost power, but are safe and dry."

"Least we can do." Her father, Doug, sat on a stool, glaring out the ice-coated window at the white-capped waves that were tumbling towards the shore. "Power goes out all the time in blows like this. I can show you those pictures once you've had a chance to drink that. We've got plenty of time to go over them."

Stephan nodded and took a tentative sip of the scalding hot liquid. "How many pens were cut?"

"Cages, and two, but they were our biggest ones; filled with salmon getting close to harvest size. With things all stirred up, there's no way we can get out there to repair 'em soon enough. Gonna lose the whole shebang. It was the new copper netting on top of it all." Doug looked resigned. "I don't see how we come back from this. Maybe we can at least get justice."

Bonita wasn't as calm as her father. "It was Joey fecking Thompson."

Stephan lowered his mug and set it on the stained and battered table that took up much of the room. "You have proof?"

She scowled. "Such as it is." Bonita pushed several papers over to him. "We blew up the images from the security cameras."

Stephan perused the pictures. They were grainy, but to his eyes, it certainly looked like the barrel-chested fisherman. "Do you have any that point to the parking area? Or the end of the dock past the cages?"

Doug nodded. He handed Stephan the images that were stacked by his elbow. "It sure looks like the *Carolina*, but none of them caught her name. He anchored at an angle that put much of her out of view."

"These date and time stamps are accurate?"

"Yes." Bonita nodded.

"As soon as I can get there, I'll pay Mr. Thompson a visit," he promised the father and daughter. "Any ideas why he'd target you?"

"We're competition in the eyes of some of the other fisher-men. They think we're cheating by farming the fish, even though most of 'em go for lobsta, mackerel, herring, and urchin. Some think we're going to wreck the fisheries if our salmon escape and others think we'll do too well and drive down prices." Bonita rolled her eyes. "This business is damned hard enough without fighting amongst ourselves."

Stephan glanced at Doug to see if he had anything to add. The grizzled man shrugged. "Bonnie's got the gist of it. I'd have thought it'd been an old-timer. Joey doesn't even make most of his money on fish, but he's a vindictive bastard."

Stephan arched an eyebrow.

"Bonnie broke up with him when he started stepping out on her. I'd wager she knows some of his shadier dealings, though she doesn't tell me nothing." Doug gave his daughter a pointed look.

Stephan looked from one to the other. "When was this?"

Bonita rolled her eyes. "Six months ago. It's ancient history. We are ancient history and you know it, Dad. He had to have some other reason for doing this. It's not like he's been sitting home nursing a broken heart over me."

Stephan picked up his mug to enjoy the soup before it got cold. The propane heater was keeping the worst of the chill out, but with the harsh wind working through every crack and crevice in the shelter, it was still cool in the room. He studied Bonita over the rim of his mug. She looked to be in her late twenties and had the no-nonsense look he'd come to associate with many of the island natives. Her dark blond hair was thick and shiny and she had expressive green eyes framed by lush lashes. What he knew of her from his time on the island was positive; hardworking, loyal, and, according to Chip, a wicked dart player. Bonita could easily do better than the man in question, as far as Stephan was concerned.

He just kept drinking his soup and waiting.

"Fine." Bonita blew out a sigh. "He got ugly when I told him we were done. Told me I'd regret it. But," —she shot her father a sharp look— "that was months ago. He's just a bully. If you stand up to him, he backs down. Aside from badmouthing me at The Point, he didn't do anything, and most folks there have his number by now. The ones who don't aren't worth my time."

Stephan nodded in agreement. "So, any ideas why now?"

Father and daughter gave identical shrugs.

"Dad's right. He has shady dealings. Maybe something's coming up and it was a warning to keep my mouth shut." She snorted. "Goes to show how little he knows me. Pulling this shit only makes me more likely to tell anyone who'll listen everything I know, which sadly, isn't much. He never told me much about how he was making his money and I didn't ask."

Stephan put his empty mug on the table and began looking at the photos again. The ice pellets hit the metal roof of the shack with rattling pings and the heater hissed. The scanner on a shelf near Doug's shoulder crackled to life from time to time with reports from the island's volunteer EMTs and fire department, as well as the coast guard. Periodic advisories from NOAA were also broadcast. It caught their attention when Colleen's harried-sounding voice came on. "10-31, repeat, 10-31. Possible armed robbery and suspected kidnapping in progress, Belfort Library. All units report to dispatch."

Stephan gripped the edge of the table. For a moment, he felt like the world had tilted on its axis and was about to throw him off before things righted and he remembered to breathe. He fumbled for the radio clipped to his belt. As he did, it crackled to life. "Kirkland respond on channel two."

Hearing Ron's voice urged him on as he switched channels and responded. "What's going on?"

In succinct sentences, the police chief told him everything they knew, from Kevin's text message to Fred and Sam's discovery. Stephan battled against a wave of helplessness as he stared out at the darkening sky. Even with the chains on the cruiser, it'd take him far too long to get back to town, and that was only if there were no trees down on the roads. Then there would be the time it'd take to track them down.

"Any idea where they're taking them?"

"Negative. All we know is they're in the tunnels, but if they busted open sealed ones the way Fred 'n Sam reported they could be heading in any number of directions."

Stephan closed his eyes and brought up a mental image of Jane's map. He forced himself to focus and thought about the tunnels that branched from the sealed one under the library. Most headed towards the western part of the island. He flicked the radio back on. "Ron, they could be heading towards me."

"Even if they are, and that's a really big 'if,' you can't get to them without a boat."

Doug had slid off his stool and now stood next to his daughter by the table, opposite the stricken-looking officer.

"Hey, Ron, I've got my skiff."

"Doug, you'd be swamped."

Doug peered out the window again. "Nah, it's not far to the big cave from here. It'll be a rough ride and we'll get wet, but she'll float."

"Negative." Ron's voice roared through the radio. "I've already got two old men traipsing through the tunnels after them. I don't need to worry about more of you. Stay put. That's an order!"

Doug reached over and muted Stephan's radio so Ron couldn't hear him. "He can't order me and Bonnie around, you know."

"Can you get me there?"

"You won't like the ride and I can't anchor safely in this mess, so you may have to weather it out in the caves for a while till we can get back, but yeah, I can get you there. If you get caught at high tide, you can ride it out down by the back wall. It never gets more than knee-deep that far back. At least you can poke around and try to find them. Better than sitting here, right?"

Bonnie started gathering up the photos to stow them back in the battered file cabinet and turned the stove off. "We'll all go. You'd better get any first aid supplies and blankets you've got in your car and leave us the keys. We can cover it with the tarps to keep the ice from freezing it shut."

"Kirkland!" Ron's voice barked through the radio's speaker again. "Did you hear me?"

Stephan looked at the radio and then at the Joneses. He nodded. "If you're willing to risk it, I'm in your debt."

"Kevin's m'nephew. He's a good kid, and Amber's a cousin." Doug reached for his wet weather gear and began tugging it on.

"Best leave that here." He pointed to the radio. "Won't do you any good to have Ron squawking at you if you're trying to be stealthy."

Stephan shook his head. "I'll turn it off, but I may need to be able to reach him. God knows if there's cell service down there."

Bonita was pulling on her own gear and suddenly waved her hand at the two men. "Shush. D'you hear that?"

They both stopped what they were doing to listen. After a moment Stephan heard the barking. "Karria," he breathed, and launched himself out the door.

Bonita and her father shared a bemused look and quickly finished dressing before following the officer out into the storm.

Stephan zipped his coat up as high as it would go and bent his head to try and protect his face from the stinging pellets as he pushed his way through the wind towards the water's edge, where a familiar seal clambered up onto the rocky wall that helped buffer the spit of land from the water. She barked again when she saw him coming.

Not knowing what else to do or how Maisy actually communicated with the animal, he gazed at her and thought hard: *Maisy's in trouble. We're going to help.* Out loud he called to the seal, "I'll be right back!"

He turned too fast and almost lost his balance before pinwheeling and catching himself on the icy rocks. As quickly as he could, Stephan headed for his vehicle and made a beeline for the emergency bag in the trunk. "Will this fit?" He called to Bonita as she gingerly made her way towards him. She nodded. Together the three of them made quick work of covering the car enough to keep it from becoming encased in anything more than the thin layer of ice that would inevitably form as it cooled.

The entire time, a small voice in Stephan's head keep chanting, "Hurry, hurry, hurry." It was agony.

By the time they approached the skiff that was bobbing up and down in the angry surf, Karria had slid back into the water and was floating near the small boat.

"Scram," Doug waved at the seal.

"No, she's here to help." Stephan was too anxious to worry about picking his words.

"Help? It's an opportunistic thief. Probably been feasting on our fish." Bonita scowled.

"Not this one." Stephan clenched his jaw as he launched himself into the craft that was bouncing up and down in the storm-whipped sea. "She's family," he shouted to Bonita over the wind once he was seated.

"That's just weird, Kirkland." Bonita was more surefooted as she hopped into the stern of the boat and yanked the engine's rip cord. It caught quickly despite the coating of ice and roared to life.

Doug finished untying the skiff and made it in just as a wave caught the small craft and pulled it away from the dock.

Once she saw they were underway, Karria leapt in front of them.

Stephan felt his gut lurch with the motion of the boat and the fear that was building inside him, but he tried to focus on the seal and where she was heading. "Follow her." He called back to Bonita.

She gave him a skeptical look and shouted, "I know how to get to the caves."

"She knows the right one."

Bonita looked at him like he'd lost his mind.

The small bay was sheltered from the worst of the swells, which were barely visible as large angry walls of gray and white in the distance. Even so, it was slow going getting to their goal, despite it being within eyesight. After cutting parallel to shore for fifteen long minutes, Bonita angled the small craft to ride the waves ashore towards the entrance to the largest of the cave openings. Karria appeared next to them and started barking furiously and slapping at the boat.

"Follow the seal," Stephan yelled.

"It's right there!" Doug gave the policeman an exasperated look and pointed at a black opening.

Karria positioned herself between the skiff and the entryway.

"Let her lead you, please." Stephan gave Bonita a desperate look.

She shook her head, but changed their heading so they were once again running at an angle rather than towards the shore. "This is crazy, Kirkland."

As soon as the boat shifted, Karria moved to the bow and leapt out of the water like a dolphin, leading them past the opening. Several minutes later she angled towards the shore. Bonita started to change course to follow and then frantically began trying to turn. "She's gonna crash us!"

A large, wall of granite loomed in front of them. Stephan narrowed his eyes as he watched the seal and then shook his head. "No, no, she's not. Don't you see it?" He pointed. "There's a gap. I think it's big enough." He leaned forward to get Doug's attention and pointed to what he saw.

"Where the hell did that come from?" The fisherman's eyes narrowed. "I know this area like the back of my hand. Ain't never seen that." He threw his arm forward and pointed for Bonita.

His daughter gave the opening a dubious look but aimed them for it.

"I dunno that we're gonna fit." Doug was frowning as they drew closer.

Light from the small craft's headlamp illuminated the opening and Bonita throttled the engine down. As they squeaked past the narrow entry, with Doug pushing at the right wall to make sure the boat didn't hit rock, she turned it off entirely.

All three felt their jaws drop as the narrow tunnel they were floating down opened into a high-ceilinged chamber. The water pooled and then ended on a gently sloping sandy bank. Karria was ahead of them, awkwardly pushing her way out of the water and up into the cavern. As they reached the water's edge, Doug hopped out and tugged the skiff forward to help it beach on the sand. Stephan clambered out after him and looked at Karria.

She tipped her head to the left.

He moved forward while Bonita and Doug got the boat settled. He played his light at the entry and eased forward into a narrow tunnel. Stephan backed out a moment later, pulled off his poncho, and grabbed his kit. "What am I going to need, Karria?"

He ignored the dubious looks Doug and Bonita were giving him and looked at the seal. Karria nosed through the bag and pulled out a multipack of foil blankets with her teeth. "Okay," He stuffed them into his jacket pocket. "You know where we need to go?"

She made a soft huff that he took as assent. He glanced back at the father and daughter and handed them the extra radio that was in the duffle bag. "If I'm not back in a half hour, radio Colleen and tell her where we are."

"We're coming with you, dummy." Bonita gave him a disbelieving look.

"I don't know what we're walking into." Stephan shook his head. He glanced back to where Karria had been and frowned to see that the seal had managed to move off without making noise. "Did you see where she went?"

"Not back this way." Doug shrugged. "She would've had to pass me. Damned odd behavior."

"And me, I know." Stephan couldn't help the small smile despite the grimness of the situation. He stared at the duo. "If I tell you to stay put, you need to do it. They have at least one gun and a bunch of hostages."

"We will." Doug agreed and Bonita nodded.

"All right." Stephan strode into the tunnel. "Come on." He began moving forward again, wondering if they were even going the right direction. It was possible they were missing paths that branched off without even realizing it. "Keep track of the wall on the left for tunnels." Stephan started moving again. A tang of smoke started wafting along the air currents as they continued forward. He instinctively began moving faster.

A scream pierced the air. Stephan blanched. He knew that voice. "Maisy," he breathed his child's name out and would have lunged forward if Doug hadn't yanked him backwards. He started to fight against the man's tight grip before he felt another hand grab his face and turn it.

In his worry for his child and fiancée, Stephan hadn't noticed the play of lights on the walls ahead. He'd almost stumbled right into the situation without any idea of what he was walking into.

"Uncle Joey, stop being so mean! You're hurting Miz M."

"Godddamn it, ya brat! I'm gonna hurt her a lot more, and you'll be next after I'm done." Joey's roar reverberated down the tunnel.

"What are you doing here?"

Soft as it was, the newcomer's words cut through the shouting and silence filled the tunnel.

Stephan clicked off his flashlight and crept forward.

"This doesn't concern you, freak." Joey's tone was harsh. "Grab her, T." He grunted. "Gonna finish this."

Stephan heard a whimper and one of the children shrieked, "Stop it, you mean man!"

"Amber," Bonita whispered.

"Bitch!" A deep voice roared.

"Who's the naked chick?" A third man's voice came to them. "Where are they all coming from?"

The noise of a gun cocking chilled Stephan to his core. He barreled into the cavern.

Several things happened all at once.

From their position, Sam and Fred, like Stephan, had flung themselves into the space the men and their hostages were holed up in. Fred held the can of Raid up and sprayed directly into the eyes of the unarmed man, who was gripping Betty Jo and Amber around their arms. He dropped to the ground, shrieking and writhing. The two girls grabbed hands and skittered away to the opposite wall.

Joey had an arm wrapped around Maura's neck and a gun pressed into her side. She was pale and her eyes were unfocused. Her jacket was ripped and a thin line of blood trickled down her neck, below where Joey was now choking her.

A naked woman with long, luxuriant black hair and a thick white streak running down the center of it was pulling children out of the room and pushing them into some unseen space behind her.

A bulky man with a gun was struggling to get a grip on a slim young woman with shaggy, short hair. Stephan recognized her as Josie from the harvest festival. The hand holding the gun was waving around.

The sound of a gunshot ricocheted off the walls. Maisy and the older boys, the only children still visible to Stephan, clapped their hands over their ears. He started to lunge for his daughter when pain blossomed in his shoulder.

"Daddy!"

Maisy pivoted away from the naked woman, who was reaching for her, and stepped towards her father.

Stephan shouted when he saw Joey lift his gun and aim it towards his child. He blinked rapidly, trying to clear away the sweat that was dripping into his eyes, and squinted. Before either man discharged their weapon, a rock whizzed through the air from behind Stephan and hit Joey in the head.

Dazed, he lowered his arm and Maura dropped to the ground.

Stephan reached for his child and yanked her behind him and into Bonita and then Doug, who pulled her further back and out of immediate danger.

"What the hell?" Joey's enraged scream filled the space. He started to lift his arm to aim the gun for Stephan when Bonita launched another rock into his right arm, momentarily weakening it and causing the gun to clatter down to the cavern floor.

Meanwhile, Josie, Sam, and Fred were dragging the big man to the ground. His gun had been knocked out of his hands and kicked to the side.

Joey turned his wrath on Maura, who lay unconscious near where his weapon had fallen. He sent a vicious kick into her back while shaking out his right arm and screaming profanity. His eyes darted around and he reached for his gun. He crouched down by

Maura and held the gun steady with both hands. He gave Stephan a malevolent smile. "I'll kill her if you move."

Maura's eyes slowly opened, the pain from the blow having roused her. She focused on Stephan and looked puzzled to see him there. She gave him a small smile before grimacing in pain. Maura was too far away to see the dark stain spreading over his jacket. She felt the muzzle of the gun press against her head and fought the urge to close her eyes in fear. She tried to make sense of what she was seeing and hearing. The only children left in her view were Mike and Kevin. Maybe that meant the others were safe. Stephan was here and Joey sounded desperate. She had to believe that meant the children would be okay. She kept her eyes on Stephan and whispered, "I love you," hoping he could hear her despite the distance and chaos.

At that moment, a haunting song began filling the cavern. It teased and taunted. The music and words seemed both familiar and otherworldly, comforting and disconcerting.

Maura felt the gun's pressure against her skull ease, but didn't dare move. Stephan was keeping his eyes locked on her and Joey so there was no indication from him as to what was happening. She did hear a gasp down past her feet, then a second voice echoing the ethereal sounds. The words weren't in a language she knew, but they sent a wash of warmth through her. The pain throughout her body flared momentarily and then began to dissipate. She blinked as a golden light filled her vision. She wondered if she was imagining it and gave Stephan a bemused look.

"What the hell?" Joey growled as a gold light seemed to wrap around his hostage like a net and his gun was forced away from her head against his will. He glared at Stephan and began to lift his arm when he heard a noise to his left. He glanced that way and caught a glimpse of a shapely, bare leg. As he tipped his head up, he started to register the large, gray shape hurtling down towards him. He felt a flare of pain and then nothing as the heavy cudgel bashed his skull in.

Maura struggled for a moment and then sat up, feeling far better than she had any right to given all that had happened. She slid away from Joey's body and bumped into a pair of legs before finding herself hauled up by strong arms hooked under her shoulders. "Come with me." The words filled her head, but not her ears.

"Okay, but—" Maura answered as she looked to see Stephan with his gun still pointed in her direction. Confusion and pain were etched on his face.

"Trust me." The voice was the same that had been singing the song that had seemingly healed her.

It clicked into place. "Karria. I trust you." She reached for a wide, long-fingered hand. She smiled at Stephan. "It's okay."

From the perspective of everyone else in the cavern, Maura and the woman melted into the wall and vanished from view.

Fred hurried over to Joey and the space Maura had been standing in. Stephan, clutching his shoulder, was trying to get there, too. He was hampered both by his injury and a frantic pair of arms that threw themselves around his waist.

"Daddy!"

"Maisy!" Stephan held her in a fierce, one armed hug.

"Maura's with Karria. She'll be okay." Maisy's eyes went wide as a drop of blood fell from his wound onto her hand. "Oh no, Daddy, you're hurt!" Tears started pouring out of her eyes. "Don't die, please don't die."

Stephan was feeling a bit shaky on his feet. He leaned back against the wall. "I'm not dying, love. Don't worry, Maisy Daisy. I'm not leaving you."

Fred glanced over from feeling the seemingly solid wall with a frown and saw Stephan's ashen complexion. He hurried to them. "Sit, lad." He looked at the girl. "Maisy, go get Sam's pack. It's by his feet."

"No need." Bonita slipped in next to them with the bright orange bag they'd brought from the police cruiser. She dropped it down next to Fred and unzipped it. "Can you put your gun down so no one else gets shot?" She eyed Stephan's weapon.

He nodded and handed it to Fred, who dropped the clip out and put it down on the flap of the bag. "Don't touch it," he admonished everyone around him. He eyed Mike and Kevin. "Don't touch any of them."

Fred then reached over and started unzipping Stephan's jacket. "Let's see what we're dealing with." He looked at Maisy. "Young lady, can you help Sam make sure everyone is safe and warm? We've got extra mittens, hats, snacks. Here, take a few of these too." He handed her some of the remaining foil blankets packed up in tight rectangles from Stephan's pack.

"Thanks." Stephan let his head rest back against the rock wall. "I'm getting cold, Fred."

"You're going into shock."

"Bonita, call Ron."

"On it," she assured Stephan as she turned the radio back on. It was staticky as she tried to find a channel that worked. "I'm just going back toward the skiff to try and get better reception. I'll be back." She pointed her direction to Sam.

"Was wondering how you all got here, since you didn't pass us." The old man patted her on the shoulder as she walked past him.

Josie stood back against the wall, watching the group. When no one was paying attention to her, she slipped into the narrow, well-hidden tunnel that Fred hadn't been able to find. She knew the path by heart and ducked and twisted when she needed to. Her pace only slowed as she reached her mother's chamber and heard Maura's puzzled voice.

Josie touched what appeared to be a solid wall with her hand and watched as it shimmered with a faint blue light and became translucent. She stepped through the opening.

The cave was dotted with chairs from varying eras, a couple of tables, and a bed draped with a colorful afghan and piled with an assortment of equally colorful, mismatched pillows. Books were stacked in an open chest alongside a guitar, wooden flute, and a stringed instrument Josie knew Maura would never have seen before. A half-completed chess game was out on one of the tables.

The pieces of intricately carved marble gleamed in the golden light that suffused the room.

Josie's mother was reaching into one of her crevice hidey-holes while Maura was looking around the room in amazement. Josie dropped into her favorite seat.

"You look shell-shocked." She chuckled when Maura jumped and spun to face her.

"Josie! Stephan, Maisy, everyone, are they okay? How did you get here?"

Josie nodded. "Stephan was shot in the shoulder. Fred is tending to him. Everyone who matters is safe." She tipped her head to the side. "Yes, mother."

Maura glanced back at the other woman in the room and then over to Josie again.

A slight smile played around Josie's lips. "Yes, Karria is my mother."

"You're—" Maura hesitated and then blurted it out. "Selkies, aren't you?"

"That's what you call us, yes." Karria's accent was unidentifiable. She gave Maura a gentle look and gestured to a folding chair that was padded with a seventies-era daisy cushion set. Karria sat across from her in a simple wooden chair. She put a leather pouch that clinked and gave a heavy thud when dropped down on the table. Her large black eyes were fathomless as she gazed at Maura. "You have questions. Another day I may answer some."

Josie's bark of laughter reverberated in the room. "I'll come over for lunch and answer more tomorrow." She grinned at her mother's frown.

Maura looked between the two as the silence dragged on, aware there was a conversation going on that she wasn't privy to. She wrapped her arms around herself, struggling with her fascination and curiosity, as well as the intense need to make sure for herself that Stephan, Maisy, and the others were in fact safe.

"Take this." Karria pushed the bag across the table to Maura. "We don't have the need. It will help you and keep the intruders away."

Maura reached for the bag and pulled it open. Her eyes widened as she took in the handfuls of coins. "This is a fortune. I can't take it from you."

Josie pushed out of her chair and moved to stand next to Maura. "We want the treasure hunters to stop. If you show up with this and Ron swears there isn't any more here, it should help. Fred and Sam will help me seal off the entrances afterwards."

"But won't that trap you here?" Maura gave them each a worried look.

"No, we have many ways in and out—well, my mother does. I'm stuck in this form, so it'll be trickier for me, but I'll manage." She gave Maura a slight shrug. "She can come via underwater passages I can't use."

Maura's eyes widened. "Oh!" She turned and gripped Josie's hand. "Stephan saw an unusual pelt."

Josie's eyes narrowed. "Where?"

"In the town offices. There's a secret room. He couldn't tell me much about it, but he told me about that. It has markings like Karria."

Both women fixed her with sharp gazes, leaving her feel distinctly like prey. She fingered the silken drawstring that was threaded through the leather.

"Your mate will tell us more another day." Karria nodded her head with a decisive motion.

"I will be at your home at noon," Josie touched Maura on the shoulder. "I'll lead you back to the others for now."

"Yes. The child is getting scared again. She needs you. So does your mate."

Maura looked around the room and saw no obvious exit. "Umm." She stood and turned to look, but couldn't figure out how to leave.

Josie picked up the bag and pushed it into her hands. "I'll take you."

Karria reached for the woman and pulled her into an embrace. "Your kinswoman saved my life. I have saved yours. The debt is paid."

"Is that all this was?" Maura felt a stab of disappointment.

Karria gave her a puzzled look.

Josie understood and gave Maura a sympathetic look. "Yes and no." There was silence again as the two selkies communicated.

Karria gave Maura a slight smile. "Jane held my heart and I hers. The debt is over but the—" she looked at Josie and then nodded. "The love is not."

"But you never spoke to me all these years." Maura felt tears pricking the backs of her eyes.

"First it was to protect my child. Then pain. It caused pain." Karria shook her head.

Josie gave Maura's arm a squeeze. "I think I can help you understand better, tomorrow. We need to go now. You've been gone too long, and I still need to show you the bones."

"Okay." Maura held the bag in both hands and gave Josie a mystified look. "I still don't see where we came in."

Josie smiled. "Follow me." She waved to her mother. "I'll be back."

Karria nodded and hesitated a moment before striding over and pulling Maura into a brief but tight embrace. She tapped one finger on Maura's chest over her heart. "Love stays."

Tears leaked out of Maura's eyes and she nodded. She was spun around. Her jaw dropped as she saw Josie touch the wall. It seemed to vanish under Josie's hand. She felt herself get gently shoved from behind and stumbled after the younger selkie back into the tunnel. When Maura turned to take a last look at Karria's cavern, she only saw impenetrable granite.

Josie reached back for Maura's hand and led her carefully through the dark, narrow passageway. Maura could hear familiar voices growing louder as they went. Lights from flashlights and lanterns were glowing ahead. She quickened her pace, eager to rejoin Stephan and the others. She would have gone right past the small alcove if Josie hadn't grabbed her and forced her to stop. "Here. You'll need to bring them back here later."

As Maura stepped towards the alcove, she could barely make out the gleaming white bones of a foot. She gave an involuntary yelp of surprise.

"You got the bag from the chest right there," Josie pointed to the left of the remains. "You don't know the woman who saved you. You followed her here and then she vanished."

Maura nodded. "Okay."

"Miz M? Hey, Miz M, was that you?" Mike's voice came from just around the bend.

"I'm here, Mike, with—" Maura glanced around and realized Josie was gone. "I'm here," she repeated in a weaker tone.

A flashlight lit the space and Mike, Kevin, and Sam all hurried to her side. Sam pulled her into a fierce embrace. "We were worried."

"Whoa," Kevin whistled and pointed to the human skeleton with the flashlight Doug had given him.

"Yeah." Maura showed Sam the leather pouch. "Whoa is right." She gripped Sam's arm. "Stephan?"

"Will be fine," Sam assured her. "Fred says he's going to need surgery to get the bullet out, but he and Bonnie slowed the bleeding. They're doing what they can for the shock. It'd do him a world of good to lay eyes on you."

Maura nodded and hurried past the man and boys to get back to the rest of the group. She flew past the two bound men and didn't spare a glance for Joey Thompson's Mylar-covered body.

"Maura!" Maisy launched herself into the woman's midsection as Maura reached the knot of people gathered around Stephan.

His skin was gray-tinged, but he managed the ghost of a smile when he saw her standing in front of him.

Maura dropped to her knees and thrust the bag into Maisy's hands so she could grip one of Stephan's cold ones in her own. Tears streamed down her cheeks. "I'm so sorry."

His hand gave a light squeeze. "I am. I didn't protect you."

"You did!" She pulled her mittens out of her coat pocket and forced them onto his hands. "You're freezing."

"I found the hand warmers." Doug came over from where he'd been rummaging through Sam's pack. "Hey, Maura. You look a hell of a lot better." He handed the warmers to Fred, who slid them under the foil blanket and onto Stephen's abdomen. Doug then moved off with a fistful of granola bars for the kids, after handing one to Maisy.

"We've got to keep his core warm," Fred explained in quiet tones in Maura's ear.

The radio near Bonnie went all staticky again. She grumbled, but went back into the tunnel and headed towards the skiff.

"Maura, this is worth a whole lot, isn't it?" Maisy had opened the bag and was gazing at the gold and silver coins. "Like treasure, right?"

"Yes, Maisy." Maura reluctantly took one of her hands off of Stephan's and wrapped her arm around Maisy to bring the girl to her lap and hold her in a half-hug. "It's for all of us here, but right now we need to keep it safe and secret."

Maisy nodded. "Okay." She unzipped the generous inner pocket of her jacket and stuffed the pouch into it before zipping it back up again.

Fred nodded in approval and gave her a wink. "You're gonna have to let me take a peek when this is all over, young lady."

"If Maura says it's okay," was Maisy's prompt reply.

Fred chuckled and ruffled the child's hair. "Good girl, listening to your mother."

Maisy's eyes were worried as she looked at her father, but she managed to give the old ranger a small smile. "I love her," she whispered to him from her spot snuggled up against the woman in question.

"I know you do, sweetheart." Fred's expression was gentle and he smoothed down the hair he'd mussed. He gave Maura an affectionate look. "Lots of us do."

Maura heard their conversation, but wasn't paying attention to it. Her attention was fixed on the crimson stain that was starting to seep through the thick layer of white bandaging wrapped around Stephan's wound.

"Cutter will be here in about 10 minutes. They were already on their way to the area. Ron, Chip, and Colleen are in the tunnels from the library direction. Jim's manning dispatch. He reckons they've already been heading our way for a half hour or so. I told him to send the cutter to the entrance that we all know, but I'm not sure how to get there from here. I figure it's that-away." Bonita pointed in the direction Fred and Sam had come from. She shot the old men a look. "What if they get lost down here?"

"It is," Sam nodded. "I'll take you there. We can get them back here. The coasties'll need to pick up the fellow Fred and I left hogtied back there too. A doctor should probably look at him. Ron's lot'll be fine. We left a trail of breadcrumbs, so to speak." He shot Stephan a concerned look. "Not sure how we're gonna get him out, but we'll manage. It won't be on a stretcher, that's for sure."

She nodded. "Thanks, Sam." Bonita glanced over at Stephan, whose eyes were closed. "The boat'll go to Castine. They're confident they can get a med flight from there to Bangor. I guess the ice's been turning to rain while we've been down here and it's going to stay that way overnight till the storm blows off. Some shaft of warm air flowed in unexpectedly." She shrugged. "It's the least weird thing about this afternoon." She gave Maura a puzzled look and shook her head. "Someone's going to have to explain what happened." She waved at the other woman's throat.

"What about these guys?" Doug pointed at their prisoners, both of whom were moaning and complaining, particularly the one whose eyes had been sprayed.

"Guess they'll take 'em by boat and decide on the way how to get 'em to Bangor." Bonita shrugged. She looked over at Joey's body, which had been covered with Mylar. "Are we sure he's dead?"

Sam nodded. "Yep." He fished around in the police kit and found some flares.

Her expression was conflicted. Sam nodded in agreement as he walked over to her. "Ayuh, I think we all feel that way. Come on. It's a walk to get to the rendezvous point. We'll set these off so they see us."

"Yeah, sure." Bonita nodded.

"Can we come too?" Kevin hooked his thumb back to where Betty Jo and Amber were crying. "It's too much here for me and Mike."

Bonita grimaced. "You should be comforting your cousin, and Mike ought to be helping his sister."

Both boys uttered deep sighs.

"Yes, ma'am," Mike sighed again.

As she and Sam were walking out of the cavern, Bonita complained. "When did I become a ma'am?"

Sam patted her arm. "You're practically a babe in nappies to me if it helps."

"You know just what to say to make a girl feel better." Bonnie shook her head at him but smiled.

"How did you get in?" Sam remembered that he still didn't have an answer to that question.

"Believe it or not, a seal." Bonnie explained why Stephan was with them and what had happened as they picked their way through the tunnel and into the cave.

Sam didn't look surprised.

Once the flares were lit, they stood in companionable silence waiting to hear the noise of the cutter. Instead, they heard voices.

"What the hell?"

Ron's annoyed voice reached them and Sam grinned. "They found our first prisoner. I'll be right back Bonnie."

Bonita heard him shout a greeting to the police as he walked away.

A moment later she heard the familiar chugging of a lobster boat. Its lights were on, but she couldn't make out the name.

"Hey, anyone there?"

She grinned at her cousin Bill's voice. "Heya, Bill," she shouted.

The engine throttled down and a big floodlight lit the area. "Bonnie? That you?"

"Yeah."

"Is Kevin okay? What the hell is going on?"

"The kids are fine. Glad to see you." She waved when the boat eased up next to the opening. "Officer Kirkland was shot. The coasties should be here any minute to evacuate him to Bangor."

On cue, the sound of a larger engine came to them and large floodlights further illuminated the area.

Bill nodded and eased the *Laney Sue* out of the way so the cutter could anchor as close to the opening as possible.

Ron and Sam arrived as the first seaman hopped into the wide entrance. "My officers are bringing a prisoner. He'll need a medic too, but I've got an officer down."

Colleen worked quickly with the crew of the cutter, Bonita, and Bill to organize how they'd get everyone out.

It didn't take long. Joey's body bag had to be pushed and pulled out. Once the body was stowed out of sight on the cutter, they quickly ferried the children, Fred, and Sam out. The children, who were past ready to be home with their families, practically sprinted to get to the boats. Dr. Taylor insisted Stephan be among the last to leave, since he didn't want him disturbed any more than necessary. Maura and Maisy both refused to go until the last possible moment.

"Daddy." Maisy's tearful voice broke Maura's heart. "Please let me stay with you. I'll be good."

Stephan was starting to slip in and out of consciousness thanks to blood loss, shock, and the injection Dr. Taylor had given him to help him rest on what was bound to be an unpleasant trip. He reached for his daughter's hand and gave a gentle squeeze. "Stay with Maura, love."

Maura put an arm around the sobbing girl's shoulders. "We'll go to Bangor first thing in the morning, Maisy, as soon as the roads are safe to drive."

Ron nodded. "I'll drive you both myself."

Stephan smiled slightly and sagged against the stretcher that had been slid off the boat and into the cavern entrance to transport him. "See you soon sweetheart."

Maura bent down, gave him a gentle kiss, and held her trembling hand to his cheek. "I love you. Stay with us."

"I will," he promised. "Call Nick."

Maura nodded and lifted Maisy up so she could reach her father. The small girl swiped at the tears that were rolling down her cheeks and gave him a kiss on the cheek. "I love you, Daddy."

"Love you, Maisy Daisy."

Maura found herself helped into the cutter and then across the side onto Bill's crowded boat. Maisy was handed over to her in short order and they moved into the cluster of children to make room for Ron as he hopped over. Maura and Maisy moved to the side so they could watch the larger vessel as it moved off and swung around to head into the open ocean. Once the Coast Guard ship was out of sight, Maisy threw herself into Maura's arms and started sobbing like her heart would break.

Neither noticed the bouncing and rolling as the boat fought its way back around the island to its berth. As the boat approached the breakwater, all the floodlights were on and illuminating the area. The whine of generators and smell of fuel filled the air. Cars and trucks lined the wall and had their headlights shining out at the sea as well. When the *Laney Sue* approached to pass by and turn into her slip, a large cheer went up. Heartened by the fact that they'd be seeing their parents momentarily as well as getting back on stable land, even the wobbliest of the children cheered back to the crowd.

Before they disembarked, Maura reached out to Sam and Fred and embraced them each in turn. "Thank you for coming to find us." Her eyes were bloodshot and her cheeks tearstained, but she managed a smile for each of them. "You saved our lives."

Both men flushed and tried to shrug off her gratitude, but then found themselves piled on by all the children hugging them.

Ron grinned at their discomfort and then shook each of their hands when he could reach them. "You're bona fide heroes, even if you disobeyed orders."

"Anyone would've done the same." Sam turned to help Bill tie up the boat so the children could be reunited with their families.

"No, Sam," Maura touched him on the shoulder and then reached for Fred. "You two are special."

"You can thank us by having us round for cake and coffee in a few days and telling us what happened when you vanished, and about—" Fred paused and noticed Ron listening. "About the rest as well." He gave Maura a quick, hard hug. "I'm glad you're safe, Maura."

Ron tapped her on the shoulder. "I hate to interrupt, but I am going to need to get statements from everyone and I need to let the youngsters go first. Bill, I already got Kevin and Amber's on the ride. You can take them home. Maura, Sam, Fred; I'm going to need to ask you three to hang at the station for a bit."

Maisy looked up at Ron with wide eyes. "I'm staying with Maura. Don't make me leave her."

"Ah, sweetheart," Ron crouched down so they were eye level. "There may be a few minutes when I need to talk with her alone, but when I do, you can play with the puppy, okay?"

Ron hopped off the boat and, with Bill's help, got everyone safely onto the pier. Parents started breaking off from the crowd to run to their children as they appeared. By the time Ron had herded the group of witnesses and associated family members to the station, his temper was starting to fray. When he saw Vicky waiting in the main room, he sighed in relief. She'd help him corral everyone. As they all stepped into the welcome warmth and light of the room, the smell of fish chowder, coffee, and baked goods enveloped the bedraggled group.

Margery, George, and Josephine emerged from the break room. Margery hurried over to Sam and Fred. She embraced Sam and then pulled Fred in for a hug before embracing her husband again. "I was so worried."

"The soup smells divine, Margy." Sam held his wife close for a long moment.

"There's enough for everyone. You all must be chilled to the bone. George and Jo brought bread and other goodies."

"We have blankets and fresh clothing for everyone who needs them." Vicky moved towards Maura and Maisy, first since all of the others had at least one family member present who had had an opportunity to bring things from home. "Come with me." She reached for their hands and brought them into a small room where a couple of cots were made up with fresh linens. Fluffy, colorful quilts were piled upon them. A stuffed bear sat on one next to a pair of child-sized pajamas and thick socks. A roomy "Belfort PD" sweatshirt was folded next to them. "Maisy, I thought you'd like to snuggle in your Daddy's sweatshirt. I got it out of his locker."

Tears started leaking from the girl's eyes again and she nodded her head.

"The bear is for you, honey. I'm sorry I couldn't get Dot." Vicky looked to Maura. "I wanted to go to your houses to get familiar things and feed the cats, but Hal and Carl spent so much time making sure the others could get here safely that they haven't tended your road. It's still a sheet of ice. They're going to work through the night to make sure you can get home in the morning. I'm sorry." Vicky looked dismayed. "We tried. Oh, Maura, these are for you." She gestured to a pair of sweatpants, a hoodie that matched Stephan's, and another thick pair of socks.

Maura felt tears prick her own eyes as it hit her that she and Maisy were safe.

Vicky saw their expressions and frowned. "Don't turn water-works or I'll start. Change and come get something to eat. Maisy, hon, I'll bring Polly over in a little while, after the other kids are gone."

After Vicky shut the door behind her, Maisy launched herself into Maura, knocking them both over onto a cot.

"Hang on, sweetheart." Maura kicked off her own boots and tugged off the girl's. She stripped off their dirty, sodden jackets and dropped them onto the lone chair in the room before slipping back onto the cot and pulling the sobbing child close.

CHAPTER 21

After an hour or so, there was a knock at the door. Maura cleared her throat and managed to croak out, "Come in."

Josephine stuck her head in. "I know you probably don't want to, but you both need to eat. Ron says you've got a big day ahead of you tomorrow, and he still needs to get statements from you tonight." She pushed her way into the room with a tray. She set it on the nightstand and sat down on the cot across from them.

The tempting smell of chowder reminded Maura that she hadn't eaten since breakfast. She spooned a bit into her mouth, but had trouble swallowing past the lump in her throat as her eyes landed on the clock. She wondered if Stephan was on the med flight yet.

Josephine gave Maisy a speculative look. "Maisy dear, you've been excellent at keeping Karria's secret." She gave Maura a placid smile when the younger woman gave her a startled look. "I've known Karria for longer than you've been alive Maura. She and Jane had a special relationship. Different from the one you have with her Miss Maisy.

"Maura's Aunt Jane was a special woman. I was blessed to call her my friend." Josephine gave Maura a fond look and then continued, "Tonight's not the night for the tale, but Jane saved her, and it was the start of a lifelong love affair for the two of them." Josephine's eyes got misty and she smiled. "Karria has never spoken to any of us except Jane, until Maisy came along. She and Josie have held part of our hearts and been a part of our community for many years."

"Can I show her Maura?"

"Sure." Maura was still looking at Josephine in shock.

Maisy sat down next to the baker and pulled the thick leather pouch out of her jacket pocket. The brown leather was cracked and dry and the silken cord was fraying with the color long faded out of it. She opened it so Josephine could look inside.

"Oh, my word." The older woman reached in and plucked out a few silver coins. "I've never seen these before."

Maisy peered into the bag too. She pulled out one that she recognized. "Karria gave me one that looks like this after Halloween. Maura's friend from the bank came over to tell us about it. They're worth a bunch of money."

"So there really was buried treasure all this time?"

A knock on the door interrupted the conversation. George stuck his head in. "Ron'd like to have a chat with you ladies when you're ready."

Maisy shot up, forgetting all about the bag of coins in her lap and sending them spilling. "Is it about Daddy?"

Maura went pale when she saw George hesitate. She was able to breathe again when she realized his gaze was fixed on the coin that had just rolled into his foot.

"Uh, no, dear. I think he's ready to get your witness statements." He bent down to pick up the coin and winced as his knees gave an audible crack. "Never seen one like this before." He spun the coin around between his fingers, looking at it from all angles.

Maura crouched down to make sure everything that'd fallen was picked up, while Josephine put the ones that'd spilled onto the cot back in the bag.

"Can I take a better look another day?" George handed the coin back to Maisy.

"Sure, if my mom says it's okay."

Maura stilled. Maisy gave her a worried look.

"Did I say something wrong?"

"No, sweetheart," Maura pulled her into a tight hug. "You just made me feel wonderful."

"Oh, good." Maisy's voice was muffled against her shoulder. "I love you, Maura."

"I love you, too, Maisy."

George smiled and dropped the coin into Maisy's hand when Maura released her. "You know where to find me. Ready, darling?" He offered a hand to Josephine.

Josephine handed the pouch to Maisy. "You might want the Chief to lock that up until you figure out what to do with it."

Maisy nodded and handed the bag to Maura. "Mom'll know what to do. She always does."

Maura was quite certain she didn't, but the child's faith in her, especially after the horrible day they'd had, warmed her. She tucked the pouch under their jackets and squeezed Maisy's hand as they joined everyone who was left in the main room. An excited puppy scampered over and began frantically licking the girl's stockinged feet and, when she sat on the floor, her face and ears.

After all the goodbyes had been said and the older folks had left, the two adults sat down at the large desk in the main room. Maura reached for the framed picture of her, Maisy, Evelyn, and Karria that Stephan kept there. Her eyes widened as she realized she'd never called Nick.

"What is it?" Ron was enjoying drinking his coffee in silence, but saw her expression.

Maura glanced at Maisy and then whispered, "I need to call Nick and their parents."

Ron glanced at the clock. "It's the middle of the night there, and we don't have any news yet. I've fielded a couple calls from the media, but haven't told them much. At least the weather's working for us in keeping the press away. They're asleep and won't have heard anything, is what I'm saying, Maura. There's nothing they can do but lie awake and worry right now. Let 'em have the rest. Call before you turn in." He took a long drink and put his mug down. "Why don't you go change while I chat with Maisy. Then we'll let her cuddle with Polly while we talk."

Maura forced herself up from the chair and back to the other room. As she went, she saw Ron sit down on the floor with the girl and dog. She heard the low rumble of his voice and Maisy's higher pitched one respond as she shut the door.

Maura went to Maisy's cot and picked up Stephan's sweatshirt. She held it to her nose. The scent of his soap still clung to the material. She inhaled deeply and felt a sob burst out of her throat. She grabbed a pillow and sank down onto the cot before burying her face into it and crying as noiselessly as possible. She sobbed out her fear, her anger, pain, and relief until she felt empty inside. After the tears trickled to a stop, Maura splashed water on her face in the small bathroom and quickly changed into the clothing Vicky had brought for her. After drawing in a deep breath, Maura stepped back into the main room. Ron was in his office with the door open. He looked over at her from his desk with a sympathetic smile. Chip had returned from the weirs and was sitting on the ground across from Maisy. They were rolling a tennis ball back and forth for Polly to romp after.

After Maura took the seat across from him, Ron commented, "I'm going to have some more questions for Maisy after she's had a chance to rest. She had some," —he hesitated— "interesting things to say at times. Actually, a few people did, and I'm curious to hear your take on things."

Maura could guess what he was referring to. "Ron, I'll tell you everything, but some of it sounds incredible and some would put," —she briefly wondered about the linguistics and then gave a mental shrug— "would put people in danger if it became public."

"Josie and Karria?"

Maura nodded.

"I'm trying to figure out how to keep them out of the official record. Fred and Sam seem to know where Josie actually lives, but wouldn't tell me, no matter what I threatened them with." He sighed. "She and this Karria woman can both be in the record as Jane Does for now, but I will need to speak with them. As to the miraculous healing and vanishing act you pulled," he spread his hands. "I'm still figuring out how to address that. Maybe you'll be able to enlighten me." He gazed at her for a moment. Ron then began to rapidly click his pen as he thought out loud. "I don't want an invasion of treasure hunters, and I want to protect these women as much as you all do. They were on the right side of things. We'll figure this out. I'll definitely need to sleep on it, though. We all do." He pulled out a clean piece of paper. "Take me through what happened from the beginning."

Maura drew in a deep breath and began reliving her day from hell. Every now and then, Ron wanted to go back over a detail or ask a question, but for the most part she spoke and he took down notes. By the time they'd wrapped up, it was almost 11 pm.

Ron's phone buzzed as he was putting the notes he'd just taken in a folder with the rest. "Chief Moore speaking. Yes, Doc. Uh-huh. That's wonderful news. Thank you. Yes. His little girl and fiancée are here. They'll be relieved. We'll be over tomorrow as soon as the roads are clear. Uh-huh." He smiled. "Yeah, she's a pain in the ass, but she means well. Kick her out if she gets in the way. Yeah, I'll call and tell her myself. Got it. Thanks again. We all appreciate it. Okay. Bye."

Maisy had shot up from the floor and was standing at the desk gripping Maura's hand as Ron was talking. Chip had joined her and all three stared at the chief while he spoke to the surgeon.

"Stephan came out of surgery with flying colors. He'll have some rehabbing to do, but they're hoping he'll get full use of his arm back. They're keeping him for a few days so he can stay on IV fluids and antibiotics. If he's healing well, he can come home and do PT in Ellsworth. If there are complications, he may need to do a stint at one of the rehabs in Bangor, but either way," he spoke directly to Maisy. "He is going to be absolutely fine, and everyone is going to work hard to get him home to all of us as soon as possible."

Maisy nodded her head and started crying again. "I'm so happy," she wailed through her tears.

Ron stood up and held the girl in a tight hug. "I know you are, sweetheart. We all are. Can you come help me take Polly for a walk before I drive home with her? I don't want her piddling in my car."

"Okay." Maisy gave Maura an uncertain look. "Will you be okay if I go?"

"Of course, sweetheart. I'll be right here with Chip. And when you get back, it'll be bedtime for both of us."

"I'll be out here all night making sure you're safe," added Chip.

"I have to get my coat."

"Ah, yes. And you and I can pay a visit to the place we talked about on our way out, okay?" Ron patted his jacket pocket as he shrugged his own coat on.

Maisy gave a solemn nod and looked to Maura to make sure it was the right thing to do. When Maura nodded back, she skipped off to get her coat and tuck the treasure pouch back into the pocket.

Chip gave them a puzzled look. "What am I missing here? You're all talking in some weird code."

"In good time, Chipper, in good time." Ron patted him on the shoulder and clipped a leash to Polly. "I'll buy you as much time as I can to make your call, Maura."

"Thanks, Ron." She gave him a grateful smile, then held her arms open for Maisy. The girl rocketed into them for a hug and kiss before joining the chief. As the duo started walking to the door, Maisy began quizzing him about the surgeon's exact words.

Maura gave a weary smile to Chip. "I need to make an international call."

"Figured as much. Here, use Ron's office."

The phone rang several times before a bleary voice answered, "Feck all. Do you have any idea how early it is?"

"Nick, it's Maura."

"Oh God." His tone changed and he began peppering her with questions. "What happened? Is it Stephan? Is it Maisy? Are they okay? Do you need us to fly over today?"

"Nick!" Maura cut him off. "Please, just listen. Maisy's fine and Stephan will be okay." Without getting into all the details, she outlined the day's events for him.

While they'd been talking, the wave of exhaustion that she'd been holding at bay overtook Maura. She barely stayed awake as Nick began discussing flight options and the best way to get from Boston to Bangor. Her eyes were closing when Ron stepped in and plucked the phone from her weak grip.

"This is Ron," he paused. "Good morning, Nicholas. Yes, thank you. Look, Maura's almost asleep at my desk and Maisy's not going to turn in without her. Yes, okay. Yes, I'll put you back on with her if that's all." Ron gave Maura a gentle nudge and slid the receiver next to her ear.

"Mmmhmm," she managed.

"Maura, I just wanted to say thank you for being there for Stephan and Maisy. I'm really glad they have you."

"Me too." She tried to keep her eyes open. "G'night, Nick." She gave Ron a bleary-eyed look. "Where's Maisy?"

"In bed waiting for you. We pushed the cots together. Hope you don't mind."

As soon as she slid under the quilt, the girl snuggled up into her and whispered, "Love you, Mom." Both were asleep within minutes.

CHAPTER 22

There was a commotion in the station when Maisy and Maura emerged from their small room the next morning. Josephine saw them come out and hustled them back in.

"The roads are clear enough that media started to arrive. Ron says you can talk to them if you want but if you'd rather avoid them, Chip will sneak you out and drive you home. Ron will come pick you up to head to Bangor as soon as he can break away. But first, breakfast, and I have more of an update to give you. Sit, stay." She gestured to the cots.

"Thank you, Josephine." Maura had no desire to talk to anyone, much less someone asking more questions. She gave Maisy a quick squeeze. "You okay, sweetheart?"

"I've never spoken to a reporter before." Maisy had a speculative look on her face. "Would we be famous?"

Maura gave her a slight smile. "For about five minutes in Bangor, maybe Portland. Or even Boston—since you and your daddy came from there, those stations might pick it up."

Maisy tipped her head to the side as she contemplated the allure of fame and then shook her head. "I don't think I'd like to. Oh no, Maura." Her eyes went wide. "Grandma and Grandpa don't know about Daddy, do they?"

"Oh, goodness." Maura looked at her in dismay. "You're right. We'll have to remedy that." She was uncomfortable calling Sophie's parents without speaking with Stephan first, but it wasn't right for them to learn what had happened via the news. She picked up her cell phone and groaned. "My battery is totally dead."

A knock came at the door on the opposite wall. Maisy hurried to open it and grinned at Josephine. "How'd you get over here?"

The white-haired woman winked at her. "I pretended I was bringing food over to Chief Dean and the EMTs. I did that before the reporters arrived, but they don't know that. Now help me put all this down on the table there." Soon, they were enjoying breakfast.

"Is the power already back?" Maura realized she didn't hear the sound of generators.

"They worked through the night to get us online. Belfort jumped to the top of the priority list thanks to your adventure. It helped that the storm switched to rain the way it did."

"Josephine, Maisy and I need to make a call. Do you think we can use the phone next door?"

"Probably not, but we can get into the clerk's office and use Bernice's. She won't mind. Eat first, though. You both need a warm meal to start the day."

As much as she was dreading the phone call, Maura still had a healthy appetite, and between them, she and Maisy devoured the meal.

Josephine made a satisfied sound when the last crumb had been eaten. "I told George you'd eat it all. Okay." She looked around the room. "I'll pack up your things while you make your call. Then Chip is going to sneak you out of here." She looked at Maisy. "Is your special bag locked up?"

The girl nodded. "*Our* bag," she corrected Josephine as she reached for Maura's hand. "Karria gave it to Maura."

"Good girl." Josephine fished a ring of keys out of her pocket and pointed to one with a yellow band wrapped around it before she handed the whole thing to Maura. "That one will get you into Bernice's office. Just lock it back up when you're done."

"Thank you, Josephine." Maura reached out and gave her an impulsive hug before squaring her shoulders. "Do you remember their number, Maisy?"

The girl nodded. "Daddy taught it to me as a song when I was little in case of an emergency."

"Good." Maura reached for her hand. "Let's do this, then."

As they left the EMS office, Josephine could hear Maisy chattering away. "You're worried about talking to Grandma, aren't you? Is it because you think she won't like that we're marrying you because she's Mama's mommy? I told her how much I love you when I talked to her last week. I also told her about how we're going to paint my room a pretty green, and how we're reading Harry Potter each night and that you explain the words I don't know." As her cheerful voice trailed off, Josephine chuckled and started to put the room to rights.

The call to Sophie's parents was as uncomfortable as Maura had feared, but they were eager to speak with Maisy and hear from her that she was safe and sound, so the time Maura had to spend on the phone with them was brief. After they reassured themselves that Maisy was safe, it was agreed they wouldn't come up until they'd had a chance to speak with Stephan.

After locking up, Maura and Maisy followed Chip out through a rear door. The morning sun was shining brightly, reflecting off the vehicles and the coating of ice that still clung to many of the tree branches and wires overhead. Four news vans lined the street in front of the building along with a few unfamiliar cars. He grinned at the surprise on their faces. "There're more on the way. Story's interesting enough it's going national. Sam and Fred are going to be famous." He gave Maura a concerned look. "I hope you're not upset by that."

Maura burst out laughing. "Not in the least Chip. They deserve all the accolades they get and more."

Before leaving them in their driveway, Chip told Maura, "Ron said to plan on having lunch at home. He's hoping you'll get to Bangor for dinner."

As they settled in, Maisy and Tim followed Maura around as she got the house warming up and took care of immediate chores, including getting bags packed for Stephan and Maisy. "Can I call Fern? There's no school today, is there?"

"No, there's not."

"Will Mrs. Dean be mad if I don't go the rest of the week?"

"No, sweetheart, she'll understand." Maura dropped a kiss on the girl's head. "I'm going to go take a shower. I can run you a bath after I'm done. Please tell Fern to tell Liz I'll call later." She handed the child the house phone.

Maura retreated to the bathroom. While waiting for the water to warm up, she examined her neck and side. To her amazement, she couldn't find a single scratch or bruise. Physically, she felt better than she had any right to. Better than she had in ages, in fact. Whatever magic Karria had wrought had been deep and profoundly healing. Maura felt a stab of guilt that she was feeling so well while Stephan was in the hospital. She understood why Karria hadn't returned to the cavern after having killed Joey in front of everyone, but seeing the blood seeping out of Stephan's shoulder and the gray cast to his face was an image she'd gladly have traded even if it'd meant keeping her own injuries, no matter how painful they'd been. Her mind started to replay Joey's death, but she forced herself away from the memory.

After a brutally hot shower, Maura got the tub ready for Maisy.

Maisy hesitated in the doorway. "Maura, do you mind if I start calling you Mom sometimes?"

"It makes me happy, Maisy, but I don't want you to feel like you have to."

The child beamed at her. "It makes me happy, too."

"Can I—" Maura gazed at her. "Can I start calling you my daughter?"

Maisy nodded her head vigorously. "I'd like that a lot."

Maura beamed at her. "Me too." She gave her a quick hug. "Hop in before the water cools."

Maura was almost done packing her bag when the phone rang.

"Hey." Stephan's voice was raspy.

"Stephan!" Maura sank down onto the bed and held the phone tight to her ear. "Oh, God. It's good to hear your voice. Are you okay?"

He gave a slight chuckle. "Aside from being shot, you mean? Yeah. I feel like I've been hit by a truck, but they keep telling me it's all the medications as much as anything." He paused to cough and she heard him take a sip of something. While he was doing that, she hurried to reassure him.

"Maisy's good. She's worried about you, but she's safe and doing well. She's taking a bath right now. We're coming over with Ron later today. We packed a bag for you, but can add to it if there's anything special you want."

"Just the two of you." Stephan's voice was weary, but clearer. "I'm glad you're coming. Damnit."

"What?"

"Colleen came back. She's a pain in the arse."

Colleen's voice was muffled, as though a hand were covering the receiver, but Maura could still make out her grumbling that he had five minutes before she came back in.

"She belongs torturing newbs at a police academy some-where," Stephan groused when he came back on the line. "You asked if there was anything I wanted from home?"

"Yes."

"Could you bring me some real tea? And maybe my razor?"

Maura smiled. "Both are already in there."

"Perfect." He was silent for a moment. "Maura, there's so much I want to say, but mostly I just want to hold both of you."

"I wish we were there already. I love you, Stephan."

"I love you too."

"Can I bring the phone to Maisy so she can say hi?"

"That'd be great." Stephan hesitated. "Did you call my family?"

"I spoke with Nick hours ago. We called the Jordans this morning. We'll call your parents once Maisy's out of the bath."

"Thank you. Tell them I'll be fine and that I love them."

"I will." Maura gave a gentle knock on the bathroom door. "Maisy, sweetheart, your Dad's on the phone. Can I come in?"

"Yes! Yes, yes!" Maisy made a large splashing sound as she climbed out of the bath.

Maura opened the door, handed the child the phone, and wrapped a towel around her. She started drying her hair with another towel while Maisy chatted away to Stephan and listened intently to his responses.

"I love you to the moon and back too, Daddy. See you soon. Bye." She handed the phone to Maura. "Colleen made him hang up."

Maura kept her thoughts about the woman's highhanded behavior to herself and instead said, "Finish up in here and then we'll call Gran and Gramps."

The phone started ringing again. When she checked the ID, she sat next to Maisy.

"They're both okay."

"We're worried about you too, darling, but thank you." Evelyn's voice was tight with anxiety.

"Is that Gran?"

Maura nodded. "I'm putting you on speakerphone so Maisy can listen and talk, too."

"We are too. How are you doing, my loves?" Andrew's voice was tense as well.

"A lot better now." Maisy snuggled up against Maura as she spoke. "Lana's dad is taking us to see Daddy later when the roads are safe to drive on."

"Nicholas told us what he knew, but there must be so much more."

Maura nodded. "There is. Maisy and I just spoke with Stephan. He's doing much better already, but they're keeping him in the hospital for a few days to make sure. We still don't know if he can come home with us or if he has to go to rehab first. I'm sorry I didn't call earlier—" Maura hesitated and Maisy interrupted.

"We weren't able to call last night because it was so late, and then I needed Maura to cuddle me to sleep, and then we had to sneak out of the station because of the reporters, and then we packed bags for me and Daddy, and I just took a bath." Maisy paused to draw in a breath.

Andrew quickly interjected before his granddaughter could keep going. "We have tickets to Boston tonight. We'll rent a car and head straight up."

"You're coming to visit!" Maisy's face lit up. "Even though you were just here?"

"Of course, love. We wouldn't want to be anywhere else."

"Karria helped save us, Gran. And she healed Maura after Betty Jo's uncle hurt her. Even though Karria kept telling me she'd be okay, it was still super scary to watch Maura bleed and then see her face change colors. But then she got surrounded by a gold light and I know it was Karria. I wish she could've healed Daddy, too." Maisy's voice trembled as she wondered why her heroine hadn't come back to heal her father.

They could hear a sharp intake as Evelyn and Andrew both gasped. Maura hadn't mentioned her own injuries to Nick.

"I'm fine now." Maura hurried to fill the silence. "Maisy's fine too. Everyone took really good care of us at the station. We're safe."

Andrew responded first. "That's a relief. It sounds like there's quite a bit of a story here."

After everyone wished everyone else a safe trip and multiple "I love yous" were shared, Maura hung up the phone.

Maisy looked thoughtful. "If the coins from Karria are worth a lot, maybe Daddy won't need to be a police officer anymore," she quietly said.

"What do you think he should do instead, Maisy?"

"Daddy loves taking pictures. Maybe he could do that for a job. I know he likes helping at the school with the big kids, too.

I guess it'd be okay if he did some police stuff, but I don't like him being in danger." Maisy was frowning and plucking at a loose thread. "It was supposed to be safe here."

"I understand." Maura nodded in agreement. She was of the same mind as the child, but knew Stephan might feel differently. And what money, if any, they'd get from coins was an unanswered question. Her income wouldn't leave room for many extras for a family of three. "Right now, we're all safe. Let's focus on that and figure the future out later, when we're together and everyone's better. How about lunch?"

As they were sitting down for grilled cheese and soup, the doorbell rang.

"Josie." Maura stepped aside so the slight woman could enter the house. "I'm sorry. I forgot you said you'd be coming over." She glanced out the door. There was no vehicle in her driveway. "How did you get here?"

"Magic." Josie's lips quirked when she saw Maura's expression. "You almost believed me, didn't you?" Her smile widened before she shrugged. "Sam gave me a small boat years ago. Your beach is easy to access."

"That makes sense." Maura's expression cleared. "Would you like some food? We just made lunch."

"Yes." Josie hesitated as she handed Maura her coat. "There are things I'd like to talk about that aren't for the child's ears."

Maura nodded. "I understand. Food first, though."

Josie followed her into the kitchen. While Maura made up a third setting, Maisy gave the newcomer a curious look. After a minute, she gave Josie a mischievous smile. "I know why you're here."

"Oh?" Josie wasn't used to children and didn't know how to respond to her impudence.

Maura arched an eyebrow at the girl.

Maisy hurried to explain. "You want to talk to my mom about your mom. It's okay. I know you don't want me around. Karria told me I need to give you privacy. But I have to eat first."

Josie calmly sipped some soup and studied the child. Finally, she seemed to come to a conclusion and nodded. "I see why my mother likes you so much. But she's right. You can't be with us when we talk."

"Okay." Maisy shrugged.

Maura eyed the girl. She didn't trust the easy agreement.

Maisy shrugged. "Karria promised she'd tell me later." She took another bite of grilled cheese and contemplated her own words. After swallowing she admitted, "I don't know when later is, but that's okay. She'll tell me, and I kinda want to snuggle with Tim while we wait to go to Bangor."

Maura nodded. "Good idea."

The three ate in relative silence for several minutes before Maisy pushed away from the table and brought her dishes to the sink. She waved to Josie before heading upstairs.

"Would you like more to eat?"

"No." Josie finished the last of her soup and pushed the bowl away. "It's hard to find all the words. I'd like to share in a way that's easier for me."

Maura gave a hesitant nod. "Like your mother does with Maisy?"

"Yes." Josie gazed at her. "It's easier."

"Okay." Maura turned so she was fully facing the youthful-looking woman. As their gazes locked, she felt herself being drawn into Josie's dark gaze. She gripped the side of her seat to try and stop the sense that she was tumbling. The feeling abruptly passed. In her mind's eye, Maura saw and heard a younger version of the human Karria, singing and dancing naked in the surf. She had recently been allowed to leave her colony and was reveling in her freedom, enjoying exploring all of the caverns and small coves of Belfort Island. There were people, but they were easy to avoid. The herring and mackerel were plentiful, and the coves and caves offered protection from predators. She'd already found the perfect cavern to make her home. She had placed a glamour over the small entrance that led to the cave and connected to another, more secret one. There was another large cave nearby that was popular with the local people. Karria couldn't put a glamour over that, since it was too etched in their collective memories, but she was confident that her home would stay hidden.

As Karria was frolicking in the surf, a young man appeared. His trousers were rolled up to his knees and he carried a bucket and clamming shovel with him. A floppy straw hat was perched on his head. Though he still had the slender grace of youth, the barrel chest that featured prominently with the Thompson men was already visible. He stopped and stared when he came upon Karria.

She sensed his presence and interest before she turned and gave him a coquettish smile. As far as selkie custom went, she was an adult, and free to mate or not as she chose. She still had years before she'd enter her breeding cycle and feel an urge to return to the colony. Karria was feeling giddy with her freedom and the power her body seemed to hold over this young man as he approached her.

Watching the scenes unfold in her mind, Maura blushed. Thankfully, Josie wasn't inclined to dwell on them for any longer than necessary to make sure Maura understood that the love affair was mutual and intense. A season passed and Dickie was head-over-heels in love with the selkie. He begged her to come home and meet his family, to introduce him to hers. Karria had been warned before leaving home not to share her secret and put him off. He became suspicious and followed her one evening after they'd had a passionate tryst. She realized too late that he was watching. The revulsion on his face when he saw her slip into her pelt broke her heart. Karria retreated to her cavern and the sea for many months. The next time she saw Dickie was by chance a number of years later, when he and a young son sought shelter in the cave near her home during a sudden storm. Their meeting was awkward, and though Karria could speak his language fluently, she said little after helping them get to safety. The child followed her when she slipped away. He saw the old skeleton. Karria had stayed in the tunnel and observed him as he studied the bones.

He didn't notice the emptied lockbox. After his father called to the child and he turned away to leave, Karria stepped forward noiselessly and plucked up a loose coin that had fallen and been left on the ground when she'd taken the purse back to her cavern soon after settling in. The coin was battered and dull, with a rough tree embossed on it. She followed the boy to the larger cave and, before he joined his father, pressed the it into his hand. She slipped away before his father saw her again.

The scene shifted to another gale. This time, Karria was holed up in her cozy cavern in the throes of a far-too-early labor. She heard a sputtering motor over the shrieking of the wind, but was far too wrapped up in her own pain and misery to pay attention to the periodic calls for help from a familiar voice that drifted in on the wind.

In the next flood of images and sounds that poured into Maura's mind, Karria had matured. The edges of her body had softened, and the blaze that made her distinctive was prominent in both her seal and human forms. Karria's loneliness came through, and tears formed in Maura's eyes as she felt it as keenly as if it were her own. There was some excitement because life was once again rooted in Karria's womb, but not too much, as there had been three more losses since the first. Maura understood that Karria was withdrawing more from the other selkies in the region and spent much of her time in her cave. It had been a foggy summer, which suited Karria just fine, but then came a glorious day. The sparkle of the sun called to her. She slipped into the water in seal form and went to a quiet beach she loved for the wild roses that scented the air with a pervasive sweetness. There was a wonderful, long flat rock that warmed in the sun. Karria spread her pelt out on the granite so it could bake in the blazing summer heat. She hadn't planned on returning to the water in human form, but the shimmer of light on the gentle swell was so inviting she couldn't resist. She dove in and let the current carry her out. On impulse, she shifted and made her way around towards the busy beach the humans loved so much. She stayed far enough from shore that only the keenest observer would notice her. She watched children shriek and splash around. Her hand touched her gently rounded belly. Would this one survive? Would she have a child in the spring? Lost in her thoughts and observations, Karria didn't notice the craft float up behind her. There was a sharp blow to her head and large hands hauled her aboard over rough wooden planks. Dazed, she found herself gazing up into the brilliant blue sky as a motor kicked on and the boat began bouncing over the waves and further out to sea. An anchor was thrown overboard and then a familiar, but different face loomed over her. His words and actions were vicious. He blamed her for his father's death. Her protestations of innocence only led to further violence and pain. Karria stopped speaking. This wasn't the innocent child she'd met years earlier. She did what she could to protect her abdomen and to fight back. In the end, her limp, bloody, violated body was rolled overboard with a weighted net tangled around her legs.

As she drifted down through the sea, the shifting light and muted colors soothed the dying selkie. It was only the unexpected quickening of the babe in her womb and the spark of magic that lit with it that drew Karria back into her body and made her fight to free herself from the net. Holding her breath as long as she could, she made her painful way under the water back around towards the beach where she'd left her pelt. If she could reach it in time, they'd survive.

She was barely conscious as the powerful incoming tide washed her battered body ashore. The shock the pretty young woman felt at coming upon Karria hit Maura like a weight. Through Josie's magic, Maura watched and felt what her Aunt Jane did to help the selkie. Karria had tried to rebuff her efforts as she crawled towards the rock, but was far too weak to get beyond the surf. She gathered her remaining energy to push the image of her pelt on the rock into Jane's mind and point towards it. After the shock at the communication passed, Jane ran and found the seal skin. She placed it over Karria and there was a tremendous golden glow. When it faded, the seemingly healthy seal made her awkward way back into the surf and slipped under the waves. Karria watched Jane examine the shredded, bloody remains of the skirt she'd used to try and staunch the selkie's wounds. Karria touched the young woman's mind with her own once more but didn't try to communicate, not then.

Karria reached out to Jane, initially with song, as the long summer days turned shorter and a chill entered the air. Karria had no desire to interact with humans again, but despite herself, she enjoyed the woman's companionship and gentle ways. She was fascinated by her weaving and yarn work. Eventually, as winter took hold and Karria's belly grew heavy with the baby, she allowed herself to be led into the small home, where it was warm and safe. She always kept her pelt close, but allowed Jane to dress her to ward off the cold. As her spirits lightened with the baby's growth and strong sense of magic, the songs Karria sang to herself and Jane became more hopeful and joyful.

She and Jane didn't become lovers right away. It was a slow progression as their friendship and trust deepened into more. By the time they shared their first kiss, Karria was heavily pregnant and spring was well on its way.

Josie was born on a calm May morning. Birds sang cheerful songs to one another as the familiar pains of labor wracked Karria's body. Jane helped her birth the baby. After, she accompanied them both to the sea, so Karria could give her child her first meal in their most natural form.

Tears spilled from Maura's eyes as she watched the relationship develop and deepen. Karria and Josie had their cavern, but often stayed with Jane in her home. Occasionally, but not often, Jane would stay in their hidden space. As Josie grew, Karria allowed Jane to introduce her to a select group of human friends who came to visit. Though they were younger versions of the adults she knew, Maura recognized several members of the historical society among them. Most of the time, Karria stayed hidden. There were, however, times she allowed herself the pleasure of interacting, though never speaking, with these intriguing humans. Even then, she often kept to her seal form.

Josie took to George and Josephine, but her favorites were Sam and Margery, who, busy with their own youngsters, didn't get to visit as often. On those rare occasions, their boys and Josie played together. The parents kept her secret. In the end, Josie spent far more time with humans than her mother did. Though Karria had reservations about this, she also trusted Jane and her friends to keep Josie safe. It was a relief to her to have support. She hadn't returned to her home colony since the attack, not wanting the attentions of Josie's father or any of the other males or any pressure from the females to raise her daughter in the colony.

Things were idyllic for Josie as a youth. It wasn't until she was a young adult that it changed.

The first thing that happened was Maura started spending more time at her aunt's house. Keeping the selkies' secret was paramount to Karria, so Maura and Josie weren't allowed to cross paths. Josie was jealous at first, but old enough that she had her own things going on.

The second thing was that she met Joey Thompson. He was a teenager, but mature for his age and charming. Josie didn't understand her mother's horror and wrath when she caught Josie embracing him. Karria waited until the boy had left for home before hustling Josie back to the privacy of their own cavern. There, she shared her memories with her daughter.

In the brashness of youth, Josie was confident that the Thompson whose affections she was enjoying was nothing like his grandfather or father. She dismissed her mother's concerns, but wasn't so foolish that she didn't take precautions. She was careful to never let Joey see her in her seal form. She made no requests to meet his family or friends. This suited Joey just fine, because his steady girlfriend in town would have been unhappy if she'd become aware of Josie.

Joey had heard stories of a strange black-haired woman who'd had to die for her sins from his father, when the old man had been drinking long and hard enough to unburden his soul to his middle son. He also talked about skeletons and treasure in the caves under the island, something Joey never took seriously until the haggard man produced a battered old coin one day shortly before his death and entrusted it to Joey—things Josie was aware of because she'd taken to spying on the fisherman.

Another thing the men bonded over was the cruelty his father showed to any seal that had the misfortune to cross his path. Joey enjoyed causing pain, but knew enough to hide it from people. When he was alone with his father, however, he could be himself. Out swimming one morning, Josie chanced upon them in her seal form, drawn by the screaming and crying of a pup. When they threw the tortured and abused corpse back into the sea for the sharks, she realized her mother's warnings were to be heeded.

Not long after that, Josie's pelt was stolen. She'd hidden out at Jane's for a time while trying to find it. Then it was summer again, and Maura was coming back from her boarding school for vacation before leaving for college. Sam came to Josie's rescue. He purchased a small plot of heavily wooded land from Molly Harrison. With George Clark's help, he built a simple two-room building with a sleeping loft. A sturdy woodstove provided heat in the winter. Sam came and refilled the propane tank himself to ensure Josie had fuel for cooking. A composting toilet and old copper tub let her take care of basic necessities. A stream a short walk from the cabin stayed flowing most of the year and provided her with fresh, clean water. Over the years, little luxuries were added. The old-timers who knew Josie would bring food by or slip her money when they could to help her purchase treats and supplies.

Though she tried to avoid contact with people, Josie couldn't live as a complete hermit on an island where everyone knew one another. Sam, and later Fred, quietly told anyone who got nosy that Josie was a harmless, mentally ill young woman who snuck out from her family in Ellsworth from time to time. They'd assure whoever they were speaking with that they'd find her and bring her home. If anyone noticed how slowly Josie aged over the years, they didn't mention it. Avoiding Joey Thompson proved to be easier than anyone expected as he spent as many days off island as on.

Josie helped Molly harvest her blueberry barrens every summer, and in return, Molly brought Josie into her old farmhouse. There, she taught Josie how to make jams and can the produce she grew in her expansive gardens. This brought Josie into contact with Liz and the two developed a friendship as they worked in Molly's kitchen. Liz was told Josie had escaped a violent home situation and was more than willing to keep Josie's presence a secret and enjoyed her easy, undemanding, company.

The siren call of the sea constantly pulled at the younger selkie's heart. When she reached maturity, her urge to travel home to mate was brutal to resist. Without her pelt, however, she couldn't make the journey or be accepted.

Josie reached for Maura's hands and clasped them in her cool ones as she eased her mind out of the woman's and waited for her to fully return to her own body and emotions.

Maura gazed at her for several long minutes before sliding forward in her seat and pulling her into a tight embrace. "I'm so sorry, Josie. I had no idea."

"They didn't want you to know. Keeping our secret was always paramount." Josie had always liked the younger woman when they encountered one another despite being displaced because of her.

"I never meant to take you away from your home here." Tears trickled down Maura's face as the residual emotions from the selkie still echoed inside her.

"It wasn't your fault any more than it was mine." Josie's voice was quiet. Sharing and reliving the memories had been draining for her. "Everyone did what they thought was best for both of us." She shrugged.

Maura drew circles on the wood with her index finger. "It wasn't right." She gave Josie an intent look. "I want to help make this right, Josie."

The selkie tipped her head to the side and considered Maura. Slowly she nodded her head. "We'll figure it out together, then. I'll find you after you get back." Josie glanced at the tabby who'd just walked into the room and patted her lap for Mags to jump up. She smiled as the elderly cat settled in with a contented sigh.

Maura's eyebrow lifted.

Josie gave her a smirk. "How do you think Mags and Tim found their way here?"

"You dropped them off?"

"They were alone and needed a good home."

Maura smiled at the peaceful expression on Mags's face. "Thank you."

The selkie nodded. "I can feed them for you when you're away."

"Oh," Maura wasn't sure what to make of the offer. She was still digesting the fact that Josie had as much claim to the house as she did. Even so, it was her private space. Or, she amended to herself after hearing Maisy thudding around upstairs, semi-private space. Still, she needed the help and wanted to forge a deeper relationship with Josie now that she understood their connection. "Thank you. I'll get you a key." She hesitated. "If you'd like to stay here, you can use my room or the art room. It has a futon I can make up as a bed."

"If you'll be longer than a few nights, I may. But right now, I can just stop by once a day and feed these furry friends. When you return, I want to speak with Stephan. If he found my pelt, I want it back."

Maura went to the drawer where she kept her spare key. She handed it to Josie. "How can I reach you to tell you when we'll be coming home?"

Josie tucked the key into her pocket. "Tell Fred or Sam. Since I don't need to stay away from Joey now, I plan on visiting them more."

"Okay."

Josie cocked her head at a noise Maura didn't hear and stood up. "The police chief is here. I'm not ready to talk to him."

"How do you—?" Maura heard a car pull into the driveway.

"Our ears are better than yours." Josie gently put Mags down on the chair she'd vacated and waved to Maura before slipping out the back door.

Maura was just locking it again when the doorbell at the front rang. Rubbing the back of her neck, she went to let Ron in. "We're packed, but I still need a few minutes, is that okay?"

Ron gave her a tired smile. "I can give you fifteen." He sniffed the air. "Is that vegetable soup?"

Maura nodded. "There's a bit left. Would you like some?"

"I'd be grateful. It's been nonstop. Some of the reporters were making noises about hunting you down for interviews. Chip and Sam are holding them off, but—" He shrugged. "Like it or not, they want to talk to you."

"We'll be ready in ten," Maura promised. She poured the remaining soup into a travel mug and handed it to Ron.

After Maisy and Maura were buckled in, Ron gave them both a smile of approval and eased the cruiser back onto the road. "They'll find you in Bangor, but at least this buys us some time to talk." He spent much of the drive back to town passing along messages.

Maura watched the waves undulate under the bridge as they crossed onto the mainland. When she told Ron the Kirklands were coming back over, she saw relief flicker across his face.

"I'm glad you'll have help," Ron admitted. He glanced in the rearview mirror and noted that Maisy had earbuds in and looked like she'd fallen asleep. "Some of the Thompsons are agitating about Joey's death, demanding we find the woman who killed him. Eliza is convinced folks know more than they're saying about her identity." Ron blew out a sigh. "I have to do an investigation, Maura, and multiple witnesses say you vanished with her."

"After she miraculously healed me from everything Joey did to me," Maura replied in a conversational tone.

"Yeah, after that. And I've got questions about that, too."

"I was pretty out of it."

"So I heard." Ron glanced over at her.

"Can it wait until it's just you, me, and Stephan?"

Ron hesitated and then nodded. "Colleen tells me you spoke this morning."

"Until she made him hang up." Maura lips curved into a wry smile.

"She has an excellent bedside manner." Ron deadpanned before adding, "She's hurting right now. She was close to Joey. You know that."

"He's not the one who actually shot Stephan—at least, I don't think he was. Maybe he was." She shrugged. "It's all fuzzy. I was struggling to stay conscious and I don't think I was the whole time."

"I was wondering about that. We had conflicting reports and ballistics testing won't be back for a while. One of the others tested positive for gunpowder residue on his hand."

Maura nodded. "I think Joey was about to, but like I said, I was mostly out of it." Her forehead wrinkled as she tried to piece together moments that were hazy in her memory.

The 50-minute drive to Bangor from the mainland stretched to two hours because of downed wires and trees. Maura answered Ron's questions as best as she could while they made their way west. The ice damage eased up the closer they got to the city.

"I made reservations for you and Maisy at the Riverside. Town's covering the first two nights. Gives us all some time to get sorted out." Ron swung the car into the hotel parking lot. The lights from the hospital next door were bright as the sun was getting lower in the sky.

A couple of state troopers were in the hallway beside two of the rooms. They looked at the newcomers with interest. One stepped into the room to his right. A moment later, Colleen stuck her head out of the door and strode down the hall to meet them. Dark circles shadowed her eyes and her normally glossy hair was dull and limp in its ponytail.

"He's with PT." She nodded in greeting to Maura and Maisy and a spark of humor entered her expression. "He'll be happy to see you two and be rid of me." She turned back to Ron. "One of the suspects is ready to be released to our tender care. There's been some disagreement about where he belongs. The other two can't leave yet. They've all been arraigned and denied bail."

Ron nodded. "How long till Steve's back?"

"Just left five minutes ago."

"All right, then. We're all getting food." He gave Maisy a stern look when she started to protest. "We won't do your daddy any good sitting here waiting, and we all need to eat something. They have pizza in the cafeteria," he added.

Maisy scowled at him but muttered, "Fine."

Maura wasn't feeling particularly hungry, but saw the practicality of his plan. She just shrugged in agreement.

"Let me check in with them and then we'll be on our way." Ron strode over to the troopers.

Colleen glanced down at the bag Maura was holding. "Is that Stevie's stuff?"

Maura nodded.

"Might as well leave it in his room. Come on."

Maura reached for Maisy's hand and gave it a gentle squeeze when she felt it trembling. "Should we put Pooh Bear on Daddy's pillow for him so he knows we're here if he gets back before us?"

Maisy nodded. "I don't like hospitals," she whispered to Maura when they put the bag down on the visitor chair and fished out the well-loved stuffed animal. Her lower lip wobbled. "I'm trying to be brave."

It struck Maura that the last time the child had been inside a hospital was probably the day her mother had died. "Oh, honey." She gathered Maisy into her arms and gave her a long hug. "No one is leaving you today."

"Promise?"

"Promise." Maura held out a pinkie.

Maisy gazed at her for a long moment and then hooked her own pinky around Maura's. "Okay." She gave Pooh a kiss, left him on Stephan's pillow, and held Maura's hand in a tight grip as they left the room with Colleen.

The meal was subdued. Colleen started to ask about Eliza, then gave Maura a sidelong look. Tired of pushing her food around on her plate while pretending to eat, Maura ignored Colleen and looked at Maisy. "Let's go find some goodies in the gift shop to bring your dad."

After picking out a few treats and a stuffed moose that Maisy insisted would help Stephan feel better, the two made their way back to the room.

"Daddy!" Maisy's shriek of delight rang through the small room. She shoved the moose into Maura's hands and raced to her father's side.

"Hey, love." Stephan reached for his daughter with his uninjured arm and held her in a tight hug. "I missed you."

He looked over her dark head and gave Maura a searching gaze and then, seeing no trace of injury, a weary smile. "I'm so happy to see both of you."

Maura leaned over Maisy's head to kiss him. She touched his cheek with her hand and frowned at the heat she felt there. "We've been worrying about you."

He tipped his head so his chin pointed at the chair. "Come sit next to me." He squeezed Maisy's shoulders. "Love, can you sit in Maura's lap?"

"Why can't I be on the bed and snuggle you instead?"

"I'm pretty sore still, and—" He pretended he was sharing a secret. "I'm pongy. They haven't let me shower yet."

Maisy wrinkled her nose at him. "I didn't want to say anything. I don't mind, Daddy."

"Love, it hurts too much right now, okay?"

"Okay, Daddy." Maisy tried to hide her disappointment as she climbed into Maura's lap. Stephan dangled his hand over the edge of the bed and wiggled his fingers at her until she reached out and held his hand. "Gram, Gramps, and Uncle Nick are coming over tonight."

Stephan arched an eyebrow. "They are?"

"They want to help."

He nodded slightly. "Okay."

Maura tried to hide her concern. She was expecting more of a protest from him.

He noticed and winked at her to try and lighten her mood. "Thanks for chasing Colleen away."

"She's in the cafeteria with Ron."

"Maybe she'll stay there," he muttered.

Maura gave a slight chuckle. "Doubtful. Ron wants to visit before he takes her back to Belfort."

Before they could talk more, Ron and Colleen came back in. They only stayed for a half hour before a gray-haired nurse chased them out, insisting Stephan needed rest. Once Maura's relationship was explained, she allowed Maura and Maisy to remain while she hustled the others out. She returned a few minutes later with a satisfied look on her face and a heavy food tray in her hands. After putting it on his table, she checked Stephan's temperature. While they were waiting for the thermometer, she commented, "I'm sure she's a lovely lady, but your colleague was driving us all nuts."

She turned to Maura and Maisy. "Now, young lady, you have a very important job." She crouched down so she was eye level with Maisy. "You need to make sure your daddy eats. Can you do that?"

"I'll try." Maisy nodded. "I want him to get better."

"He will, but his body needs food to do that." She gave Stephan a stern expression. "Cooperate, and I'll see what I can do about getting you a shower tomorrow."

"Yes ma'am."

Color streaked through the sky as the sun set. After Stephan had made a real effort to eat his meal, Maura and Maisy split the half of a sandwich he'd left untouched while he dozed. Maura got a text message from the Kirklands that they were at the airport and would let her know when they landed in Boston. When the troopers guarding the prisoners and keeping an eye on Stephan's room changed shifts, Maura exchanged a few words with them while Maisy colored. They called Sophie's parents and Maisy told them she wanted to spend her school vacation with them. That, and a long conversation with father and daughter, comforted the worried couple.

Eventually, they both kissed him goodnight and made the short trek back to their own room. Once Maisy was sleeping, Maura, shaken by Stephan's weakened state, indulged in a private cry in the bathroom before slipping into her own bed.

CHAPTER 23

In the morning, they stopped at the cafeteria to grab breakfast to bring with them. As they were leaving, a trooper entered and made a beeline for them. Maura felt a knot form in her gut as he approached. His expression was impassive and gave away nothing. Sensing the shift in Maura's mood, Maisy pressed up against her side.

"Good morning, ma'am, Maisy." The young man nodded his head at them each in turn. "Lieutenant Brown wants you to meet with the press as soon as possible."

Maura closed her eyes in relief and drew in a shuddering breath.

The officer gave her a quizzical look before he suddenly realized what she might have taken his approach to mean and his eyes widened. "I'm sorry. I didn't mean to scare you." He looked at the laden tray. "I can take your food and Maisy up."

"I want to see Stephan first."

"Uh, he really wants you to join him in the briefing room ASAP."

Maura looked at the man. His blond crew cut, uniform, and stocky build gave him an intimidating look. But up close, she realized he was still young. She fixed him with the look she gave teenagers when they were annoying the older patrons at the library.

"I will speak with him after I've had a chance to see Stephan and get Maisy settled."

"Okay." He shifted uneasily. "We'd better get going, then." He hurried them towards the elevator.

Maisy looked up at Maura. "Didn't Lana's dad say you didn't hafta speak with the reporters if you didn't want to?"

Maura nodded. "No one has to speak with them, but if you don't, then they don't know your side of the story. Like it or not, what happened to us is interesting to people right now."

Maisy saw the cluster of police officers near her father's room before Maura. "Uh-oh." Her hand tightened around the woman's.

Maura frowned.

"Damn." Their escort shoved the tray back towards Maura. "They're discharging one of the prisoners. I'll get them to wait till you're in Officer Kirkland's room." He jogged down the hall to intercept an older, grizzled looking man.

They both looked back to Maura and Maisy.

After an initial expression of annoyance flitted across the older man's face, his gaze softened and he nodded in agreement with whatever the younger officer was saying. He spun on his boot heel and strode into the doorway the troopers were clustered by. The younger man waved Maura and Maisy towards Stephan's door. Once they reached it, he opened it. As he moved to shut it, he commented, "I'll let you know when it's all clear."

"What's going on out there? No one will tell me anything. They told me to eat my breakfast and shut the door." Stephan's voice held an uncharacteristic edge of petulance.

"One of the bad men is being moved." Maisy clambered up onto the bed by her father's feet while Maura found a space for their breakfast tray. "They also told Maura she has to speak to some reporters. Oh, and Daddy, Gran, Gramps, and Uncle Nick are in their car."

Maura gave Stephan a weak smile. "Good morning." Dark circles under his eyes and a tightness around his lips concerned her as she gazed at him, but he managed a weary smile in response.

"Good morning, love." He reached for Maura's hand and tugged her close so she could give him a kiss. "You don't have to speak with them, you know."

She bent down to kiss his forehead and felt a surge of relief that it felt closer to normal. "I think…" She spoke slowly as she thought it through. "I think I should just get it over with."

Stephan gave her a searching look. Finally, he admitted, "I hate sending you out to face it alone."

"If me doing this now helps them lose interest in us, then it's worth it." Maura shrugged. "Maybe it won't help, but we won't know unless I try."

Stephan brought her hand to his lips and gave it a tender kiss. "Anything you don't want to answer, just say no comment or that you don't know. You have no obligation to answer anything, no matter what anyone tells you."

Maura nodded. Her stomach started flip-flopping around now that she'd committed. Her mouth felt dry. She reached for her coffee and then thought better of it. She was already on edge. Caffeine might not help matters. She gave Stephan a grateful look when he pushed his cranberry juice towards her and handed her a slice of toast from his tray.

"You can't face them on a completely empty stomach, love."

"Okay." She did her best to choke down some of the drink and cold toast.

From her spot at the foot of the bed, Maisy had been listening. "Mom, just tell the truth, except for about Karria and Josie, and you'll be fine."

Maura's eyes glinted with amusement. "Should I lie about our friends?"

"No." Maisy shook her head. "No, lying's bad, but no-commenting would be good, right, Daddy?"

"Mom?" He looked from the girl to woman and back.

Maisy's face fell. "Isn't it okay? Maura said she doesn't mind."

Stephan let go of Maura's hand and reached towards his daughter. "It's more than okay, Maisy Daisy. You just surprised me. It makes me happy."

"Oh, good." Maisy squeezed her father's hand and then dropped it to reach for the donut Maura had let her get along with her oatmeal. "It makes me happy, too."

The young trooper reappeared in the room. "Ms. Ballard, Lieutenant Brown's getting impatient."

Stephan drew in a breath, but Maura rested a hand on his uninjured shoulder. "I'm almost ready." She bent down and gave Stephan a gentle kiss. "There's so much I need to tell you when you're feeling up to it," she whispered. Straightening, she added in a normal tone, "I love you, sweetheart."

She followed the young man out the door.

When Maura returned an hour later, she was pale.

Stephan slid as far to the side of the bed by his IV as possible and patted the vacant space. "Sit and tell me about it." He looked at his daughter. "Maisy, can you go ask Nurse Katie for a coffee with cream and sugar for Maura?"

"Sure, Daddy." Maisy gave Maura a hug before skipping out of the room.

"What happened?" He held her close with his good arm.

"They had so many questions and a few kept insinuating it was all some twisted love triangle. I think Eliza's spoken with them. Others wanted to know if any treasure was found because of the skeleton. There were a bunch of questions about how I healed so quickly when they were told by Mike and Betty Jo that I'd been hurt by their uncle." She sucked in a deep breath and felt herself relax as she let it out and listened to the steady thumping of Stephan's heart. "I said I don't know an awful lot. A few times Lieutenant Brown interrupted and told them I couldn't answer because of the ongoing investigation. Afterwards, he wanted to grill me too, but I told him I needed the restroom. When he turned away, I used the stairs to come back here instead." She lifted her head so she could see Stephan's face. "That's not breaking any law, is it?"

"No," he assured her. "It will annoy the crap out of him when he realizes you slipped away, but you're not obligated to talk with him. Isn't Ron still in charge of the investigation?"

"I don't know." Maura rested her head back down against him. "I thought he was, but I haven't talked with him since the drive over yesterday and he spent much of that gently interrogating me himself."

"I'm sorry I'm stuck in this bed, Maura. You shouldn't have to face this by yourself."

"I'm sorry you're stuck in this bed because you came after us, but, Stephan, I'm also so grateful you did."

"Me too."

A second armchair had been brought into the small room overnight, so Maura and Maisy were each able to curl up in their own chair while Stephan dozed.

Around noon, there was a knock on the door and Katie came in with an orderly. They had just set the lunch trays down when three people hurried into the room.

"Stephan!" Evelyn flew to her son's side, almost knocking Katie into Maura's lap.

A new trooper hurried in after them. "Hey! You can't be in here!" He addressed Nick because the tall man was closest to the door.

Nick arched an eyebrow. "The hell we can't."

"These are Stephan's parents and brother," Maura quickly explained to Katie as the orderly slipped past everyone to get out of the crowded room. "They flew in from England this morning."

With the room far too crowded, Nick and Maura decided to get Maisy lunch. Because he'd been driving all morning, Maura sent Nick and Maisy back to the hotel while she picked up takeout. When she returned, Nick was stretched out on his bed, hair damp from a shower, with Maisy snuggled up to him, talking about Joey's death in great detail.

Their lunch was subdued as Maisy continued to tell Nick about everything that had happened from her perspective. Periodically he asked questions, but for the most part he listened intently.

Maisy smiled when she saw Maura finish her meal. "I'm so happy you ate, Mom. You needed to."

Nick arched an eyebrow and then gave Maura a warm smile. He reached out and patted Maura's hand before moving it to cover his mouth when a yawn snuck up on him. "Would you ladies mind letting me sleep for a couple of hours?"

Evelyn and Andrew stayed with Stephan until he fell asleep in the later afternoon. After they each had a shower, they invited everyone into their suite. Andrew suggested Maisy spend the night in their room. When Maura hesitated, Evelyn smiled at her. "Let us help tonight."

"I—well, thank you." Maura had to admit she was craving some privacy. "That'd be lovely."

Andrew squeezed her shoulder as he passed by to help Nick and Maisy, who were struggling with the door.

Maisy was bursting with excitement. "Mom, Mom, you're on the TV in the lobby!"

Maura grimaced when Andrew gave the girl permission to turn on the television. Maisy flipped channels until she found a news station showing excerpts of the press conference. Maura studied her own image for a moment. She looked pale and tired. Lieutenant Brown was just as intimidating onscreen as he'd been in person. "Glad that's over," she muttered to Andrew.

He put down the plates he'd been holding so he could envelop her in a long hug. Maura felt her shoulders start to drop down as she let herself relax in the caring embrace. "Thank you," she murmured against his chest.

Andrew gave a gentle squeeze of acknowledgement and then released her a moment later after his stomach rumbled. The noise made them laugh. "Breakfast was many hours ago." He smiled. "We were both too upset to eat with Stephan."

Evelyn had put a plate with a slice of pizza in Maisy's hands and was helping herself to one of her own, when the child complained, "They're lying!"

"Who is lying?" She looked at her granddaughter in confusion.

"The people on TV."

Nick plucked the remote out of his niece's hand and clicked the television off. "What were they lying about, love?" He thanked Maura when she passed him a plate.

"About Mr. Thompson loving mom. You should've seen him. He had such an awful, mean look on his face, but he also looked really happy about hurting her. It was super scary." Maisy put her plate down and the moment Maura sat on a chair, climbed into her lap. "Karria told me it'd be okay, but I was worried anyway."

"They're just trying to make the story even more interesting to people." Andrew hoisted her out of Maura's lap and put her between himself and Evelyn on the sofa.

Maura felt her appetite slip away. She didn't care what strangers thought, but she deeply cared about her relationships and, yes, her reputation on Belfort. Her phone vibrated in her pocket and she surreptitiously slid it out to see numerous texts were coming in from friends throughout the region, as well as from summer residents. She pushed it back into her pocket.

Nick dragged his chair next to Maura's. She gave him a sidelong look, half expecting him to be eying her with suspicion or disdain. Instead, his expression of concern looked so much like his brother's that her breath caught in her throat for a moment.

When Nick saw Maura look at him, he gave her an encouraging smile. "You should eat something. Gotta keep up your strength." He waited until his parents had diverted Maisy's attention and leaned close to whisper. "We all know what they're implying is a load of shite. Don't let it get you down." He gave her a one-armed hug and then winked at Maisy when he saw the child watching them.

After they cleaned up their meal, Nick looked at Maisy and Maura. "Fancy walking back over with me? I'd like to visit Stephan for a bit."

When they stepped out of the hospital elevator, all three were surprised to find Stephan standing there, holding a metal IV pole. He grinned at them. "Becky made me a deal. I can shower if I do five laps."

"What number are you on now, Daddy?"

"Three. I was just taking a break."

Maisy reached for his wrist. "Come on. I'll help you."

As they turned around, it became clear that the ties on the back of Stephan's gown had loosened. Nick started chuckling. He whistled at his brother and grinned when Stephan shot him a crabby look. "I can't tie the blasted thing properly with my arm."

Maura quickly stepped forward and redid all of the strings in the back of the gown so Stephan was fully covered.

"Thank you." He gave her a kiss and then scowled at Nick. "Some people don't kick a man when he's down."

Nick gave him an unrepentant grin. "Got you all fired up to get that lap done."

Stephan turned away and muttered under his breath while Maisy led him back down the corridor.

After they'd moved off a bit, Maura glanced over at Nick. The older brother's expression was troubled. When he saw her gaze, he shook his head. "I hate seeing him like this."

"Me too," she agreed as she watched Stephan move with slow steps past the nurse's station. "But it's good he's up and about. And he doesn't feel as feverish as he did yesterday." She tipped her head towards the nursing station. "I'd like to find out how he's doing from his nurse."

After Stephan made his way back to his bed, he was fatigued. Pleased to have had some alone time with him, Maisy didn't make a fuss about saying goodnight. Maura helped him get settled and promised to text him after they were at the hotel. As they were leaving, she saw Nick reach for Stephan's hand.

Alone in her room, Maura replied to some of texts that had piled up. She listened to voicemails and deleted the ones from reporters. She took advantage of her privacy to return calls to friends both on and off island. It was after ten when she heard Nick's door gently close.

Her phone pinged and Maura smiled to see Stephan's text.

ru up

Yes

dressed?

?

pjs or reg

It took Maura a moment to puzzle out what he was asking.

Haven't changed. Been on the phone. Liz sends her love.

visit?

Aren't you exhausted?

no

Okay. Give me five minutes.

She recognized the trooper guarding the remaining prisoner. He nodded in acknowledgement when she waved. Maura slipped into Stephan's room. The lights were dimmed, but she could easily see where she was going.

"Hey." He smiled at her from the bed.

"Hey yourself." Maura sat on the edge and leaned over to give him a kiss. He was out of the hospital gown and wearing the zippered hoodie and sweatpants she and Maisy had brought. His skin smelled of antiseptic soap and the IV was disconnected. "You finally got that shower."

"It was heaven." Stephan's expression was more relaxed than she'd seen in days. "Snuggle with me."

Maura kicked off her shoes and wiggled her way onto the mattress so she could join him. They both sighed in relief as her head rested on his good shoulder and his arm encircled her.

"You said you had a lot to tell me."

"I do, but aren't you too tired right now?"

"I've been sleeping on and off for the past two days. The shower was refreshing. And," she could hear the smile in his voice, "I might have had Nick swap out the decaf tea they brought me with supper for some you brought."

"I see," Maura tried not to laugh.

"It's the first privacy we've had and likely the last for a while. Unless you're too tired," Stephan's tone shifted as it dawned on him that she probably hadn't dosed up on caffeine.

"I'm happy to be here." Maura took in a deep breath. "I don't even know where to start."

"How about with when you disappeared, and then we'll go back to the rest."

"Okay." Maura closed her eyes as she relayed all that happened, both in Karria's cave as well as what Josephine had shared and Josie's visit the next day. Periodically Stephan asked questions to clarify something, but for the most part he let her just talk. When she finished, Maura opened her eyes and pushed herself up so she could see his face. "What do you think?"

"Wow. That's a whole lot to take in." He hesitated a moment. "Did you tell Ron all of this?"

Maura shook her head. "Not Karria and Josie's stories. I wasn't ready, and I don't know how much of it is really mine to share with him anyway. But he wants to talk to them."

Stephan was quiet for several minutes. "I've been thinking about it while I've been stuck here. I think we need to tell Ron the truth about Karria. He can't force her to speak. Hell, he can't even coerce her into changing to human form to bring her in. But he has to do his job and close the case. No one in their right mind would file charges against her. She was defending children as well as a downed police officer. He would have killed one or both of us if Karria hadn't intervened when she had. She didn't beat him, just gave him one really good, well placed, whack on the head. It's not going to go away until Ron gets answers. Too many different people saw what happened. The Thompson family is going to be on his back about it, even if Joey wasn't beloved by all of them." He urged Maura to relax against him. When she did, he continued thinking out loud. "Fred may have blinded the guy next door permanently and no one's talking about charging him with anything. Ron needs to tie it up, though, or more people are going to insist on getting involved—like Brown here. I haven't heard from Ron at all today. Has he been in touch with you?"

"No, and I expected to see him today."

"Wonder what that means." Stephan ran a hand down the back of Maura's hair when she yawned. He urged her to put her legs under the blanket and then snuggled her close again.

"I should go back to the hotel and let you sleep," she murmured.

"Later. Keep me company."

"I'm awfully tired myself."

"Rest, then." As Maura's breathing evened out and deepened, he adjusted the angle of the bed for sleep and shifted a bit to get more comfortable before drifting off as well.

When Becky came in at one to check his vitals and see if he needed any pain medication, she discovered the couple nestled up together. Both were deeply asleep. Using a penlight, she checked his bandage. Since he hadn't registered a fever the last two checks, she opted to use a forehead thermometer rather than wake him up. She maneuvered her stethoscope adeptly to listen to his heart and lungs without disturbing either of them. Sleep could be hard to come by in a hospital and seeing him smiling in his was, in the veteran nurse's opinion, the best medicine he could get.

When she left, she turned the lights all the way off and gently shut the door behind her. It stayed shut until Katie came on at 7.

The young nurse called out, "Rise and shine, my sleeping beauties," as she entered the room carrying a breakfast tray. She was followed by an orderly who carried a second tray.

Stephan came awake and oriented faster than Maura and smiled at the cheerful nurse while Maura blinked at her and tried to figure out exactly where she was. She blushed when she did, which made the others smile.

Katie reached out to help Maura sit up and slide off the bed and then helped Stephan adjust the angle, since his good arm had fallen asleep in the night. "You've got a busy day, my friend," she commented to Stephan. "PT, OT, and the surgeon want to check you out. Your boss called to say he's going to be here in an hour.

Lt. Brown's angling to have you both meet with a couple reporters, too. Best of all, Dr. K is talking about releasing you if you stay fever-free through all of that."

"To go home?"

"As long as PT and OT sign off, that's the plan I just heard."

Stephan grinned. "That's the best news, Katie, thanks."

She nodded. "I thought you'd like it. Now you two eat up. I have to get your vitals first though."

Maura sipped her coffee while the young nurse did her job and kept up a steady stream of conversation.

Maura's phone pinged as she was finishing her meal. "Maisy wants to know where I am."

"If Ron's coming, maybe you should keep her away for a bit."

"Good idea." She gave him a wry smile. "I think I'm going to get out of here before Ron comes, too, if you don't mind."

"Not at all, love." He reached for her hand and gave it a squeeze before tugging her close. "I'm glad you stayed last night. It's the best I've slept in days."

"Me too." Maura gave him a gentle kiss. Her phone pinged again in rapid succession and she groaned. "I'd better go. Your parents—"

"Are just fine handling her." Stephan interrupted. "But you definitely don't want to be here when Brown shows up. I love you."

After another, lingering kiss, Maura reluctantly left the room. She reached the hotel lobby at the same time as Nick. He was sweaty and wearing running clothes.

Nick took in her disheveled hair and noted that she was wearing the same clothing as the day before. He smirked at her. "Late night?"

"A peaceful one."

Nick's expression softened. "Good. You both needed it." He caught her arm before she could enter the stairwell. "Maura, I'm a wanker. I never really asked how you are." His expression was serious. "I mean, you and Maisy told us what happened and said Karria healed you, but are you all right?"

She understood what Nick was getting at and reached out to squeeze his arm. "Thank you." She started to say she was fine, but stopped and gazed off at a point over his shoulder for a moment before sighing. "Honestly? I'm still not sure. Physically I feel great, and I'm grateful we're all safe." She worried her lower lip as she tried to find the words. "I'm torn. I haven't really let myself stop to think about everything that happened. I've had to keep moving. I can feel it bubbling up inside sometimes, though. It was terrifying, Nick. And an ugly, part of me is grateful I never have to worry about Joey again. He always made me nervous. But then I feel awful, because I never, ever wished him dead. I still don't." Maura's expression grew troubled. "I feel like I can't let myself stop to really think about any of it until we're all home." She shrugged. "Does that make any sense?"

Nick nodded. He reached for her hand and gave it a gentle squeeze. "I can take Maisy off your hands when we get back to Belfort so you've got some quiet to think."

The morning passed relatively quickly. Ron brought most of the group back to Belfort in his car after lunch while Nick stayed with Stephan to wait for his discharge paperwork.

As Maura was getting sorted out downstairs, the doorbell rang. She wiped her hands on a dish towel and peeked out the window. She hurried to let George and Josephine in when she saw them waving to her. The comforting smell of fresh, hot bread wafted in with them along with the familiar tang of lasagna. "We weren't sure what you had in the house for dinner." Josephine walked back to the kitchen and put the food down. "Josie said you needed milk."

George took a carton out of the bag he was carrying and put it and a couple of bags of cold cuts into the fridge, then placed some ice cream in the freezer. "We won't stay, but we wanted to make sure you're all comfortable tonight. Is Stephan with you?"

"No, he and Nick are just leaving Bangor now and still have to stop for his medicine."

Josephine nodded. "How is he?"

"In some pain, but doing much better. They were worried about infection. The new antibiotics seem to be working, though."

"Good." The couple shared a look. "Uh, Maura," George's voice was gentle. "Has anyone talked to you about Eliza?"

"Not really." She gave them a wary look. "She blames me, doesn't she?"

Josephine nodded while George looked uncomfortable. "At the moment, yes. Betty Jo, Isabelle, and Mike have swayed most of the other Thompsons over to recognizing that Joey was to blame for his own death. They all knew Joey ran with a rough group and many half-expected something like this. But Eliza—" She shrugged.

"Was blind to his faults." Maura sighed. "I figured as much, but it still hurts to hear it."

"The cold cuts and ice cream are from Jack. He wants you to know he's worrying about you. He wanted to call, but was concerned you'd be mad they didn't realize what Joey was up to and stop him before it got out of hand."

Maura's expression softened. "I'll call him in the morning." After a few minutes of chatting, the couple gave her affectionate hugs. They spoke briefly with Andrew and Evelyn as they passed on the path to Maura's door before leaving the family to settle in.

CHAPTER 24

Maura and Stephan could hear voices greeting one another before the doorbell rang. Nick let the newcomers in and helped Maura collect their coats. Once Ron, Jackson, Adam, George, Josephine, Stephan, Nick, and Maura were all seated around the table with warm drinks, the police chief reached into the inner pocket of his jacket and dropped a cracked leather bag onto the wood. It hit with a heavy clinking sound. He pulled out a list and nodded to Adam, who pulled out one of his own.

"Before we get to this, Colleen and I searched a storage unit Joey was renting. We found all the missing maps and books except a few, but those were located at his house. There were also a number of items that had been reported missing when the old historical society building was broken into years ago. Vicky is going to help coordinate getting everything back to its proper place. We also came across an old coin that looks like one of these." Ron pointed at the bag. He then looked around the table. "I asked Adam to document them with me, both for security and so he could do some preliminary research for Maura."

Adam grinned at Maura. "I'm so jealous that you found the *Molly Ann*'s treasure, but if anyone other than me got to find it, well—I'm glad it was you."

"You think it really is?"

"From the *Molly Ann*? Yeah. James Wylie must have managed to make it to the caves. I think Ron sent the bones off to the medical examiner, right?" When the chief nodded in agreement, Adam continued. "Hopefully they confirm the age, but the coins fit the tale." He pulled on white gloves and opened the sack. Adam then carefully placed the coins on the table. "We need to go through our lists again first."

Once the men confirmed that the coins on the table matched the ones on their lists, Adam grinned at everyone. "It's a real-life treasure, and because Maine honors the treasure trove doctrine, you, Maura, are now a very wealthy woman."

"How wealthy are we talking, Adam?" Ron asked.

"Retire and move to a tropical paradise if she wants. It's preliminary, but these," he said, pointing to a pile of smaller coins, "are New England sixpences, and several are in outstanding condition. They can fetch upwards of 400 thousand each. Maura's got eighty-three of them. These Pine Tree shillings are bigger and have more silver, but aren't as valued by collectors. Still, they add up. By the way, Ron, this is the kind you showed me from Thompson's house. As exciting as these all are for history buffs and New England collectors, it's these beauties that are the motherload." Adam pointed to a small stack. "These are New England threepence. Until now, there was only one known in existence, and it's held by the Massachusetts Historical Society. These are going to create quite a stir when word of them gets out. Four are in mint condition." He looked at Maura. "They're going to fetch at least a million each, or I'll eat my hat. The rest are interesting, but not rare. I haven't looked up their values yet. You're going to want an expert and not an amateur like me valuing the collection and helping you sell them."

Stephan reached for Maura's hand under the table. When she turned her wide eyes towards him, he nodded. "Do you still want to do what we talked about, or does this change things?"

A smile bloomed across her face. "I think it makes it even better, don't you?"

"I do, but I want you to be sure."

Maura nodded her head. "I am. Are you?"

"Yes, love, I am."

"You are better people than me," Nick muttered, but he gave his brother and future sister-in-law looks of admiration as he sat back in his chair to see how the others reacted to their plan.

Maura looked at each in turn as she explained. "We think that everyone who was in the caves, either as a hostage or in the initial rescue—so us, the children, Sam, Fred, Doug, Josie, and Bonita— should all get a coin that's of similar value, such as the sixpence. If these," —she pointed to the Pine Tree shillings— "aren't worth much sold, perhaps we can keep a few for the town to display, or not, depending on what people think. We certainly don't want to create more problems. The rest..." She drew in a deep breath and plowed forward. "We think the rest should be sold for the highest prices possible and all of the proceeds go into a fund. We hope Jackson will manage it, and that a board made up from the community will oversee it."

"What would this fund's purpose be, dear?" Josephine leaned forward with an intrigued look on her face.

"Everyone has different needs. We'd like to see it be used as a sort of grant fund to give everyone who lives here year-round a helping hand when needed." Maura gave Stephan's hand a squeeze. "The only stipulation I have is that the first round of funding include a greenhouse for the library and the construction of a community garden."

"A couple of requests could quickly deplete something like this, even with a cushion of millions," Adam pointed out.

"True. There would have to be restrictions. And Jackson would, if he's willing, guide us on how much could be given away each year while still preserving the bulk to keep it generating interest as long as possible. I'd love for this to last many years. A lawyer will need to help and I think the whole town should have some say, but wouldn't it be wonderful to be able to have somewhere to turn if there are unexpected medical bills or if work is slow and someone's having trouble making rent or paying their electric bill? Or maybe to help with repairs if a boat's engine goes during the slow season, or to help someone go to school?" Maura looked around the table again. "What do you all think?"

"I think you're bloody generous, and I'm damned proud to have you becoming a member of our family." Nick was the first to break the silence that had settled over the room.

Maura beamed at him.

"I think it's going to be a helluva headache at the town meeting we have for this, but then it'll be a godsend to many people." Ron gave her a nod of approval.

Jackson nodded. "I like it, Maura, and I'd be honored to help manage the fund. Once we have a lawyer, I'll work with them to draw up proposals we can share with everyone at town meeting. If this is all worth what Adam thinks it is, I can definitely grow it into something that should be self-sustaining for years to come."

"I think you're nuts." Adam gazed at the couple for a long moment before sighing. "But it'll do a lot of good for folks who could use it, and it seems like an equitable solution. But please tell me you're going to keep some extra money for yourselves. You deserve a break. Have a wedding. Take a honeymoon. Splurge a bit, and maybe stop working so damned hard."

Josephine and George nodded in agreement with Adam. "Honey, it's such a generous thought, but you really should keep more. There's no shame in it. It was given to *you*. Go back to your art. You're going to be raising a daughter. She needs your time and attention, too. You'll want to have it to give her." Josephine reached across the table and squeezed Maura's arm.

Maura and Stephan shared a look. They'd had a similar conversation themselves the day before, and then again with his parents and brother after Maisy was in bed. Stephan laced his fingers through Maura's. "We think we've found solutions that will work well, but we both need to speak with our employers first." He glanced over at Ron to find the chief frowning at him.

"I'm going to hate this, aren't I?" Ron muttered.

"I hope not." Stephan met his gaze. "I think it's a good solution, given the limitations I'm going to be left with."

"They're certain?"

"Not entirely. I'm hoping that I can regain more mobility when I can do more vigorous PT, but some of the damage is going to be permanent."

Ron nodded. "I was afraid of that." He glanced around the table. "I'll come back another time when we can have a more private talk."

Stephan nodded in agreement.

"Besides," Maura broke in. "This is all just hypothetical right now. There could be relatives who come claim this." She waved at the coins.

Adam shrugged. "I'm not sure. I did some research on that. Neither of the spies had children, near as I can tell. I suppose the Queen of England could make a demand on it, but that's a stretch. It's all just folktales in the end. It's derived from a trapper who also believed selkies inhabit our waters, so the credibility is already rocky. You okay?" He looked over at George, who had choked on a sip of coffee.

The older man waved off Adam's concerns as he coughed.

"Is there anyone else who could lay claim to this?" Maura eyed George and relaxed when he winked at her.

"Well, there's some precedence that the town can claim half of the treasure in Maine. Given your plans involve effectively giving the town far more than half anyway, I'm not sure it matters. Of course, the Select Board might feel differently, and God knows what'll happen at town meeting. The state will want their cut in taxes along with the IRS when the coins are sold, and there will be the fees for the lawyers and coin dealer."

"So, we won't be as rich as it seemed."

"Yes, you will." Jackson's voice was quiet. "This is one thing I'm very good at." His gray eyes sought out Maura's gaze and held it. "I have connections. Given the philanthropic intents behind the bulk of the sale, I think I can interest a reputable dealer. I can't promise, but she's honest, wealthy, and a history buff. She does what she does for pleasure. The bonus is, she's a lawyer."

Maura searched Jackson's face. There was pain there. The offer seemed to be costing him something emotionally. She had her suspicions, but she didn't want to probe in front of everyone. "Are you sure?" She hoped he understood the deeper intent behind the question.

Jackson gave a small nod of acknowledgement. After a fraction of a moment, he added, "I am. I'll call her later today."

"We need to find out if we have to advertise this. If that happens, we're going to have to be prepared for even more treasure hunters." Ron looked like he was getting a headache just thinking about the possibility of inexperienced people from all over descending on the caves and tunnels.

"We block them off." Stephan shared Ron's sentiments. "We block the tunnels off. Maybe Adam and a few others go back and explore to make sure nothing was left behind and then we block off the tunnels."

"But not the caves," Adam objected. "They're part of the island, and they provide refuge that fishermen and boaters use."

"I think," Josephine broke in, "it's too late to put this genie back in the bottle. Like it or not, word will get out. When those men go to court, it'll be clear they believed there was treasure down there."

"You need to move quickly to control the narrative, then." Nick's expression was thoughtful. "You need to focus on the story you want told, and get it out as far and wide as possible, as quickly as possible. Like it or not, you two," —he indicated Stephan and Maura— "are the best mouthpieces to do it at the moment, since reporters are still looking to talk with you about what happened and the imagined connection with Thompson."

"Bloody hell, this is getting complicated." Stephan's shoulder was aching. He saw the time and realized he'd missed taking his pain medicine. He got up to make a small snack to take it with. Maura joined him and quickly cobbled together a plate of cheese and crackers for the table.

Adam stacked the coins back up and counted them out loud as he put them back in the pouch.

George and Josephine were sharing a meaningful look. Josephine leaned over to catch Ron's eye. "Ron, has Vicky talked to you about the historical society Christmas Party?"

The police chief gave the older couple a curious look. "No. She started to say something to me and then stopped." He turned to face them. "Is it relevant to this?" He gestured to the coins. Jackson let out a snort of amusement.

"Perhaps." Josephine's smile was regretful. "Maura, Adam, Nicholas, I'm sorry, but we need you to give us privacy for a little bit."

Stephan started to argue and then shook his head. "You don't care what I have to say anyway, do you?"

George nodded. "We do, lad, but it doesn't matter until the whole board convenes and takes a vote. Until then, we only have permission to speak with Ron."

"And four of us doesn't make a quorum." Jackson's disgruntled expression mirrored Stephan's.

"Just so."

"Will you be okay?" Maura put a gentle hand on Stephan's good arm.

His expression softened and he nodded. "I'm just going to sit here with Greta." He nodded to the cat, who was patiently waiting to jump into his lap.

Maura looked at Nick and Adam. "Why don't we go upstairs, I guess?" She shrugged. Being kicked out of a room in her own house was an uncomfortable experience.

Adam was being unusually quiet. When they reached the upstairs landing, he put a finger to his lips and pointed towards the crafting room, which was located above the kitchen and then to the heat register in the floor. Nick grinned when he saw Adam lie down and put his ear near the opening. Maura rolled her eyes at them both and left them to their eavesdropping.

Maura went to her own room and gazed out at the cove. The rhythmic movement of the waves lulled her into a meditative state. She didn't know how long she stayed that way before she heard the floorboards creak and looked up to see Nick and Adam standing there. Nick looked amused. Adam simply looked shocked. She arched an eyebrow at them.

"Selkies? There really are selkies on the island, a *colony* of selkies?" Adam's flabbergasted expression made Maura smile.

She gestured to a nearby chair. "There are, Adam, but two hardly make a colony." Maura looked at Nick. "They told Ron?"

"About Karria and this Josie woman? Yeah. And those old-timers in your historical society have apparently been hoarding a bunch of treasure of their own. Ron's more than a bit miffed at them, especially Stephan and his own wife for not telling him the moment they found out."

"There've been too many secrets on this island. Until recently I thought it was impossible to keep much hidden around here. I was clearly wrong." Maura was privately glad it was all coming out into the open. "Does this mean the pelt Stephan saw really is Josie's and that they're going to give it back without a fuss?"

Nick nodded. "Sounded like it. Josie confronted some of them while you were in Bangor. Apparently, Maurice had found it hidden in the rocks at Barrel Cove years ago. He thought it was interesting and tucked it away. He knew Josephine and Molly both are scrupulous about cleanliness so he didn't mention bringing it in because he figured they would worry about germs. Then he forgot about it. That's all Stephan cared about, and Josephine kept reassuring him they would get it back to Josie quickly. She sounded more than a little miffed at Maurice herself."

"They should have done it already."

"Not only did you know they exist, but you know these creatures on a first name basis?" Adam gazed at Maura. "Why didn't you tell me? You know I've been fascinated by that legend my whole life."

"It wasn't my secret to share, Adam. And, I didn't truly believe it until the caves. It's a difficult thing to accept."

"So that trapper wasn't crazy." Adam sat back in the chair and absently pet Mags when she made a graceful leap into his lap. "And those tunnels that were blocked off, the ones Joey blew up, that was that done on purpose?"

"Yes, according to Josie it was to protect them. Sam and George did it."

There were heavy footsteps on the stairs and Ron poked his head into the room.

"Maura, are they all insane? Is it some sort of mass delusion? Stephan's been on some powerful pain medication."

She gave the police chief a sympathetic smile. "I don't know what George and Josephine told you. Stephan only told me about the pelt because it looks like Karria's. But if you're asking about Karria and Josie being selkie, then yes, it's true."

"How the hell am I going to file this in my report?" He sank down on the foot of her bed. "You think you know people. You think you know your own town, and then, bam!" Ron shook his head. He eyed Adam and Nick. "Why aren't you two looking more curious?"

"We eavesdropped." Adam shrugged.

Ron rolled his eyes. "I should've guessed."

"Ron." Maura hesitated and plowed ahead. "Can we say Karria was a mentally unbalanced woman, or maybe a drug addict, who'd been using the caves for shelter?"

"How do we explain your miraculous healing, Maura? The kids all swear they saw Joey hurt you. Sam, Fred, Stephan, Doug, and Bonita have also provided witness accounts that corroborate this to one degree or another. Hell, even one of Joey's coconspirators shared that in his statement. And then several of them saw you get healed by some golden light and vanish with the naked lady, what'd you call her, Karria? Who you're all telling me is Blaze, the seal?"

"I don't know how to explain it, Ron." Maura shrugged. "An act of God?" She stopped Tim from climbing up around her neck. "No one will believe the truth, anyway."

"Eliza already assumes we're all covering up to protect you."

"She thinks *I* killed Joey?"

"You or Josie." Ron shook his head. "Because you emerged without a scratch on you, she's convinced herself that everyone's lying about him injuring you to cover for you killing him."

She gave Ron a troubled look. "Are a lot of people seeing it the way Eliza does?"

"No." He shook his head. "She's pretty much alone in this when it comes to islanders. Her theory has gained a bit of traction on the mainland and on social media." He sighed. "I'm hoping we can get a couple more interviews out there to quell it. Stephan did a good job the other day. He's credible in the public eye. It doesn't hurt that he's photogenic and has an adorable kid."

"Gee, thanks." Stephan had wandered into the room while Ron was talking. He eased down onto the bed. "George and Josephine are off to talk with the other board members. Jackson's going home to make his call."

Maura got up to help Stephan prop some pillows behind his shoulder so he could sit back in more comfort. "It's a conundrum," Maura commented to Ron while smiling at Stephan. She felt a surge of relief when Stephan chuckled softly. Some of the tension around his jaw eased up.

"I'm beginning to like the idea of portraying her as an itinerant druggie. We could plant some paraphernalia in one of the small tunnels."

"Did you just advocate planting evidence, Chief?" Adam's eyes glinted with amusement.

"Can it, Beals. These are extraordinary circumstances."

Adam grinned. "Indeed. And might I add, I'm really not sorry the homophobic prick is gone?"

Nick gave him a fist bump.

Ron scowled at both of them. "You're not helping."

"Just keeping it real, Ron."

"Adam?"

"Yes?"

"Don't you have somewhere else you need to be?"

"Can't go without you. We have to lock the coins up together, remember? Besides, you drove me here."

"For Christ's sake. I managed to forget that for five minutes." Ron ran a hand over the top of his head. His eyes landed back on Maura. "How the hell do we explain you?"

She shrugged. "A miracle? Divine intervention? Mass hallucination?"

"Hallucinogens? Hmm. No, that won't fly, since four of you got medical care, at least three had extensive lab work, and Thompson had a full autopsy."

"Maybe it will just have to be left as one of life's unsolved mysteries," Nick suggested.

"Ron hates unsolved mysteries." Adam grinned.

"I've about had it with you today Beals. You can be a real pain in the ass."

"You love me anyway."

"Not really."

"I amuse you."

"Occasionally." Ron tried not to smile at the younger man.

"Couldn't send you home to Vicky and Lana with that scowl on your puss."

Ron rolled his eyes at Adam. "Just because you're Vik's cousin, don't think I'll keep taking your sass."

Adam grinned at him. "I'm her favorite cousin."

"God knows why." Ron's smile crept out.

"Is anyone not related to someone else on this rock?" Nick shook his head. Before anyone answered, he heard a car door shut and looked out the window. "Mum and Dad are back with Maisy. I'm going to go help them unload everything."

"I'll come too." Maura started to move away from the bed but stopped when Stephan grabbed her hand. "Maybe Adam could lend a hand."

Adam looked from Ron to Stephan and back again before blowing out a sigh. "Yeah, I can help. Keep your little secrets."

After the two men had left the house, Stephan looked at Ron. "You can ask Maura. I won't."

Ron frowned at him. "Because you're on medication I'm going to write that off." He looked at Maura. "I need you to help me bring Karria and Josie in for questioning."

"Why would I do that?"

"Because they're integral to a police investigation into a murder and kidnapping. For crying out loud, Maura, it's not like you to be like this either. What's wrong with you two?"

"Ron, they've suffered enough at the hands of the Thompson men. I can't ask them to risk their freedom and lives."

Ron grumbled under his breath for a minute and stared out the window at the cove. He sighed. "What about here? Do you think they'd be willing to talk here or even there?" He pointed at the beach. "I can't close the investigation without speaking with them. And that's all I want to do, talk."

Maura chewed her lower lip. "I can ask Josie."

"What about her mother?"

"She only communicates with Maisy, and hasn't since everything happened."

"I see." Ron's tone indicated he didn't really, but also knew he didn't have many options. "Do what you can. I'll make the time for them."

Maura nodded. "I'll pass the message along the next time I see Josie."

"When will that be?"

She spread her hands out. "Your guess is as good as mine. But she did promise to come back after we came home and I haven't seen her yet, so I expect it'll be sometime soon."

"Well, that's something." Ron looked at them both. "You both really believe this selkie business?"

"When it hits you right in the face, it's hard not to, Ron." Stephan's voice was mild.

Maura nodded. "What they shared with me—" She struggled to find the words. "It was like nothing I've ever experienced before. I lived those moments of their lives, and some of what they showed me about Aunt Jane—well, hang on." She went to her closet and rummaged around until she pulled out a small wooden box with a seal carved on the top. "Here, look for yourself." She put it on the bed so Stephan could see the contents when Ron opened it.

Inside, there were remnants of fabric with rust-colored stains soaked into the floral pattern, a lock of long black hair, and a series of photographs— Karria and a young Jane, the two with a baby, and then a teenage-looking Josie. There was a shiny sixpence coin and a journal. "I know none of this is definitive proof, Ron, but look at Josie. Look at Jane and their clothing. You've seen Josie with your own eyes. She only looks like she's aged five years from this picture, yet it was taken decades ago. You can read the journal. If you need to do DNA testing on this fabric, take it and some of the hair. I don't know what selkie DNA looks like, but I imagine it's neither wholly human or seal."

"When did you find this, Maura?" Stephan was gazing at one of the photos.

"Last night. I was trying to find a blanket for your mom. I was going to show it to you today. Josie must have left it here. I've never seen it before, and I've been through that closet a million times."

Ron had taken the journal and sat down in the arm chair to start thumbing through it. "Huh." He paused and began reading in earnest.

"What does it say, love?"

"I don't know," Maura admitted. "I started to read it, but felt like I was invading Aunt Jane's privacy, so I stopped."

"Your aunt is filling in a whole lot of blanks about how the historical society's come by their valuables and why they hid them away."

"That's good, I guess, but can't the others tell you?"

"They can, but it's good to have verification from someone who can't change their story."

Maura shrugged. "If you say so."

She turned and felt Stephan's forehead, causing him to give her an exasperated look. "I don't have a fever. Stop fretting."

"I can't." Maura sat down beside him and held his hand as he drifted off to sleep while Ron quietly read the journal.

CHAPTER 25

When Maisy returned to school on Monday, Maura forced herself to go back to the library. She ducked under the yellow crime tape that still cordoned off the building and joined Colleen by the doors. She drew in a shaky breath as she gazed at the building that had, for so much of her life, been a sanctuary. Now, it felt tainted. She frowned when she realized her hand was trembling as she went to insert the key into the lock.

Warmth hit the two women as they stepped inside and Maura felt a sliver of relief. She'd been anticipating it to be as cold and raw as the day of the kidnapping. Maura held a hand to her mouth when she realized there was an important library resident she'd forgotten all about in the trauma. "George!" She hurried to the turtle's tank and her expression crumpled when she saw his tank had been broken. "Oh, George, I'm so sorry." Tears leaked from her eyes as she started to look for his carcass.

Colleen looked at her askance and then realized what Maura was crying about. "Chip and Matt have the turtle, Maura."

"They do?"

"Yeah, Chip found him wandering around when we first came here. He came back for him after he brought you home. You know

Matt and critters." She shrugged. "They've made it their apartment mascot. I think Liz's kid has been helping feed it."

"Thank god." Maura sagged against the wall in relief.

Colleen shook her head, not understanding the fuss over a turtle, but glad the other woman had stopped crying.

Maura wandered around the library, investigating every nook and cranny aside from her office, until she had nowhere left to explore. She stood inside the doorway and looked at the destruction. The knickknacks she'd collected over the years were strewn about, many smashed on the ground.

She leaned against the doorframe and glanced over at Colleen. "What about him appealed to you?"

Colleen was quiet as she tried to gauge why Maura was asking. Eventually she shrugged. "A few things. There was something compelling about him physically that drew me. Also, a bit of rebellion. My father hated his father and would never tell me why. It made Joey tempting, and I was flattered when this older man paid so much attention to me. And," she glanced at Maura. "I know you won't believe me, but he could be tender and kind, especially after we stopped dating. He's the one who encouraged me to go to the academy. Dad didn't want me to apply, much less go after I got accepted. Joey supported me and helped me." She looked down at Maura. "I always wondered why you played so hard to get. It took me a long time to realize you weren't playing and that you really didn't like Joey. I wondered if you were gay, but then when you went gaga for Stevie, I realized we just have very different taste."

"Gaga? Gay? Seriously, Colleen?"

The tall woman shrugged. "You fell hard fast, don't deny it. And, yeah, for a while I wondered if you were gay. We both did. Neither of us understood why you weren't interested in Joey. He said your aunt must've rubbed off on you. I figured that meant because she didn't date, like maybe you were both asexual or something, but he insisted it meant you preferred women."

Maura kept her thoughts to herself. There was no need to hurt Colleen's feelings, but how anyone would pick the likes of

Joey Thompson over someone like Stephan, or most anyone else if it came down to it, was beyond Maura's comprehension. "You should've asked me. We just have very different taste." She shrugged. "Makes the world go 'round, right?"

"I guess." Colleen stepped into the office and picked up the pieces of a broken Buddha. "Bud Collins brought this back from Japan, didn't he?"

Maura gave the pieces a sad look and took one from Colleen's hand. "He did. He wanted to thank me for showing him the world was bigger than Belfort before the Navy did." The smiling figure had always brought comfort to Maura when she was feeling frazzled with some of the more challenging kids. No single child had ever given her as much trouble in the afterschool program than Bud had that first year, until she'd discovered he had a previously untapped passion for geography.

So many meaningful things had been smashed to the ground. She knew her memories were safe in her heart, but it still hurt. The arrogance and entitlement that Joey had felt was evident in the tantrum he'd thrown in the room. Even with the evidence in front of her, Colleen couldn't acknowledge how awful he'd been.

She tried to tamp down the surge of anger. Colleen was, she reminded herself, grieving. But as she picked up shards of a broken mug Jane had bought on their trip to France, it bubbled over. She threw the largest remnant at the plywood as hard as she could. It helped marginally, but not nearly enough. She gritted her teeth. "Colleen, leave me alone."

"I'm not supposed to let anyone be here alone right now. It's still a crime scene." She shifted on her feet and gave Maura an uneasy look. "Actually, I need to ask you not to do that."

"Do what?"

Colleen edged away slightly at the fury in Maura's voice. "Uh, throw things. Please don't destroy any evidence."

"They. Were. All. MY. Things. *HE* already trashed them." Maura's voice reflected her outrage.

The officer held her hands up. "Yeah, I know, but until the chief clears it, this is also still evidence in an open investigation."

Maura tightened her grip on the Buddha piece until the jagged edge pierced her skin. The urge to lash out warred with her good sense. She drew in a ragged breath and dropped the destroyed statue into Colleen's hand along with several drops of her own blood. "Fine. I'm leaving."

It wasn't until she was halfway out the doors that Maura realized she was bleeding. Cursing, she spun on her heel and stormed back into the library. When she saw Colleen, she held up her other hand. "Not a single word."

After she'd taken care of the small wound, she stalked back out of the library and into the business district. The cold air helped, but she was still seething. Maura proceeded to take a brisk walk up and down the two streets. There weren't many people out and about. The handful she encountered took one look at Maura's stormy expression and simply waved from a distance. She did two loops before her pace started to slow when she reached the old municipal building. She stared at the large covered windows. Lost in her thoughts, she didn't hear Nick's approach.

"It'd make a wonderful gallery."

"Stephan told you?" She glanced at him.

"Told me what?" Nick gave her a confused look.

"About this building." She gestured.

"We've never talked about it. I saw you standing here. I can leave you alone if you need space."

"No." Maura sighed and shook her head. "Don't leave. I just came from the library. It put me in a foul mood."

"Fair enough. So, what did you think Stephan told me?"

Maura waved a hand towards the building. "Ever since the new town offices were built, I've thought this would make a wonderful gallery and artists' cooperative. There's room for classes, studios, small shops." She sighed. "It's been sitting vacant for so long when it could be a vibrant part of the community."

"If only someone had money to sink into that sort of venture, and the good will of the community behind them." Nick's voice was nonchalant.

"Yeah." Maura sighed again. Then her eyes narrowed and she looked over at Nick.

The Englishman was grinning at her. "Took you long enough."

"Huh." Maura looked at the building with fresh eyes. "I wouldn't pay what that jerk in Boston wanted even if I could. He's let it sit neglected for so long."

"Bet he'd be happy to get it off his hands, then." Nick's eyes glinted and he grinned at her again. "Especially if someone made a cash offer, say, before news of the town's sudden wealth became public knowledge."

Maura nodded. "Price probably will change even more." She kicked at a loose pebble. "Doesn't matter. I don't have the kind of cash to make an offer like that."

"I do." Nick's voice was serious this time.

"I don't even know how much we'll end up with from the coins, or if we'll be able to keep them, Nick. I know what Adam said, but until they're sold and we have the money in hand, it's all a gamble, isn't it?"

He smiled at her. "Maura, you have no idea how much I'm worth, do you?"

She frowned at him. "Why would I?"

Nick slung an arm around her shoulder. "I was so wrong in December. I'm going to love having you in our family."

She wondered if he'd stopped for a drink somewhere along the way.

Nick saw the look she was giving him and laughed. "Come on. Let's get a peek inside, unless you have somewhere else you need to be."

"No, your dad's taking Stephan to PT today, and your mom—"

"Threw everyone out this morning." Nick nodded decisively. "Excellent timing, then." He peered at the fading real estate listing in the window and punched the number into his contacts. "Let's get a coffee and make a call."

He led Maura towards Jack's and gave her a quizzical look when she hesitated near the door. "What's wrong?"

"Joey's uncle owns this place. I meant to call him our first real day home and forgot. Now it's awkward." Her voice was wistful. She cared for Jack.

Nick put a hand on the small of her back. "Gonna have to do this at some point. Let's get it over with." He gave her a little nudge and steered her into the café.

The heavy scent of coffee and fried potatoes hit them in the face along with a blast of hot air.

"Maura!" Jack Thompson's eyes lit up when he saw her come in. He left Maurice standing at the counter and hurried over to envelop her in a bear hug. "I've been worried about you."

"Mmmmmmmphnmmm." Maura's face was partially mashed into his white apron. Luckily, she could breathe through her nose.

"What's that?" Jack loosened his hold a bit so he could look down at her.

Maura sucked in a gulp of air. "I was worried about you, too," she finally managed.

Jack gave her an understanding nod and pulled her along by the hand back towards the register. Nick trailed them with an amused smirk on his lips.

"Hold yer horses, old man," Jack grumbled when Maurice started to complain at him. "June, Maury wants his usual!"

"I figured. It'll be up in a minute." She beamed at Maura. "I'm so happy to see you, honey. Are you hungry? How 'bout your brother there? I'll fix up something special for you both."

"And it's on the house," Jack refused to let go of Maura's hand as he finished getting Maurice his change.

When the other man started to talk to Maura and moved to embrace her as well, Jack scowled at him. "You can have your turn later. Scram."

He pulled a stool up and patted it. "Sit. We need to talk." He eyed Nick. "Mind giving us a few minutes of privacy, young man?"

Nick wondered what sort of privacy the café owner thought they'd have sitting by the register, but shrugged. "Sure. May I have a coffee cup first?" When a large one was thrust towards his hand, he grinned. "Cheers. Maura, I'll be back there making that call." He gestured towards a quiet spot in the back corner.

"Thanks, Nick."

"Fred 'n Sam told me everything. Betty Jo, Izzy, and Mike had quite a bit to say as well."

She nodded and studied his face with an anxious expression. "Jack, I'm so sorry."

"For what? You didn't do anything wrong! It was that good-for-nothing nephew of mine and his cronies who are to blame. I'm sorry none of us realized how seriously he took my brother's drunken ramblings." He shifted uneasily. "Some of my family thought he walked on water." He looked chagrined. "I'm afraid they still do. They think his uh, feelings, for you colored his judgement." Jack shook his head. "The rest of us all know that's horse shit. He was cruel even as a kid, like Cal was." Jack pulled her into another hug. "I just want you to know that most of us know who he was." He gently let her go. "A few of us are feeling some relief he's gone, truth be told. And we're all thankful that you, Officer Kirkland, and all the kiddies are safe. ALL of us are glad about that. How's Steve doing? I wanted to bring food by, but wasn't sure how welcome a Thompson would be." Jack's lips turned down into a frown.

"You're welcome anytime, Jack." Maura reached for one of his beefy hands and held it in both of hers to give it a squeeze.

June joined them at the counter and pulled Maura in for a tight hug before nudging a tray piled high with food towards her. "Go eat before this gets cold."

Nick stood up to help when he saw her coming. "I'm not sure I can eat all that." He eyed the overflowing plates.

"Me either," Maura admitted. "No one asked what we wanted."

"Well, we've got an hour to kill before Mr. Jones meets us, so we might as well stuff ourselves." Nick's expression was cheerful as he doused his eggs with pepper. "So, not all the Thompsons hate you."

"I guess not."

Nick nodded in satisfaction. "They shouldn't. You didn't do anything wrong."

"Joey was good at manipulating people."

He flushed. "Yeah, I remember."

Maura lifted a forkful of eggs to her mouth, but before eating them asked, "I thought you were a software programmer. Is that wrong?"

"No, it's just incomplete."

"Stephan told me you have your own business."

"Yes, I contract out my services. My bread and butter is creating aps for estate agents, but ten years ago, I started branching out and flipping property in London. I got lucky with my first building, and it's enabled me to diversify and deepen my investments."

"Do you have tenants, too? Do you do the renovation work yourself? Is it just you, or do you have partners?" Maura was fascinated to learn this about Nick.

Used to Maisy, Nicholas wasn't fazed by the rapid-fire questions. "No, too much of a headache. I tried being a landlord for a couple years and wanted to tear my hair out. Sometimes, but mostly I farm it out to a crew who does work I like. Just me and sometimes a mate, or Mum and Dad will go in on a project with me. I've tried to convince Stephan to join me, but he's risk averse; ironic given his profession." Nick shrugged. "Sophie nixed everything I approached them with." He took a moment to eat. "It always disappointed me because I knew I wouldn't lose their money, but I didn't want to cause problems, so I didn't push." He grinned at Maura. "I know you want to ask, but won't." He took a swallow of coffee. "If they'd gone in with me the last time I offered, they would have pocketed half a million."

Maura stared at him in astonishment. "That's more than simple house flipping, Nick."

"They're not single-family homes. I have a knack for it, and I don't have to sell right away. My first one made enough to let me do that." He shrugged. "The tools I create are effective, especially if you understand how to use them to their full potential."

"And you think the old muni is a sound investment?"

"It wouldn't make money as a flip, but as an investment in the community? Absolutely. We'll need to check it out with an inspector, but there aren't any glaring concerns outside." He saw the hope on Maura's face even though she wasn't verbalizing it. "You and Stephan both have artistic gifts. You both care about community and are good at fostering it. You won't get rich with this scheme, but that's not the point anyway. I think it could let you both quit your jobs or at least cut back. It would give Maisy as much time as she needs with both of her parents." His expression was contrite. "I'm really sorry I was such a prat at Christmas, Maura."

She reached across the table. "It hurt, but I understand where your concerns were coming from." She held his hand for a moment and the gave a slight squeeze before letting it go.

Nick grabbed it back and looked at the bandaged cut. "When'd this happen?"

"At the library. I might have lost my temper." Maura shifted uncomfortably in her chair and pulled her hand back. She stuffed some food in her mouth.

"Did Colleen say something to upset you?" Nick was amused by the way the pretty officer got under his brother's skin, but recalled she had a relationship with the dead man.

Maura shrugged and continued to chew her food.

Nick arched an eyebrow and waited for her to swallow. When she proceeded to fill her fork again, he nudged her leg with his booted foot. "What happened?"

She blew out an annoyed sigh. "She doesn't see how awful he was. She also told me I wasn't allowed to throw my own destroyed property against the wall." Maura's lips quirked into a smile as she was finally able to see humor in her own reaction. "First I was sad at what they did to my office. Then I was angry, really angry, and Colleen acting like I shouldn't be made me even more mad."

"They trashed your office?"

"Yeah, on purpose. I heard him doing it, but hadn't seen it until today." Tears sprang to Maura's eyes and she felt her temper start to kindle again. "None of it was valuable to anyone but me. They didn't have to do that. They were already planning on killing me at that point."

Nick felt his own temper spark at that reminder. He tamped it down. "You have every right to be furious at him and anyone defending him."

"Thanks, Nick." She gave him a lopsided smile as they resumed eating.

Both looked at his phone when it pinged. "Shall we go indulge our curiosity?" Nick gathered up their garbage.

Bimy Jones was sitting in his car, waiting. When the realtor saw them, he turned off his old Buick and stepped out into the cold. The car creaked and rose several inches. "Miss Maura, it's good to see you looking so well. And you must be Mr. Kirkland. Your brother is a fine, brave man." He stuck a hand out to give Nick's a firm shake and then gently squeezed Maura's fingertips.

As he opened the key box on the door, Bimy apologized for the coolness of the building. "Mr. Jacobs doesn't like to spend more than necessary. Still, we'll be out of the wind." He smiled at them as the lock opened. The door creaked from sitting unused for so long, but when he closed it, it had a good seal.

Dust motes floated in the air and the plywood protecting the windows kept the space unnaturally dark. Bimy went to the light switch. After flickering uncertainly for a moment, the fluorescents turned on with a humming noise. Maura grimaced. Nick moved off and started testing the floorboards and grilling Bimy about the construction. As he drew him around the space, peppering the agent with technical questions, Maura wandered around on her own. She'd been right. The space would work beautifully for the vision she'd long held in her mind's eye. The changes Jacobs had made in anticipation of turning the building into a coffeehouse and bookstore had brought warmth and openness to the lower level. The old cannery shop's character remained, with the original wide pine planks and simple shelves built into the brick walls. The wall between the two spaces had been removed and replaced with a wide, graceful archway. It would make a wonderful teaching space. There was even a large sink and countertop along the far wall.

On the second floor, Maura's eyes gleamed as she considered the possibilities for classrooms and exhibition spaces. Because it had been a public building, there was a tiny elevator, which would make it all accessible and allow larger works to be moved. Finally, they trooped up to the third floor, which Jacobs had converted into a loft-style apartment with a kitchen and luxurious bathroom.

"As you can see, it's a special space. With the right vision, it could be a gem in our community." Bimy looked at Maura.

When they stepped back outside, Nick offered her his arm. He spotted Maura's car in the library's parking lot and began heading towards it.

"The list price seems awfully steep for around here. But it is a wonderful building." Maura's voice was wistful. "I'm guessing he won't go down once word gets out about the coins."

"Probably not, but you know, it's really not worth more than $600,000 and that's only because of the size, elevator, and location. Honestly, he should count himself fortunate if he gets $500K for it, and that's even when news of the coins gets out. Jones is right. It really will take a very special buyer and vision. It has the potential to be a money pit."

They crossed the street and Maura glanced over at him; disappointment evident on her face. "So, you think my idea probably wouldn't work?"

"Did I say that?" Nick smiled and shook his head. "Between that space and this community, I think your idea is one of only a handful that *would* work."

Relief flooded her features. "So maybe before you go home, you could come back with me and Stephan and we could all look again?"

"Sure, if you'd like that, I'd be happy to." Nick nodded in agreement.

"Thanks, Nick." Maura gave him a wide smile.

"You're welcome, Maura." Nick cleared his throat. "I need to go to Ellsworth to take care of a few work things. Do you need anything?"

After Maura requested more kibble for the cats, Nick gave her a quick hug and kiss on the cheek. "I'll see you at dinner."

"See you later, Nick, and thank you for everything." She pulled him close for another hug. "You really helped me today."

"It was nothing, but I'm glad if I did." Nick waited till she was in her car before jogging down the street to his rental.

When Maura got home, she saw Fred's Outback parked in front of Milly's. The fragrance of baking bread and chocolate cake filled her nose as soon as she stepped through the doorway. A heavy, meaty scent and the tang of fried onions also permeated the air. Maura stood and breathed in the aroma while tugging off her boots and hanging up her coat. In her thick woolen socks, she quietly padded into the kitchen.

Evelyn saw her first and smiled. Her hands were wrist deep in dough. Fred was frowning in concentration while rolling a pie crust out. He didn't notice Maura at first, but when the floor creaked, he glanced up. His smile warmed her heart.

"Maura! There you are." Fred glanced at his flour-dusted hands. "I'd hug you but, well—" He tipped his head towards the dough.

"That's okay. I can still hug you." She was thrilled to see him looking healthy and happy. She wrapped her arms around Fred in a fierce embrace. She felt him awkwardly pat her back with his forearms and released him.

"Shall I make tea?" She saw Evelyn didn't have her customary mug.

"That'd be lovely, dear. Mr. Foley, will you have a cuppa?"

"I'd like that but please, I keep asking you to call me Fred."

"Just so." Evelyn nodded in agreement. "Forgive me. My thoughts keep scattering away today."

Maura put the kettle on and gave a covered pan simmering on the stove a curious look. She then looked at Evelyn with some concern. Stephan's mother had been napping far more than the last time she'd visited, and she'd snapped at her husband and Nick more than once. "Would you like to take a break and rest, Evelyn? I can finish that up for you."

"No, thank you, dear. I'm almost done. If you'd like to fill the pie and help Fred put the top crust on it, I'd appreciate it. The bottom half is in the oven."

"Sure. What're you making?"

"Steak and kidney. It's Stephan's favorite."

Maura hesitated.

Evelyn looked up from the dough she was mixing and saw Maura's expression. "Spill it."

"Nothing." Maura shook her head. "The filling's in that pan on the stovetop?" She turned to look.

Evelyn stopped working and pierced Maura with a sharp gaze. "You know something."

Fred's eyes darted between the women.

Tears leaked out of Evelyn's eyes.

Maura gave her a horrified look. "Oh, no, no please don't cry. I'm sure I'm wrong. He probably loves steak and kidney pie."

"No, he doesn't." She started sobbing. "He hates it, always has. I knew that because he finally told me last year. I promised I wouldn't make it for him again. Then I got so confounded today that I went and did it out of habit." Evelyn's crying increased.

"I happen to love steak and kidney pie, and haven't gotten to enjoy it in years." Fred offered.

Maura beamed at him while Evelyn lifted eyes that still shimmered with tears and looked at him. "You don't need to humor me, Fred."

"But I'm serious," he protested. "I haven't had a good one since my wife died. She used to make it for Sunday dinner once a month."

"Well, we'll fix that, then. You're staying for supper."

"I'll need to call Sam and Margy, but they won't mind me canceling. I eat there too often as it is."

"Invite them here."

After getting mugs of tea for everyone, Maura convinced Evelyn to sit at the table and take a rest. She then proceeded to help Fred finish up the pie and get it baking in the oven.

Fred excused himself to call Sam. While he was out of the room, Maura put the biscuit dough in the refrigerator and sat down across from Evelyn. She reached for her future mother-in-law's hand.

"Want to talk about it?"

"I hate his job," Evelyn confessed. "He never intended to become a police officer. I know he's good at it and he's helped loads of people over the years, but I wish he'd quit. I don't want him in harm's way anymore." Tears started leaking out of her eyes again.

Maura held her hand in silence.

Fred walked back in and picked up his mug before joining them at the table. He gazed into the milky tea for a long moment before looked looking at the women. He reached for Maura's free hand and covered it with his own. "You gave us quite a scare, young lady."

"Not on purpose, Fred."

"No, of course not. Who would've thought the library would be such a dangerous place to work? My wife used to worry about me and in the end, she was the one whose job killed her."

"I thought she died of cancer." Maura looked at him in surprise.

"She did; lung. Never smoked a day in her life, but she was a counselor in a treatment center. Most of her clients were chain smokers. For years, they were allowed to smoke in the therapy rooms. She'd come home with the stuff clinging to her hair and clothing."

"That's awful."

"It was," Fred agreed. "But it brought me here, and I can't regret the past twelve years. I've made good friends, I've explored new places, and I like to think I've done some good."

"You helped save the children, Stephan, and me. You and Sam are heroes."

"We're two old men who had nothing to lose and were in the right place at the right time."

"Were you listening in on our conversation?" Evelyn queried Fred.

"No, ma'am. After I hung up with Sam—oh, he and Margery are delighted by your invitation—I came right back. I've been struggling with how we almost lost some wonderful people for such a senseless reason. People like me and Stephan know there are risks when we take our jobs, but Maura here, well, libraries are supposed to be safe places for learning and community. Her job was supposed to be a safe one, like my wife's."

Evelyn reached out and put her hand over the one he still had over Maura's. "So, you think my son shouldn't quit his job?"

"Is that what you were talking about?" Fred's eyebrows rose in surprise.

"I was telling Maura how much I wish he would."

"I can understand that sentiment." Fred used his free hand to drink some tea. After a moment, he met Evelyn's gaze. "Does Stephan know how you feel?"

"Of course not. Parents need to let their children live their lives. But it's eating me up inside."

Maura slid away from the table and stood up to gaze out of the window into Milly's backyard. She wrapped her arms around her waist. "What about spouses?" Her voice was soft, but both heard her.

"Spouses need to talk."

"Tell him how you feel."

"I don't want him to feel like I'm pressuring him to quit because I'm afraid." Maura turned to face them. "I hate this."

Evelyn stood up and held Maura. "Oh, lovey."

Maura's phone started ringing and interrupted them. She apologized and slid it out of her pocket. "I'd better take this." Maura answered. "Hi, sweetheart."

The call was brief.

"They're going to stop at the school to pick Maisy up so she doesn't have to take the bus home today. They know to come here."

"Very good." Evelyn patted her own cheeks. "I'll go freshen up. I don't want any of them knowing I've been crying."

Fred's voice was gentle. "It's not a bad thing for people to know you cry for them, Evelyn."

Evelyn looked at him for a long moment and nodded her head. "Perhaps, but it matters to me."

After Evelyn had gone upstairs, he and Maura worked together to clean up the kitchen.

"How are you doing, Fred?"

"I'm fine." He handed her the pan he'd just dried. "I regret that that young man may have lost his sight, but I don't feel bad about doing what I did."

Maura nodded. "Have you seen Josie?" She put the pan away. "Ron wants to talk with her and Karria to try and close the case. He agreed to meet them at my house or the beach."

"So, he knows their secret now?"

Maura nodded. "He doesn't really believe us."

"Sometimes seeing is required," Fred observed. He leaned his long body against the counter. "If Josie wants me or Sam there, we'll be staying, regardless of Ron's preferences."

Maura privately wondered if the police chief was losing his patience with all of them, but couldn't fault Fred. Karria and Josie needed their support and protection far more than Joey Thompson's supporters did. "You won't get an argument from me."

"Didn't think so." He urged her to join him back over at the table. "When does Josie get her pelt back?"

"We're still waiting on the historical society. They're dragging their feet for some reason."

Fred nodded. "Maurice or Terry most likely. Ron can apply some pressure to them if he wants his interviews. It's not fair to ask Josie to do this while holding her pelt ransom."

"I hadn't thought about it in those terms," Maura admitted.

Fred patted her hand. "You've been a bit preoccupied." His phone pinged and he glanced down. A slow smile spread across his lips. "Do you think the Kirklands would object to one or two more at dinner?"

"Probably not," Maura's tone was cautious. "But Stephan still tires easily. If it's someone who will expect him to socialize, it'd be best not."

"No, they won't, and perhaps it will do him some good."

"Do you think they'll like steak and kidney pie?" Maura glanced at the oven.

Fred laughed. "Possibly. What's Stephan going to eat?"

"Good question." Maura thought about what she had stowed away in her own freezer. "I have another lasagna that Josephine brought by yesterday. We can heat that up."

"Any estimates on when the library will reopen?"

Maura looked at Fred. Neither noticed Evelyn in the doorway. "I'm struggling to even care. I went back today. It was…difficult. I'm not sure how I go back and work there."

Fred nodded. "We saw what they'd done." He was quiet as he gathered his thoughts. "It's just a building, Maura. Your work is about people and helping them."

"Fred, I kept waiting to hear the door bang open and see a man with a gun. I don't know if I can be there alone or feel safe with children there. And I know it's not rational. I know this was an aberration, but—" She shrugged. "I'm not sure how to get past it."

"Time will help. Having the space cleaned up and maybe rearranged might help." He sighed too. "It's still fresh. You're not always going to feel this way. You know that."

"Not going to allow me a moment of self-pity, are you?"

"I'm just trying to help." He gave her a small, crooked smile.

"We've forgotten how you suffered in all of this too, haven't we, Maura?" Evelyn stepped into the room. "Because your injuries are no longer visible, we forget you suffered them." She moved to gather Maura into a hug.

"Oh, no. I don't feel that way at all." Maura protested and then found herself locked in a motherly embrace.

The front door opened and Maisy's high-pitched voice floated in while Andrew's baritone responded. Evelyn gave Maura a squeeze and then let her go so they could greet the others. Stephan was pale and quiet, but he had a loving smile for Maura and his mother as he sat on a chair to push off his shoes.

Nick arrived moments before the rest of the guests and found a cheerful group laughing and chatting in the living room. Stephan looked tired but relaxed as he held Maura's hand. They sat on the couch looking at a paper Maisy was showing them. Nick grabbed a beer before joining the group. He perched on the sofa arm. Seconds after he did, Maisy's head shot up and she beamed. "Karria's here!" She looked at Fred. "Mr. Foley, is she one of the special guests?"

He nodded and stood up. "Mr. and Mrs. Dodd are bringing her and Josie to dinner."

Maisy dropped her paper on the coffee table and dashed for the door.

Curious, Nick, Evelyn, and Andrew all followed. Stephan and Maura held back, not wanting to overwhelm the two selkies.

There was a chorus of hellos from Sam and Margery and then Josie's voice hesitantly joined in.

Maura reached for Stephan's hand when she felt a presence enter her mind. His startled look let her know he was experiencing it too.

Karria's greeting was tentative, nothing like her forceful mental voice in the cave.

Maura tried to project a feeling of welcome.

Stephan looked at a loss and whispered to Maura, "What do I do?"

"I think just share what you feel with her." Maura shrugged. Of all of them, Maisy was the one with the most experience communicating with the elder selkie, and she was in the foyer jabbering away.

Stephan furrowed his brow and stood up. Maura joined him and they both turned to see Karria in the doorway watching them.

She was wearing a simple blue shift and had a pair of thick knit socks on her feet. Her black hair with its silver blaze gleamed in the soft light.

Maura stepped forward. "It's lovely to see you again, Karria."

The selkie nodded. She met Maura's gaze before shifting her eyes to Stephan. She glided towards him with an intent expression.

Stephan stood still. His expression was wary as she approached him.

Maisy came skidding into the room. "Daddy, isn't it great that Karria's here? This is so exciting!" She slid to a stop next to Maura and looked from her father to Karria and back again. She cocked her head to the side. "Daddy, you don't need to be scared. She's going to help."

Stephan ignored his daughter's chatter and kept his eyes locked on the selkie's black gaze. When she started singing softly and reached a pale hand up to his injured shoulder, he instinctively moved to protect it.

Karria ignored his move and stepped forward again. She put her palm over his bandage. A golden glow formed underneath and Stephan let out an involuntary "Oh," as warmth spread into his healing flesh from her touch. He hissed in pain when the light flared, and then his expression relaxed.

By now, everyone else in the house had filtered into the room. Evelyn started to move forward, but Josie grabbed her arm and shook her head.

Stephan swayed where he was standing. When the glow under Karria's hand faded, he stumbled backwards and sank down onto a nearby chair. Evelyn broke away from Josie and hurried to her younger son's side.

"You feel better now, don't you, Daddy?" Maisy had her arms wrapped around Maura's waist.

Stephan remained pale, but the pinched look around his eyes and lips was gone. He flexed his fingers, then slid his left arm out of the sling and moved it in small, experimental motions. When they didn't cause pain, he progressed to some of the stretches he was doing in physical therapy. When those were done without the restriction he'd become accustomed to, he smiled. Moving carefully, he swung his arm in a circle and then laughed in delight. "Thank you, Karria!"

Karria nodded.

Maisy released Maura and ran to Karria. She gave her a fierce hug. "Thank you for helping Daddy. I knew you would."

"You are welcome, sweet child." Karria's voice held a melodic quality that was compelling to listen to. "I could not before." She touched Maisy's cheek and the girl got the expression she usually did when they were communing telepathically.

Maisy nodded. She then looked at her grandmother. "Gran, I'm going to wash up and set the table."

Within twenty minutes, they were all seated around the large table in the dining room. Conversation was stilted at first, but as Nick and Maisy joked and Margery and Evelyn found common things to talk about, things began to ease. Soon Andrew was chatting away with Sam and Josie while Fred and Stephan spoke in quiet tones about the ongoing investigation. Maura was filled with conflicting emotions as she took it all in and mostly moved her food around on her plate. Karria caught her gaze. Suddenly an image and the sensation of peaceful companionship filled Maura as she watched a younger version of Karria, Aunt Jane, and the Dodds around the table in her kitchen. Maura sighed at the contentment Karria had felt and tears formed in the corners of her eyes as she found she could orient the vision to focus in on her aunt. She felt as though she could reach out and touch her. It wasn't until Stephan gently clasped her hand and drew it back down that she realized she'd moved to try and touch Jane once more. His cerulean eyes were focused on her. "Are you okay?" The whisper was for her ears only. Maura blinked away the tears and nodded.

"They were so happy together."

Karria nodded. She reached out and touched Maura's chest above her heart with a cool, gentle hand. "Love." She imbued the word with a wealth of emotion.

Tears leaked from Maura's eyes. "Thank you, Karria."

The selkie slid her hand away and resumed eating her second serving of pie. After she finished, she gave Stephan a placid look. "You may call your alpha. We will meet with him now."

"Alpha?"

Maura figured it out first. "Ron. Your superior officer, the alpha."

"Ah, of course." Stephan coughed slightly.

Fred gave Karria a surprised look. "I thought you were waiting until Josie had her pelt back."

Josie stood up. "We have faith you'll make sure the others do the right thing. Once I have my pelt," she glanced at Maisy and then back around at all the adults. "I will be leaving for the colony. It's long past time for me to meet them, and—" She glanced again at the child and then shrugged. "And experience my adulthood. I think that once I touch it, well, the sea has been calling to me for so many years. I am tired of resisting the song. Speaking with Chief Moore is not a high priority to me, but it matters for all of you. And you do matter to me." The younger selkie shrugged.

Everyone was silent for a moment. Then Maisy's wavery voice drew their attention. "Karria is leaving us, too?"

Josie gave the child a sympathetic look. "Yes. She needs to accompany me. I've never met the others. To ensure I'm accepted, she needs to come with me."

"But then you'll come back, right?" Maisy stood up and rounded the table to stand next to Karria.

The older selkie rested her hand on the child's shoulder. Tears pooled in Maisy's eyes and spilled down her cheeks. "But that's so long. Do you have to leave me?"

Maura gathered Maisy up into her lap. "Sweetheart, Josie needs to be able to live her life, and meet the rest of her family."

Maisy started sobbing. "I know, but I thought everything was going to be happy now."

Karria gently pulled Maisy from Maura's lap and into her own. She rested her hands on the child's temples for a few minutes, and then on her heart. Maisy's tears and sobs slowed. She hiccupped. Then a smile appeared on her lips. "Really?" She looked up at Karria. "Are you sure?"

Karria put her hand over Maisy's heart again and closed her eyes. The child stilled and her breathing deepened.

Maura felt Stephan tense next to her and reached for his hand.

Josie leaned down between them. "She's visioning with her. The child is safe. It's a rare gift. Let her enjoy it."

"Visioning?" Stephan's voice was wary.

"Sharing images of the future."

"Of possibilities?"

"No." Josie's voice was soft. "These are certainties."

"But that's impossible." Stephan turned in his chair to look at the dark-eyed woman.

Her grin was mischievous. She poked his shoulder where the bullet had entered. She waited a beat for him to notice. When understanding flashed across his face, she arched an eyebrow. "We are impossible. Your healing should be impossible, but here we are, and here you and Maura are, hale and whole."

Stephan nodded and turned his gaze back to his child, who had just let out a soft sigh and was opening her eyes to gaze at Karria.

"Thank you, Karria." Maisy threw her arms around the selkie and drew in a deep breath. Before she could speak, Karria placed a finger on the child's lips and shook her head.

"Only for you. It's a gift just for you, Maisy."

"Oh." Disappointment flooded the girl's face, but after a moment she nodded. "I understand."

A sniffle from further down the table drew everyone's attention. Margery had her head turned into her husband's shoulder and was quietly crying while Sam rubbed her back.

Karria pushed away from the table and went to embrace them both.

Fred gave Josie a sad look. "I'm going to miss you something fierce."

"I'll miss you, Fred." She reached for his hand. "I'll say a proper goodbye before I leave."

He nodded and held her hand in a tight grip. "You'd better."

Sam looked at Stephan. "Why don't you call Ron? Get the interrogation over with so these ladies don't have to waste any more of their precious time on Joey Thompson."

Stephan and Maura brought Karria and Josie across the street, where there would be more privacy.

Karria hesitated a moment before entering Maura's home and then stepped in with a sigh. She greeted Mags and proceeded to roam from room to room while the elderly gray tabby walked beside her, chatting away.

"Josie." Maura reached out and touched her arm. "Are you sure there aren't things you want from here?"

Josie's laughter was a series of barking sounds. When she stopped, she was still smiling at Maura. "I don't know if I'll ever take this form again once I get my pelt back." She shook her head. "You mean well, but I have no need that you can help me with. Enjoy your home. Enjoy your things. Be happy here with your family."

Ron questioned the women one at a time and then together. Stephan stayed with them for the duration. Eventually, Ron said Maura, Sam, and Fred could join them and went over things one more time, including the evening's healing. Finally, he let out a deep sigh and stared into his mug of coffee. "I have no idea how I'm going to write this up, but come hell or high water, I will figure out a way to officially close this case tomorrow in regards to the investigation into Mr. Thompson's accidental death." He eyed Stephan. "And I sure as hell don't know how I'm going to fix your disability paperwork. Miracles aren't a checkbox the State of Maine offers."

Karria gave him a slight smile. "You don't truly believe." She and Josie shared a look.

"Maura, please have your daughter join us at the beach. Anyone else who wishes may come, but my mother would like Maisy and Ron there."

Maura and Stephan exchanged a glance and when he nodded, she stood up. "Okay. Give me a few minutes to bundle her up." She slid on her boots and coat and hurried across to the other house. Her invitation drew curiosity from everyone except Maisy, who seemed to understand what was going on. The girl raced for her boots and outerwear. The others followed. Quiet conversations continued as they topped the small rise. The tide was coming in and a full moon hung low in the sky.

As they gathered in a knot against the bitter wind sweeping in off the water, Karria gave Maisy a long embrace and then, in a fluid motion, stripped off the dress she'd been wearing. She handed it to the girl. Josie opened the backpack she'd brought and shook out a seal pelt.

"Is that—?" Evelyn's voice was filled with awe.

Karria gave her a smile and then stood in front of Ron, whose embarrassment was obvious. She waited until he met her eyes, then opened the pelt up and slid the seal head over her own.

There was a faint glow as it wrapped around Karria's body and enveloped her. Within moments, the woman appeared to have been swallowed entirely by the black pelt. Karria slid to the beach and stared up at Ron. Her barks sounded vaguely like laughter as she watched him. Ron crouched down and gazed into the seal's eyes. "I have to believe you now, don't I?"

She huffed in agreement and butted his hand once with her head before making her awkward way back to Maisy to give the child a quick nuzzle. Then she slid into the cold, dark waves.

"Anyone want coffee?" Andrew broke the silence that had fallen. "Or something stronger?"

The group all moved back towards the big house, but Josie touched Maura's arm. "Can we go back to your house?"

"Sure." Maura quickly let Stephan know and then broke off with Josie from the rest of the group when they reached the houses.

Once inside, Maura kicked off her boots and followed Josie into the living room. She sat on the chair opposite her and waited.

Josie was stroking Mags and gazing at the flames in the woodstove. For several minutes, the periodic popping from a log and Mags's purrs were the only sounds that broke the silence. Eventually Josie spoke. "You and I both always wished for bigger families. I wish they had chosen to raise us together, here. I would have liked to have known you."

"I would have loved that." Maura slid forward in her seat and let her hands dangle between her knees. "I'm sorry you'll be leaving so soon, but I understand. At least, I think I do."

Josie nodded. "I expect I will see you again, but not for many years." She gave Maura a thoughtful look and then nodded. "Yes, our paths will cross again. And yes," she nodded to Maura's unspoken question, "you will see Karria again." She gently put Mags off her lap and onto the chair. "May I take a last look around?"

When they went across the street, Josie sat down between Sam and Fred while Maura perched on the edge of Stephan's chair until he snaked his arms around her waist and tugged her into his lap. She instinctively pulled away from his injured shoulder, but he urged her back. "It feels better than, well, ever."

Maura carefully lifted the edge of his shirt and peeked at his now smooth skin. "Amazing," she whispered.

"Look who's talking," Stephan gently stroked her unmarred neck.

Maura sighed, snuggled into him, and looked around the room. "Where's Maisy?"

"She wanted to be alone for a while." He saw her concern and shook his head. "She's fine, love. I think she just needs some time to absorb tonight's events. Stay with me." He slid further back into the chair.

Maura felt cocooned and safe. She idly listened to the conversation flowing around them and let the images of Karria's transformation play through her mind's eye. It was like nothing she'd ever seen before. It hadn't looked painful, but it was hard to reconcile seeing Karria as a woman one moment and a seal the next.

Josie leaned over and whispered something to Fred. He nodded in agreement. After a few minutes, he cleared his throat. "I've had a delightful and fascinating visit, but I have an early morning at St. Croix tomorrow, so I need to call it a night. Sam, Marg, I'll bring Josie home."

"Won't fight you on that tonight, Fred." Sam gave Evelyn and Andrew a chagrined look. "I'd love to continue our conversation, but it's been a long week for us as well, and it's started hitting me hard."

"I think that goes for all of us." Andrew stood up and covered a yawn.

After a flurry of goodbyes, the Kirklands and Maura were soon alone. Stephan went to check on Maisy and came back downstairs a couple of minutes later. "She's sound asleep." He shot Maura a questioning look. "Where would you like to be tonight?"

"Why don't you two catch some rest at your house? I can get Maisy on the bus in the morning. I don't feel like giving up your bed for the sofa." Nick smiled at his brother.

"How thoughtful of you." Stephan grinned back before moving to hug his parents.

When they finally settled in their bedroom, Maura gently eased Stephan's shirt up over his head and examined his shoulder thoroughly, first with her fingers and eyes and then her lips.

By the time they tumbled into the bed, neither was thinking about injuries.

Later, Maura was drifting off to sleep with her head on Stephan's chest. He, however, was feeling great. After having rested so much for the past week, Stephan's mind was jumping from thought to thought. He twined a lock of Maura's hair around his fingers as he let things filter through his brain. "Maura, are you still awake?" He kept his voice quiet in case she'd fallen asleep.

"Mmmmhmmm. Why?" Her voice was sleepy.

"I want to rethink our jobs. Adam's right. We won't have to work the way we do."

"What if the money isn't what he thinks it'll be?"

"We don't need much, do we? There's no mortgage on the house, and I have enough to pay for the addition. Maisy has a college fund that should see her through with plenty to spare. I already checked—if I stay at 28 hours a week on the force, we keep our health insurance. I think Ron would go for it. My pension won't be amazing, but it should be adequate if we don't go crazy." He let the silky strands of her hair flow through his fingers and moved his hand down to gently stroke her back. "I know you love the library, but you don't have to work at all. You could spend time on your art."

Maura lifted her head and rolled so she was resting on her elbow and looking at him. "Did you and Nick talk about today?"

"Did something happen?"

"I visited the library."

"How'd it go?" Stephan moved so he was able to give Maura his full attention.

"Could've been better. I lost my temper with Colleen."

Stephan chuckled. "Welcome to my world." He drew her close. "Was it awful? I'm sorry I wasn't there."

"I needed to do it alone. I would have preferred to do it without Colleen, but Ron still has everything roped off." She traced idle circles and lines along his chest and shoulder as she thought about it. "They destroyed my office. I know it's just stuff, but it was mine.

They were things that mattered to me. God, she wanted to defend him, Stephan. She still doesn't see him as the monster he was."

"She loved him, Maura." His voice was gentle.

"It makes it worse. I want to be angry at her, but I know I shouldn't. I know this is hard on her too." She lifted her head. "They talked about me. They thought I was gay just because I didn't find him appealing."

Stephan couldn't help the rumble of laughter that filled his chest.

Maura's lips quirked. She started laughing with him. "The island's full of gay women, by that standard," she snorted.

"He did seem to cut quite a swath through the population even so." Stephan thought about Bonita.

"I never understood it. You just had to look in his eyes and—" Maura shivered in his arms at the recollection.

Stephan shrugged. "Abusers are good at what they do. They're really good at twisting people's thoughts and emotions around till they can't see a way out, even when they're given a life preserver or shown the exit." He couldn't count the number of domestic calls he'd gone on. "He might not have hit these women, but he did manipulate and use them."

"I guess." Maura's warm feelings were fading rapidly the more they spoke about Joey.

Stephan could feel the tension coiling in her shoulders. "You mentioned Nick."

"Oh." In a voice that grew with excitement, she told him about her outing with his brother.

Stephan agreed that they should go back to look at the building together. "Does that coin in the box change things for you, Maura?"

"It's ours, free and clear. If we can sell it for what Jackson thinks those are worth, it would cover a lot of the asking price." She smiled in the dark. "We could actually do this if we want to."

CHAPTER 26

It took another week, but finally the historical society held the promised meeting early on a Tuesday morning. It was contentious. Maurice and Terry tried to hold out and insist the entire collection, including the seal pelt, needed to stay intact and hidden. It wasn't until Karria herself showed up and forced herself into their minds that the two men backed off. Once she had Josie's skin in her hands, she nodded to Maura, who—along with Sam, Fred, George, Josephine, Molly, and Stephan—followed her out the door. Stephan stopped at the school to get Maisy.

By the time they reached home, a number of vehicles were clustered at the end of the road.

Tears filled Maisy's eyes. "Thank you for bringing me to say goodbye."

He gave his daughter a sympathetic look and pulled her close for a hug after she'd released her seat belt. "I love you, Maisy Daisy."

"I love you too, Daddy." She snuggled into Stephan's arms for a moment before wriggling free. "I don't want to miss saying bye."

"They won't leave without you."

Maisy shook her head. "Josie will want to go as soon as she sees her pelt."

Stephan wanted to reassure her, but knew it was an empty promise. Instead, he squeezed her hand as they walked towards the beach. "I'm really proud of you, love."

Maisy ran down to join the knot of people clustered on the beach. Stephan saw Nick and his parents standing together to one side, with Maura, Fred, and the Dodds nearby. George, Josephine, and Liz, with Molly leaning on the willowy blonde's arm, were on the other side. Karria and Josie were in the center of the group in human form. There were a couple of large garbage bags in front of them. Maisy threw herself into Karria's arms but, by the time Stephan made it to the group, she'd already let the selkie go and was snuggling up to Maura.

Karria and Josie nodded to acknowledge his arrival.

"We have a few things we'd like to give each of you before we leave. Maybe you'll get some pleasure from them and remember us fondly." Josie nodded to her mother.

Karria reached into the first bag and took out several books. She and Josie handed them to Stephan, Liz, Evelyn, George, and Margery. Next came the chess set, with its intricately carved marble pieces. This was handed to Fred with a smile. Sam was handed the guitar. Andrew and Josephine were each given spectacular green crystals that required two hands to hold. Molly was given a lovely flute. Karria paused before Nick with an amused expression on her face. She leaned over and whispered something to him that made him blush. She then handed him the stringed instrument Maura had puzzled over back in the cave. Karria and Josie then reached into the last bag, and holding their hands behind their backs, approached Maura and Maisy. Karria reached for the girl and held her in a tight embrace, then put a delicately carved figurine into her hand. Tears rolled down the child's cheeks, but she smiled and nodded. Josie gazed at Maura. "Jane made this for me when I was a baby and added onto it every year until I was eighteen. I know you'll treasure it as I did." She put a soft, heavy bundle into Maura's arms. Both selkies embraced the humans, then Karria drew two pelts from the bottom of one of the bags. Fred grabbed the empty bags before they blew away.

Few eyes were dry as Josie was reunited with hers. The joy and relief that exuded from her was palpable. She quickly stripped out of her clothing and settled into the pelt, which after a few seconds, glowed and began swallowing her. Karria gave Maisy a last hug and kiss and slipped into her own. The mother and daughter splashed in the shallow waters for a few minutes and then pushed off into the waves. They turned when they were offshore and bobbed in the current. They took a long look at the humans standing there, then dove under the waves.

The group slowly spilt up. The elder Kirklands invited Liz and Molly back to the house with them when they saw Molly shivering. Fred, the Dodds, and Clarks all said their goodbyes. Stephan, Maura, and Maisy stood staring out at the cove until Maisy's teeth started chattering. By unspoken agreement, the trio veered off to the smaller house. Once inside, they settled on the sofa.

Maisy showed her parents the delicately etched and stained wood. The small sculpture was set in a base of blue tourmaline. The image of a young, slender woman and barrel-chested man holding hands and smiling was sweet and beautifully rendered. Dickie and Karria were easy for Maura to make out. "Oh, this is the man Karria loved when she first moved here." Maisy looked at the adults. "She told me he was really special to her, but that they weren't right for each other. Did you know she loved Maura's aunt? That makes Josie and Maura a bit like sisters, doesn't it?"

"A bit like that." Stephan nodded. "This is a precious gift. You need to take good care of it."

"I will, Daddy. I'll put it in my room here tonight, but I want to show Gran and Gramps first."

"Of course."

"Are you going to open your gift, Maura?"

Maura's smile was slight. "Yes." She reached for the bundle that was tied together with some twine and easily undid it. She unfolded the blanket. With Stephan and Maisy's help, she spread it out on the floor so they could examine it. The center was a black seal with the familiar blaze on her forehead. A smaller seal with similar markings was snuggled against her side. They were on a gray-blue background, and the entire baby-blanket-sized rectangle was edged with clusters of crocheted pink and white roses. The blanket spread out from there, with new borders of differing colors and patterns. Some held imagery like others of Jane's more complex work, others were simple and colorful.

"Did your aunt make you one like this, too?"

"No, sweetheart." Maura shook her head. "Nothing like this."

"Oh." Maisy was quiet for a moment. "Now you have one!"

Maura hugged the child. "That's right." She carefully folded it up. "I'd like to see Liz before she leaves. Ready to go across the street?"

"Sure!" Maisy gave Tim a quick hug before dashing out the door and across the street.

Stephan looked at Maura. "Are you okay?"

"A bit sad," she admitted, "but yes. How about you?"

"Truthfully?" When she nodded, he continued, "Relieved. I'm grateful, beyond grateful, don't get me wrong, but Maisy's obsession with Karria worried me."

Maura squeezed his hand. "She's going to be just fine, great even."

He smiled at her. "Keep telling me that as she grows up, will you?"

CHAPTER 27

Jackson stopped by the next morning with a proposal from his cousin. She'd made an exceedingly generous offer to purchase Maura's coin outright and was willing to help them with the sale of the others, as well as the proposals they wanted to make to the town. After he left, Maura looked shell-shocked.

"Let's go for a walk. It'll clear our heads." Stephan urged. "How about the big beach?"

As they walked, the crisp, sweet smell of pine needles being crushed under their feet and the chattering of birds and squirrels around them helped center Maura. When they were five minutes out, she let out a heavy sigh.

"Better?"

"Yes." Maura looked at Stephan. "I guess selling to Cora's the right thing to do."

"I think it is." Stephan nodded in agreement.

"We could take a really nice honeymoon."

He grinned at her. "We could, or we can make your artists' co-op a reality."

Her eyes lit up, but then she slanted him a questioning look. "Is it a crazy thing to do? It'd use up the money."

"I think it's something the community could get behind."

"Can we check out the building together with Nick?"

"We can go over to the big house and talk with him after our walk." They broke through the woods and the wind coming off the open ocean hit them in the faces. It blew stinging sand with it. "Which," Stephan grimaced, "I'm happy to cut short if you are."

Maura nodded and turned back into the protection the trees provided.

"I had a lot of time to think in Bangor. I know we've been talking about a summer wedding. With everything that's happened, well, would you consider getting married now while my parents and Nick are here?" He hurried to add, "We could still have a big party and even a second ceremony in the summer if you'd like." He took in the surprised look on Maura's face. "I know I'm springing this on you. Don't answer, just think about it."

"Okay." Maura nodded. "I will."

Stephan smiled. "Great." He pulled her close into a loving embrace until his phone began ringing. "Nick," he groaned as he heard the ringtone. The conversation was brief. When they reached Maura's yard, they kept going and slid into Stephan's car.

The drive to town passed quickly. Maura sat, lost in thought, while the brothers talked over the phone about Cora's offer.

Nick grinned at them as he keyed open the door to the old municipal building. "Let's go check it out. I convinced them to turn on the heating system so we could see how well it works."

"Where's Bimy?" Maura looked around for the portly real estate agent.

"He gave me the key so I could meet with the building inspector this morning."

"Why would he do that?" Stephan narrowed his eyes at his brother. "Seems weird."

Nick hustled them inside and shut the door behind them. "If you haven't noticed, more than a few folks on this rock are pretty barmy." He flicked on all the lights.

"Those have to go." Maura pointed to the bank of fluorescents.

Both men nodded in agreement, though Stephan was still shooting his brother a look of suspicion as he led them on a tour of the downstairs. "You know an awful lot of details about the building code and requirements for what we're thinking about." He finally grabbed Nick by the arm. "What gives?"

Nick shrugged. "I get off on this stuff. Besides, I'm just trying to be helpful so you and Maura don't have to chase down all the information. You've got a home addition to plan, a wedding to organize, a child to raise, job situations to sort out, a town meeting to plan for…shall I continue?"

Stephan closed his eyes. "No, please stop." He opened his eyes and rubbed his forehead. "When you put it that way, feel free to knock yourself out with this."

By the time they made it to the upstairs space, Maura had already listed a bunch of projects she wanted to do to make the building fit her vision. Nick had been quietly making notes on his phone while Stephan was calculating costs in his head.

"What do you see up here, Maura?" Nick leaned against the wall of the kitchen area.

She glanced between him and Stephan and then drew in a deep breath. "I've been thinking about it. I'd like to keep it as an apartment. You could use it when you visit so you'll have more privacy and space than at the house. It would give us a place for guest instructors to stay, and maybe tempt them up here with some sort of artist-in-residence type program.

"I was thinking you could create a small studio apartment in that quarter of the room back there and incorporate the bathroom into it. Then leave the rest as is." Nick gestured towards the back corner of the room. "Visitors, or myself," —he smiled, pleased that she'd been thinking about him—"can share the kitchen with everyone here. You could rent it to tourists when it's sitting empty to earn cash. You won't make a profit for yourselves if you don't charge a real rent for the rest of the spaces too." Nick leaned against the countertop. "I can help you create a business plan if you'd like. Right now, however, we have more important discussions."

"To say the least."

Maura shot Stephan a concerned look. "You think it's a bad idea?"

"No, I don't. It's new to both of us. We'll have a steep learning curve and, well," he ran a hand through his hair and gave her a wry smile. "I'm risk averse."

Nick snorted. "No kidding." His phone pinged. "Ah, the bloke we've been waiting for just arrived."

"We were waiting for someone?" Maura looked at Stephan.

He shrugged.

They followed Nick as he ran down the stairs to the first floor.

"Brad!" Maura was pleasantly surprised to see the congenial contractor. "What are you doing here?"

He pushed his ball cap back and glanced at Nick. "I thought you knew I was coming over."

Nick cleared his throat. "I thought Brad could go through the punch list we've been creating here to get an estimate put together before he heads over to the house with you two. That addition's never going to be done if you don't get on his schedule. Besides, you'll want to know exactly what you're getting into at both places before making any decisions, right?"

Maura and Stephan glanced at each other. "That was thoughtful of you, mate." Stephan nodded at Nick before he reached out to shake Brad's hand. "Thanks for fitting us into your schedule."

"For you two, well, I'm happy to bump any project you have to the top of the list. Amber had nightmares for days, but she also kept telling us how she felt less scared down in the tunnels because she was with you, Maura. She's always felt safe with you. Nat and I are grateful."

"Please give her a hug from me." Maura felt a wash of guilt that she hadn't checked in on the children yet beyond brief conversations early on with their parents.

"I will." He nodded and then reached for the pencil behind his ear and flipped his notepad open to a clean page. "So, what've we got here?"

As they drove back to Briar Road, the couple bounced from topic to topic. Brad had been enthusiastic about Maura's vision and Nick's practical suggestions. Stephan had offered opinions from time to time, but mostly took it all in. When they were about ten minutes from home, Maura turned in the passenger seat to study Stephan's profile. "Let's do it."

He glanced over at her. "Build out the bedroom on the third floor to include a sitting room? I liked what you and Brad sketched out. It'll make renting the space easier."

Maura smiled and reached for his hand. "Thank you, but that's not what I was talking about. Let's get married while your parents and Nick are still here. I do want a big party with our friends and family, but I don't care about a fancy white dress or saying our vows in front of anyone other than family. I don't want to wait."

"Are you sure? I don't mind waiting so you can have the traditional bits and bobs that go with a wedding. I'm sure Maisy would love to plan with you."

"She can help us plan an epic party to celebrate."

Stephan grinned. "We can go back to town to get a license sorted out as soon as Brad leaves."

"Which days are you working next week?" Maura smiled.

"Ron has me down for Tuesday, Wednesday, and Thursday so I can be at the school and then the 3-11 on Sunday. Nick's heading for Boston the Tuesday after and taking a night flight."

"I'll miss him."

Stephan laughed at Maura's wistful expression. "Who'd have thought, huh?"

"Hey!"

He grinned at her offended look. "I'm going to miss him, too, but he'd go stir-crazy too much longer out here. He loves London."

"So, we could get married next Friday." Maura observed.

"We could." Stephan's smile grew.

CHAPTER 28

When Friday came, Maisy was sent to school, despite her protests. Andrew and Evelyn took Stephan's car and went into town early for lunch with Fred and the Dodds.

Well before they were scheduled to leave, Nick started hurrying the couple along.

Stephan grew exasperated with his brother and told him to stop nagging Maura. Both were surprised when the bride interrupted their brewing fight and suggested that leaving early was all right with her. When Stephan scowled at Nick, Maura explained that waiting around was only making her jittery.

Nick beamed. "Thanks, Maura. I just want to take care of this before the wedding."

"Are you going to tell us what 'this' is?" Stephan gave his sibling a disgruntled look.

"Not yet," was Nick's cheerful response as he hurried them into the back of his rental car. "I'll play chauffer."

Maura grinned and slid in without protest. Stephan eyed Nick. "You're up to something."

"What if I am?" Nick shrugged. "Get in the car already."

Maura laughed. "Come on, let Nick have his fun."

"Listen to your bride."

Stephan muttered something under his breath that earned him a punch in the shoulder as he was getting into the car.

Maura reached for his hand. She tugged him over towards her side of the car. As they started down their bumpy, winding road, she whispered, "We're getting married."

Stephan's entire expression lightened and he ran a finger down her cheek. "So we are." He leaned over so he could kiss her lips. "I can't wait."

When they reached the business district, Nick parked in front of the old muni building.

"This isn't town hall."

"I know." Nick smiled at Maura in the rearview mirror. "But there's something I need to show you both." He turned the car off and opened Maura's door. He offered her his arm. After they were all standing on the sidewalk, he hustled them to the wide front door.

Maura noticed the plywood in front of the windows had come down. She gave him a quizzical look.

Nick's face was lit with excitement as he unlocked the building and ushered them in. The heat was on and the afternoon sunlight poured in through the windows. Maura and Stephan both turned to him.

"What's going on, Nick?" Stephan looked at his brother.

Rather than replying, Nick handed Maura a thick cream-colored envelope. "Open it."

Stephan stood slightly behind her so he could look at the contents over her shoulder. Both gasped at the same time. "This is too much, Nick." Stephan looked at his brother in shock. "It's amazing, and beyond generous, but—" He spread his hands out trying to find the right words and not hurt his brother's feelings.

"Here's the thing." Nick looked back and forth between them. "Every time I offered you an opportunity to go in on a purchase with me, and you turned it down, I set a percentage of the profits aside in pretty aggressive investment funds. My intent was to give it to you for Maisy's college. Then when Sophie died and you socked away so much of the settlement money, I realized Maisy wouldn't need it. After our visit over the holidays, I decided I'd give it to you both as a wedding gift. I just changed my mind a bit in how." He shrugged. "Giving you a check felt strange anyway. With everything that's happened, well, I want you all to be safe and happy. Knowing I can do something to help pave the way makes me feel better. I wasn't expecting you to be able to do it all by yourselves, but now you can save that money for your family. Please let me do this. Please accept my wedding gift. You're both happy to give to others. Let me give this to you."

Maura's eyes widened as she took in the enormity of what Nick had done. She thrust the deed into Stephan's hands and threw her arms around his brother. "Nick!"

He smiled over her head at his brother. "Brad's crew will start work on Monday. They'll want to go over the choices for finish work with you, but that's all you need to worry about. Everything's been taken care of. All I ask is that you keep being the wonderful brother and sister that you are."

He started laughing and patted Maura's back. "Are you soaking my shirt?"

Stephan saw Maura's shoulders shaking and hurried over to them. "Love, it's okay."

Nick peered down at Maura and gave her a gentle shove towards Stephan. Her gales of laughter became audible.

Maura grabbed Stephan's arm and leaned against him as she gasped for air.

"Might want to rethink the wedding, mate." He winked at Stephan.

"You. Called. Me. Sister." Maura finally got out.

"I did." Nick grinned at her. "Better go make it official." He checked his watch. "Mum and Dad'll be picking Maisy up in a few minutes and expecting us over at the town hall."

Maura felt a sudden fluttering in her belly and looked over at Stephan. His slow smile brought one to her own lips. "We're doing this."

He nodded and bent his head so his words were for her ears alone. "Did I tell you how beautiful you are?"

Maura found his hand and laced her fingers through his. "Maybe, but you can tell me again."

He squeezed her hand in response. "I love this dress."

Maura smoothed down the front of the sheath that she'd worn on their first date. "It seemed appropriate."

"Lots of great memories." He nodded in agreement and grinned when her cheeks colored.

Nick shook his head. "Come on, you two."

Stephan ignored his brother and tugged Maura close for a kiss. "I love you."

"I love you too." She smiled against his mouth. "I don't want to be late to my own wedding."

He pulled up and chuckled. "Two against one. Let's get going, then."

Nick grinned at Maura. "Better get you to the altar before you change your mind."

"That won't happen." Stephan and Maura both spoke at the same time, which made Nick chuckle as he hustled them out of the building. He locked up and handed Maura the key before he bent down to give her a kiss on the cheek and Stephan a quick embrace.

The frigid air hurried them along as they strode down the street to the newer town offices.

"Daddy! Mom!" Maisy was standing by the doorway to the clerk's office with Andrew and Evelyn. She waved to them both and then threw her arms around each in turn when they reached her. "I'm so excited! I could barely sit still all day! I'm so happy we're getting married today! Mom, Mom, Gran has a surprise for you!"

Evelyn laid a gentle hand on her granddaughter's arm. "Love, may I?"

"Oh, right." Maisy grinned. "I'm just so, so, so, so excited! I thought I'd jump out of my skin all day. Do you feel that way, too?" She looked at her parents, who both nodded in agreement, and then grinned at her grandmother.

"Are you quite done?" Evelyn laughed and then smiled at Maura. "I know you have something old with your aunt's shawl, but if I may." She reached out and fastened a simple gold bracelet with small sapphires in it around Maura's wrist. "I wore this on my wedding day as my something new and blue. I'd love it if you borrowed it for the day."

"Oh." Maura felt tears prick her eyes. "Thank you, Evelyn." She embraced her.

"Mom, don't you need something new, too? Lana told me you had to have something new, old, borrowed, and blue or it'd be bad luck."

"My stockings are new." Maura gave her a fond look.

"Will this do, Maisy Daisy?" Stephan fished out a ring box from his trouser pocket and showed her the simple gold bands he and Maura had found in Bar Harbor when they'd snuck off-island several days earlier. "They're new."

Maisy's eyes were shining when she looked up from the rings and then at her parents. She nodded. "I think so."

"So, are we ready? Ron's inside and waiting." Andrew reached out to squeeze Maura's hand and gave her a kiss on the cheek.

"You'll remember to take pictures?" Stephan looked at Nick.

"Of course." His brother gave him a slight shove towards the door. "Let's get moving here, people."

Andrew reached for the door and held it open. Evelyn and Maisy slipped in first, then Nick.

Maura's soft gasp of surprise drew Stephan's attention away from his father. He turned his head to see what had caused her reaction and felt a burst of warmth inside when he saw the room was jammed full of people.

"You didn't think we'd let you get married without us, did you?" Liz's eyes danced with laughter as she took in her friend's surprise.

Fern beamed at Maura and offered her a simple bouquet of colorful roses with a single daisy in the middle. Pale green ribbons fluttered down from the knot that held it all together.

Maura hugged the girl, then Maisy, who was grinning from ear to ear.

"Did we surprise you?"

"So much." Maura wiped a tear away and gave the flowers an appreciative sniff.

Lana ran over to join her friends and gave Maura a hug as well, while Vicky waved to her from across the room where she was standing with the Dodds, Fred, Jackson, and the Clarks.

Maura was touched to see the library trustees and volunteers there as well.

"Are we about ready to get this show on the road?" Ron's voice cut through the excited chatter in the room. He nodded when everyone turned to look at him. "Everyone can socialize after we make these two legal."

Stephan and Maura met each other's gazes from across the room. They moved to stand in front of Ron, who gave them a fond look. "Dan's handling any calls so all three of us could be here." He tipped his head towards Chip and Colleen. "I don't want to take advantage."

"Of course."

Maura smiled at Maisy, who stood next to Stephan, and handed her bouquet to the child to hold.

The ceremony was simple and sweet. After vowing to love and honor one another, Maura also affirmed with Maisy that she'd love and cherish her for the rest of her life. Stephan and Maura exchanged their rings and a kiss, which was met with much cheering and teasing from their unexpected audience.

Ron again cut through the noise and suggested everyone move down to the large conference room for food and refreshments. The crowd cleared out quickly.

Stephan and Maura looked at his parents and Nick to see if they knew what Ron was talking about and were met with smiles.

"Your friends wanted to make the day special, even though you opted for a small family affair." Evelyn clasped Maura's hands.

"I'm so happy to have you officially in the family, darling." She pulled her in for a long embrace. "We're all chuffed."

When she released her, Maura found herself immediately wrapped in Andrew's warm embrace. "We're so happy, love." He wiped away a tear and reached for his wife's hand.

After a few quick photos, the group made their way down the hall to join the others.

"Surprise!" A cheer went up and Maura started laughing when she realized even more people were crowded into the spacious room than had attended their ceremony. She saw all of their neighbors, Adam and Michael, a number of public safety employees and volunteers, Jack and June, fellow town employees, and the rest of the historical society. A row of tables had been pushed up against the far wall and was loaded down with a potluck of hot and cold dishes and a two-tiered wedding cake as the centerpiece. Maura's hand went to her mouth when she saw the cake, and she looked for Josephine and George. When she caught Josephine's eye, she mouthed "Thank you," before she found herself caught up in a whirlwind of congratulatory embraces.

As Maura tried to wend her way to the bakers, she was set upon by an enthusiastic group of children. Her eyes widened and tears pooled in them as she found Betty Jo, Kevin, Mike, Amber, Tommy, and Isabelle all hugging her, followed by an assortment of parents and guardians. She noticed Stephan surrounded by a number of teenagers he was working with at the high school. They smiled at one another as they accepted congratulations and hugs from one member of the community after another.

When they finally met back up again, Stephan pulled Maura close. They only had time to whisper "I love you," to one another before more friends spilled into the room, wanting to congratulate and celebrate with them.

EPILOGUE

Late August

The music from the DJ's speakers was thumping, but as Stephan and Maura, with their arms wrapped around one another, made their way down to the cove, it became background noise to the shushing of the waves. The heavy scent of roses was redolent through the air. Stephan plucked a vibrant pink one and threaded it into the colorful wreath that crowned Maura's hair.

"It's been quite a year, love."

"It's hard to believe that's all it's been."

He nodded in agreement and led Maura over to their favorite rock. Stephan sat and drew her down onto his lap as they looked out at the waters. "Are you happy?"

Maura sighed with pleasure as she leaned back against him. "Do you even need to ask?" She turned her head and smiled at him. "A year ago, my big dream was for a greenhouse. In my wildest imaginings, I dreamt of transforming the old muni into what it is now. A husband and children were a fantasy I kept locked away, and the trust—well, that wasn't anything I ever conceived of." She gave a light laugh. "I obviously didn't have my sights set nearly high enough."

"Clearly not, since I wasn't even on your radar." Stephan started laughing when she rolled her eyes at him. He gently tucked a lock of her silken hair back behind her ear. "It hasn't been easy, but if we had to go through all of that again to get to this—well, I wouldn't complain." He rested a hand on her swelling abdomen. "I'd even take getting shot again, knowing it'd lead to Karria's healing."

She chuckled. "The depth of that was unexpected, wasn't it?" Maura shifted as one of the babies pushed against Stephan's hand. "This morning, Maisy told me she knew this would happen before the wedding, that Karria had shown her."

Stephan gently caressed the spot where the baby was rolling and pushing. "She insists Dr. Beals is wrong and that they're a boy and girl, you know."

"I'm going to take Maisy's word over the ultrasound on this one." Maura's eyes slanted out to the cove. Her voice was soft, but Stephan heard her. "I wonder how they're doing."

He wrapped his arms around her. "Has Maisy ever told you anything else Karria showed her?"

"No, you?"

"No. I think it's the first secret she's ever managed to keep. All I can get out of her is that there was more to it than the twins, and that it all made her so happy in her heart."

"There's something lovely about knowing there's magic out there." Maura waved her hand around. "Even if it's not a part of our lives anymore, I feel blessed for being allowed to see all that we did, you know?"

"I do. Karria and Josie gave us so many gifts, but just learning about their existence was the biggest."

"Exactly." Maura turned in his arms again. "I'm grateful for the healings, beyond grateful." Her hand settled on Stephan's and her smile widened as the baby bumped hard enough to bounce their hands off her abdomen briefly. "The wealth is amazing, too, but really, the biggest gift was simply them."

Stephan smiled. "Mrs. Kirkland, I think we've played hooky from our guests long enough. What do you say we go back to our party?"

Maura slid off his lap with a smile. "I suppose we should." She reached for his hand and twined her fingers around his. "I do miss knowing there's magic around us. It sounds ungrateful to say it out loud. Maybe it's just missing them. I wish I'd been able to get to know them better."

Stephan pulled her close for another kiss before they started walking off the beach to head back to the party, which had spilled out of their yard and across the street. "Maisy insists we'll see them again. Until then, we'll just have to make our own magic."

COMING IN 2021

Please enjoy a sneak peek at *Flatlander*,
the next book in the Belfort Island series.

The wind had a bitter edge to it, pushing Liz to jog to her truck. Once inside the cold cab, she tugged off a glove and fished her keys out of her pocket. She jammed it into the ignition and turned it. The engine whined at her for a moment before falling silent. "No, no, no," Liz muttered under her breath. She gave it a moment and then tried again. All she got was a clicking noise.

She swore and let her head fall back against the seat. Her eyes skimmed the parking lot. There wasn't anyone out but her and most spaces were empty. "Damn it." Molly was counting on her.

Liz slid out of the cab and slammed the door shut behind her. She hurried back around to the front of the building and scanned the sidewalk to see if there was anyone she could get a jump from. Her eyes landed on a familiar rental car in front of the old municipal building. She sighed. There was nothing else to be done. Liz briskly made her way down the wide sidewalk and dashed across the street.

She peered into the windows of the building, hoping to see Nick. With no one in sight, she took her glove off and pounded on the wooden frame of the door. After a minute of this she gave up and let her head fall against it. She'd have to call Molly. Resigned, she started to turn around when she heard an amused voice behind her.

"The newlyweds are home taking advantage of the school day."

Liz jumped. "God you startled me."

A tall man stood smiling at her. His light brown hair was being ruffled about by the wind and laugh lines crinkled up at the corners of his cerulean eyes. "Good morning Liz." He looked at the door she was leaning against. "Did you need something?"

His British accent charmed her, but there was no way Liz would ever let him know that. She nodded. "Actually, I was looking for you Nick. I need a jump."

His amused expression remained. "I'm not sure I follow. What sort of jump are we talking about?"

Liz narrowed her eyes. "My truck's battery is dead and I need to get Molly to an appointment." She hated having to ask him, but she was out of time and options. "Can you give me a hand?"

"Ah, that sort." Nick nodded. "I don't know if I've got cables though."

"It's okay, I do." Liz was feeling edgy about the minutes slipping away. "Please, I've got to get to Molly. I don't want to make her late."

"Of course." Nick clicked the fob to unlock the SUV's doors and waved her towards it. "You'll need to direct me."

Liz nodded and headed for the silver Explorer. She stopped in surprise when he beat her to it and opened the door for her. "Uh, thanks." She gave him a small smile and slid inside. While Nick was rounding the car and getting in, she tucked a lock of her thick blond hair back behind her ear and pulled her knit cap back down.

She quickly directed him to her old Ford. It looked sad and lonely in the parking lot with its blue paint rusting out in spots and years' worth of dents and dings mottling it. She tried not to worry about what the sophisticated, wealthy man next to her would think about it. A surge of annoyance that the thought had even entered her mind filled her.

When he stopped his vehicle next to hers and angled it so the hoods were as close as they could get, Nick glanced over at Liz. He was taken aback to see the anger that flashed across her face. He knew he was awkward with people at times and mentally reviewed their brief conversation. He didn't think he said anything that would anger her. Nick gave a mental shrug. Maybe she was upset about the car. He reached down to pop the hood and left the rental running. "How can I help?" He'd had enough interactions with the proud woman to know she wouldn't appreciate him taking over.

Liz forced herself to draw in a deep breath. She handed him her keys. "Let me get the cables hooked up and then when I say so can you try turning her on?"

"Her?"

She flushed. "Maybelle. Fern named the truck when we first got her."

"Ah," Nick tried to hold it in, but a smile crept out anyway. He gave the truck a considering look. "Like blue bells in May?"

Liz paused in surprise. "That's exactly what Fern said." Her chocolate brown eyes gave him a long, considering look.

Nick shifted uncomfortably as she studied him. "So, Molly has an appointment?"

"Right," Liz hurried to get the cables. After several minutes she had to admit it was hopeless. The battery was dead.

Nick had remained quiet, but hated seeing the defeated look on Liz's face. "Where's Molly's appointment?"

"Her cardiologist in Ellsworth."

Nick tipped his head towards his car. "I can drive you both. I'm free for the next few hours."

"I can't," Liz hesitated. This wasn't about her. She thought of how frail Molly had grown over the past couple of months. They'd waited weeks for this appointment. She stopped herself.

"Thank you, Nick. I'd appreciate it." She disconnected the cables and locked them back up in her truck.

Once she was back his car, Nick swung out of the parking lot and gave her an expectant look.

"Oh right, you don't know where she lives." Liz shook her head at herself and proceeded to direct him out to the isolated end of the island where the elderly lady's farmstead was.

When he wasn't watching the road, Nick alternated between stealing looks at the lovely woman sitting next to him with a pensive look on her face and out at the increasingly windswept and beautiful scenery that lined either side of the road. Finally, he broke the silence. "I didn't realize there were blueberry barrens on the island."

"Hmm?" Liz was pulled out of her reverie. She glanced out the window and then over at Nick. "Yes, only on this end. There are patches of berries here and there all over but these are the only barrens." She gave the brilliant scarlet plants a fond look. "They make the winters more tolerable."

Nick nodded. "They're beautiful."

Liz gave him a surprised look. "I thought you were a city boy."

"Boy?" Nick started laughing. "I'm 44 Liz. Just because I love the hustle, bustle, and conveniences of London doesn't mean I hate nature." He glanced at the sea as it became visible over the rise. The juxtaposition of the blue green water undulating in the distance with the slashes of red under a brilliant blue sky was striking. His voice held a touch of reverence as he returned his eyes to the road. "It's gorgeous here. The wildness has its own appeal."

"Are you planning on moving here too?" The question slipped out before she realized she was asking it. Liz hoped her tone was casual.

Nick slanted her a look and then focused on maneuvering around a frost heave. "I toyed with the idea of getting a small vacation cottage, but don't want to hurt Maura's feelings. She's asked my opinion on every single detail of the apartment that Brad's fixing up in her building."

Liz nodded. "Turn left here." She pointed at a rutted dirt driveway.

Nick nodded and admired the rambling white farmhouse that came into view. "Has Molly lived her long?"

"Her whole life. This is her family's homestead. Her brother and sister left as soon as they could. She stayed and cared for their parents and the farm."

"Did she raise her family here?"

"She never married."

"Why not?"

Liz shot him an amused look. "Why haven't you ever married?"

Nick felt a flush creep up his neck. "Fair enough." He pulled around into the half circle in front of the house and cut the engine. "Shall I wait here?"

"Come in. Sometimes she needs some help. It could be a few minutes."

He nodded and followed Liz up a couple of steps and onto the generous porch. As she was ringing the bell, he admired the wide pine planks and took in the sturdy wood and stone construction of the house. The paint was flaking and his experienced eye noticed cracks in the shingles and spots where wood was starting to rot, but overall, the house looked well-constructed. Though he never talked about it with anyone for fear of sound like a nutter, Nick enjoyed tuning in to the energy of buildings. The lifelong fascination had led to him to using his programing skills to develop real estate aps and, in recent years, to rehabbing properties. The sense he got from this home was deep satisfaction and rootedness. The farmhouse wasn't going anywhere and had been well loved. It brought a smile to his face and he patted the exterior wall as they stepped inside.

Liz gave him a quizzical look when she saw his action.

Nick gave her a bland smile and nodded in greeting to Molly when the frail woman came into view. She looked distracted by something in the kitchen. But her attention fixed on him quickly enough.

"I wasn't expecting to see you again so soon Nicholas."

"My truck wouldn't start," Liz hurried to explain. "Nick offered to bring us."

"Oh my." Molly tutted. "Liz dear, I keep telling you to take my car. It's just sitting there. I know you love Maybelle, but she's old and giving out, just like me." She shook her head and looked at Nick. "I have a perfectly good vehicle sitting in the garage."

Liz's face flushed. She wished Molly wouldn't bring this argument up in front of Nick. She planned on buying the car in the spring when work picked up again and she could scrape together enough money to not feel like she was stealing it entirely. "Can we talk about this later Molly? We're running late because of me. Do you have your insurance card and the medication list I made for you? What about your hat?"

Molly gave the younger woman an affectionate smile as Liz hurried around the expansive foyer gathering up her warmest coat and a pair of thick, knit mittens. "I double checked. I have everything I need in here." Molly patted the large leather purse she had cradled in her arms before offering it to Nick. "Would you carry this for me?"

"Of course." Nick reached for it and arched an eyebrow at how heavy it was.

Molly noticed. "I like to be prepared."

He gave her an amused smile. "It feels like you have a fruitcake in here."

Molly laughed. "Only in December." Her watery blue eyes twinkled in delight. "Believe it or not, I carry one around so Iris can't foist one of hers off on me. I show tell her she already gave me one. Her memory's starting to go so she believes me."

Nick's rich laughter brought a smile to Liz's lips even as she fought against it. She took advantage of Molly's now free hands to help the woman into her coat. She handed her the mittens while she quickly zipped her up.

"I can do that myself Elizabeth. I'm not infirm yet."

Liz flushed. "I'm sorry."

A bony wrinkled hand patted her arm. "I know you care and don't want us to be late, but Dr. Perkins always is. He can wait on me for a change." She tugged her mittens on and gave Nick a stern look. "No speeding to try and make up time. I cannot abide with reckless driving."

"No ma'am." Nick bit back his smile and nodded. "Shall I get the door?"

Molly beamed at him. "I'd rather take your arm and let you help me down the stairs. Liz knows how to lock up."

"Of course." Nick winked at Liz when Molly turned towards the door and hooked the old lady's purse over his left arm while he offered her his right.

Liz rolled her eyes but gave Molly an affectionate look that Nick noticed before he gave his full attention to getting the frail woman out of her home and into the SUV.

"We didn't used to bother locking the doors you know. With all the drugs, it started becoming necessary. Then with that nasty business with your brother, Maura, and littles at the library, well can't be too careful anymore I suppose."

Upon reaching the clinic, Nick pulled up to the main entrance and helped out. "I'll park and wait in the lobby."

"It might be a while," Liz gave him an apologetic look.

"No worries."

Once he'd taken care of the car, Nick found a corner seat and sank down onto the uncomfortable chair. He let his long legs stretch out. Rather than study his phone, Nick watched the ebb and flow of people in and out of the building. When a middle-aged man and woman passed near him as they headed for the exit with their arms wrapped tightly around one another and tears rolling down both their faces, he felt a pang of sympathy followed by profound gratitude that his brother was better. A police officer on Belfort Island, Stephan had recently been shot in the line of duty and his fiancé, now wife, Maura and daughter Maisy had been kidnapped along with a group of children under Maura's care at the library. Getting the early morning call from Maura telling him

Stephan was in the hospital was terrifying enough, but having to call their parents and share the news with them had been gut wrenching. In the end all had ended well for the victims. For their kidnappers, not so much. One, a local fisherman, Joey Thompson had died at the hands of a selkie, Karria, and another had been blinded by one of the old men involved in the rescue. Along with the blinded man, two other coconspirators were in jail having been denied bail.

Normally Nick would be restless sitting in a waiting room, but the past few weeks had taken a toll and he was content to relax. In the morning he'd be heading for Boston and then home to London. Once there, he'd throw himself back into his work and rugby league. As the time dragged on, he got bored people watching and scrolled through the photos on his phone. One of his favorites was Maisy, Fern, and their friend Lana mugging for the camera a few days ago while Maura and Stephan were gazing at one another by their wedding cake, oblivious to the girls' antics. Fern, looking much like a smaller version of Liz, was the tallest in the group despite being the youngest. She normally carried herself with a quiet, reserved air, but the image had caught her with a look of delighted glee on her face that warmed Nick's heart. It bothered him how difficult life was for her and her mother. Liz had made it clear, however, that he was to butt out. Pity and charity, no matter how well intentioned, were not appreciated.

Nick sighed and kept scrolling. He paused at one with two women with lustrous black hair with silver markings in it. The smaller, Josie, looked like she was in her early 20s at most but was, in fact, older than him. Her mother, Karria, looked his age and was at least 80. He'd snapped the picture of the selkies surreptitiously. He also had one of the pair in their seal forms moments before they'd entered the frigid waters for parts unknown.

When Liz and Molly appeared in the corridor, the elderly woman was moving slower than before and Liz's eyes were red rimmed. Nick strode over to them. Wordlessly, he offered Molly his other arm. She patted it as she slid her arm through. He felt her hand trembling. Once they reached the exit, he ran to get the car. It was a silent ride back to Belfort, but once they crossed the bridge onto the island, Molly let out a heavy sigh. "I've had a good run." She patted Nick's hand as she tried to shift in her seat to catch Liz's eyes. "Liz dear, don't be sad."

Liz roused herself. "Don't say that Molly. He said he could be wrong. He said it was just an estimate."

"Sweetheart, I know what I feel in my bones. This was my last Christmas."

Nick glanced in the rearview mirror and saw tears streaming down Liz's cheeks. He quickly averted his eyes so she wouldn't see his gaze.

"Now," Molly glanced over at him. "Liz and I have quite a few things we need to discuss. I'd like her to make sure the car is running before you leave so she can drive herself home later, but then we'll need some privacy."

Nick nodded. This time he looked in the rearview until Liz met his eyes. When she gave a slight nod, he offered, "I can swing by the school if you call them and bring Fern home with Maisy. Mum had plans for a big meal and Fern's always welcome."

Liz nodded. "Thanks Nick. I'd appreciate it."

He felt a swat on his arm.

"Eyes on the road," Molly chastised him. "I don't want to meet my maker today."

He grinned a bit as he focused back on the road.

After Molly got settled in the house, Nick and Liz opened the garage. His eyes widened in surprise at the cherry red vehicle inside. Despite her heavy heart, Liz smiled at his reaction. "Not what you expected?"

"I figured it'd be an old tank." Nick ran an appreciative hand along the sporty lines of the Lexus. "This looks like a sweet ride."

Liz shifted uncomfortably. "I'll just borrow it until I can get a new battery for Maybelle."

"Uh huh." Nick was busy peering through the window.

She shook her head when she realized he was paying no attention and nudged him out of the way so she could open the door. "Let me just make sure it's running."

Nick felt a jolt of electricity when Liz's hip bumped against his. As the car purred to life, he stepped back to get some space. After a moment, the engine was silenced but Liz didn't step out. Nick glanced over and saw her holding her head in her hands. "Oh, no." He whispered the words out loud. His instinct was to go comfort her, but he wasn't sure she'd welcome it. While he was dithering about what to do, Nick saw Liz visibly pull herself together. She wiped her eyes with her gloves. Before she could turn and see him staring, Nick swiveled so his back was to her and studied the old tools hanging on the wall. He heard the door shut and slowly turned.

"You can stop pretending." Liz gave him a wry smile.

"Huh?"

"I saw you."

"Ah," Nick ventured a step closer to her. "May I give you a hug then?"

She hesitated and then nodded. "Yeah, I could use one." She took a half step towards him.

Nick quickly bridged the gap and wrapped his arms around her. The top of her head came near his own and he inhaled the sweet summer scent that wafted up from her hair.

For her part, Liz let herself, uncharacteristically, melt into his firm embrace. It felt nice to be held, even if it was just for a moment, rather than being the one always holding it together for others. Nick's cologne had an appealing woodsy tang she couldn't identify. She breathed it in.

Liz's breath tickled his neck and Nick shivered as he tried to contain an ungentlemanly giggle.

She misinterpreted the reaction and on an impulse she didn't stop to examine, Liz placed a gentle, fleeting kiss on his neck.

Nick's arms tightened around her in response. "Liz," his mouth had gone unaccountably dry. He shifted to move his left hand up to gently cup the side of her head. He felt her freeze and time stood still for what felt like ages before, seconds later, she turned her head and kissed the palm of his hand and then moved so she was gazing at him. He swallowed hard. Since his visit at Christmas he hadn't been able to get the single mother out of his head. It was an unusual and uncomfortable experience for Nick. For years he'd managed to have an active social life that involved no entanglements that stretched longer than a week or two and while he thought of most of those women fondly, he rarely thought of them at all after they parted ways. He simply buried himself in his work and rugby until his next attempt at dating. Liz couldn't be a simple fling though. She was his sister-in-law's best friend. Her daughter was his niece's best friend. His entire family loved her and her child. He had to tread very carefully.

A smile flitted across her lips. "You're overthinking this Nicholas," her voice was whisper soft before she bridged the slight distance to his mouth with her own.